THE CONJURER'S CURSE

STEPHANIE COTTA

Copyright © 2022 by Stephanie Cotta

All rights reserved.

Names, characters, places, and incidents are the product of the author's imagination. Any resemblance to actual events, locations, or persons, living or dead, is purely coincidental and not intentional unless otherwise stated.

Copyright © 2022 by Stephanie Cotta

Publisher: Monarch Educational Services, LLC

Developmental Editor by Kelly Martin; Line edits by Polly Harris; Lead Editing by Haley Hwang

Cover Design - saiibookcoverdesigns.com/

Full Spread Images and Header Image: Licensed Adobe Stock Photos

Tahira - Illustrator, Stephanie Cotta

All rights reserved. No part of this book may be reproduced in any form or by any electronic or mechanical means, including information storage and retrieval systems, without written permission from the publisher, except for the use of brief quotations in a book review. Thank you for respecting the work of authors. www.monarcheducationalservices.com

For Alan,
whose life and love has been an inspiration

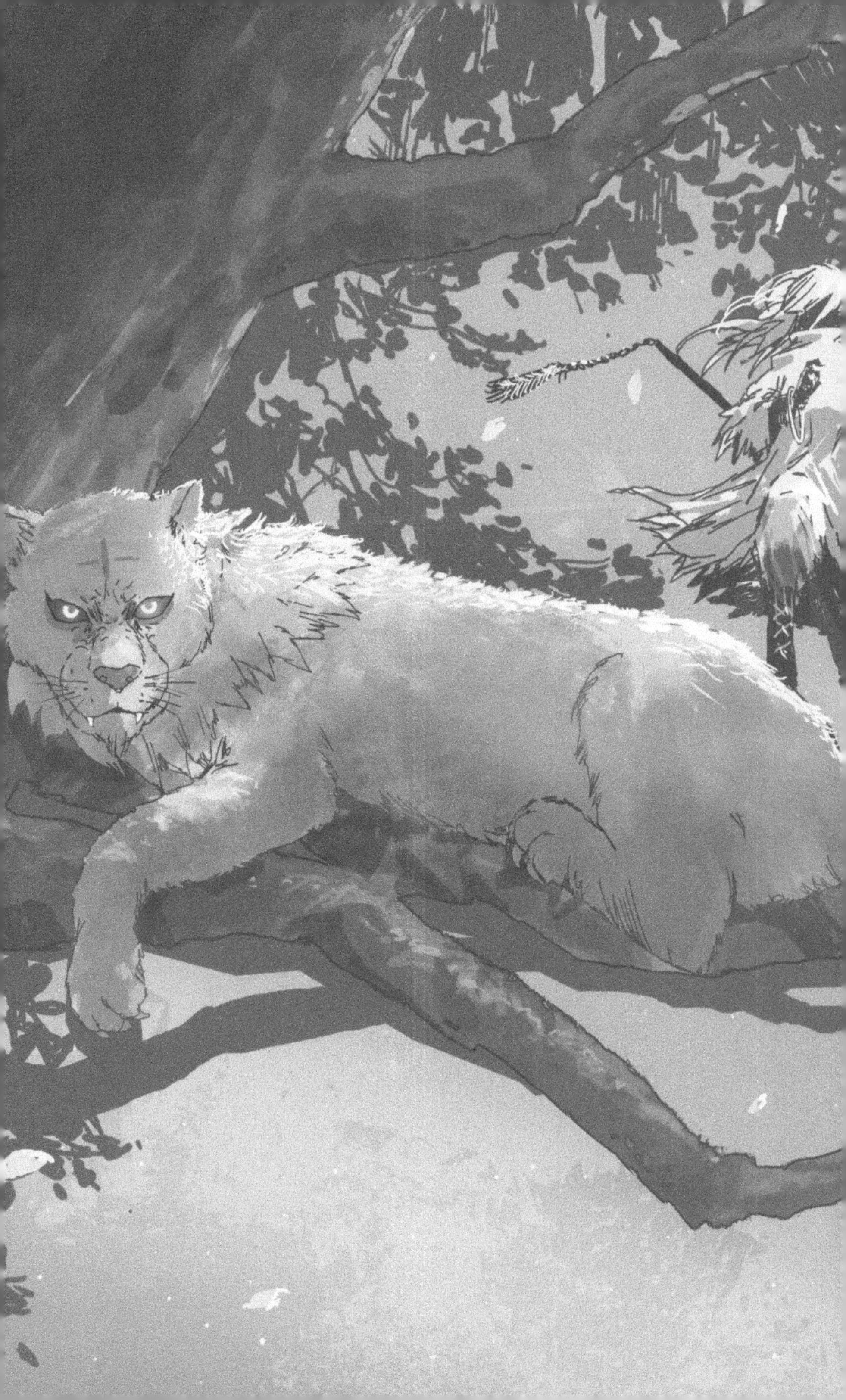

PROLOGUE

Rowan clutched his shortspear and approached the Thulu Jungle. The dense, tropical wilds teemed with echoing bird calls and low, guttural growls. The air, wet and heavy, thrummed with swarms of buzzing insects. Thick and slitted shadows darkened the emerald ferns masking the ground. Life in strange abundance dwelt therein, and Rowan was about to stalk it.

His blood pulsed with the thrill.

Naja, his guardian-mother, strode alongside Rowan garbed in a short, sleeveless dress made from her latest kill—the creamy hide of a twin-tail panther. She circled him, fingering the black pearl necklace hanging above her shapely bosom.

"Lower your heart rate," Naja instructed, easing her palm over Rowan's tanned, leather breastplate. "I know you're anxious to begin, but slow it down. You don't want the twin-tail detecting your racing heart."

Rowan exhaled a calming breath, steadying his pulsating heartbeats and relaxing his taut muscles. The balmy breeze swept his long, ivory hair over his stark-white face. Naja snatched the loose strands between her nimble fingers and gathered them behind his neck.

"Remember what I've taught you," Naja said, weaving Rowan's hair into a warrior's braid, "and you'll pass the trial."

The Moran'ysi njahi. The warrior trial to vanquish his first twin-tail panther on his own. Three years of training and preparation came down to this pivotal feat. He could not fail—not if he wanted to earn the validation of the villagers in Karahvel.

Rowan fidgeted with his leather bracers, fixating on the jungle's shrouded vines jumbled like a clump of seaweed. "If I defeat the twin-tail, will the villagers finally stop calling me a *dikyli*?"

"We can hope," Naja said, wistfulness stealing into her alto voice. Then her usual constructive tone reengaged. "But don't focus on the villagers. Focus only on the twin-tail."

Naja tied off Rowan's braid, then faced him. "You're ready for this," she said, her own rows of coiled black hair swaying with her movements. She gripped him by the shoulders, her ebony face shadowed by the twisting tree limbs. "Stalk the twin-tail to its den and claim its hide. Hold to my instructions."

Rowan nodded, slowing his breaths. "Set the bamboo spears, lure it out, and strike unseen," he recited, cinching his grip around his shortspear.

"And remember, Rowan," Naja said with a solemn stare, "still water, steady heart. See the beast as an equal, and be fearless in your strike."

Rowan nodded, drew in a long breath, then entered the dense woodland, pushing past lofty palms with deft strides. Though lean in frame, Rowan prided himself in being nimble where it counted—his mind and body honed for this swift jungle chase.

A twin-tail could smell a hunter from afar, so when Rowan came upon the first mud pit, he coated his pale skin, masking his scent, and blended in with the shadows. He scoured the damp dirt at a measured pace, searching under the swath of leafy foliage for twin-tail tracks. Paw impressions were often hard to spot, but last night's rain softened the soil, revealing a set of fresh tracks.

Rowan followed them, which led straight to a burrow obscured by a mass of twisting vines. The panther retreated there to feed. A trail of blood indicated an animal had been dragged through the tramped brush.

Rowan fashioned his traps. He stuck a dozen cloven bamboo reeds into the moist ground, angling each one upward like a thrusting spear. He circled them around the twin-tail's den, leaving the creature with only two options: risk leaping over the sharp bamboo or seek escape over its burrow—where Rowan would stage his ambush.

Rowan grappled his way up a canopy tree's spiraling vine to higher ground. From there, he dropped onto the mounded burrow, crouching low in the ferns wet with dew.

The disturbance to its home summoned the twin-tail. Its furry head poked out from the hole, and the creature spread its wiry, white whiskers. Rowan held his breath. The panther approached the circular row of bamboo reeds, belly low to the ground, dragging its two whiplike tails through the variegated ferns. It inspected the deadly barrier with several deep growls and swatted at the bamboo. The reeds wouldn't come free with ease; Rowan had buried them well. The twin-tail then attempted to squeeze its body between the tightly arrayed bamboo, and that, too, failed. The creature scrambled backward, shaking its creamy head, whipping its tails in an agitated tangle.

It flicked its amber eyes, seeking a safer route, and turned about face. The creature stalked back toward the den, its gaze transfixed on the mound. The twin-tail chose the path Rowan wanted. He swallowed an anxious lump and lifted his shortspear, readying his stance.

The creature leapt upon the mound, and Rowan came face-to-face with his quarry. The twin-tail's eyes dilated into black pools. Its blood-smeared jaw dropped open with a challenging snarl, and with claws spread, it sprang into an attack.

Rowan thrust his spear, striking the panther high in the chest. Its scream ricocheted through Rowan's eardrums. The twin-tail crashed into him, raking its claws against his shoulders. Rowan hissed in pain, gritting his teeth. He squirmed beneath the thrashing beast and hurled kicks to its belly. His heartbeats thundered as he crammed the spearhead deeper. The twin-tail's wild screams drawled into internal growls, losing spirit. Breaking free, Rowan pulled out the spearhead, and the twin-tail rolled off the mound, falling at the entrance to its den.

Rowan's heart pounded in his ears as he peered over the mound's rounded lip. The creature laid still. The blood-wound at its center seeped into the surrounding fur.

Burning skies, I beat it!

Hands shaky, Rowan rappelled to the ground and steadied his

racing heart before his kill. The twin-tail was his equal in spirit. Vanquishing it signified he surpassed it in strength.

Naja arrived at the kill site, her shortspear strapped to her back. She shimmied between the bamboo stakes and embraced the muck-covered Rowan. "You did well." Her dark lips curved into a proud smile. "Were you wounded in the fight?"

Rowan rolled his shoulders, wincing. "Only some grazes."

Naja pulled away and regarded his trap. "I see you heeded my instruction and used the bamboo spears."

"They worked exactly as you said."

Naja lifted a hand to Rowan's mud-caked face, and her smile broadened. "You need to wash off before we head back to the village. Otherwise, you might scare everyone."

Rowan snickered. "Yeah, 'cause they've never seen a mud-covered albino before, huh?"

"They haven't, Rowan." Naja laughed. "You might confuse their prejudices."

"Then maybe I should encase myself in mud on a daily basis."

"That's one strategy. Though, they might start complaining about the smell." Naja wagged a hand over her broad nose.

Rowan sniffed his armpits. "Is it that bad?"

"Like a twin-tail, I could smell you from a distance."

"That's a joke, isn't it?"

Naja flashed a wry smile. "Head for the waterfall and wash," she instructed, prodding him forward. "I'll make a sling for us to carry your kill. It won't take me long, so no dawdling."

Rowan soon reached his favorite waterfall, cascading into a wide, glistening pool. He shuffled behind the underlying cliff face and into the deafening downpour. The plastered mud peeled away, and he was back to his alabaster, painted self. His red eyes flooded as he tilted his head back, rinsing out his hair. No one else in the village shared his peculiar features, his oddities—the crescent-shaped birthmark on his neck the most unusual of all—and the villagers never let him forget it.

After the rinse, he returned to Naja, and together, they hefted the twin-tail back to Karahvel. People gathered around the outskirts of the coastal village. Chieftain Haraz stood with drooped shoulders at the forefront, distinguishable by his ceremonial headdress boasting bright feathers and ivory adornments. The elders who comprised the *majiri*—Karahvel's governing council—clustered around the chieftain. Each wore long colorful tunics cinched at the waist with braided belts.

Like curious jungle birds, they came closer to inspect the kill, as was the custom when a youth successfully performed the Moran'ysi njahi. Haraz's wrinkled face showed neither enthusiasm nor disapproval, but the majiri couldn't mask their surprise. Rowan didn't know if it stemmed more from his feat or from his lack of injuries.

Naja stood at attention before the chieftain and the majiri, her long arms and legs as taut as thick bamboo. "Rowan has killed his first twin-tail," she announced. "I, Naja, his guardian-mother, ask he be recognized among the Karahvelans."

Haraz turned to the elders, and with hushed voices, they deliberated their verdict. The majiri's spokesman, Menka—a bald, older man with a mangled upper lip and a perennial scowl—stepped forward and addressed Naja. "The majiri will recognize the boy's achievement. However, his status as a dikyli remains."

Outsider.

Rowan hated that word. All his life, he heard it whispered as a reminder of how different he was from everyone in Karahvel.

"As such," Menka continued, "he won't be joining the ranks of the Karahvelans."

Naja stabbed her spear tip into the sand. She thrust a judging finger at the elders. "You all know he's earned his place. Or am I to understand you're refusing to recognize my boy's warrior status because he's not like us?"

"He's not *your* boy, Naja," Menka shot back, quick and harsh as a viper's strike. "Just because you refused to accept a husband, it doesn't make that white leech your son."

Rowan bristled at the insult.

Naja's muscles bulged as if she'd been slapped. "I chose not to accept *your* son as husband—let's be clear on that, Menka. A warrior's life suits me better, as does instructing *my* boy. I thought it was our custom to rear any motherless child." She shot a firm stare at Haraz. "It's why I fought to have him placed in my charge, Chieftain. We don't abandon children, for it would make us no better than *lynasi.*"

The implication wasn't lost on Rowan. In the jungle, female lynasi were known for abandoning their young when endangered. In Karaḥvel, the rearing of children was one of their most sacred undertakings; neglecting a child was unthinkable.

"It is for that reason the boy still remains in our village," Haraz said, his voice wooden.

"Yes, but what if this boy is the source of woes?" Menka persisted, leveling his finger at Rowan. "There are many who believe the dikyli is a plague."

"Stop hiding behind that word," Naja snapped, her tone matching her sharp glare. "Rowan has lived amongst us for thirteen years. When will you accept him as one of our own?"

"With all the suspicion surrounding his origins, how can we?" an old, croaky-voiced elder said. "He was born under a red crescent moon! A fact we can't ignore."

"Nor the ominous mark on his neck," a short elder interjected, squinting his dark, nebulous eyes.

"It's a bad omen," Menka said, nodding along with his fellow elders. "The death of his first three guardian-mothers is a troubling phenomenon. Have you forgotten what happened to Sylda? Her skin *aged* beyond her twenty-five years!"

Rowan cringed, forced to hear every condemning word the elders uttered. The majiri was no different from everyone else in the village. They voiced their frank thoughts as if Rowan didn't exist, unconcerned if he heard them or not. The overwhelming urge to retreat back into the jungle—far from these scornful stares—rooted in his mind.

Haraz remained conveniently quiet as the elders continued their railing. They respected Naja's position as a warrior but held too many qualms to grant her wish.

"Be wary, Naja," Menka warned. "If things continue as they are, you're next to follow Sylda. You die, and we'll all know what he really is—*cursed*."

Naja turned away from the majiri in a huff. "Come, Rowan, back to our hut. These fools can stew in their superstitions. You and I are going to celebrate."

Rowan ignored the animosity dripping from the elders' scowls, lifted his chin high, and with Naja's help, carried his kill toward their hut. Along the way, coalescing murmurs drowned out the quiet lull of the sea. Villagers halted their chores and eyed the slain twin-tail. They knew what it meant: He was a warrior.

Rowan and Naja reached their hut and worked together to prepare the animal. They divided the carcass, stripping away what they would use for ornamental items and clothing. Naja removed the organs; Rowan skinned the twin-tail's hide. A nagging question pressed at his thoughts as he slid his knife between the layer of animal skin and muscle. He couldn't shake Naja's argument with the majiri out of his mind—or Menka's harsh words.

"Is Menka right about me?" Rowan bent his head, rubbing at his crescent-shaped birthmark. "Am I . . . cursed?"

"Ignore Menka," Naja said with a sharp tsk, her dimpled chin tightly drawn. "It's village superstition and not for you to worry about."

Except Rowan did worry. He wasn't ignorant of the villagers' whispers—nor their harsh looks. As the village freak, he was blamed for every bad thing, and well, lately, he wondered if the majiri might be right. "But what Menka said about Sylda—it's hard for me to ignore. How can I, after what happened to her?"

The frustrated fire in Naja's eyes dissipated. "Her death was a tragedy, but you must understand something—when inexplicable things occur, people look to attach blame. And since the majiri insists on regarding you as a dikyli, it makes you the ideal target for their suspicions. So spare them no thought."

Naja's directness ended the topic. She disappeared into the hut and came back with a cowl hood, woven from multi-colored thread, draped over her arm. "This is for you."

Rowan accepted the cowl and read the weavescript to himself: *"In honor of your Moran'ysi njahi, may this cowl forever speak of my pride in your accomplishment. I see you as warrior and equal."*

Naja took it from Rowan's hands and placed the cowl over his head. "The majiri may not count you as one of us, but in my eyes, you've earned your place among our warriors." Pride glimmered through her onyx eyes, enlivening their dark luster with soft light.

Rowan basked in Naja's love and praise. She instilled him with courage and skills he could rely upon in the face of danger. He couldn't imagine life without his guardian-mother's daily instruction.

Night settled, speckling the cobalt sky with stars. Naja and Rowan cooked strips of meat on sticks over the fire. Their spotted *kalb* lounged between them, wagging its long, pink tongue in the evening's humid air. The hound usually accompanied them on hunts, its nose and ears excellent for tracking. Rowan petted the animal between its raised ears as more of Naja's clash with Menka filtered through his mind.

"Why didn't you marry, Naja?" Rowan asked, rotating the meat sticks. "You could've had a child of your own, instead of watching over a freak like me."

Naja admonished him with a sharp look. "You're not a freak. You're different, like everybody is." She softened her expression after making her point. "As to why I never married, it's no great secret. I never found a man who could better me. I was well past the marrying age when I took you under my supervision—something I believe Sylda would've wanted. It's then I realized the way to better myself was to help shape you into a man. You've been a thrilling challenge."

Rowan blushed beneath her warm smile. "You don't regret it? Even after what happened today with the majiri?"

"Nah," she drawled, "and I never will."

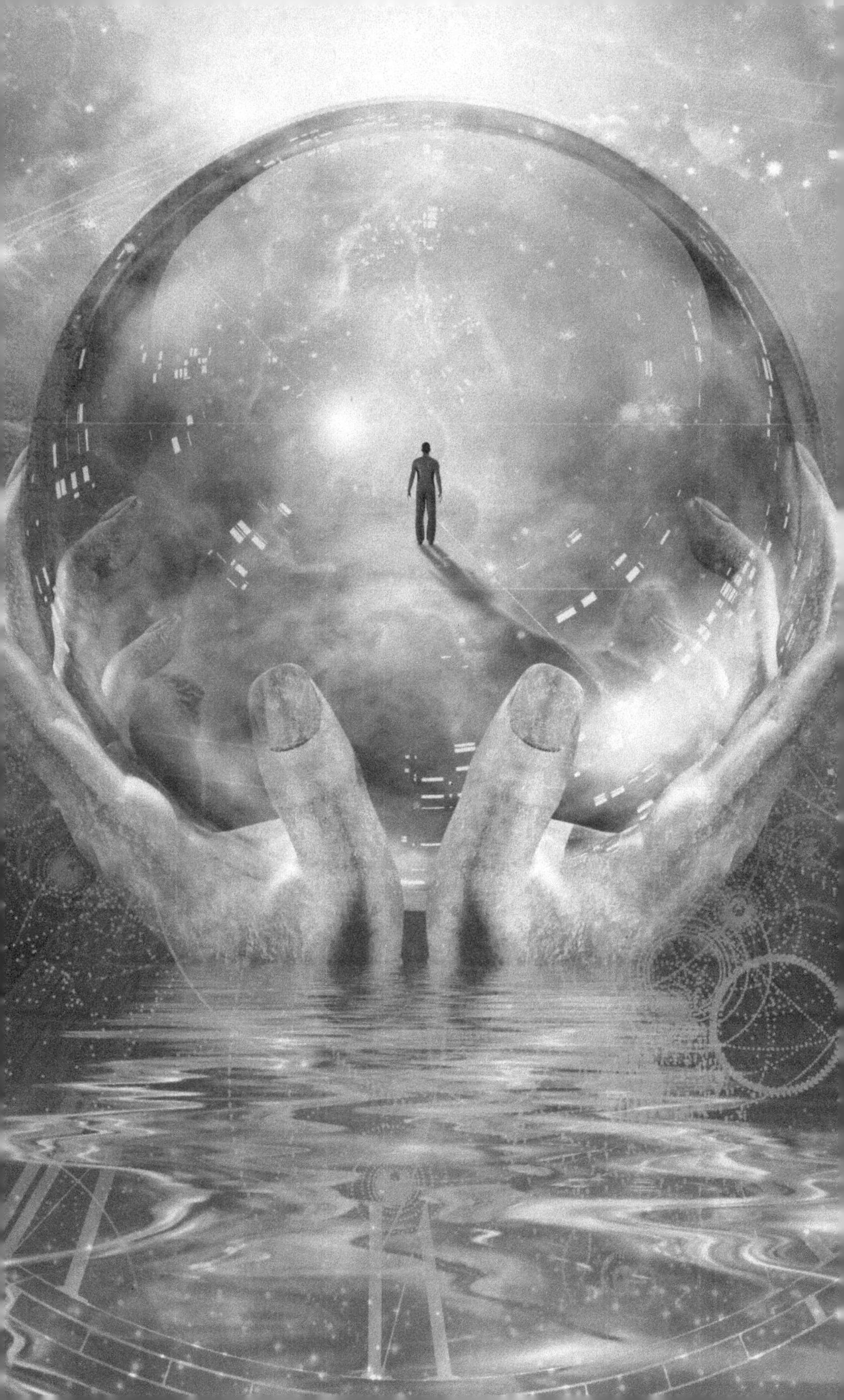

CHAPTER 1
OUTCAST
FOUR YEARS LATER

The scorching sun bled Rowan's crimson eyes dry. Sweat beaded upon his brow as he gathered a bunch of barley stalks and severed them at the base with a swift swing of his sickle. He shuffled forward and collected another bunch, his beige, full-sleeve tunic clinging to his skin. He stood out among the bare-backed laborers, the harvest sun less threatening to their ebony skin.

Rowan's own translucent forehead burned under the harsh rays. He secured the cowl hood covering his neck and brow and continued working, soon outpacing the laborers on either side. He stood for a moment to stretch his back and tilted his head toward the expansive azure sky.

A trail of smoke marred the horizon. It came from the jetty's direction.

Has someone died?

No, that couldn't be. Everyone would be at the shore for a funeral procession and not hunched over the field. Yet, the more Rowan stared at the smoke trail, the more it pricked at his thoughts.

"Hey, Red-Eyes," snarky-mouthed Lesca mocked, smacking his sickle against Rowan's leg. "Stop daydreaming and get back to work."

"Your row isn't gonna harvest itself," Tolas said with a sneer, his dark eyes and freckled face obscured by his frizzy, black hair.

Rowan scowled at the nasty twins. "I wasn't daydreaming—only waiting for you to catch up. If you don't like my pace, just say so."

Lesca pursed his thick lips and shifted his gaze to his twin, as if seeking input. Tolas contributed nothing, except an indignant grimace. They grumbled their annoyance and trudged ahead, swinging their sickles.

Rowan shook the smoke trail from his mind and crouched again next to the barley. His sickle severed another bunch as the hard stomp of the field overseer grew louder.

"Dikyli," an older man hollered, motioning with a quick snap of his hand. "Chieftain Haraz wants to see you."

Rowan frowned. "Why?"

"He didn't say. Leave your sickle and go at once. You're done for the day."

Something wasn't right; Rowan felt it in his bones. The twins tilted their big, bushy heads, suspicion evident in their eyes. Lesca couldn't mask his sneer; Tolas showed naked relief.

Rowan dropped his tool and hurried from the field, his brows knitted. He removed his cowl, regathered his loose hair, and tied it back with a leather cord, then covered his head once more. He kept a hand raised, shielding his face from the midday sun. Even still, his eyes watered anew. This time of day was the worst for his eyes, and so, he welcomed a break from the fields.

Rowan entered the village center and shuffled toward Chieftain Haraz's bamboo hut. He picked at his fingers and nails, removing dirt.

Why does the chieftain want to see me?

No reason was given. Though, the scathing eyes of the villagers filled Rowan with unease. Did they know something he didn't?

Questions nipped at his mind as Rowan pulled back the reed-woven flap of the chieftain's dwelling and entered. Haraz sat cross-legged on a plush, rouge cushion, wearing his headdress and flaxen robe, belted at the waist with a dual-toned cord. Colorful rugs woven by the village's best weavers blanketed the earthen floor. Each rug told a story in the threaded colors, line by line. Weavescript was an ancient tradition known only to the villagers of Karahvel—an artform Rowan's guardian-mothers also taught him.

"You wanted to see me, Chieftain?"

"Sit down, Rowan." Haraz extended a gnarled hand to the cushion across the unlit firepit. A shaft of sunlight gathered there, pouring through the open sunroof, bright and blinding.

Rowan, apprehensive, kept his gaze downward and took a seat.

The solemn sheen in Haraz's hooded brown eyes was less inviting than ever. "You must leave the village," he said through thin, weathered lips.

A sickening knot formed in Rowan's gut. "Why must I leave? What have I done wrong?"

Haraz's eyes darkened. "You are cursed."

"W-what?" Rowan stiffened like hardened clay. Had Menka finally persuaded Haraz to accept his superstitions as true? "Why do you say this?"

"Death clings to you like a net," Haraz said with a heavy tone, like he'd suspected this dark truth for many years. "In the past seventeen years, while you've lived in Karahvel, four women have served as your guardian-mothers—all of whom have died before their time."

Rowan shook his head and raised his fingers. "It's only been three. Naja is alive."

Haraz scrunched his lips, then delivered grave news. "She died this morning."

A horrifying chill swept through Rowan's body. "Naja's dead?" His lips quivered. "No, that can't be. She appeared fine when I left her. I don't understand—"

"I think you know." An accusatory glint shrouded the chieftain's eyes. "It's *you*, Rowan."

Rowan's mind whirled with disbelief.

No, this can't be happening.

Not again. Not. Again. He had to see the truth for himself.

Rowan darted out of the hut in the next hitched breath. Haraz shouted for him to return. Rowan ignored his calls and raced to the village's edge, heart hammering against his chest. His stomach churned like floodwaters as he reached his and Naja's hut—only to behold a disturbing sight. All of his guardian-mother's belongings—loom, weavings, clothes, and hunting spears—were gone, removed as if tainted with a sickly aura.

Where was her body? Where were her things?

Don't tell me they burned them —

Then he remembered the smoke he saw while in the fields. Had that been her pyre?

Devastating anger clouded and overwhelmed Rowan's thoughts. He sprinted back to Haraz's hut and burst past the flap.

"What have you done with Naja's body?" Rowan demanded.

"Her ashes have been spread."

Rowan's heart pulsed with shock. "I should've been the one to do it!" Outrage and grief pulled him to his knees. "You didn't even let me say goodbye. She was my guardian-mother!"

"You are not one of us, Rowan. That is why the majiri handled the pyre. The villagers desire you to leave. The majiri has weighed the evidence and decided."

Rowan's voice hardened. "What evidence?"

The chieftain gave him a long, troubling stare. "It seems the longer people are near you, the shorter their lifespan becomes. Naja's death confirms what the majiri has suspected for years—you are a poison." Haraz dispelled a shuddering breath. "Understand, now? You don't belong here. You're a dikyli."

The searing word stung like bile in Rowan's throat. After seventeen years, he still couldn't escape it.

"Look at yourself." Haraz pointed at Rowan with a mangled finger. "Your hair and skin are as white as sea foam, and your eyes are bloody red."

Shame dipped Rowan's head. He'd known this stark truth all his life—yet knew nothing of his true origins. He fingered the vivid weaves near his feet, reading the message. It spoke of the chieftain's life, his many deeds, and his family line. "How did I come to be here? I want the truth, Chieftain—not the vague answer I've heard all my life."

Haraz sighed, wispy brows drooping, his gaze heavy. "It's true we found your mother, Zurie, washed upon our shore, pregnant with you. But the moment you were born—when your mother saw the ominous mark on your neck—she uttered these words: 'He really is cursed.' She named you, then fled the following morning and never returned."

Rowan's throat tightened. His mother had abandoned him?

Why? Because of a curse? "You told me she died after giving birth to me." He narrowed his eyes at the chieftain. "So, that was a lie?"

"I thought it kinder than the truth."

"Kinder? You lied!" Rowan dug his nails into the mark's crescent-shaped bulge. "So, everyone believes I'm cursed. Even you?"

"Four guardian-mothers dead is hard to ignore, and hardly a coincidence," Haraz said, his voice low and forlorn. "By now, you should be aware of the illness you bring."

"If you thought me cursed," Rowan scoffed, throwing up his fists, "why keep me inside the village all these years?"

"I thought your mother's words were merely words," Haraz explained, fiddling with the strand of black pearls around his scrawny wrist. "Over time, I began seeing them differently. Since you started working the fields this year, our yield hasn't been as bountiful. Certain bundles from the harvest show signs of disease, as if the stalks were . . . *corrupted*. Not to mention every kalb you've had died within a year under your care."

Rowan opened his mouth to object, but no words came. He didn't know why his hounds always died. He assumed they ate something harmful in the jungle.

I can't be the cause. Rowan covered his face with his hands, shaking. *I can't be!*

"And then there are your guardian-mothers, the first of whom was my own beloved granddaughter Kialla . . ." Haraz hesitated, his grizzly-bearded mouth quivering, on the verge of weeping. "They're all reasons for the villagers to look upon you with dread."

"I'm not a plague." Rowan's hands curled into fists against his toned thighs. "None of this was my choice. I didn't ask to be this way."

Haraz's bony shoulders sagged. His gaze held a vestige of genuine sympathy. "It's best you leave at once to prevent any unwanted violence. The people hold you responsible for Naja's death."

Rowan's breath hitched, and a nauseous ache burrowed in the pit of his stomach. Like a loose thread in an unfinished weave, his entire world unraveled before him.

"I've n-never been outside Karahvel," he said, his voice quaking. "I know nothing of the world. Where will I go?"

"Search for your kind. Find who cursed you. Perhaps there's a way to break the curse. If you don't, people will continue to die around you, and you'll forever be alone."

Rowan trembled at the cruel reminder. He'd never been entirely alone. He always had a guardian-mother to watch over him. The pain of their deaths clawed at him—a fresh, gaping wound. He couldn't bear the thought of being responsible. They'd raised him, showed him kindness—but their love was gone. Now, only animosity existed in this place he called home.

"Please, Chieftain, let me stay." Tears clung to Rowan's eyes, swallowing his vision. "I-I'll move outside the village—build a shelter in the Thulu Jungle—just don't banish me!"

A twinge of sorrow creased Haraz's brows. "I fear even then, your nearby presence will draw warriors into hunting you as a twin-tail. You must go far away."

Rowan's heart plummeted into his stomach.

This can't be happening!

Haraz's stance went rigid, as if passing judgment before the majiri. "I'll have Gesu ferry you to the Luvarian port in Kadern. From there, you can secure passage to Eldon. Someone there may direct you further. Whatever happens to you, you are dead to us. Don't ever return."

Haraz's final statement was a blunt spear driven through Rowan's heart. A gut-churning pain overtook his body. He stood, legs shaking, and hastened from the hut. Tears burned in his eyes as he dashed toward his home. Hateful gazes followed him like knives to his back. Whispers began at once, chittering like a field of crickets.

"The plague's finally leaving."

"Our village will be free of his poisonous taint."

"We're yielding a meager harvest 'cause of the freak."

"A pity the dikyli didn't leave before Naja died."

Shame seized Rowan by the throat, urging him to hide. He felt exposed, like everyone could see his freakish flaws, and their condemning black eyes pounced with judgment. He fled inside his hut, laboring to calm his breath—an impossible feat. His legs, as heavy as boulders, crumpled beneath him. He succumbed to his knees, arms clenched around his chest as his body shook like palm leaves caught in a gale.

Get a hold of yourself!
He forced out a strangled breath, then another.
Still water, steady heart.
His gut tightened. His chest heaved under his tunic, which billowed like a sail.
Burning skies, this pain ... it's flooding every vein.
Rowan forced down a hard swallow, and his saliva burned like hot coals in his throat.
His eyes welled with tears at the sight of Naja's cot, wishing his guardian-mother rested there, napping. It lay empty.
It's as Haraz said. She's really dead.
A scream tore from the depths of Rowan's lungs. His banishment wasn't the worst of it. No, being unable to say goodbye to the woman who watched over him these past seven years formed a chasm in his heart. Rowan wanted to crash in a motionless heap and grieve, but Haraz's stern words echoed in his ears. *"It's best you leave at once."*
It would be dangerous to linger.
Rowan stood, swiping at his tears with a sweat-soaked sleeve, and stuffed what few belongings he possessed into his sack. He cinched his purse at his braided belt and grabbed his shortspear.
He exited his hut and found grumpy-eyed Gesu already waiting for him. Haraz's man kept his distance, as if being within six feet could signal his sudden, combustible death. Rowan hurled a silent curse.
Superstitious fools! The lot of them!
Gesu flicked his shaven head, gesturing for Rowan to follow him to the quiet inlet bordering the Thulu Jungle. The offshore breeze was balmy and comforting, and the crystalline waters swelled gently with the tide. For years, Rowan had harvested black pearls in the nearby estuary alongside Naja. He would bid this entire place a bitter farewell.
Rowan dashed across the golden coast to the dock and stepped onto the small barge. He gave the village a final glance. People gathered on the shore in their colorfully woven vestments, watching him depart, their dark pleasure written as clearly as weavescript on their faces. None wore it more blatantly than the nasty twins. Lesca and Tolas snickered on the shore as if they themselves were the masterminds of this shameful exile. Their black, malicious eyes

burned right through Rowan as they mouthed a snide *"So long, freak."*

Rowan spun around and concealed himself against the short bulwark. Unfortunately, it gave him a perfect view of the earthen jetty. Smoke still billowed from Naja's pyre. It funneled upward in surging torrents, coalescing in the sky with Naja's ashes.

A dark heaviness settled in Rowan's chest.

My guardian-mothers are dead because of me . . .

The unbearable truth plummeted like a jagged stone into the depths of his soul. Rowan pried his eyes from the jetty and stared out at the horizon's vast emptiness. More unfathomable truths swarmed in his mind.

I'm an outcast, without a home—nowhere to belong.

He banged his head against the wood, groaning. He rocked back and forth, arms wrapped tightly around his legs.

Nobody who loves me remains in this world.

"Did anyone really love you?" a sinister voice inside his head taunted. "Your guardian-mothers must've known you were cursed—that you'd be the death of them. Secretly, they reviled you."

That's not true! Rowan hurled back, gripping his head. *They didn't know.*

"Oh, but your real mother knew the truth and abandoned you. You are alone . . . forever alone."

Rowan banged his head harder against the bulwark, silencing the dark voice. He'd gone through this agony before, each time he lost a guardian-mother. No matter how traumatic the loss, he only had so much emotional stamina. Exhausted, he curled into a ball, dropped his head against his sack, and sought escape from this betrayal.

CHAPTER 2
ACROSS THE ARDRUIN SEA

"Wake up, dikyli." Gesu jabbed Rowan in the shoulder with the butt of his spear. "We're at Kadern Port."

Rowan stirred, mind groggy, muscles stiff.

Did I really sleep through the entire trip?

Exhausted from grief and his banishment, Rowan had found solace in sleep.

The salt in the air enriched his lungs, reminding him of Karahvel. He tried opening his puffy eyes only to be met by the jarring morning light, and he squeezed them shut again. The groan of ships tacking filled his ears. Seagulls squawked. Sailors murmured. Waves lapped against the barge.

His heavy eyelids fluttered open once more. Squinting against the blinding sun, Rowan beheld a bustling harbor boasting a row of gargantuan ships, the size of which he'd never seen. He stared up at the sleek, palmlike masts flying their colors, and his jaw dropped.

Rowan pointed in amazement. "These ships are enormous!"

Gesu didn't show a hint of astonishment. He kept on task, guiding the barge toward an opening at the pier. "Board one heading for Eldon. That should be the only thing on your mind."

"And there, I'll find someone like me?"

"Don't know." More like Gesu didn't care. His stiff jaw and stern brow revealed how badly he wanted to be far away from his cursed passenger.

Rowan tried not to let it get to him. His village had forsaken him. Soon they would be a passing thought. He leaned against the bulwark, wind swishing his hair. "Have you ever seen anyone with my red eyes and pale skin before?"

Gesu grunted, like the answer was obvious. "Your mother was the first, and she didn't stay long enough for us to learn her origins. You're on your own." He readied his pole, fingers twiddling with impatience, and fixed Rowan with a nudging stare to get off his barge.

Rowan shouldered his sack and leapt onto the pier. Gesu pushed off without another word.

Several swarthy men dressed in colorful silk robes bumped against Rowan's shoulders, shooting him irritated glances for standing like a twit in the middle of the pathway. Rowan felt completely out of place, like a phoenix in the water. The more stares he received, the more he pressed his head down and scuttled farther along the dock.

Stay on task. Find a ship.

He overheard many people using the common tongue. Naja had insisted he learn it. She must've known this day would eventually come—when he would be outcast and forced to find his place in the world of Tarcia.

Rowan approached the nearest vessel, where a dark-skinned Luvarian sailor oversaw men loading cargo. "Is this ship bound for Eldon?" he asked.

"Naw, we makes for Soltorra."

"Where can I find one heading to Eldon?"

"Try de *Silver Star*. Dey frequent Eldon. De ship's at dock eleven." The sailor pointed toward the port's south end. "Dat way. Dough, yous best hurry. I can sees dat dey're raising de mainsail."

Rowan thanked the man and hurried down the pier, pushing his way through the throng. He arrived at dock eleven, out of breath, sweat pouring down his neck and back. *Silver Star* was painted in flowy, white script along the ship's bow beside the sculpted figurehead of a woman with long, flowing hair that swirled around her curvy body, mimicking waves.

A jumble of noise grabbed Rowan's attention, and he twisted his head toward the sound. The gangplank was lifting off the dock.

Rowan raised his arms and shouted, "Wait! I need to board this ship!"

Two tan-skinned sailors, with their hands gripped around ropes, halted raising the gangplank. They gave Rowan bemused stares. "Why this boat?" one of them called out.

"Are you heading to Eldon?" Rowan asked.

"Aye, we are, laddie."

"Then let me aboard. I can pay." Rowan held up his purse.

The two men exchanged glances, pausing for only a moment before lowering the gangplank back onto the dock. "Hurry up, laddie. We're castin' off whilst the wind is strong."

Relief coursed through Rowan's veins as he rushed across the wooden plank. As soon as his feet struck the deck, the ship hoisted anchor and pulled away from the pier. Rowan steadied himself against the bulwark and caught his breath. His stiff posture relaxed.

I made it in time.

The two sailors approached; one strolled with a merry gait. They both wore open waistcoats with wooden buttons and linen trousers chopped off at their shins. The jolly one had a flashy, scarlet cummerbund tied around his sculpted waist, while the other man's was silky blue.

"Welcome aboard the *Silver Star*," greeted the man with the red sash. "Ma name's Tozrah." He was of average height, with a muscular build, and wore his dark, long locks loose around his face. "This here's Talek, our helmsman."

Rowan straightened, intimidated by the bulky helmsman, who had the beefiest arms he'd ever seen and stood a full head taller than Tozrah. "I'm grateful you let me aboard. I'm Rowan."

"Look here," Talek said with a phlegmy, gruff voice, unfurling his massive arms, "we're only lettin' ye aboard 'cos ye said ye could pay. So, let's see yer marks."

"Marks? All I have are these." Rowan pulled out several black pearls from his pouch.

The hope in Tozrah's cheerful eyes deflated. "Those aren't marks, laddie. I dinny know what they be."

Rowan placed the pearls back in his purse. "They're all I have."

"If that be all ye have," Talek said, his chunky dreads swaying in the breeze, "we'll have t'chuck ye overboard."

Rowan detected no remorse in the helmsman's words and panicked, thrusting his hands in front of him. "Please, no—don't. I must get to Eldon. These pearls have to be worth something. It's what we use to buy and trade in my village."

Talek eyed him with suspicion. "An' where in the stars is that?"

"Karahvel."

Talek's long nose and big lips scrunched in a befuddled frown. "Never heird o' it." He looked to Tozrah. "How aboot ye, Toz?"

"'Tis ringin' a bell." Tozrah scratched at his thick mane. "'Tis a remote village from what I heird. I dinny know folk still lived there."

"People do," Rowan said, lowering his head and glancing sideways, "though they don't look like me."

"I'll bet," Tozrah said with a chortle, pointing a callused finger to indicate all of Rowan. "Ain't no one this far east lookin' like ye. Ye'd need t'heid far, far southwest if ye wanna see any Shandrians."

Rowan perked up at the unfamiliar term. "Who are they?"

Tozrah slapped his sunburned forehead, flabbergasted. "'Tis what ye be, laddie! Dinny ye know yer own race?"

Rowan shrank back, a rush of embarrassment reddening his cheeks. "I don't know what I am. I've never been away from Karahvel before." His world before all of this was undeniably small. He was only now beginning to realize how wide it truly was.

"Ye're Shandrian, a'right," Tozrah proclaimed with a merry chuckle. "No mistakin' it."

Rowan's heart soared with hope. One piece to solving the mystery of his origins had been discovered. "Where can I find more Shandrians?"

Tozrah stared at him like he was a freshwater lout. "Weel, in Shandria, o' course."

Rowan felt more and more like an idiot. "And how do I get there?"

"Weel, not by boat, if that be what yer askin'." Tozrah chuckled, the lilt of his voice rising and falling like mild waves. "From Eldon, ye must go by land. 'Twill be a long journey."

Rowan drooped his head. "Doesn't matter. It's where I must go."

Tozrah snapped his fingers, drawing Rowan's gaze. "Hey, noo, laddie, yer forgettin' one thing: Ye dinny have marks fer this voyage."

"Please, let me stay," Rowan begged. His fear of being cast out again reared its shameful head. "I'll earn my keep, I swear."

Tozrah and Talek exchanged glances again. Talek shrugged, like it didn't matter much to him. He sighed and said, "I'll go explain this to Cap't Saville." Talek tromped off, disappearing up the aft deck.

"If yer gonna stay, then yer gonna work. I'm holdin' ye to it." Tozrah turned, searching for someone. "Izak! Fetch a swab bucket an' broom. We have oursels a new cabin boy fer this voyage."

Izak was burly and brawny, and scraggly black hairs covered every inch of his bare torso. He brought the items and plopped them at Rowan's feet. "Get t'swabbin'."

Rowan picked up the broom, holding it like he would his spear. "How do I, uh, swab?"

Tozrah threw back his head and guffawed. "Izak, show the lad how it's done."

NIGHT CAME LIKE A BLESSED SONG, ESPECIALLY AFTER A LONG, grueling day swabbing the main deck. Izak took Rowan to the galley for a bowl of Soltorran stew, which he learned meant it consisted mostly of a chewy meat called mutton. Rowan didn't care what it was and slopped up every drop in a manner of minutes. He hadn't eaten a morsel since he left Karahvel.

"Fer a skinny fella, ye sure can eat," Izak remarked, spooning up his stew.

"I'm not *that* skinny," Rowan mumbled.

Burning skies, will I be teased by everyone I encounter?

"I have muscles," Rowan said, straightening his shoulders. "They just, uh, aren't bulky."

"Weel, compared to us sailors, ye're as skinny as an eel." Izak took the liberty of showing off his thick biceps, as if Rowan needed reminding. For men who hauled cargo, hoisted sails, and manned rigging, it was little wonder how they got their strong physiques. "Say now, what sort o' work did ye do in yer village?"

"I harvested oysters and barley, but I also did a fair bit of hunting in the jungle."

Izak pointed his spoon at Rowan's belongings nestled at the foot of the table. "So, that spear o' yers isny jist fer show, eh?"

Rowan shook his head, flushing. "One of my guardian-mothers was an expert with the spear. She taught me how to wield it."

"Guardian-mother?" Izak frowned at the title. "How many o' those ye have?"

"I had four. They're all gone now. I'm on my own."

Izak grew quiet. He scratched his wiry black hair, then stood. "C'mon, lad. I'll show ye where ye can bunk fer the night."

Rowan grabbed his sack and followed along in silence. Mentioning the past cast a shadow of grief and regret upon his mood. Had he understood the effects of this "curse" early on, could he have done things differently? Somehow prevented his guardian-mothers' deaths?

Such futile thoughts. Rowan hurled them aside. Dwelling on them did no good. One couldn't alter the past.

They entered the berthing quarters where sailors lounged in canvas hammocks slung between beams. Several men were already passed out and snored louder than the groans of the ship.

"Here ye are," Izak announced, indicating an empty cubbyhole where Rowan could sleep.

Rowan stared at the small, rectangular opening in the floorboards and wondered how he'd make his body fit. Two adjacent cubbyholes stored rope, tools, and a collection of bundled goods.

"Rest up," Izak said, covering his palm over his wide mouth, yawning. "T'morrow, ye'll be swabbin' the forecastle and sterncastle deck."

Rowan didn't groan or complain; it was the bargain he'd struck. "Uh, thanks for teaching me the ropes, Izak. Sailoring isn't easy work."

"Aye, but 'tis rewardin'. One gets t'see the most wondrous o' places." Izak smiled, then wandered off to his own hammock.

Rowan retrieved his woven blanket and, using his sack as a pillow, he scrunched into the slot, tucking in his knees. He no sooner had sunk his head to rest when a jolly face wreathed by thick locks popped into view from above.

Rowan jolted in fright. "Burning skies! Don't scare me like that!"

"Sorry aboot that." Tozrah's chapped lips curved into an apologetic grin. "I jist wanted t'see how yer gettin' on."

"I'm fine." Rowan turned sideways, pulling the blanket up to his chin. "I've done laborious work most of my life."

"Good, good. I can see ye aren't a softie," Tozrah said, shifting positions in his swaying hammock. "So, what's yer story? I know ye have one. Why else would ye be so anxious t'climb upon this boat?"

Rowan sighed, resting his arm upon his forehead. "I was banished from my village."

Tozrah's dark violet eyes widened. "A nice laddie like yersel'? Whatever fer?"

"'Cause I'm different. The villagers didn't want me around." Rowan didn't mention the curse. The last thing he needed was to spook these sailors and give them reason to toss him overboard like spoiled cargo. "The chieftain told me to leave and never return. He tasked me with finding my own kind—it's where I belong."

"Belongin' somewhere, aye, 'tis a special feelin'." Tozrah's tone grew wistful, like he knew the feeling well. "Me an' ma mates have our homeland in Soltorra, but 'tis the sea that calls our hearts. 'Tis where we find we most belong. Every Soltorran is taught the wind an' tide when they're a bairn. Chartin' stars, hoistin' sails, 'tis in our blood. 'Tis who we are. 'Tis what we do. We sail beneath the goddesses' light."

"Dinny fret." Tozrah gave Rowan a lopsided grin. "I'm sure ye'll find a place t'belong. Ye have the look in yer eye o' one who be desperate fer answers. They'll come if ye keep yer heidin' straight. Though, ye best watch oot fer black sharks. The world o' Tarcia, 'tis like the sea. 'Tis wide an' vast an' filled with creatures who'd kill ye an' fer no other reason than it bein' their nature. Shandria isny the loveliest place from what I heird. Watch yersel', laddie."

"I don't know what to expect," Rowan admitted. A wave of nervousness stole over him. His body shivered beneath the blanket. "I only hope I can find someone who knew my mother. That's all I have to go on."

"'Twill be enough, I'm sure. If not, then ye can start afresh."

Tozrah made it sound so simple. To Rowan, starting a new life filled his mind with every fear he could imagine. What if his people didn't welcome him? What if the curse killed more people? What if everything that happened in Karahvel repeated in Shandria? What if he never learned who cursed him?

This dreaded noose around his neck dragged him beneath a whirlpool of worries.

I've come this far. The only choice is to keep traveling forward. Whatever it takes.

ROWAN PLUNGED THE MOP INTO THE SWAB BUCKET, SWISHED IT around, then scrubbed at a stubborn piece of seaweed stuck to the deck. A horde of the smelly, slimy-green substance was strewn across the sterncastle, baking under the sun. He had a pile shaped in a mound ready for chucking.

"When ye finish wi' this deck," Izak said, overseeing Rowan's progress, "ye can start on the forecastle deck. 'Tis got bits of seaweed an' muck from the journey a'ready."

Rowan swiped his forehead, readjusted his cowl, and kept swabbing. Tozrah and Izak, along with several others, were applying a goopy mixture to the ship's wood siding. Rowan wrinkled his nose at its strong odor.

Tozrah cracked a wide grin and held out his pitch bucket. "Wanna see?"

Rowan came closer and peered into the bucket, turning his nose at the dark, oozy substance. "What's it for?"

"Keeps the wood lookin' nice an' shiny."

"It reeks," Rowan said. "What's it made of?"

Tozrah rambled off the ingredients. "Pine tar, boiled linseed oil, turbine, an' beeswax. We make it oursels."

"And you use it on the entire ship?" Rowan asked, watching Izak apply the substance with liberal strokes.

"Jist aboot," Tozrah said, dunking his brush into the bucket. "Takes some time. 'Tis why we only do it once a week. Gotta keep the *Silver Star* lookin' her best."

Rowan picked up a loose clump of seaweed and flung it over the bulwark. "Sounds like you love this ship."

"Aye, she's a comely lass. She's home t'me an' ma mates."

Home. The one thing Rowan didn't have anymore. He hung his head and settled back into work. At least this hard labor kept his hands and mind occupied from dredging up the past.

The first day on this ship was tough. Day two, even worse. Not only did he have two decks to swab, but the cook snagged him to assist in delivering meals. And when it suited Captain Saville, he sent Rowan relaying orders to the crew on deck. By day three, he felt like a kalb tugged back and forth on a leash. He didn't even finish one chore before another landed in his lap.

"You sent for me, Captain?" Rowan asked, peeking his head into the ship's cabin.

The dark-bearded captain, whose navy-blue eyes were shadowed by his feather-festooned hat, glanced up and motioned to Rowan with a pudgy hand. "Take this to Talek." He pointed to a small note on the edge of his desk. "We're adjusting our course. A storm is approaching. I'm hoping we can bypass it."

Rowan raced onto the main deck, flew up the steps to the helm, and delivered the captain's note.

Talek eyed it and grunted with satisfaction. "I was wonderin' if he'd seen those dark clouds. They look nasty."

A shiver snaked through Rowan's bones. "Will a storm sink this ship?"

"It could," Talek said, stuffing the note inside his pocket, "but we're good at keepin' cool heids when things get hairy. Dinny worry yer heid. The *Silver Star* can handle whatever the sky hurls at her, jist ye watch."

Rowan didn't have to wait long. An hour later, the cloudburst hung overhead.

"Brace yersel', lad," Talek said, gripping the helm. "'Tis goin' t'be a rough ride."

Rain poured from the sky in a frenzy. The sea raged, tossing the ship. Waves climbed high as mountains. The wind howled as deafening as the pounding surf. The sailors hurled commands at one another, manning the rigging. Some lashed themselves to the bulwark to avoid flying overboard.

Rowan stumbled as he made his way off the sterncastle deck. Dizziness swirled inside him, and his stomach lost its contents. He crawled on hands and knees, his head reeling. He'd managed his seasickness up until now, but the rocking ship put his head in a violent spin.

A wave spilled across the deck, hurling Rowan clear across the main deck and against the starboard bulwark. Pain lanced through his back. The boat dipped forward, and Rowan went airborne. He yelped, scrounging for something to grab onto lest the sea swallow him in its raging jaws.

His fingers clawed at nothing; panic took hold. He veered over the side.

A pair of hands grabbed his waist and yanked him back against the deck. Rowan's stomach launched into his throat as Tozrah thrust him back on his feet.

"Lash yersel', laddie!" Tozrah shouted in his ear, steering him toward the mast. "Ye'll get eaten by a sea serpent if ye fall in." He threw a rope across Rowan's body. "Pull tightly. Ye won't be flyin' off if ye hold fast."

Fingers trembling, Rowan knotted the rope tightly around his waist. Tozrah dashed off to his post. Talek battled at the helm, arms bulging as he steered with all his might.

Rowan's frantic breaths coalesced into mist before his eyes. A terrible fright seized hold—body quivering, hands shivering, vision blurry from the relentless deluge. Despite the fear rampant in his nerves, Rowan gawked in awe at the sailors fighting the sea. Never had he seen such dauntless courage. Chaos surrounded them. Rain and sea were two relentless opponents, yet each sailor did their part, keeping the ship sailing forward.

"Keep that rigging secure!" Captain Saville belted, standing steely-faced near the helm. "We are on the tail end of this storm. Hold fast!"

"Hold fast!" Talek repeated, beginning a chant for the sailors. "Hold fast!"

When the storm at last subsided, Rowan still clung to the mast, teeth chattering. Sloshy footfalls approached from behind. He cocked his head and spotted Tozrah.

The smiley sailor tousled Rowan's drenched head. "Ye can let go, laddie. The gale has passed."

"Will it return?"

"I dinny think so. 'Tis smooth sailin' from here on oot."

Rowan breathed easier. He hoped Tozrah's prediction proved true.

"Steady as she goes, Talek," Captain Saville said from the helm. "Send the cabin boy to alert me if the weather changes again. I shall be in my cabin."

Rowan released his grip on the mast, his knuckles sheet-white, and untied the rope's knot to the sound of Tozrah's increasing laughter. He shot the sailor a testy glare. "What's so funny?"

"Why *you*, laddie!" Tozrah beamed. "With all yer soaked clothes, ye look like a drowned goat!"

Rowan grunted, and his cheeks reddened. He removed his cowl and gave it a tight wringing.

"Aye, noo," Tozrah slapped Rowan hard on his back, "give yersel' a hearty clap. Ye survived yer first sea storm!"

Rowan didn't feel an ounce of exuberance. "I never want to go through that again."

Tozrah wrung out his sash. "T'wasn't so bad."

"I almost flew off the ship!" Rowan exclaimed, his voice pitchy.

"I was there t'catch ye. Couldn't let the sea have ye, not when ye must reach Eldon, aye?"

Eldon, yes — a return to land. It couldn't come soon enough.

Tozrah waved him below deck. "A bowl o' hot stew 'tis jist what yer shiverin' bones need. Eat yer fill, 'cos afterward, the decks'll be needin' swabbin' again." The sailor jabbed an elbow against Rowan's ribs. "'Sides, there also be that pile o' vomit ye left behind. In case ye forgot."

Cheeks aflush, Rowan hung his drenched head. A cabin boy's work never ceased.

CHAPTER 3
ELDON

"Land ho!" the lookout hollered from the crow's nest.
Rowan rushed the bulwark with excitement, catching his first glimpse, in the distance, of a land mass with rugged cliffs and rolling hills. A massive, circular, walled city nestled along the raised coastline sprinkled with clay rooftops, ivory towers, and green pasturelands. To the southwest, vast grass plains buffeted by the wind stretched along the landscape like thread, and farther south lay a dark forest with lofty trees of the varieties Rowan had never seen.

He had reached a new world.

At the port straight ahead, ships' colors danced in the breeze. And far, far in the distance, glittering like a mound of white shells, stood a marvelous bastion with a host of spires piercing the cerulean sky.

Mesmerized, Rowan pointed. "What's that building at the top of the city?"

"'Tis Castle Roidel," Tozrah said, winding up a rope. "Home o' the Immortal King."

The very name sent a shudder through Rowan's bones. "Um, who's that?"

Tozrah sniffed. "Oh, jist the ruler o' the world. Near aboot, anyway. Yer homeland o' Shandria be under his domain, same as mine, same as most."

"Eldon must be a prosperous place, then?"

"Aye, 'tis so. As the capital o' Mestria, Eldon has its share o' lucrative exports, but like any large city, 'tis got a murky underbelly. Steer clear o' the slums, if ye dinny want t'get snatched or mugged."

"Where should I head then?" Rowan asked.

"The Merchant District. 'Tis jist beyond the port. Ask 'round the taverns—"

"Taverns?" Rowan interrupted, frowning. "What're those?"

"Er, weel, they be ale houses, places fer drinkin', that sort o' thing. Keep yer eye oot fer signs, they'll steer ye right. Inside a tavern 'tis the best way t'find other travelers. Ye might get lucky an' find a caravan headin' south. 'Twill be yer best bet."

Rowan smiled, grateful for Tozrah's input. "Thanks for the advice."

Tozrah hung up the rope and found another task to occupy his hands.

The *Silver Star* sailed into the port and dropped anchor. Lowering the gangplank, the sailors set to unloading their cargo.

"Guess this be farewell, laddie." Tozrah's violet eyes twinkled like gems in the bright sunlight. "May the goddesses' light watch o'er ye on yer travels."

Rowan blushed. "Uh, and yours, Toz. Will you give the others my thanks?"

Tozrah's chapped lips curved in a cheeky grin. "Give it to 'em yersel'!"

A pair of beefy arms engulfed Rowan from behind, lifting him clear off the deck. The surprise barrel-hug choked his breath until he landed back on his sandaled feet. Talek and Izak laughed in his ears like boisterous seagulls.

"That be a Soltorran send-off," Izak claimed with a hearty chuckle.

A far better send-off than I received in Karahvel.

Rowan returned their merry smiles. He'd been fortunate to sail with this jolly crew across the Ardruin Sea. Now the next leg of his journey awaited.

After thanking the three sailors, Rowan shouldered his sack and strapped his shortspear at his back. He disembarked, then gave the crew of the *Silver Star* a final wave before leaving the pier.

He followed a group of Luvarian peddlers who looked like they knew their way around the sprawling city. The scent of the sea lingered through the streets. The farther Rowan roamed, the more he was thankful for the peddlers, as they kept him from getting lost. Every street resembled the next, crammed with tall buildings.

Did one family live in each one?

The high rooftops casting shadows upon the well-traveled roads dwarfed the huts back in Karahvel. There, everyone spent the majority of their time outside in the sun, working the fields, harvesting pearls in the estuary, or tending their gardens. The bamboo huts were used primarily for one thing—sleeping.

What kinds of things did Eldonians store in their huge homes? Rowan was tempted to peek. Despite his curiosity, he kept from staring at any window in particular—his first priority was finding a tavern. He hadn't seen a sign indicating one yet. Perhaps he was on the wrong street.

He stopped for a moment and glanced back the way he'd come. The port was no longer visible, let alone the sea. How far inland had he traveled?

The peddlers he followed found a place to set up shop. A line of stalls cluttered the street, along with a mass of folk in every size, shape, and skin color. Rowan had never seen so many people in one place. He wandered down the thoroughfare, intrigued by the handmade crafts and exotic foods that made his mouth water. Merchants called out bargains on their wares and sundries.

Rowan reached the edge of the street only to find several branching alleys.

Now where to go?

He picked the left route and hoped it led him to a tavern—any would do. There, he could get a hot meal and a means to travel onward. He already didn't like the feel of this city. It was much too big, too crowded, too . . . *foreign*. A quiet shore and a warm breeze would be a welcome comfort.

He needed lodgings for the night. He doubted anyone would be setting off on a journey this late in the afternoon. Then he remembered a major problem: He had no marks. He couldn't buy a meal, let alone a bed for the night. He was out of luck.

Rowan grumbled under his breath. "When did I ever have luck? I've been cursed all my—"

"What do we 'ave 'ere? A lost Shandrian pup?"

Rowan jolted. A row of cloak-wearing urchins perched upon the roof right above him. Tozrah's warning raced through his mind.

"Steer clear o' the slums, if ye dinny want t'get snatched or mugged."

Had he accidentally wandered into the slums? And was the hooded bunch lurking above him a pack of thieves?

"I don't have any marks," Rowan said, edging backward, "so leave me be."

One of them cackled, his mischievous grin half-shadowed by the willowy urchin looming behind him. He threw back his gray hood, shaking his wavy, brown hair in mirth. Short, with glinting, blue eyes, he exuded the crafty visage of a streetwise knave. "Yeah, we know ya got no marks. I've been trailin' ya for a good bit and figured that out early on. What ya look like is lost to me. Where ya headin'?"

Rowan came straight out with it. "I'm trying to find a tavern."

The chatty thief cocked his head. "Ain't ya a bit youn' for ale?"

"It's not to drink," Rowan retorted, cheeks blushing. "I need to find travelers heading to Shandria."

"Ah, well, in that case," the thief said with a cheery pep, "I can save ya the trouble. I know of a caravan goin' there. Leaves t'morrow, which gives ya plenty of time to hang with us."

Rowan eyed the group with suspicion. "And why would I do that?"

"'Cuz ya look like ya could use a friend on the street."

The cocoa-complected urchin stooped his coily head over the thief, chuckling. "He gots de look of a first-timer written all over 'im."

"I'll say," the short thief agreed, sharing a grin with his pal. "Eldon can be dangerous for a newcomer. Best stick with us. We'll keep ya safe. Wouldn't want some thug snaggin' ya off the street."

The urchin and his friends dropped to the cobblestone in a synchronous swoop.

"The name's Curren, by the way," the thief said, approaching Rowan with a welcoming gait. "I'm the leader of this crew, and who might ya be?"

Rowan eased backward as he shared his name.

Curren roped an arm across Rowan's shoulder as if they were close friends and flicked a finger toward the tallest member of his crew. "That there's Casir."

The young man's lanky build reminded Rowan of a lean beanstalk, and the black mop of kinky hair sprouting from his scalp were the flowering spikelets.

Casir sent Rowan a casual wave, wiggling his long, ebony fingers. "Welcome ta de fold," he said, his cadence skipping like a rock across a stream.

The golden-haired girl loitering behind Casir narrowed her edgy gaze in Rowan's direction; a standoffish gleam dwelt in her dark-brown eyes. It wasn't the same scornful glare he received from the villagers in Karahvel, but something else—a distrust of some kind. Rowan couldn't say he blamed her. It wasn't like he trusted these young urchins.

Curren shot the unfriendly girl a pointed look. "Hey, Thura, stop starin' daggers at our new friend. Would it kill ya to smile?"

"Smile?" Thura rolled her eyes and maintained a scowl. "I don't give those out as *freely* as you do." She half-turned with a flip of her fishtail braid and kept a lookout, sliding her fingers along the helves of the two, sleek hatchets secured at her hips.

Curren clicked his tongue. "Don't be put off by Thura's frosty nature," he told Rowan. "She's like this 'round everyone."

A girl with sun-kissed skin sashayed up to Rowan, her flouncy orchid dress swaying with the pitter-patter of her footsteps. "Well, I think it's nice to meet ya," she said in a coy, overeager voice. "Call me Daejah."

Unlike the aloof blonde, Daejah offered a bright, inviting smile. Her dark-brown hair held up by a flowery hairpin slid from one petite shoulder to the other as she tilted her head back and forth, surveying Rowan's face. "Y'know, we don't see many Shandrians in Eldon," she said. "So, ya're kinna a treat for the eyes."

The way Daejah's dazzling violet eyes twinkled brought a torrid flush to Rowan's face. His shoulders tensed, and he tried to look anywhere but into Daejah's eyes.

Curren must've sensed Rowan's discomfort and wagged a finger at Daejah. "Back up, Dae. I think you're makin' 'im uncomfortable."

Daejah glided a slender finger over her red-painted lips. "Sorry, darlin'," she said, sending Rowan a teasing wink. "I'll spare ya from gettin' the wrong idea. I'm already taken." She looped her arms around a fiery-haired young man, who stood nearly as tall as Casir but boasted a more muscular frame. "Aren't ya gonna say hello, Hal?"

It didn't seem that Hal heard her. He did nothing but stare as though Rowan had sprouted horns from his head.

What's with him?

Hal's russet eyes were unsettling, unnerving, even soul-piercing. Rowan's entire body recoiled with distrust. He instantly wanted space.

Rowan snaked free of the rambunctious thief and backed away from this group of strangers. Sure, they were a bunch of youngsters, probably near Rowan's age, but Tozrah's words evoked caution.

Curren lifted his arms in a show of good faith. One hand held a juicy, red apple. "Jumpy fella, ain't ya?"

Rowan thrust his arm out in a warning gesture. "You shouldn't touch me."

Curren gave him a funny look before sinking his teeth into his apple. "Why not? Ya carryin' some kinda disease?"

Rowan's eyes lowered to the street. "Well, no, but people around me tend to die earlier than they ought . . ." he trailed off, withholding any mention of his curse.

Curren raised an eyebrow. "Must be somethin' serious then?"

Rowan's shoulders tensed as he shrugged. "It's the reason I'm here. I was banished from my village."

The intrigue drooling on Curren's lips turned into a wild grin. "Great, y'all fit right in with us. We're all outcasts! We could use a Shandrian in our company." He threw a thumb over his shoulder. "Hal 'ere killed the last one."

Rowan jerked his head, warily looking at the red-haired youth. "You killed someone?"

"Flames, Curren." Hal shot his friend a testy scowl. "Ya can't say somethin' like that outta context! He'll think I'm a heartless murderer."

"Don't worry," Curren reassured Rowan with another friendly shoulder clasp. "That slithery snake deserved it. We're thieves, not butchers."

Rowan didn't feel any less comforted. He hadn't quite formed an opinion about these Eldonian urchins yet. Despite their friendliness, they possessed a dangerous energy. Thura radiated ferocity even without her pair of hatchets. Several knives hung on each of the male's belts, and those were only the visible ones. Under their worn cloaks, Rowan assumed they carried more. These thieves had likely seen their share of alley fights and knew how to tread these streets, unlike Rowan.

At least they didn't cast him off, even after hearing of his banishment. It earned them an ounce of trust, but Rowan remained cautious. After getting exiled from his village, he wouldn't trust anyone fully for a long time. Maybe never.

"Say, ya must be hungry," Curren said, with another mouthful of apple. "'Ere, 'ave some meat." He slapped two pieces of dried jerky in Rowan's hand. "And don't give me that look. We didn't steal it. We paid for it fair and square. We may be thieves, but that don't mean we steal everythin'. That there's the best jerky y'all find in the district."

"'Course, in de past, ya did try stealin' it," Casir said, flashing a cheeky grin.

"I learned my lesson," Curren said with a cavalier huff. "I couldn't swindle a thin' under the eyes of the shop owner—think he could sniff out my intentions. Anyhow, we always pay if wantin' anythin' from his shop."

Rowan eyed the thief. "And the apple?"

"Oh, this I stole." Curren finished it off, then tossed the core aside. "C'mon, back to the hideout. We've idled long enough on these streets. Don't wanna attract any unwanted attention."

"Go on ahead of us," Hal told Curren, coming alongside Rowan. "There's somewhere I wanna take our friend beforehand."

"Do as ya like." Curren waved for Casir and Thura to follow, and the three of them dashed off.

Rowan was left alone with Hal and Daejah, and unease pitted in his stomach. He eyed Hal, scrutinizing every detail. His straight red hair gathered in a low, messy bun and his fair complexion—blemished with sooty smudges—seemed contradictory with his purposeful gait and the dignity elevating his broad shoulders. Rowan couldn't explain it, but something seemed *off* about him.

Or maybe it's me who's off.

Rowan had never interacted with youths his age who didn't harass him. His awkward behavior toward their friendliness had to be painfully obvious.

The couple strolled back the way Rowan originally came.

"Um, where are we headed?" Rowan asked, picking up his pace to match Hal's earnest strides.

"To a friend of mine," Hal answered, his titian eyes alight with an enigmatic luster. "He runs a stall along the thoroughfare on Market Row. If you're gonna go to Shandria, ya gotta look the part. We'll start with your clothes."

Rowan glanced down at his tunic's tan, baggy sleeves. "What's wrong with my clothes?"

"Everythin'," Hal blurted, wagging his finger up and down at Rowan's attire.

Rowan bristled. "Hey, they keep my skin from getting burned."

"So will actual Shandrian attire," Hal said, "and then you'll look like ya belong. That's what ya want, in'n it?"

The thief's words took Rowan aback. "How do you know that? I never said anything—"

"Ya didn't 'ave to," Hal interjected, exchanging a good-humored smile with Daejah, who glided along beside him, holding his hand. "It's written all over your face."

Rowan stared sideways at the thief, dumbfounded.

Daejah leaned behind Hal and gave Rowan a reassuring smile. "Don't be bothered—that's just Hal. He's got a knack for knowin' what people think."

How could Rowan not be bothered?

Am I the only one who finds that unnerving?

"So, in other words," Rowan said, "he's nosy."

"As nosy as they come," Daejah said with a giggle.

"The booth's right 'round the corner." Hal's steps hastened, and an eager grin illuminated his face. "Aha! 'Ere it is—The Nimble Weaver. Come take a look."

Rowan wandered inside the small, enclosed stall, finding tables and shelves arrayed with an assortment of neatly folded clothing. Leather boots and everyday slippers were stacked in wooden cubbies for easy display and accessibility.

"Good day to ya, Gunther," Hal said to the shop owner lurking behind the rustic-wood counter.

A man with an untrimmed beard and dark, oily hair pulled back in a ponytail rose from a wooden chair, holding a simple cane for support. Rowan couldn't take his eyes off the black patch that covered the man's left eye. A scar peaked above the eye patch, gnarly enough to make him shiver.

Daejah leaned in close and whispered, "Don't stare. It makes Gunther grumpy. He used to be a soldier—'tis how he lost his eye."

Rowan whipped his gaze to the cobblestone before the shop owner caught him staring.

Gunther limped around the counter, favoring his right leg. "What brings ya by?"

"I brought a friend in dire need of new clothes." Hal grabbed Rowan by the forearm and thrust him forward so Gunther could get a good look at the obvious apparel problem.

A gruff chuckle escaped the shop owner's uneven lips. "I'll say. His clothin' is quite worn. What do ya 'ave in mind for the lad?"

"An outfit or two fit for a young, strappin' Shandrian."

"Oh, is that what he is?" Gunther lifted his scruffy eyebrows. "I was distracted by all the layers of woven Luvarian cloth. Thought he might've been bleached by the sun or somethin'." Gunther's dull eyes scrutinized Rowan like he was the oddest oddity the man had ever seen. "Ya look like a lad who's confused."

"Go easy on 'im, will ya?" Hal said, stifling a chuckle. "He's new to our corner of the world."

Hal and the shop owner shared some jests at Rowan's expense.

And the teasing continues.

Hal's laughter faded, and he asked, "So, can ya help us out?"

"I've got several thin's that might fit the lad." The shop owner set upon his task, rummaging through one stack of clothes, picking up an item, and then another, until he held a complete outfit.

Gunther handed Rowan several folded items and a pair of boots, then pointed to a partitioned area. "You can take off your worn clothes and try on these new threads in there."

Rowan went over to the small, enclosed area and undressed. After a week of sea travel, his outfit had seen better days. He didn't have any qualms about discarding his old clothes. They were a piece of his past—a past he wanted to forget and forever leave behind.

Taking hold of the first item, he donned the scarlet undertunic, then the same colored overtunic, followed by a gray tabard. He slipped his legs into the charcoal trousers and wriggled his feet into a black pair of leather boots that cinched below his knees.

Rowan fiddled with the ruby sash around his waist and stepped out from behind the curtain. "I'm not sure this is right."

"Almost." Hal grinned and came behind Rowan to assist. "The sash should be tied to the side like this."

"My, what a handsome Shandrian," Daejah commented, her lips curving into a vibrant smile. "These clothes suit ya well."

Rowan blushed and quickly glanced at the hanging mirror, only to discover his cheeks were as red as pottery paint. He twisted from side to side, admiring his new attire. The fabric was simple and comfortable, and the dark red brought warmth to his albino skin.

"What of a hooded cloak?" Hal hollered to Gunther. "He'll need one for his long journey."

Gunther glanced at Rowan. "Does the lad 'ave a color preference?"

"Um, blue, perhaps?" It would remind him of the sea and his time with the Soltorran sailors.

"Let's see what I got." Gunther searched through the cloaks hanging at the back of the stall. He selected one colored midnight blue. "This should contrast nicely with the red of your tunics. Try it on."

Rowan slid the cloak across his shoulders and placed the hood over his head. "Well, what do you think?" he asked Hal and Daejah.

They flashed satisfied grins. Daejah snuggled her lithe frame against Hal and grasped his arm. "I think he looks ready for his journey, don't ya, darlin'?"

"Agreed." Hal twisted his head and got Gunther's attention with a snappy whistle. "We'll take whatever else ya picked out."

"I've got several outfits on the counter. Take a look and decide what ya think."

Daejah gamboled over, radiating a smile of pure delight. "I like these," she said, setting several items aside. "Rowan should look quite fetchin' in 'em."

Rowan hid his blush behind Hal's taller frame. Daejah's every word and glance heated his skin. All his life, he'd never experienced a girl's flirtatious attention.

"Don't be embarrassed. Daejah has a magical allure on men," Hal whispered, somehow knowing exactly what Rowan was thinking.

"So, it's not just me, then?"

"Nah. She's made me blush more times than I thought possible."

Gunther tallied up the cost; it brought a stab of panic to Rowan's insides. Swept up in the moment, he entirely forgot about the payment.

"Um, Hal?" Rowan whispered over the thief's shoulder. "How am I going to pay for this? I don't have any marks, remember?" The red-haired sleuth wasn't planning on stealing, was he?

"Never ya mind 'bout that. I got ya covered." Hal's attention turned back to Gunther, and he dropped a handful of shiny coins onto the counter. "That oughta cover 'im."

Gunther picked up the coins, chuckling. "Helpin' out more strays, eh?"

"Only those in desperate need," Hal said, like it was no special undertaking. "This one got 'imself lost in the Merchant District. Me and my friends saw his obvious need and decided to assist."

Gunther placed the coins in his lockbox beneath the counter. "Well, come 'round again whenever ya find a stray in need of new threads."

Hal bid the merchant farewell and exited the stall. Rowan chased after him, finding his new boots surprisingly comfortable. As much as he enjoyed his sandals, they were better suited to the sand and not for extended travel. Hal had done him a great service.

As Rowan walked, he kept fingering the softness of his tabard's cloth. What exactly was it made from? No material in Karahvel came remotely close.

Daejah wandered ahead, poking her slim nose into a stall boasting colorful hair ribbons. Hal watched her from a distance, an amorous glow filtering his titian eyes.

Rowan took advantage of the moment and asked the question that had been weighing on his mind since they'd left The Nimble Weaver. "Hal, uh, why'd you do this?"

"Hm?" Hal said, distracted. "Do what?"

"Why'd you go out of your way to buy these clothes for someone like me?"

A frown spread across Hal's face. "Someone like you? You make it sound like you're somehow different from all of us."

"But I am," Rowan insisted, his body tensing. "People are . . . *dead* because of me."

Hal's eyes narrowed in an enigmatic way, peering far past Rowan's skin and into his soul. "And 'cuz of that, ya think ya don't deserve to be shown kindness?"

Rowan didn't acknowledge it, but somewhere in the dark recesses of his mind, the insidious shame he carried wouldn't let him think otherwise. "I oughta give you something in return."

Hal turned and put his hands on his hips. "Like what?"

"Er, well, I have these black pearls." Rowan pulled one out and showed it to Hal. "Interested?"

The thief's eyes lit up like bronzed amber. "Where'd ya find such a fine beauty?"

Rowan's tension eased at Hal's sudden delight. "From my village. We farm the oysters that make these pearls."

"Really?" Hal's eyes gleamed with fascination. "It's exquisite!"

"Here, have one then. It's the least I can offer for all your help."

Hal took it and held it up in the sunlight. "I know a girl who'll love this. Gotta make it into a pretty piece of jewelry first." He placed it in his pocket, then dipped his face close. "Keep those pearls somewhere safe, Rowan. They're worth far more than ya think."

Rowan shook his head, perplexed. "I thought they were no good?"

"Who told ya that?"

Rowan shrugged. "The Soltorrans aboard the *Silver Star*."

"Well, they're no good in Soltorra, but in Shandria, one of those'll buy ya a horse and carriage. A bagful like what ya got would get ya land with an estate, makin' ya a baron."

Rowan's brows scrunched. "What's a baron?"

"A rich landowner."

Rowan nearly choked as he swallowed. "Wait, did you say rich?"

Hal laughed with delight. "Welcome to your new station in life, Rowan. Your luck's 'bout to change."

Rowan spent much of the night and morning mulling over Hal's words. Could his life truly take a drastic turn when he reached Shandria? It seemed too good to be true. Even if his pearls granted him wealth, he was still cursed. He wouldn't consider himself lucky in any way until he threw off this noose hanging around his head.

Rowan waited on the edge of the dirt road leading out of Eldon as Hal and Curren spoke to the leader of the caravan, a man with dark skin, bushy hair, and even bushier eyebrows. Curren suavely handled the negotiations, chatting it up like he and the Luvarian caravaneer were old friends. Perhaps he was that way with everyone.

Securing Rowan's passage, Hal dropped marks into the caravaneer's hand. The man gave an approving nod, and then pointed to one of the wagons for Rowan to board. Business concluded, the Luvarian moved to the lead wagon, securing the horses.

Hal approached, sporting a satisfactory smile. "You'll be ridin' in the rear wagon. It won't be too comfy."

"It's fine. My cramped cubbyhole on the *Silver Star* was worse," Rowan admitted, giving his back a long stretch. He still had a trove of knots and kinks from the voyage. "I guess this is goodbye, then."

Curren sauntered next to him and gave his shoulder a friendly clap. "If your people don't want ya, ya've got a home 'ere. The door to our hideout will always be open to ya."

Rowan could have broken into tears. "Why're you all being so kind to me?"

"Ain't it obvious?" Curren thumped a finger against Rowan's chest. "You're like us—a stray. And we strays gotta stick together. It's what makes us a family."

The word touched Rowan's heart in a way he'd never quite known. "A family, huh?" A place to belong. He smiled, his heart brimming with emotions. "Thanks for the offer. It means more than you know."

"Hey, now, don't go gettin' all mushy on us—right, fellas?" Curren received a host of nods from his friends before continuing.

"Get yourself sorted in Shandria, and come back for a visit. Casir 'ere will prepare a savory fare that'll make your tastebuds sing and dance."

Casir gave a big, lopsided grin. "I'll makes my spicy curry for ya. It'll be an explosion of flavor beyond imaginin'."

Rowan laughed, enjoying how it felt to be unburdened. "For that, a return trip would be worth it."

The thieves took their turns giving him farewells and sage advice for his journey. When Daejah's turn came, she fixed Rowan with a bold smile and a parting wink.

Even Thura unscrewed her lips long enough to force out a sentiment. "Watch your back out there."

Daejah cast Thura a less-than-enthused expression. "Ya call that a goodbye?"

Thura smacked her cool lips together. "It is where I'm from. He's lucky to get even that."

"Um . . . thanks, Thura," Rowan said, trying not to sound as rigid as the blonde looked. "It's not bad advice."

The sharp edge in Thura's dark eyes softened, and she dipped her chin in a small nod before joining Casir.

Then, one-by-one, the thieves turned and left, until only Hal remained. His demeanor shifted to a serious stare, like the one he wore at their first meeting.

"I know what afflicts you." Hal's statement caught Rowan off-guard. "You harbor a life-draining curse."

Rowan's throat clamped, and he leaned backward. "How do you know this?"

"Because I can *see* it."

Rowan's mouth dropped. "H-how?"

"Like you, I am different." The timbre of Hal's voice changed. Its lilt was more refined, as though—all along—this was his normal way of speaking. He circled Rowan, arms folded, gaze penetrating. "A black miasma surrounds you, visible to my eyes. It is harmful to every form of life." Hal pointed at the ground. "Even the grass beneath your feet is already decaying. It is the reason people sicken around you and slowly die."

Once again, the reality of his situation crashed in like a breaking wave. Rowan balled his hands into fists. "So, it's really true, then?"

"Afraid so."
The majiri was right all along.

Rowan clawed at his crescent mark, wishing he could pry it free from his skin. "Is there any hope for me?"

"There is always hope." Hal's encouraging smile held a comforting assurance. "Believe me, if anyone understands your dilemma, it is I."

Rowan gave a sarcastic grunt. "Don't tell me you've got a curse as well?"

Hal's smile faded. "Not like yours, no, but a fated curse I aim to break. I will not stop until I rewrite my future, nor should you."

His powerful words stirred awake something inside Rowan. Like a warm wind, it passed through the chambers of his heart and lit a flame. Was it hope? Or conviction?

"Fates are not etched in stone," Hal went on. "Your curse does not define you. It is merely an obstacle you must crush to alter fate."

Rowan grinned despite himself. "You really aren't like the others. Why is that?"

Hal's eyes gleamed. "Are you asking to know my secret?"

Rowan nodded with earnest curiosity. "There shouldn't be any harm in it. You know mine, and I'm headed to another country and likely won't return."

"That is a good point. Then here it is." Hal dipped his head in close with a cheeky grin. "I am Mestria's Crown Prince."

Rowan's eyes widened. "Y-you're a prince?" he said, flabbergasted. Did this mean he lived in that glittering castle with the Immortal King? Then why would he tromp the streets with a bunch of common thieves? Was it solely out of amusement or for a greater purpose?

"Ashes, you should see the shock on your face," Hal said, chortling.

Rowan closed his gaping mouth and raked his hair, grappling for something to say. "I'm guessing your, uh, thieving friends don't know about this, do they?"

Hal shook his fiery-red hair, his mysterious air returning. "Alas, they are in the dark."

"Well, whatever reason you're hiding it from them, it must be important."

Hal released a heavy sigh. "We all harbor secrets. Not all can be shared with whomever we want. Be mindful who you tell about your curse."

Right. It wasn't information he should unwisely announce. "I'll bear that in mind."

"Oh, and one more thing." Hal removed a sleek, cross-hilted knife from his belt and held it out to Rowan. "Take this."

Rowan hesitated. "I have my spear."

"Something tells me you will have need of a knife." Hal pushed the hilt into Rowan's hand. "Trust me: A man should never travel without a knife. It might save your life. Or another's."

Rowan took the weapon and concealed it beneath his sash.

Hal stepped back, a kind smile softening the intensity in his eyes. "Farewell, Rowan. I hope you find a way to lift your curse."

Rowan returned Hal's smile. "You as well." He found his place among the procession and boarded the wagon.

As he rode out of the city, a question drifted into Rowan's mind: *What other new sights am I bound to see before reaching Shandria?*

CHAPTER 4
WHERE SHADOWS STRIKE

When night fell, the caravan stopped and made camp alongside the East Sea Road. The travelers pitched their tents far from the shadow of the forest. The Grimwood. Folk in the camp spoke its name with fearful shudders. A cool wind snaked through the ominous trees, rustling the mangled branches. They groaned as if gasping for breath, and a foreboding quiver crawled up Rowan's spine.

Kirani, the leader of the caravan, noticed Rowan staring and barked, "Dan't get close ta dat forest, y'hear?"

Rowan turned to face the caravaneer lounging by the fire. "Why not?"

"Foul things lurk inside." Kirani took a swig of ale. "Moonshades could attack, devouring your soul 'n bones quicker dan yous can scream for mercy."

A harrowing chill swept through Rowan's veins even as he took a seat beside the blazing fire. "Um, how do they devour souls?"

Kirani's thick unibrow lifted as he tapped his moccasin-style boots together. "Haven't yous heard de stories?"

Rowan shook his head and pulled out a piece of dried meat; Curren had given him two generous bundles. "This part of the world is new to me. There's much I don't know."

Kirani's sable-brown eyes peered over the lid of his mug, spying the woods. "Let's hope yous never learn how'a Moonshade feeds. It'll scar yous for life—er, dat is, if yous live through de encounter."

Rowan fought the hard lump in his throat as he swallowed his bite. After Kirani's disturbing tale, he wanted far away from these gloomy woods. "How long until we clear this forest?"

"Two more days," Kirani said, firelight dancing on his dark skin. "De East Sea Road hugs de Grimwood at every stretch for many miles. Once we're clear, we shan't hav'ta worry about dose cursed demons. Rarely do dey leave de darkness of dose woods."

Cursed demons, huh?

Rowan chewed at his jerky, deep in thought. What made Moonshades cursed? Was it anything like his curse? If people in this caravan knew of Rowan's situation, would they call him a cursed demon as well?

Such dour thoughts drew Rowan to eat in silence. He spent the better part of the following day keeping to himself. He feared if he opened his mouth to speak, his entire reason for heading to Shandria would spill out of him. So he avoided eye contact with every traveler in his wagon and, instead, kept his gaze affixed to the Ardruin Sea. The ebb and flow of the tide against the cliffs mesmerized him. He was awed by the way it crashed and pounded the rocks, splashing mist high into the air. Such power.

"Water is the most destructive force in nature," Naja told him once, during his spear training. *"Its power is unmatched. And yet, when it's still, there's untold tranquility. It's a balance we, as warriors, would do well to emulate."*

Still water, steady heart. It was Naja's faithful mantra, evoked during their hunts inside the Thulu Jungle.

Rowan removed the cowl hood from his sack and read the colored thread telling of his victory over his first twin-tail. Tears moistened his eyes when he came to the affirming phrase: *I see you as equal and warrior.* His fingers tugged at the tight weave. The pain of losing Naja gripped his heart. He missed her reassuring smile, the way her dark lips lifted whenever he wrote her messages in weavescript—a cherished game between them.

He could never write her another message. Her smile was gone —*she* was gone. He sank his head back and lost himself in the passing clouds of the twilight sky.

When the stars revealed themselves, the wagons once again stopped for the night. Travelers built fires on the edges of camp. From what he overheard from Kirani, flames often deterred the Moonshades.

Rowan prepared his spot near a small fire. He draped Naja's hood over his sack to serve as a pillow and snuggled beneath his woven blanket. He slept under the shining stars and dreamed of Naja, of when they hunted and gathered food inside the jungle. It brought a smile to his sleeping face and a somber longing to his heart.

ON THE THIRD NIGHT OF TRAVEL, ROWAN AWOKE TO SCREAMS. HE bolted upright and threw back his blanket. His eyes darted after the frenzied shapes. People stampeded like a wild herd, forsaking their tents and belongings, as ominous shadows sliced through the camp with coiling claws of black smoke.

Rowan squinted in the darkness. A murky monster attacked, and then another, striking with fangs glinting beneath the silver moonlight. A pair of stark-white eyes approached in the darkness, causing Rowan to freeze in his tracks.

What are those things?

"Get de wagons ready!" Kirani yelled out. "We must leave!"

"Horses are spooked!" a pale-faced Mestrian man responded in a panic. "They're not cooperating."

"Make dem!" Kirani shouted. "We can't stay put. Moonshades are on de prowl."

Rowan's blood chilled at the caravaneer's words. He reached for his sack, stuffed his blanket and hood inside, then grasped his spear. He didn't know what they faced, but he'd rather do it with a weapon in hand.

Leaves from the trees scratched at the air—a discordant buzz. And then he smelled something foul. A strange, sulfuric stench permeated the camp, twisting Rowan's gut.

A sleek creature bathed in swirling blackness burst from behind a tent. Its mane of snaky tendrils teemed and slithered around its feline-shaped skull and bladelike canines. Swift and agile, it pounced on a fleeing girl, knocking her to the ground. She screamed in frightful terror.

The pitch of her wail raked at Rowan's ears, shackling his bones. He *needed* to help her, but his legs wouldn't budge.

Naja's voice came to him in that paralyzing moment, a balm upon his nerves.

"*To kill a predator, you can't behave as prey. Still water, steady heart. See the beast as an equal, and be fearless in your strike.*"

Still water, steady heart. Rowan repeated the mantra under his breath, calming his spirit. Instincts returned in a flash, and the fear drained from his veins. His legs unclamped, and they carried him right before the beast.

Rowan whipped his spear forward with white knuckles and drove the weapon into the creature's skull. Bone crunched, and black blood oozed from the wound. The creature flung open its unhinged jaw and belted a deafening eldritch scream.

The girl scrambled away from the ghoulish monster, nursing a shredded arm. The creature flicked its nebulous mane, tracking her movements. It crouched low, preparing its attack.

"Stay back, demon!" Rowan hissed. He swung his weapon and buried the spearhead into the creature's white, lidless eye. Another baleful scream assaulted his eardrums.

Rowan reared back, ripping the spearhead free. The creature swung its canines like daggers, then lunged for Rowan's head with a quick snap of its jaw. Rowan spun, avoiding the attack, and buried his spear in the back of the monster's neck.

The move bought him a moment.

He dashed for the girl, grabbed her uninjured arm, and yanked her to her trembling feet. "Quick! Run for the wagon!"

The girl sprinted as Rowan covered her retreat. He backed away, his spear tip swishing like a whip in front of him. The creature didn't give chase. Instead, it shirked away. Rowan returned his attention to getting the girl to safety.

Several of Kirani's workers hurled torches at the moving shadows. Two caught flame. The beasts' screams echoed all around, swallowing every other sound as they fled into the woods.

"Get'ta de wagons!" Kirani shouted, waving his arms. "Quickly, we leave!"

Rowan sucked in sharp breaths and hoisted the girl into the caravaneer's wagon.

She tore off a section of her hem and wrapped it around her bleeding arm. "You saved me—thought I was gonna die." Terror brimmed in the girl's vermillion eyes, her pale face bleached with fright.

Rowan blinked, noticing only then that she was like him—an albino Shandrian with red eyes. "You're—"

Another scream pierced the air. Rowan spun around. A shadow sprang from the woods—this one a behemoth possessing a row of twisted horns protruding from its oversized skull. It crashed upon an elderly man who was hobbling toward their wagon. Faster than lightning striking, the monster ripped apart bones and sank its fangs into the man's rib cage. A blue, spherical light left the man's chest, swallowed by the creature's jaws.

Rowan stumbled against the wagon. "Burning skies! How's this possible?"

"It's what Moonshades do!" the girl shrieked. "They devour souls!"

Rowan snaked his body to the rear of the wagon. Terror infiltrated his bones, and his muscles seized. His heart pounded against his chest, causing the collar of his tunics to pulse. More harrowing screams pounded his eardrums. Each one wrenched his soul, compelling him into action.

"Stay here." Rowan turned toward the chaos, when the girl tugged at his shoulder.

"Don't leave me!" she cried.

"But the others—they're going to die!"

"Dey're done for," Kirani yelled from the front of the wagon, seizing the reins. "We stay any longer, 'n we'll be devoured! Climb in, or stay 'n die."

"Do as he says," the girl insisted, tightening her grip on Rowan's shoulder.

With pained reluctance, Rowan leapt into the wagon right as

Kirani whipped the reins with a loud smack. The wagon hurtled down the road at reckless speed. Rowan jostled around like loose cargo, smacking from side to side. Fraught with fear, the girl grasped Rowan's arm, tucking herself close. He clutched her body tight against his, an anchor in the madness as they sped farther and farther from the gripping sounds of death and carnage.

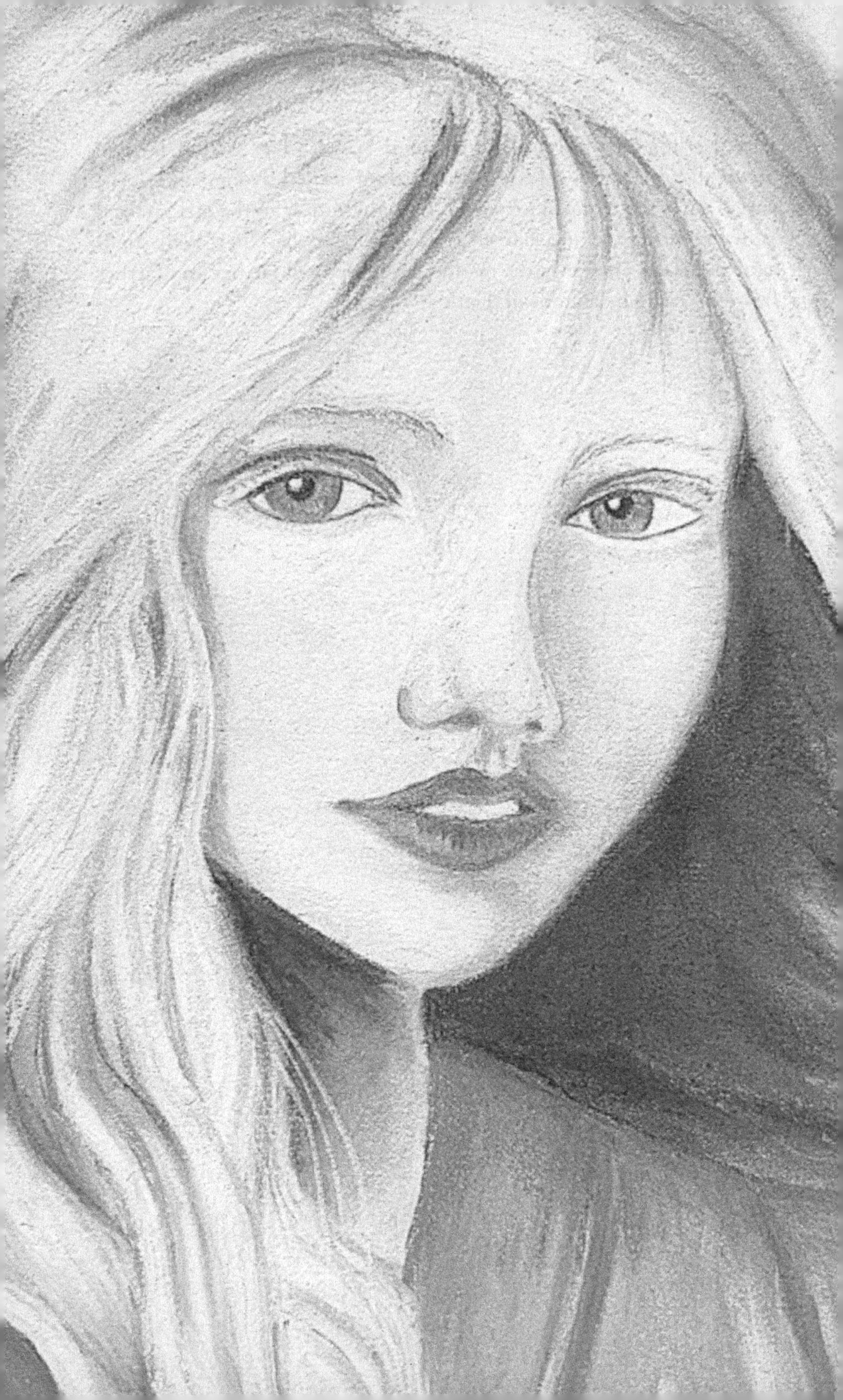

CHAPTER 5
TRAVELING COMPANIONS

The wagon came to a jarring halt at daybreak. Another wagon in the caravan arrived moments later, its wheels rattling as if their axles were on the verge of snapping. The husky, brown-skinned driver brought the wagon to a sudden stop near the edge of the bluff, and the crammed occupants—more than a half-dozen—shared beleaguered groans.

Rowan clambered out of his wagon on unsteady legs and retched. He wasn't the only one. Four others scrambled out of the second wagon and heaved over the cliff. Rowan wiped his mouth with his sleeve and straightened his back. The sea breeze washed over him, bringing a familiar peace to his spirit.

Kirani gave his horses water before taking a swig for himself.

Rowan returned to the wagon and reached for his waterskin, only to find it no longer in his sack.

Burning skies, had it flown out during the jostling ride?

"Here, have some of mine."

The feminine voice surprised Rowan, and he glanced up. The girl he rescued from the Moonshade stood above him with a spunky smile. Soft white lashes, batting like dove wings, framed her bright vermillion eyes.

She favored her right arm as she eased from the wagon and patted the dust from her rose-colored hem, the pleated collar of her short emerald dress, and matching green tights. A cream-colored headband kept her cascading, ivory hair out of her face—a face Rowan found most arresting. Her every feature enchanted him like a white orchid.

The girl's heart-shaped lips curved the longer he stared. "What?" She laughed, tapping the tips of her tan sandals against the ground. "Do I have blood on my face or something?"

Her plucky question snapped him out of his daze. Rowan swung his eyes toward his sack, which only made him look more like an idiot. "No . . . um, there's not," he said, hoping his face wasn't turning scarlet-thread-red. "I, uh . . . I've just never seen another Shandrian before."

"Wait—so, I'm the first?" The bewilderment in her voice sounded sprightlier than a jungle songbird.

It still couldn't persuade Rowan to grant her another glance—yet. And not because he lacked the courage; he simply didn't know how to act. In the end, a mute nod was all he mustered.

"Well, I don't bite," the girl teased. She tapped his shoulder and offered him her flask. "Here. There's enough to share."

Grateful, Rowan took a long sip. The water, cool as the air, coursed down his parched throat.

The petite, coltish girl eyed him with curiosity. "I'm Tahira. What's your name?"

"Rowan." He handed her back her flask. She scooped it from his grasp, her fingers brushing across his, soft and pleasant as the breeze. A thrilling yet nervous twinge pulsed within his heart, constricting his throat. "Um, thanks for the water."

Tahira smiled with an appreciative nod. "I owe you after your heroics."

Rowan was quick to deflect the praise. "I wouldn't call it heroic. You nearly died." He stared at her shredded dress sleeve and bandaged arm, noticing the blood stains. "How's the arm?"

She cringed, bending her forearm. "It smarts like you wouldn't believe."

Rowan bit his lip. Guilt spiked his chest. "I should've acted sooner, but fear had me by the throat."

"And yet you still managed to save me from that Moonshade. I didn't see anyone else bravely fight one off. This," she held up her arm, wincing, "will heal. But having my soul devoured? There's no coming back from that. A fate you prevented."

Rowan didn't know where to look to avoid the distracting twinkle in her eyes. Inwardly, he squirmed. Did all girls on this continent possess such wiles? He slid a hand through his hair and sought a change in topic. "So, you, uh, traveling alone?"

Tahira shook her head. "No, I came along with my uncle, but I don't know if he survived the attack last night."

"Have you asked anyone if they've seen him?" Rowan glanced at the survivors huddled by the bluff and pointed in their direction. "One of them might know."

Tahira's gaze flickered toward the group of fair-skinned Mestrians, but she didn't leave to inquire.

Rowan studied her unconcerned expression. "You don't seem too worried about his fate."

Tahira's eyes flashed, and a surge of emotion creased her delicate brow. "He knocked me into the Moonshade's path to save himself. Why should I care what happened to him?" She stiffened her shoulders, but her calloused expression remained. "Sounds bad, doesn't it?"

Rowan shrugged. "I won't judge." He lowered to the grass and stretched out his legs. "I don't have any family. Been on my own since leaving my village."

"Hm, then we're similar." She took a seat beside him, braiding her hair. "If my uncle is dead, then I, too, am without family." She glanced at him, her eyes curious. "If you have no family, why are you heading to Shandria?"

"I have unresolved business there." It seemed the simplest and vaguest answer he could conceive on the spot.

Tahira appeared amused. "You have business there?"

"Is that surprising?"

She chuckled. "Well, yes. You're what, sixteen?"

"Seventeen," Rowan corrected, flushing. "And what does my age have to do with it?"

She shrugged, finishing her braid. "You just seem too young to be caught up in Shandrian affairs."

"You can't be any older than me," Rowan retorted, his tone guarded. "What do you know of Shandria anyway?"

"Far more than you, I gather." Her voice held an edge of bitterness. "I was born in the capital, Arjun, and lived there for thirteen years until my parents moved to Eldon with my uncle for some speculative scheme of his. It ended up proving disastrous. We lost everything and fell into poverty. My parents took ill and died within a year. I lived alone with my uncle after their death. He soon became a drunk and a gambler . . ." Tahira rubbed her arms, her gaze lost in a void. "When he lost, he took his anger out on me—that's the reason I don't mourn him, understand?"

Rowan swallowed and gave a silent nod. Much in her final statement gave rise to horrible thoughts. He let them lie and didn't pry.

"We all harbor secrets," Hal had said. *"Not all can be shared."*

Including mine.

Tahira glanced away, then peeked back at him, her slender eyebrows scrunched. "Hey, what's that on your neck?" She touched his skin, and he flinched, every muscle tensing. "Were you scratched by the Moonshade?"

Heat flooded Rowan in anxious waves. He brushed her hand aside and concealed the mark with his palm. "It's nothing. Just a birthmark."

"That's a strange-looking birthmark. It's red and shaped like a crescent moon—"

"I said it's nothing." Rowan pulled his hood on and fled, desperate to escape her probing questions, and more than that, her far-too-curious gaze.

When he retreated a few yards, his mind filled with sulking thoughts.

Well done, Rowan. The first person you meet who looks like you, and you scamper off like a frightened kalb with your tail between your legs.

But should he have stayed? After all, he was cursed. Curren and his crew hadn't minded, but then, they hadn't known of his curse—save Hal. If people knew they'd die having Rowan near, they'd stay far away, and they'd be right to do so.

I need to keep my distance from everyone.

He didn't know how long it took the curse to latch onto an individual before drawing life from their body. Kialla, his first guardian-mother, died two years after being with him. Sadly, Rowan couldn't remember her, or picture her face. He remembered Telula fairly well.

She lasted three years with him and instructed him in basic weavescript. After her death, Sylda was assigned as his guardian. She continued his weavescript education and introduced him to the spear. She, like Naja, was counted among the warriors in Karahvel. Sylda's death came five years later when he was ten. Her death was a severe blow, and that was when the whispers first began.

His seven years with Naja were quite different. Well-aware of the villager's increasing suspicion, she kept him more isolated. They spent most of their time occupied in the jungle or in the estuary, harvesting pearls. Had she done so solely on account of the whispers, or had she suspected something troubling about him?

More questions emerged.

Why did Kialla die quicker than the others? Was it because she spent more time around him in his earliest years? As an infant and toddler, he would've needed nursing, constant care, and supervision.

Poor Kialla . . . no wonder Chieftain Haraz insisted I leave.

He must've concluded this the moment Naja died and put it all together.

I bring death wherever I step.

The morbid thought unearthed something far more disturbing.

The Moonshade . . . had it perceived the curse's miasma? Is that what repulsed it? That even I ought to be avoided?

Burning skies . . .

Rowan glanced over his shoulder, spying the direction from which they had come. The Grimwood was now a small, dark blight in the distance. The Moonshade and its dripping fangs flashed in Rowan's mind. He steadied his heart with a quick, deep breath and took comfort that the Grimwood lay behind him. Who knew this world held such horrible creations? They defied everything Rowan thought possible.

Tozrah was right. It really is a vast world filled with creatures aiming to kill.

THE CARAVAN TURNED WEST, AND THE GLISTENING SEA WITH THE

silver blue horizon became a distant memory. They journeyed through a wide-open stretch of low-lying hinterlands festooned with violet bushes growing in clumps. Their floral and herblike notes floated on the mild breeze, teasing Rowan's nostrils.

"The heather smells so pretty," Tahira said, sitting beside him. "Don't you think?" Her gaze searched for his, a hopeful request for conversation.

Rowan turned his head, avoiding eye contact. "It's nice," he mumbled, trying to scoot over. Unfortunately, his body was already pressed against the edge of the wagon. Stuck with nowhere to retreat, he pulled his hood past his forehead, shading his eyes, and kept his back turned so no one would speak to him.

The maneuver worked. Tahira didn't pester him again, and the five other peddlers in the wagon busied themselves by discussing their trading plans in Shandria. Their bulging canvas sacks consumed all the leg room. Rowan felt like mud squished between two fists.

After another four days of travel, they reached a small outpost called Westerlund and restocked provisions for the next leg of their journey. Apparently, an arid desert lay in their future, and for the crossing, they needed water in abundance.

Rowan waited not far from the two wagons, stretching his legs beneath the shade of a flowering tree. White petals flitted like leisure butterflies in the wind. Several landed on his shoulders. He brushed them off as soft, shuffling footsteps approached him from behind.

"Aha, found you!" Tahira beamed, holding up two water flasks. "I got us some—"

Rowan took off in the opposite direction before she could finish.

"Hey!" she called out, quickening her stride. "Why're you avoiding me?"

"I'm not avoiding you," Rowan hollered back, making for a small grove of fruit trees as if they could somehow obscure him from sight. The tactic was complete idiocy, and so, he slowed his steps.

Tahira caught up to him several seconds later. "Running away at the sight of me kinda proves you're trying to avoid me," she said in a pert tone.

Rowan groaned under his breath. "Look, I'm avoiding everyone, all right?" he said, leaning against the tree's smooth bark. "There's a difference."

"Why?"

The pesky word irked him. "I don't feel like being especially chatty. Is that a problem?"

Tahira's long lashes fluttered with irritation. "You're a strange one, you know," she said, tucking the flasks in the linen sack draped across her body. "You've been reclusive ever since I mentioned your birthmark. Are you embarrassed by it?"

"I'm not embarrassed," Rowan shot back. His answer hardly sounded convincing. Burning skies, what could he say to silence her curiosity? "Look, it's complicated, and I don't feel like discussing it, all right?"

Tahira rolled her eyes and folded her arms against her chest. "Fine, forget I even asked." She relaxed her brow and stared at him. "The thing is . . . I don't like seeing you all lonesome."

"I'm fine on my own." Rowan paused and narrowed his eyes. "Or is it *you* who doesn't like being alone?"

Tahira's eyes widened for a split second, and then quickly lowered. She kicked at the fallen petals, flushing. "Guess you figured me out easily enough."

Rowan raked his nails along his birthmark and grimaced. He *had* been a bit insensitive. Anger about his own situation had slipped through his tongue and bitten back. "Face it, we're alone. Those you loved in life are gone. All we can do now is stand on our own and move forward."

"I mean to," Tahira said. A pleading wish colored her eyes a deeper shade of crimson. "Just stay beside me for the remainder of this journey. That's all I ask."

Rowan inched backward, blood heating. "I can't." He swallowed. "You should keep your distance from me. I'm not well, you see."

Tahira seemed to scrutinize his face. "You look fine to me."

Rowan held in a caustic grunt. "Looks can be deceiving."

"Yours aren't." Her eyes twinkled, and she cracked a winsome smile. "You're kinda handsome when your eyes are downcast."

Rowan's face flushed. "Burning skies, you're persistent."

"Well, I can't abandon you with that lonesome gleam in your eye," Tahira teased.

"Be careful," he warned, drawing his arms snug against his chest, a barrier over his heart. "You don't know me."

"And I never shall if you keep this reclusive act up."

"It's my intention," he stressed, circling to the other side of the tree. Sunlight peeked through the emerald leaves and formed shifting patterns on the mossy grass.

"I don't buy it," Tahira said, following him like a loyal kalb. "No one actually wants to be alone. Sure, we pretend we do, 'cause it makes us feel safe and in control, yet all the while, our hearts scream with yearning to belong. To someone—anyone. Even a stranger."

Her words pulled at Rowan. He stared at her. Everything she said came from deep within her. She held his same desire. His reluctance dissipated the longer he stared into her eyes. The sunlight brightened the swirling gold flecks in her irises.

His face warmed. "You're a strange one."

Tahira's giggle blossomed into a sprightly laugh. "Well, now, since our strangeness has been established, can we be traveling companions?"

The appeal of her offer overruled Rowan's objections. He'd met someone like him, and he didn't want to drive her away—as his village cruelly had.

His shoulders relaxed, and he gave her a friendly nod. "We can be companions on one condition."

"Name it."

"Don't ask about my birthmark again—and if I tell you to keep your distance, do it without question."

Tahira's smile turned into a frown. "That's two conditions, y'know, but yes. I promise I shall adhere to both."

She ambled back toward the caravan, giggling like she'd succeeded in some great endeavor. Rowan tilted his head back against the tree, letting the petals fall wherever they desired.

Great. Who have I let into my life?

CHAPTER 6
THROUGH THE SAND SEA

The caravan departed from Westerlund. Throughout the next day, vistas of thriving grasslands and leafy-green trees faded into sparse, dry terrain.

Rowan directed his eyes south, spying the flatlands ahead. Not a hill or mountain in sight. Bright white clouds hovered overhead, stretching for miles. The sweltering heat choked the air from Rowan's lungs. As the sun climbed to its zenith, its rays baked the ground and radiated off his clothes. Beads of sweat formed beneath his collar. Rowan removed his tabard and overtunic and stuffed them into his sack.

The grinding sounds of the wagon wheels grated Rowan's eardrums.

A sea of sand stretched across the horizon. Rowan stared at the peculiar terrain with strange fascination as his wagon passed by a cluster of wind-beaten boulders that peaked above the golden waves like giant fingers scooping up sand.

"What is this place?" Rowan asked their driver, nodding toward the jutting crags.

"De Omaran Desert," Kirani answered, chewing on a grip of dried meat. "Takes near'a week'ta cross if de weather's fair."

"And if it isn't?" Rowan feared the answer.

"No telling, sonny, especially if dere's a sandstorm. Easy'ta get lost 'n travel aimlessly 'til dying of dirst."

Rowan cringed. "That sounds terrible."

"Could happen'ta de inexperienced. But I've done dis route a hun'red times. I know it like I know my ma's face. We'll get'ta de other side. Dan't yous worry about a ding."

Kirani telling Rowan not to worry only made him worry more. People only said "not to worry" when trouble was imminent.

The ride remained trouble-free the first three days of their sand-sea crossing. Midway through the fourth day, everything changed.

A massive sand cloud stretched over the horizon.

Rowan's jaw dropped. "Um, Kirani, what's with the wall of clouds?"

"Dose aren't clouds," Kirani responded, his slight shoulders noticeably tensing. "It's a sandstorm."

Like a predator on the prowl, the whipping winds headed straight toward them.

"We're doomed!" one of the Mestrian peddlers screamed, quivering.

"No, we're not," Kirani snapped. He twisted his bushy head and glared at the peddler. "It'll simply delay our trip, 'n dat's all."

How could the caravaneer treat the incoming threat so lightly? The sandstorm surged at wicked speeds. The winds funneled in a fury, swirling sand in wild torrents. The wagons rattled, and the horses nickered in alarm.

"Easy, easy, girls," Kirani said to the horses in a soothing voice. "Keep your heads. It's just'a bit of flying sand—"

A wind shear struck the wagons, launching everyone from their seats and overturning their rides like a capsized barge. Rowan flew several yards before landing face-first against the sand. He ate a mouthful of granules, then spit them out in a frenzy.

Tahira groaned beside him. "Ugh, that didn't feel so good."

"You hurt?"

"I'm fine"—she wheezed—"but my stomach isn't. I think I'm going to be sick."

A scream, pained and panicked, echoed over the wind.

"Someone's in trouble." Rowan leapt to his feet and raced toward the overturned wagon.

The Mestrian traveler—the one who thought they were doomed—was pinned beneath it. His skinny fingers gripped at the boards crushing his hips. "Help me!" he screamed. "Can't get free . . ."

"Hold on," Rowan said, quickly assessing the situation. He needed a way to lift the wagon.

He searched for his sack amongst the flown cargo and found it crushed beneath one of the peddler's bags. Unlatching his spear, he returned to the wagon and leveraged it beneath the bottommost board. He strained, gritting his teeth, but the wagon wouldn't budge.

More hands rushed to help. Kirani grunted beside him, using a staff to counter the weight. Together they lifted the wagon enough for the man to be pulled free. He wailed in pain, unable to stand on his legs. Two of his companions provided assistance, shouldering him between them.

"We need shelter to ride out the sandstorm," one of the companions said, "lest these winds shred the skin off our bones."

"Can anyone see anything?" someone else called out. "A landform, or an outcropping?"

"We press ahead," Kirani yelled over the prevailing winds, unhooking the horses. "Dere's a group of crags not far from here—a mile at most."

"What about the wagons?" said one of the peddlers.

"Leave 'em. We comes back when de storm pass and recover 'em den." Kirani pulled his horses along, trudging through the rushing sand. "Follow me, 'n stay close."

Everyone scrambled for their belongings. Rowan shouldered his sack and joined Tahira at the rear of the group. They stayed on the heels of the pair in front of them. Sand bombarded their hands and faces.

"It stings my eyes!" Tahira cried.

"Keep them closed. I'll lead." Rowan positioned his body in front of her, hoping it helped deflect the buffeting wind.

"We crests dis hill 'n de shelter lie a half mile more," Kirani hollered, his voice distant and muffled.

How could the caravaneer even tell what was near or not? Rowan could scarcely see two feet in front of him. Tahira circled her hand in his, shielding her eyes with the other.

All of a sudden, her hand slipped from his grasp, and she shrieked, "I'm sinking!"

Rowan whirled on his heels.

"It's got my leg!" Tahira screamed, her fingers raking at the shifting sand.

Something unseen dragged her down into a sand trap.

Burning skies!

Rowan dashed toward Tahira, but each of his steps forward seemed to push her further away from him. The terrain dipped, funneling downward into a sand-spiraling maw. Rowan swore he saw the dark jowls of a reptilian creature lurking in wait for its prey.

He snagged a bush's brittle branch—it kept him from sliding down the newly formed embankment—then flung the end of his spear toward Tahira. "Grab it! Quick!"

She stretched out a hand, her fingers extending in vain. "I can't reach it!"

Rowan slid his hand farther up the staff and gripped the spearhead, extending his reach. Tahira's fingers latched onto the end, and Rowan pulled with all his might. The edges of the spearhead sliced into his palm. He gritted his teeth against the pain.

Can't let go—not until I have her.

Rowan continued pulling, backing away from the slope, and dragged Tahira free. She found stable footing and raced toward him. He pulled her in against his chest, then propelled her forward, taking off at a sprint. "Come on, we must hurry!"

"Where's Kirani?" she said in a panic. "I don't see him."

"Keep moving." Rowan put distance between them and the sandpit. "We'll find him."

Kirani and the group couldn't be far. The crags lay a half mile away . . . somewhere in this veil of wind and sand.

Suddenly, a section of sand shifted before his feet, revealing another sand trap. A squat, four-legged reptile emerged, all beige except for an orange swath along its lower mandible. Two crescent-like horns crowned its broad head, and a row of armored ridges lined the curvature of its spine.

Rowan swung his shortspear and struck the reptile directly across its scaly face. In mad retaliation, it whipped out its long, serpentine tongue and ensnared his spear, ripping it free from his grasp. The weapon flew far out of reach. Rowan couldn't get to it, not with the reptile blocking his path. The creature slithered forward on its belly, blending in with its environment. It launched its tongue once more—a muscled lasso aiming for Rowan's throat.

He flung his bloodied hand to his waist and seized his knife. He slashed the incoming tongue, then buried the blade into the reptile's protruding snout. It hissed as the whirling wind carried off its severed tongue, and Rowan came within inches of a row of razor-sharp teeth.

"Rowan!" Tahira shouted, fumbling with Rowan's weapon—to his shock. "I have your spear!"

"Don't just stand there—use it!" he yelled, dodging a biting snap.

"Me?" Tahira shrieked, edging closer. "You can't be—"

"Stay behind it!" he warned, keeping the creature's attention engaged. The ferocious slits of the reptile's black eyes tracked Rowan's shuffling movement—and Rowan could tell from the animal's perspective, Tahira stood in its blind spot.

That's right. Keep your eyes on me.

Its jaw snapped forward like a cobra's strike. Rowan dashed out of its path, knife raised, biding his time for an opening. Its stout claws swiped in rapid succession, forcing Rowan into a dodging roll. Sand blasted his face.

"What are you waiting for?" he yelled to Tahira. "Stab it already!"

Her voice rose in pitch. "Where?"

"Anywhere!" He found an opening and struck again with his knife, this time piercing the animal's orange throat.

In the same breath, Tahira let out a sharp peal and thrust the spearhead into the creature's ribs. "S-stabbed it—like you said!"

Rowan spun away from the beast's bleeding mouth and closed in on Tahira, the blood seeming to drain from her fear-stricken face. "I'll take that." He retrieved the spear from her quivering fingers and joined her in a mad dash. With the sand flinging in every direction, he didn't know from where the creature would strike again.

A long moment passed, then another, with no sign of the reptile. Hopefully, it had crawled back to its sandpit to lick its wounds. Still, Rowan remained vigilant.

They slowed their frantic pace, and together, they shouted over the roar of the storm, calling Kirani's name.

No response.

"We should've reached them by now," Tahira said, a look of worry shrouding her face. "I think we're lost."

Rowan stopped and grabbed her by the hand. "There's no use in wandering aimlessly. We seek whatever shelter we can find and wait for the storm to pass."

"See anything?" Tahira asked.

Rowan squinted against the whirling sand before leading them toward a dark mass not far off. A cluster of boulders stood strong against the storm. Rowan guided Tahira under the concave formation, tucking themselves tight against the wind-beaten surface. They huddled close, recovering their breaths.

Rowan brushed off sand from his face and irritated eyes.

Tahira burrowed her head against Rowan's shoulder, her face turned toward the rocks. "You seem remarkably calm."

"This isn't my first storm," he said, eyes trained on the violent wind flinging over their heads. "On my way across the Ardruin Sea, we sailed into a storm. I nearly flew overboard and had to lash myself to the mast."

"Really?" She chuckled. "What a sight you must've been to the sailors."

"They called me a drowned goat."

Tahira laughed louder. At least she could find amusement in this stressful situation. Maybe it was her way of staving off her nerves.

"Thanks for the help back there with that sand beast," he said. "You, um . . . surprised me."

Tahira shivered against him. "I surprised myself. Next time, try not to drop your spear," she chided.

"Are you actually scolding me for that?" he said in a teasing tone. "How was I to know its tongue could ensnare things?" No creature he'd ever faced in the Thulu Jungle possessed such a bizarre skill.

"That was wildly unexpected, wasn't it?" She giggled about it now, but in the moment, Rowan had seen the terror in her eyes. "But you know what? I bet that creature didn't expect us to fight back. We make a good team, don't we?"

"If you say so," Rowan said, not wanting to overindulge her usage of the word *we*. "It's an unexpected surprise."

"A good one, I hope."

The unmasked earnestness in Tahira's voice rendered Rowan mute, but the way her eyes panned to find his tugged at his emotions.

Burning skies, this could become a problem. Not a bad one—a cruel one.

He didn't want to be alone forever—feared the prospect—but he couldn't risk developing an attachment to anyone while cursed. Tahira was better off moving on without him once they reached Shandria.

Rowan broke eye contact and stuffed his hands under his knees. Scrunched tight against Tahira, he didn't know where else to put them. She kept her head against his shoulder, clueless of the war raging inside his chest. He intended to keep it that way.

Tahira expelled a long sigh. "Hopefully the others are safe and didn't get caught in a sandpit like us."

Rowan feared for them as well, especially Kirani. If they couldn't find him when the storm lifted, they wouldn't survive.

HARSH SUNLIGHT BEAT AGAINST ROWAN'S FACE, BAKING HIS forehead and burning his eyelids. No flinging sand or coarse wind assaulted him.

The sandstorm must've passed.

"Oi, yous alive?"

Rowan stirred, blinking, blinded by the brilliant light. He shielded his watering eyes and found a cluster of people standing near. Kirani stooped above Rowan, swatting sand out of his kufi cap.

"We're alive," Rowan said with a cough, spitting sand from his mouth. His throat was parched and gritty, as if coated by sand. He shook Tahira awake. She lifted her head, leaving behind a spot of drool on Rowan's shoulder. She wiped her mouth, blushing.

Her abashed countenance brought a smile to Rowan's face. His heart pulsed with a sudden feeling of endearment.

Now none of that, Rowan.

Rowan redirected his eyes to the caravaneer.

Kirani shook his head in wonder, staring at them with a crooked grin. "Yous look pretty wrecked."

"We stumbled upon a reptile's sand trap," Rowan said, giving the cuts on his palm a cursory look.

"Ah, a sand drake," Kirani said. "Disturbed one, didja?"

"It's not like we meant to," Tahira retorted. She raked her hands through her tangled hair, shaking it free of sand. "The traps were impossible to spot in the storm."

"Yous lucky," Kirani said. "We lost two travelers 'ta dose traps. Sand drakes got 'em. So, I'm glad'ta sees yous both in one piece. We all thought yous were goners. Luckily, yous found dis crag for shelter."

Yes, they had been fortunate, and even luckier to escape the sand drake's trap.

Kirani offered a hand to help them stand. "Come along. We makes for de wagons."

They trudged back in the direction of the wagons on tired legs and with sand-beaten brows. It took hours to unbury the wagons, which were submerged halfway beneath the sand, and get them righted on their wheels. Kirani and the other driver hitched the horses, and everyone climbed aboard.

"And we're off." Kirani slapped the reins and remarked over his shoulder, "Let's hope we dan't hit another storm, eh?"

"Or awaken any more sand drakes," Rowan said, shooting Tahira a look.

His comment earned him a scowl from Tahira, who kicked his shin. "Don't give me that look."

"What look?"

"The look that says it was my fault."

Rowan scratched at his itching neck, grinning. "Well, it kinda was..."

CHAPTER 7
SOMEWHERE TO BELONG

With the Omaran Desert behind them, Rowan's curiosity turned toward his final destination and what his place of origin would reveal. Did he have any family there? How would he go about finding them? He only knew his birth mother's name—Zurie. Hopefully, it provided the answers he sought.

As the wagon rolled through a hilly countryside, Rowan stole glances at Tahira, admiring her Shandrian features—her skin as lovely as white-glittering sand. Burning skies, she astounded him. Meeting her altered everything he had believed about himself.

I'm not a freak.

In Karahvel, he lived a lonely existence, ostracized and scorned. Despite his obvious differences, his guardian-mothers nurtured him with tender affection, and he vowed to never forget their love. But soon, he would reach the place he truly belonged—among his people.

"What's Shandria like?" he asked Tahira.

"Mountainous." She took a sip of her water and stared at the passing woodlands. "It's surrounded by crags and sprawling steppes. The land is poorer and harsher compared to Eldon's fertile region."

"How does the country survive, then?" Rowan asked, grabbing his flask from his sack.

"With metallurgy. Mining iron ore is Shandria's chief industry—that's why it's known as the Iron Kingdom. My father and uncle tired of working the mines and aimed to try their hands at something different in Eldon." Tahira lowered the flask to her lap. "Sometimes I wonder what would've happened if we never left—maybe my parents would still be alive." Sorrow clung to her eyes like raindrops on red lilies.

Rowan didn't know what to say and kept silent. Loss tended to dredge up what-ifs. He'd done it enough already on this trip and found it to be a useless and morose pastime. And so, he shifted the conversation. "What do you hope to pursue when we reach Shandria?"

"With my uncle gone, I honestly don't know. He had intended to mine again." Tahira snorted with contempt. "Though, whatever he earned, he would've just blown on ale. I had to work as a tavern girl in Eldon to help us scrape by. I saw my share of lewd riffraff, vermin thinking they could grope me as easily as they did their mugs."

Tahira's brows angled at the memory. She was silent for a moment before she continued. "I hated it, every night masking my disdain by donning a smile whenever a drunkard needed a refill. Still, it was better than waiting to get smacked by my uncle's back-hand. I want no part of that life ever again."

Between their backgrounds—though hers differed from Rowan's—seemed to be a common thread, a shared suffering.

"What kind of life do you want?" Rowan asked.

Tahira blinked, taken aback by the question. "Why do you ask?"

"I'm only curious."

Tahira's countenance warmed. "I want what I lost when my parents died. A joyful home. To wake up every morning knowing I'm not alone." Her cheeks reddened, and her words tumbled out faster. "I would also love to have a garden to tend. We had a small one back at our old home in Arjun. I have fond memories of helping my mother till the ground and planting the seeds, watching them sprout."

Tahira's cheeks remained flushed, like she'd never spoken aloud these desires to anyone. "It may sound silly to you—"

"It doesn't," Rowan said, and he meant it. "It sounds nice. I, too, want somewhere to belong. I was told it's a special feeling."

Tahira broke into a wistful smile. "Maybe one day, if we're lucky, we'll experience it for ourselves."

Rowan wanted to believe her, but he didn't dare dream of such things—not while cursed. He couldn't bear to grasp at hope only for it to remain unattainable.

Their wagon slowed, drawing to a halt near the shore of a tranquil lake bordered by stately trees. Kirani turned in his seat and announced, "We stops here for de night. Feel free'ta bathe in de lake 'n wash your clothes."

Travelers disembarked, banishing their beleaguered expressions with eager grins, and ventured for the lake. Blasted with sand for nine days, a good washing was what everyone needed. Most of the men stripped off their tunics, then waded into the lake. Kirani and the other driver led the horses to water before undressing themselves.

Tahira stumbled out of the wagon, turning her gaze away from the bathing men. As the only female in the group, Tahira looked mortified, a tinge of rouge blossoming on her neck and cheeks.

"This way." Rowan pointed to a grassy grove. "We can pass the time over there."

"Wait—you're not joining the men to wash?" Tahira asked with surprise.

"A wash can wait till later." He glanced over his shoulder. "When the lake isn't so crowded."

Tahira nodded with relief, walking alongside Rowan to the shelter of the golden-leafed trees. "I think I will have to wait until dark for my wash."

"I noticed a secluded spot surrounded by reeds. It should shield you from sight—" Rowan's face flushed, and his shoulders tightened like weaving thread stretched on a loom. He cleared his throat. "Er, I mean, if that's what you're worried about."

"It is." Tahira blushed, her cheeks now as vermillion as her eyes. "I suppose in the meantime, we can be sandy and itchy together. Hope you don't mind it a little while longer."

"It's not the worst thing I've experienced," Rowan said, forcing his taut shoulders to relax. "Where I'm from, sand gets everywhere, so this isn't the first time I've been covered. These nasty twins back in my village thought it 'good fun' to trap me in a roasting pit in the middle of a monsoon." He pursed his lips at the unwanted memory. "I had muddy sand in my ears for weeks."

"That sounds awful!" Tahira's earlier embarrassment faded as she let out a laugh. "When I was eight, I once told my father I wanted to be a snow sprite. So, one night, he left me outside in a snowstorm during supper to see if I would change my mind. My ears almost froze off."

Rowan had no idea what she was talking about. "What's snow?"

Tahira's jaw dropped. "It sometimes falls from the sky when the weather is cold.... You really don't know what snow is?"

Rowan shook his head. "My village was always hot and humid. The only thing that ever fell from the sky was rain."

"Well, remain in Shandria when winter comes, and you'll find out."

Rowan frowned again. "What's winter?"

Tahira's answer came steeped in laughter. "You have a lot to learn."

An hour passed under the gentle shade. The travelers finished their baths, built their fires, and pitched their tents.

Tahira's nervous expression returned as she stared at the distant lake. "When the time comes . . ." she paused to scratch the itch on her forearms, "can you make sure no one follows me?"

This time, Rowan blushed hotter than a branding iron. "Um, of course—yes, I can do that."

Tahira smiled. "I'll owe you a big favor for this."

NIGHT DESCENDED, AND TAHIRA TOOK HER LEAVE, SNEAKING under the cover of darkness toward the secluded reeds. Rowan kept a watchful lookout by the orange light of their fire, positioned so no traveler could trespass without his notice. The waning moon's silvery image reflected upon the lake's glassy surface. Like an evening tide, its shimmering stillness lulled Rowan's thoughts toward the Karahvelan shore—to the aquamarine estuary where he and Naja harvested their black pearls.

He closed his eyes and pictured her warm, affirming smile, wishing he'd been allowed the chance to honor Naja's life or say his farewells at her funeral pyre. But that right had been denied him. His heart ached to show his gratitude—especially now after overcoming his battles with the Moonshade and the sand drake. He owed Naja for the survival skills he possessed.

An idea formed in his mind. He couldn't cast her ashes to the sea, but he could perform his own honoring ritual—one reserved for Karahvelan warriors.

Rowan donned his woven cowl and stabbed his shortspear into the pebbled ground. He knelt beside the weapon and gave a thankful blessing for his guardian-mother. Taking weaving thread from his sack, he tied them around the spear's shaft. His weapon served as a fitting anchoring point while he composed a prayer of gratitude for Naja's invaluable lessons.

He knotted each memory in colored sequence, deftly weaving a braided cord. Even though it was the most basic form of weavescript, it symbolized a weaving together of people and memory. When the cord reached the length of his hand, he untied the anchor point and reread the weavescript.

Tears pooled in Rowan's eyes, and he wiped them away with his sleeve.

Quiet footsteps approached. Rowan quickly cast the cord toward the lake, where it would sink and find its place of rest in the way Naja's ashes had.

Tahira returned in fresh attire, wearing a cozy, blue dress cinched with an ivory sash. Her brows furrowed. "What're you doing on the ground like that?"

Blushing, Rowan scuttled to his feet and secured his spear in his hand. "I was . . . um, performing an honor ceremony for someone."

"An honor ceremony? That sounds really . . . *sacred*." Tahira stepped closer, and her curious eyes marveled at Rowan's hood. "I've never seen such unique weaving. Did you get this in Eldon's Port Market?"

"No, uh, the woman who taught me the spear weaved it for me." His chest constricted at the painful memories. They strayed dangerously close to the truth of his banishment.

"Ah, so I should really be thanking her then for your heroic fighting, shouldn't I?" Tahira's breezy tone teased Rowan's ears like the night wind did his skin. "I imagine this spearwoman is a fearsome warrior to behold. I've witnessed enough of your skills to say that much."

Rowan blushed, and his heart swelled like a breakaway wave.

Burning skies, this girl...

In the night's quiet allure, Tahira's smile and winsome nature mirrored an ocean's tide, drawing Rowan nearer—though only enough to hover at the shoreline. Much like a hermit crab needing to abandon the security of its shell for a new one, Rowan feared the backlash from ever exposing his shameful past.

And so, he stayed inside his shell, his heart craving its protection, and remained silent. He didn't want to speak of Naja or anything pertaining to Karahvel—not when it could lead to the mention of his curse.

Tahira gathered her damp hair to one side and twisted the strands into a tight braid before finding smooth ground beside the fire. "That bath was so refreshing," she said.

Rowan returned his hood to his sack and retrieved the bundle of dried meat, ready for a meal. "Wait till you try this jerky." He handed her two chunky strips, then took a seat with several feet of distance between them. "Your stomach will thank you."

Tahira took her first bite, and her eyes lit like stars. "It's delicious! Where'd you get it?"

"From a thief in Eldon."

Tahira choked, covering her mouth with her palm. "How did that happen?"

Rowan filled her in on his adventures in the Mestrian capital and the first friends he'd ever made. He didn't mention meeting the Crown Prince, only the name he knew him by.

"You're lucky you found such amiable thieves," Tahira said after hanging on to Rowan's every word. "Most urchins are soiled rats scrounging around for whatever morsel they can steal off you and aren't likely to leave you in a pretty state. Eldon may be a shining pearl in the eyes of the world, but the land of the Immortal King is a cesspit of greed and corruption—much like everywhere else, I imagine. Shandria isn't so different."

"I've been warned it isn't necessarily the nicest place..."

"It depends on who you cross." The fiery luster in Tahira's eyes held a stern warning. "Don't get on an Iron Baron's bad side. That's some free advice for you."

Rowan wanted whatever advice she could offer. He'd been fortunate to find friendly acquaintances to steer him along his journey, but what would happen when he reached his destination? He couldn't continue to rely on Tahira, not with the cruel nature of his curse. The last thing he wanted was another death on his conscience. And so, their companionship would need to end.

Beyond the surrounding rough-hewn hills, a series of dark mountain ranges punctured the skyline. By wagon, it would be a few days before they reached them. And then Rowan would be in Shandria — his new home.

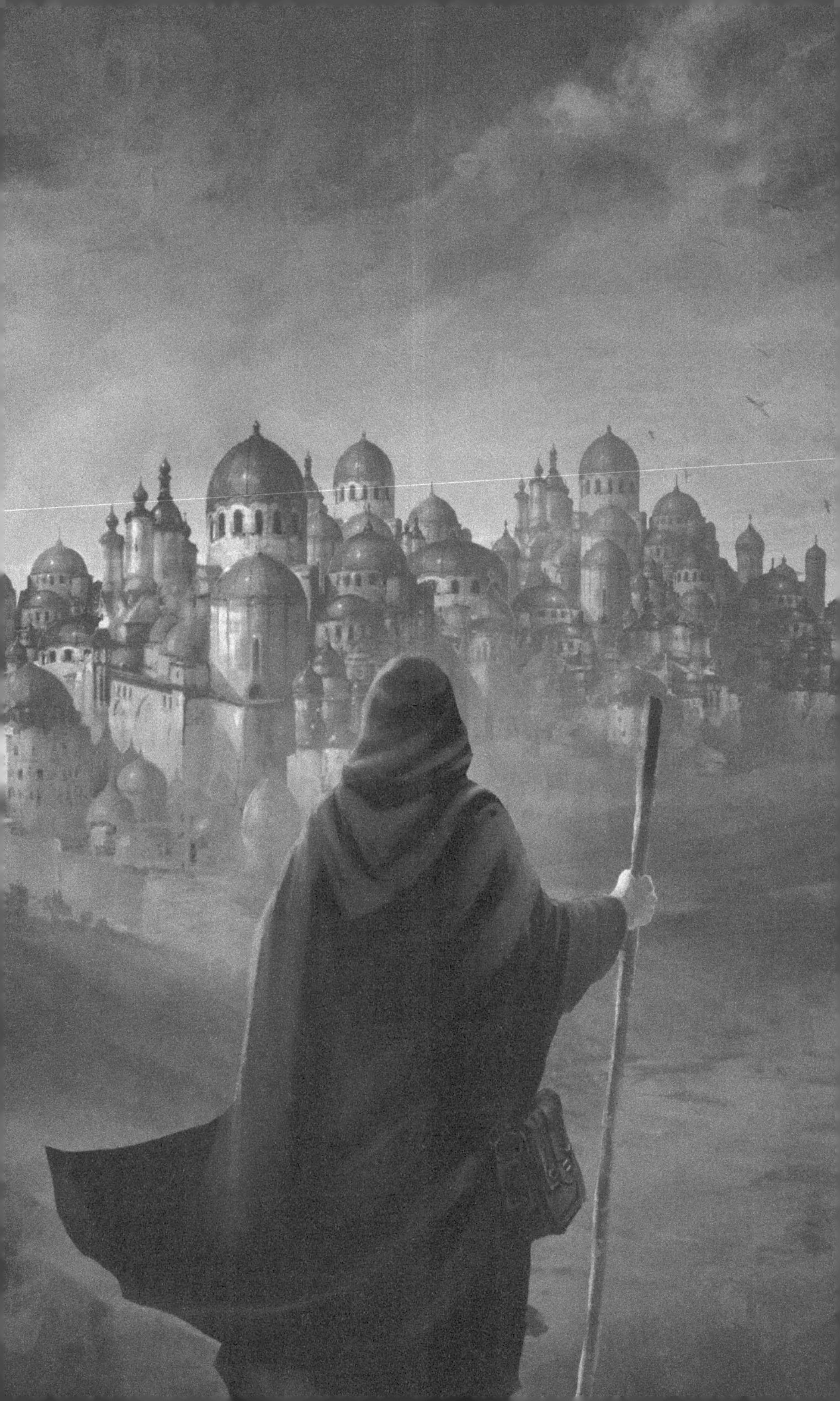

CHAPTER 8
SHANDRIA

They entered the Shandrian capital of Arjun, hunkered upon the slopes of a gigantic, craggy mountain. A bustling marketplace rested at the base, shadowed by the ridged peak shaped like a jousting spearhead. Dark, stone mansions dwelt on high outcroppings, overlooking the city below and the valley beyond. Twisting lanes split off in numerous directions, leading to different slopes of the chiseled mountainside where Rowan spied simple stone-hewn houses. Those nearest the marketplace doubled as storefronts, their wide window slats open for business.

"Dis is where our caravan disbands," Kirani said with a sublime lilt. "May your business here be prosperous 'n bountiful."

The travelers grabbed their belongings and ambled toward the market. The peddlers from Rowan's wagon sauntered off with wistful smiles, eager to earn their desired profits.

Tahira shouldered her small, linen sack. Rowan opened his mouth to say something, but she beat him to it. "I know what you're going to say, so I'll make this quick. Watch yourself, all right? Arjun has an unspoken hierarchy here. Cross the wrong baron, and you'll likely be buried in a mining shaft and never seen again."

Rowan eyed her in a playful manner. "Is that your way of saying I oughta keep you around?"

She smiled coyly. "Now there's a thought."

Rowan sighed, not surprised by her persistence. "From here, I must go it alone. There's family I hope to find."

"Ah, reuniting with long-lost family," Tahira said with a hint of melancholy. "Say no more. Good luck, Rowan." She left him with a parting smile and turned toward town.

Rowan followed shortly thereafter. The strong odor of industry and smelting iron clung to the air like oil. Metal clanged against metal in rhythmic patterns. The fire from forges lit the mucky road. Stalls smeared with ash and soot housed grimy smithies, smiting red-hot iron upon blackened anvils. Tahira hadn't exaggerated their passion for metallurgy.

Rowan passed a half dozen forges before spotting an ale house. It may not have been remarkable for Arjun, but for Rowan, one thing stood out above all others: everyone he passed bore his features.

My people.

All his life, Rowan never imagined a land existed where people sharing his physical characteristics lived and thrived without continuous consternation. For the first time, he knew without a doubt he belonged here, in this mountainous country.

Now to see if he could find anyone who knew his mother.

A sign with a depiction of a frothing cup caught his attention.

The Golden Chalice, huh?

Rowan wandered inside the tavern. The sound of boisterous conversation blasted him like a gust of hot wind.

A busty woman with spirals of curls and a short, voluptuous frame waved him over to the bar's counter. She sized Rowan up with a quick swoop of her effulgent eyes. "You look like you could use a drink, handsome. What's your poison?"

Rowan tensed at the word, frowning. "My . . . *poison*?"

"Your drink of choice," the barmaid clarified, giving him a funny look.

"Oh, uh," Rowan fumbled, blushing, "no, that's not why I'm here. I'm searching for someone. Have you heard the name Zurie before?"

The woman pressed her puffy lips together in thought. "Sorry, can't say that I have." She looped her fingers around a jug handle, sloshing the liquid inside. "Feel free to ask around. If you change your mind and want that drink, you know where to find me." She left him with a hospitable smile and moved farther down the counter, refilling two patrons' mugs.

Rowan turned to face the sea of sloshed faces.

Where to start?

With a nervous swallow, he approached the first table where three men with sooty clothes slumped, chins stooped over their mugs. "Excuse me," Rowan called from behind their shoulders.

The men didn't turn their heads.

Rowan cleared his throat and tried again. "Excuse me, but have any of you—"

"Can't you see we're talking?" one of them barked. "Bother someone else." The man shot Rowan a cold glare before drowning his face again in his mug.

Rowan moved past the disagreeable men and tried another table. The couple seated there shook their heads at his question.

He moved onto the next tavern . . . and the next, learning nothing.

On the next block, he shuffled toward a small inn set upon an outcropping. Rowan eased his way inside, surveying the rows of occupied tables. A rotund innkeeper worked behind the counter, clopping down a tray of mugs filled with a dark amber liquid. Rowan waded past a huddle of intoxicated customers and approached the older innkeeper with a white, leathery face and a sunken chin.

"Greetings, traveler," the man said in a gravelly voice. "What brings you into The Red Canary?"

"I'm seeking information." Rowan leaned against the counter. "I'm looking for anyone who might've known a woman named Zurie."

The innkeeper hesitated, passing his tongue over his chubby lips in a slow, ponderous manner. "Zurie, you say?"

"Yes, have you heard the name before?"

"I've heard the name," a voice interjected from nearby.

Rowan turned in surprise.

A tall, muscular young man stood with a self-assured gleam in his gaze and motioned to a lone table. His stylish white hair hung mere inches above his well-set shoulders, angled in a way that accentuated his sharp cleft chin and dented nose. Rowan's eyes were drawn to the man's crimson sash, black tunic, and tabard, which was well-tailored to streamline his impressive frame and made him appear more refined than the other clientele.

"Who's that?" Rowan whispered to the innkeeper.

"A regular patron who's known for being an avid pugilist. His name is Akaran Keliss. His family owns the most lucrative mine here in Arjun."

Rich, in other words, and perhaps savvy enough to possess actual information regarding Rowan's mother. Rowan considered it prudent to present himself as calm and unemotionally invested.

Still water, steady stream, he reminded himself.

Rowan left the innkeeper and strolled toward the young man. After introductions, Akaran offered him a glass of some scarlet beverage. Rowan kindly refused. Drinking would only come after he learned the information this man shared.

Akaran poured himself a drink and came straight to the matter. "So, why're you looking for Zurie?"

"She's my mother," Rowan responded, matter-of-factly.

"Is she now?" Akaran's ember-red eyes lit with an intriguing fire. "My, that's quite interesting."

"How come?"

Akaran set his glass down, tapping it lightly against the table. "My uncle spoke of a woman named Zurie often when I was younger."

The admission piqued Rowan's interest, but he didn't let it show. "What did he say about her?"

"Hm, that she was remarkably beautiful with eyes as mesmerizing as fire." Akaran paused to take a long sip of his drink. "I'm certain he can tell you more about her if you wish. Care to meet with him?"

Rowan held in his shock at the fortuitous opportunity.

A solid lead, finally.

Perhaps his luck really had changed. "Yes, I'd like to speak with him."

Akaran swigged the contents of his glass. "Great, let's head out then." He tossed a coin to the innkeeper. "As always, Yorn, thanks for the hospitality."

Outside, Akaran approached his shining black stallion and mounted. "You have a steed?"

Rowan shook his head. "I traveled here by caravan and only just arrived."

"Ride with me then. It won't be a problem."

Rowan hesitated. "Um, I've never ridden before."

Akaran frowned, seeming perplexed. "No matter. My horse won't buck."

Akaran offered his hand, and with his help, Rowan mounted.

"My uncle's manor lies outside of town on a steeper part of the mountain."

As they neared the edge of town, they came upon a fortified structure architecturally different from the surrounding limestone buildings. Soldiers garbed in uniformed surcoats stood guard upon the outerwall, like hawks ready to swoop at the slightest provocation. None possessed a single Shandrian trait—all dark-haired with either fair or ruddy complexions.

Rowan tapped Akaran's shoulder and pointed. "What's that place there?"

"It's the Mestrian Garrison," Akaran answered with a notable snarl. "This city, like all in Shandria, is under Mestrian occupation. Their foreign magistrate resides therein, and with the arm of the Mestrian military, he enforces the Immortal King's laws here in Arjun."

Rowan remembered the name. Tozrah had mentioned him with unmasked disdain.

"You see, Shandria is tributary to the kingdom of Mestria," Akaran explained, his tone steely. "Once a year, on the anniversary of our defeat one hundred years ago, a tribute is collected."

Such kingdom politics escaped Rowan. Nothing like it existed in Karahvel. "I imagine it must be a grim day."

"It's a reminder of our lack of self-governance," Akaran said, like an absolute truth. "No one likes being subject to another, especially to a foreign king from another land. Regrettably, Shandria's days of fighting ended long ago. We don't even possess a formal army. Far too many have settled into our longstanding role of paying service to the Immortal King. The iron we mine feeds his military might. I doubt it will change anytime soon."

As the horse trotted, Rowan studied the arid countryside's dreary hills and serrated peaks. Mountains upon mountains—shaded in deep blues as evening drew near—jutted into the luminous clouds. Rugged furrows stretched across the windswept valley, yet no evidence of stalks or vines of any kind grew. A winding river cut across the valley, flowing from the mountains.

"Out there is the Valley of the Fallen," Akaran mentioned, tilting his head. "It's where the final battle in our war against Mestria occurred. Every Shandrian knows it well. My great grandfather was amongst the men who fell that day. See the lone stone spire on that hill's crest"—Akaran pointed—"that's our monument to the fallen. Though the battle marked our defeat, the monument stands tall as a reminder of our pride."

Rowan absorbed every intriguing detail of this land and its people. His curiosity compelled him to learn all he could. "What else can you tell me about this country? Do we have a king?"

"Not anymore. The last king of Shandria, King Wilkar, was slain in battle a century ago. Most of his kin were rounded up and put to the sword. I've heard rumors that some still live in exile. As it stands, Shandria is leaderless. Iron Barons insert their sphere of influence, and the magistrate is content to let us mine in peace as long as we deliver the yearly tribute."

So, this is how things work in Shandria.

Rowan needed to learn, and learn quickly, if he wanted to carve out a livelihood.

They trotted up a steep hill toward a stone manor nestled in the crags. Its dark and dramatic walls appeared hewn from the mountain it bordered, including its squared tower.

Akaran left his horse to the care of a stable hand before leading Rowan into the manor's main hall. Painted murals of silvery trees and misty crags spanned the stone walls. Dark, fringed curtains framed the slender windows. Flickering light shone from a pair of wrought-iron chandeliers suspended above a long, wooden table running the length of the room.

There, a man in his mid-forties sat alone, eating and drinking. Flames from the broad hearth cast harsh shadows across his keen, intelligent face. From a sharp widow's peak, his white, wavy hair hung to his shoulders, tucked behind his flared ears as he shoveled a forkful of meat into his mouth.

"Good evening, Uncle Adelkar." Akaran's greeting caused the man to look up from his meal.

Adelkar chewed, eyeing the pair. "Nephew, who's your guest?"

"His name is Rowan. He claims to be Zurie's son."

"Does he indeed?" Adelkar lowered his fork and clasped his hands together, giving Rowan a deep, inquisitive stare. "So, Zurie's son has at last returned home after seventeen years. This is most auspicious."

Rowan cleared his throat, drawing his shoulders back, and addressed the wealthy baron. "I came here hoping to know what has become of her."

"Of course, it is to be expected, and we shall answer your questions." Adelkar extended his arm, motioning toward a vacant chair. "But first, have a seat and enjoy a meal. You look weary to the bone."

Akaran pulled out the chair. Rowan took it with a grateful nod as a demure-eyed girl hastened into the hall and set dishes and goblets before the two young men. Akaran strutted to the buffet to grab a glass decanter—which contained more of the mysterious red liquid—and filled both of their cups.

"How far have you traveled?" Adelkar asked, his eyes reflecting eager interest.

"I've traveled for nearly a month to reach Shandria."

Adelkar set aside his meal, appetite forgotten. "I gather that means you haven't been living in this region, then?"

"This is my first time among my people." Stomach growling, Rowan stared at the roasted meat on his plate and dove in, then gulped from the goblet, satiating his thirst and hunger.

Adelkar leaned back in his chair, his deeply set, scarlet eyes glistening with fascination. "I see there is much to learn. Please, tell us about yourself and where you come from. It must be quite the tale, don't you think, Nephew?"

The two men shared a brief glance before Akaran nodded. "Indeed, Uncle."

Rowan kept his story brief, forgoing any mention of his guardian-mothers or his banishment. He only mentioned the little he knew of his mother, and how life had been in Karahvel.

"Raised by tribal Luvarians," Adelkar remarked with apparent amusement. "You must've been a strange curiosity to them."

That's putting it mildly.

"More like an oddity they'd rather not deal with," Rowan said. "It's why I left."

Adelkar raised a thin, questioning brow. He folded his hands, resting his elbows on the table. "And what exactly set you upon this quest to reach Shandria?"

"I wanted to find my people and see if I could learn anything about my mother." Rowan took another gulp of his beverage, surprised by its acidic freshness. "So, what can you tell me about her?"

Adelkar's firelit face spread into a mercurial smile. "Well, it will depend on one thing: How's your head?"

Rowan frowned. "What do you—"

Without warning, Rowan's mind descended into a fog. As if back on the *Silver Star*, getting tossed and turned by the sea, his head swayed and his vision spun.

What's happening to me?

A rush of wooziness swallowed Rowan. He dropped his cup, staring in disbelief as the spilled, ruby-red liquid bloomed on the rug.

I've been drugged.

CHAPTER 9
TRUTH OF THE CURSE

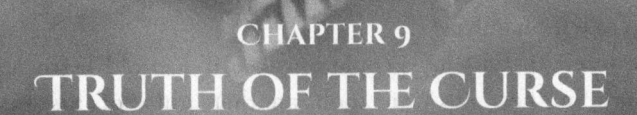

"What did you do to me . . . ?" Rowan's words slurred. He stumbled from his chair, drowning in a mind-warping haze.

A jabbing fist flashed before his eyes, and his head exploded with pain. A second strike to his face dropped him to the cold, stone floor in a dazed heap. The pain didn't stop there. Violent kicks crashed against his ribs and gut. Rowan cradled his knees to his chest, shielding his ribs.

His mind reeling, Rowan spied Akaran's hazy visage. "You tricked me!"

"How else would I get you to come along?" Akaran drove a hard kick into Rowan's side. "You're a fool to blindly trust someone you just met."

Adelkar rose from his seat and approached like an unthreatened predator. "Come, Nephew, is this any way to treat your younger brother?"

Rowan froze.

What did he just say?

Akaran spat in Rowan's face. "Half-brother." His fists delivered another round of blows.

"Akaran," Adelkar said with measured authority, "that's enough, I think. Don't want the boy thinking we intend to kill him."

"Why shouldn't we?" Akaran snarled, pulling back his fists. "He's cursed. We owe it to my father to be rid of this creature along with his mother."

"Don't forget, Nephew," Adelkar said, his tone coarse and bitter, "his mother is also *yours*."

"She's no mother of mine," Akaran said. "She can rot in disgrace, for all I care."

Rowan's insides twisted. He had a half-brother who hated him and their mother. His battered mind struggled to fully grasp this sudden and unfathomable truth. He felt like an utter fool for his blind ignorance. These men had known his identity before he even sat at the table. Even his curse hadn't been a mystery. He'd been enticed with their niceties and led right into the heart of their stronghold.

"I always wondered if this day would come, when Zurie's illegitimate offspring would resurface." Adelkar hovered above Rowan with a basilisk's stare. "What a callow creature you are. Did you honestly think we'd welcome you with open arms after the stain your mother brought upon this house?"

"I don't know what you're talking about," Rowan spat through bloodied teeth.

"So, you know nothing of her terrible deed?"

"She left right after I was born!" Rowan hissed, nursing his ribs. From the continuous lancing pain, one had to be broken. "I know nothing of her deeds, save one—abandoning me."

Adelkar's smirk was a dangerous abyss. "Probably due to the curse, I imagine."

"How do you know about it?"

Adelkar stooped his head like a vulture, clutching at Rowan's collar. "You bear a cursemark on your neck. It's plain to see. This is what brought you back. You seek to break your curse."

At this point, Rowan wouldn't deny it. "Yes. I do . . ." He took shallow breaths between the stabs of pain. "How do I break it?"

"By killing the one who cast it," Adelkar said. "It's no great secret."

Rowan's voice hardened. "Was it you?"

"Of course not, no." Adelkar cackled, his eyes glinting with wicked amusement. "Do I look like a Conjurer to you? Oh, right, you must be unfamiliar with the Conjurers of Drakmort. Yes, one of them cast the curse upon you."

"Why?" Rowan growled, the smarting pain fuel for his anger.

Adelkar drew up straight, his face a mask of hate. "Your mother tarnished the family name. As punishment, she was cursed, along with the child growing in her womb. You see, Zurie had once been married to my brother, Kainan. Two years after their union, Akaran was born. The couple's happiness ought to have been in full bloom, but it was not so. Zurie soon grew secretive, spending her time away from the manor. We sent spies to follow her movements, and guess what we discovered? She had been meeting in secret with a rival Iron Baron. She lied with a viper's tongue to exonerate herself, but once the evidence grew in her belly, everyone knew the sordid truth.

"Ah, I'm rambling. I'll sum up the tale for you." Adelkar's voice lost all emotion. "She betrayed my brother when she took up with her lover. Her actions led to Kainan's and her own lover's deaths. They died dueling one another, and she now spends her days in ruin."

"She's alive?" Rowan said, his voice shaking.

"If you can call her existence that." Adelkar peered down at Rowan with derision. "Don't think she'll rejoice at ever seeing you. You're the little wretch who made us all aware of her unseemly liaison. It's little wonder why she ran off. She couldn't live with the fact she'd given birth to a cursed bastard like you."

Rowan's heart seized as if stung by a nest-full of hornets.

"Understand now, little brother," Akaran said, curt and bitter, shoving a bloodied finger in Rowan's face. "You're the cursed result of our mother's sin. Everything is your fault."

The drug seeped like tar into Rowan's consciousness. His vision darkened—a wish granted. He wanted nothing more than to escape from these two condemning faces. They bore the same judgment in their eyes as the villagers of Karahvel. Again, the curse tightened its noose around Rowan's neck, squeezing without mercy until he wanted to scream in a fitful rage.

"I hope you've learned a sharp lesson here tonight," Adelkar said with evident scorn. "The hazards of dealing with this family."

Light footsteps entered the room. "What is happening here?" a croaky, female voice demanded. "Who's that boy?"

"Oh, him?" Adelkar said, nonchalant. "It's Zurie's bastard."

"Fools! Don't stand there in his midst. Cast him out! His curse could infect us all."

Rowan couldn't form a thought concerning the woman before a pair of hands gripped him by the shoulders and dragged him from the room. His mind slipped into oblivion. He landed against a rocky surface, at last succumbing to the darkness.

WHEN ROWAN CAME TO, A SINGLE LIGHT SHONE IN THE NIGHT sky, the stars and moon hidden behind a veil of dark, ghoulish clouds. He glanced around, eyes hazy, and found himself lying somewhere off the road alongside a mountainous escarpment. His sack and spear rested beside him like pieces of discarded trash. He checked the sack's contents—nothing had been taken, not even his pearls.

He sighed with relief.

Adelkar must've assumed I possessed nothing of value.

Rowan felt lucky and insulted at the same time.

With a pained groan, he lumbered to his shaky feet. Anger seethed inside him. He couldn't understand why they treated him with such cruelty.

I've done nothing to them.

And yet, they had brutalized him for his mother's actions. The callous thoughts baffled him and made him sick to his stomach.

Rowan hefted his sack and winced as it pressed against the fresh scrapes on his shoulder. He squinted and trudged back toward the dim lights of the city. Every step of his trek ignited internal pangs. He reached the edge of town when the sun crested the mountaintops. The workday commenced with the loud clanging of hammers.

Rowan kept his head lowered under his hood. He didn't want anyone to see his beaten face. Exhaustion overtook his mind and body. He needed some place to rest and recover, yet he doubted he possessed enough strength to stay standing long enough to broker lodgings.

"Hey, Rowan," a sprightly voice called out from a distance. "I thought it was you entering town."

A lissome form dressed in green floated toward him. The nasty drug still slithered through his system, clouding his vision. He blinked, and the girl drifted into focus.

Tahira planted her feet in front of him.

"How was the family reunion?" She dipped her head to peer beneath his hood and caught sight of the gashes to his face. "Oosh!" she gasped. "What happened to you?"

"Apparently, I have a half-brother who hates my guts."

Tahira's brow furrowed, and her lips parted.

"Questions later." Rowan took another pained step and grimaced. "Get me to a bed."

Tahira rushed to relieve him of his sack and offered a steadying arm. "Consider this the favor I owed you."

With Tahira's assistance, Rowan limped to The Red Canary and secured a room. Yorn took one hard look at him, and his plump cheeks inflated with a bewildered breath. He then shook his rotund head, as if he'd suspected all along this might happen. Yet another reminder that Rowan knew nothing about this city and its unspoken hierarchy.

Tahira delivered him to the comfort of a bed, and then waited before him, hands on her slender hips. "Now, will you explain to me why you've been pulverized?"

As much as he didn't want to come clean, he owed her an answer for the help. Seconds passed, and his mouth refused to open. He wanted to blame it on his inflamed jaw—burning skies, he did—but the reason lurked far deeper.

Shame fettered his tongue. This honest answer Tahira desired required him to leave his protective shell and expose the awful truth of his cursed existence. Everything he kept hidden would be revealed to the girl he couldn't bear to see turn against him. His aching heart seized in the stillness and braced for another blow.

"Well?" Tahira's tone was both persistent and concerned.

Rowan turned his face away. Once he started, there'd be no stopping this tidal wave. "I'm a stain upon the family name. My half-brother, Akaran, felt a beating was a lesson I needed to learn so I'd never forget our mother's great sin. She tarnished her reputation with a rival baron and brought shame upon the Keliss family. As punishment, she was cursed, along with her unborn child." He reached an unsteady finger to his neck. "That's why I have this red crescent mark—been there since birth."

Tahira lowered onto the edge of the bed. "A cursemark. I'd thought it might be that, but I wasn't certain."

He gave a stiff nod, fighting the brimming of tears. "I'm doomed to kill anyone close to me."

"H-how?" she stammered, taken aback.

Rowan swallowed, his throat a taut, knotted rope. "There's a black miasma surrounding me. It acts as an unseen killer, slowly infecting any form of life that's near. It's already claimed the lives of four women . . . my guardian-mothers." Hot tears raced down his cheeks. "The woman who taught me the spear . . . Naja—she was the latest victim. It's why I was driven from my village. They feared my curse and made me an outcast."

The hate in his half-brother's eyes resurfaced in Rowan's mind, igniting the shame within his soul. What would Tahira think of him now? He'd unveiled the curse's terrible truth. She would surely leave, and he wouldn't blame her.

Rowan waited for her to stand, hurl a soul-destroying insult, and flee the room. Seconds passed, yet she still remained. "Did you not hear what I said?"

"Oh, I heard," she said, swallowing hard. "I just need time to digest it."

How long did it take to absorb? "You should leave me alone."

"I should . . . but I won't."

"This isn't the time to be persistent."

"I'm persistent in most things," she said, her fingers laced in her lap. "This is no different."

"No, you're being stubborn—plain and simple. I'm trying to keep you from an early grave. Do you want to die?" Rowan hurled the question as harshly as he could. "That's what awaits if you remain with me."

Tahira surprised him by grasping his chin and yanking his gaze to meet hers. "Enough of this gloomy talk. I'm tired of hearing you mope like a man without hope. I'm sure there's a way to break the curse."

He held her gaze before responding. "There's a way. . . I'd have to kill the one who cursed me."

Tahira visibly shuddered and clamped her bottom lip. "Don't tell me it's a Conjurer of Drakmort?"

Rowan nodded. "It is."

Tahira blew out a troubled breath. "That's gonna be a hefty task."

Rowan figured it wouldn't be easy. "Who are they?"

"Conjurers are a rare group of Shandrian women who alone have received the gift for the dark arts. They once served the Shandrian king, but with him and his line gone, they now only serve themselves and whoever is willing to pay for their services. For a hundred years, they've been allowed to operate unchecked by the Mestrians. Even the soldiers steer clear of their abandoned bastion in Drakmort."

The breadth of knowledge in her answer surprised him. "How do you know so much about them?"

She shrugged. "My mother used to tell me stories. We had one in the family. Her name was Durene."

"What happened to her?"

"She died in the great battle against Mestria long ago—many Conjurers did. Only a few of their number remain alive today. They keep their true identities a mystery. It's a way to safeguard themselves from the Mestrian military."

Rowen swallowed hard. "I'm guessing they're not easy to kill."

"Trickery is their way, orchestrating their schemes behind the shadows." Tahira paused, and a spark of hope illuminated her countenance. "But all is not lost. We will figure a way out of this."

His head jolted up from the pillow. "*We?*"

"Yes, we," Tahira said with determination. She eased Rowan's head back against the pillow. "You're stuck with me now. I leave you for a day, and you come back beaten. So, while you recover, let me work my own kind of magic, all right?"

Rowan's brow furrowed. "What magic?"

"This kind." She leaned in close and kissed his lips.

Rowan didn't see it coming. He blamed it on the drugs. Moreover, her kiss only dazed him further. The ephemeral touch assuaged the pain wracking his skull, causing it to fade like a bad memory. He stared into her spirited eyes. How long had she wanted to kiss him?

Probably since we survived the sandstorm. Burning skies, I should've done a better job steering her off. Too late now.

With one kiss, Rowan's heart netted to hers.

Tahira smiled with the barest hint of a blush coloring her powdery white complexion. "Thought we should get that out of the way. Spare us any awkwardness."

"I don't think it worked," Rowan admitted. His blood burned like the sweltering heat of the Thulu Jungle during monsoon season, and it had nothing to do with his injuries. "I'm still feeling awkward."

She kissed him again, and her lips curved into a winsome smile against his. "How about now?"

He grinned. "A little less awkward."

She kept her face close. "Never shared a kiss before, eh?"

"I wasn't a sought-after catch in my village." Rowan laughed. It pulled at his ribs, and he winced. "A girl had never smiled at me until I reached Eldon."

Tahira's fingers twiddled with his disheveled hair. "Your village must've been a dismal place for you."

"It had its moments in the sun," Rowan recalled, wistful. "The times I shared with my guardian-mothers."

Tahira eased back and peered at Rowan. "I'd love to hear about them, but for now, you should rest. Your eyes are as lucid as a drunkard's. Trust me, I know the look well."

"I wouldn't know," Rowan admitted with a weak chuckle. "What will you do?"

"Poke my head around the city a bit." Tahira rose and grabbed her violet cloak. "I need to familiarize myself with Arjun's social climate before we figure out our next step. After what happened to you, I'd rather we steer clear of Akaran and his fists."

"That sounds wise . . ." Rowan trailed off, his eyes drifting closed. He didn't even hear Tahira leave the room. Sleep smothered him all too swiftly.

CHAPTER 10
NECESSARY DISTANCE

Rowan slept all day and night before feeling fit enough to sit up in bed. His jaw ached, and his ribs throbbed. Regardless of how awful he looked or felt, he refused to let Akaran's beating force him into running or hiding. Rowan aimed to fight back, make something of himself. He had means—his bag of pearls—and if Hal's word proved accurate, he possessed enough to purchase his security here in Arjun.

Tahira returned with breakfast. He stared at the steamy plate of scrambled eggs and sausage, and his stomach growled.

Tahira grinned and strolled toward him. "Yorn was concerned about you and had me bring this up."

Rowan's fatigued spirit lifted at the innkeeper's kind gesture. "He must find me pitiful."

"From what he told me, you're not the only one Akaran has deceived. He has a propensity to pick brawls. You were simply his latest mark."

Rowan broke into a sardonic laugh. "Oh, and I suppose being the half-brother whom he despises had nothing to do with it."

"All I'm saying is he's known as a bully around here, and he pummeled you good." Tahira placed the plate in Rowan's hands and took a seat in the room's sole chair.

Rowan picked up the fork but, despite his ravenous hunger, didn't dive into the meal. Difficult things needed to be said before another moment passed. "Look, about the kiss—don't make a habit of it." It pained him to say, but what else could he do? He didn't want Tahira's life to be in jeopardy on account of his curse. "My second condition still applies. There must be distance between us."

"Right. Distance." Tahira folded her arms. "I'll try to remember that pesky barrier." She shot to her feet and pushed her chair back several feet, her face painted with irritation.

Rowan sighed. "I don't mean to be an arse, but it's for your safety. The curse will kill you, slowly, without notice."

"All the more reason I want it gone."

"It's not your burden—"

"Yeah, well, I'm making it mine. Accept it, and eat your breakfast." Tahira pointed at the untouched food.

Rowan gave in. "Burning skies, you're pushy when you're upset."

"I'd help it if I could, but this really bites, you know." After a prolonged moment, she smiled, seeming to shake off her irritation. "So, where do we go from here?"

Rowan pondered, chewing a mouthful of eggs. "Well, we're going to need prospects. We can't stay at this inn indefinitely."

"It's a poor Shandria we've returned to," Tahira said with a somber nod. "Taxes sky high, wages in the gutter. Quite a few mine closures. So, it might be difficult finding work as a miner."

"What about as an owner?" Rowan proposed, dead serious.

Tahira's milky-white lashes fluttered with surprise. "You mean, purchase a mine?"

"Yes. I've given it some thought," Rowan said, forking up another bite. "Suppose I aimed to purchase a mine with land and an estate. What would I need?"

"Um, well, uh . . ." Tahira said, her lips and brows scrunched. "You'd need quite a bit of capital."

"Then we're in luck. I have what we need."

Tahira blinked in disbelief. "You do? Where?"

Rowan grinned, pointing to his sack with the fork. "In there, you'll find a pouch of black pearls."

Tahira's eyes widened, and she scurried to see for herself. She loosened the purse's drawstring and released a burst of laughter. "Well, aren't you a trove of secrets?" She fingered the pearls with fascination. "With these, we could purchase a mine and get it running again. I'm sure of it."

Again with the "we."

This time, he didn't mind it. "And what do you know about running a mine?"

"Plenty," she said, raising her chin. "My father was the mine captain at Iron Crossing. I learned enough to be useful."

Rowan bit into the sausage, which held a surprising blend of spices and tang. "While you were out, did you happen upon anyone selling a mine that could interest us?"

"As it happens," Tahira said, returning the purse inside the sack, "Rahn Myras, the baron my father worked for at Iron Crossing, is secretly looking to pass on his estate and mine to the right buyer."

Rowan swallowed his bite. "Why's it secret?"

Tahira wandered back to her chair, a glint of gossip in her eyes. "Apparently, Adelkar Keliss has been after the mine for ages, and there's a bit of bad blood between them. Adelkar has a habit of buying up mines and closing them down, as a means of suppressing competition to his own mine. This is why Rahn is seeking to sell to someone who won't be in Adelkar's pocket."

A shrewd grin bloomed upon Rowan's face. "He sounds like the perfect prospect. How do we set up a meeting?"

"Leave that to me. As my father was once his mine captain, I should be able to drop his name and get us an invitation, assuming people remember him. It's been a few years . . ." Tahira didn't let that sway her for long. "I'm sure someone will listen to me."

She stood and grabbed her cloak. "Don't go anywhere until I return." She flung open the door and dashed into the hall.

Rowan continued his meal with a chuckle and considered his good fortune. He wouldn't give luck the credit for Tahira's willingness to assist him. Perhaps fate had taken pity on him, bringing him a resourceful companion to help him weather the next obstacles. He hadn't known it during their journey, but Tahira was more resourceful and self-reliant than he expected. She once lived here, after all, and possessed connections. Rowan's relations had proven to be treacherous.

In all honesty, he needed her. His first day in Shandria had been abysmal. With her wherewithal, hopefully, she could steer him away from any more harm.

Rowan never wanted to suffer another beating from Akaran's fists again.

Tahira strolled amidst the tenant houses hunkered along the rugged hillside leading to Iron Crossing. When she reached her old home, she lingered, drawn to the cherished details of her memories: the conical roof she'd leapt off to land in the hay wagon; the dented door her father kicked open when he returned home from work; the small garden her mother nurtured with a horticulturist's obsessive care.

The warty birch Tahira used to climb and maim with fanciful scribbles still stood at attention next to the cobblestone fence. As a child, she'd spent hours beneath its shade, watching her mother tend the vegetables. The green shoots breaking through the tilled dirt had been the most splendid sight to her budding imagination.

The garden's current state—lying in untidy shambles—would've killed her mother. An unmistakable sign that a different family dwelt within the limestone home. The giggles of several children filtered through the paned glass. The gleeful laughter chipped away at the melancholy encasing her heart. At least it remained a cheerful home—a bittersweet solace for the one she lost.

Tahira missed living here. Only in this place had she experienced joy. Despite the allure Eldon offered, it had only exposed her to hardships that sapped her spirit. Her uncle's grand speculation led to ruin, and her parents paid the price, leaving her alone to mind a hopeless scoundrel who did nothing but exploit her for marks—all so he wouldn't have to be sober enough to work.

Those dark days were behind her now. A fresh start laid before her, one with a good, sure-handed, and—not to mention—easy-on-the-eyes companion at her side. She blushed remembering how willfully she'd kissed Rowan. Her heart sank seeing him so low, so grief-stricken. The shame in his eyes compelled her to unveil her feelings, to draw him out in the surest way possible—with a touch needing no explanation.

His life-draining curse unsettled her—but not enough to abandon him. How could she in his hour of need? On their journey, Rowan fought off monstrous creatures to protect her and had even dispelled her fears at the lake. They'd relied on each other and established trust. Now it fell to Tahira to seize the reins and display her gumption.

Tahira continued on her way and focused on the task at hand: speaking with the mine captain. At the top of the hill, a singular crag with two jutting peaks loomed, casting a wide shadow that shielded the sun from her eyes. Miners lounged around the mine's gaping entrance, eating their lunch above grass. Tahira squinted at the distance and hoped she recognized a face from her time living on Kaklin Hill. One stood out—a middle-aged man named Keld, who had been their neighbor and a friend of her father's.

He caught Tahira approaching and left the miners. He dusted off the grime from his splotchy work tunic with his broad fingers as he met her at the well. Even with a layer of dirt, the built-up calluses upon his palms shone a buffed white. He tipped his dingy cap atop his curly head in a greeting.

"Can I help you find someone?" Keld asked.

"I came to speak with the mine captain."

"You're talking to him."

Tahira held in her surprise.

Keld must've received Father's job after we left Arjun.

Tahira's chest swelled with budding hope. "Well, then, Keld, you're the man I'm here to see."

The mine captain frowned, but then faint recollection dawned in his widely set eyes. "Do I know you?"

"You knew my father, Orman, and my mother, Farla."

"You're Orman's daughter?" A quirky smile brightened Keld's soot-smeared face as he took in her appearance. "It's uncanny how much you've grown. Tell me, how're your parents? Have they returned to Kaklin Hill?"

Tahira braced her emotions and shared the hard news. "They died in Eldon—my uncle, also." It was easier to say than the brutal truth—that her uncle had likely been devoured by a Moonshade. "I'm here on my own."

Keld's smile melted into a grimace. "I'm saddened to hear they passed. Orman was a good friend." The mine captain released a heavy sigh, and the glum air passed. "So, what brings you back to Iron Crossing?"

"Business. I've learned of Baron Myras's dilemma and have a way to solve it."

Tahira's words must've been the last thing Keld expected to emerge from her lips. His smile returned, along with an amused twinkle in his eyes.

"I know a trustworthy buyer for this estate whom I believe Myras will want to meet." Then she dropped the irresistible line. "He's no friend to the Keliss family."

Keld's smile broadened. "Now that's what I was waiting to hear. Tell me more about this buyer."

Tahira could say a great deal, but she stuck to the basic details: Rowan's desire to place roots in Arjun and his capital to make it happen.

"I'll set up a meeting. Bring the buyer here at noon tomorrow." Keld's smile faded, and a cloud passed across his gaze. "I'm trusting you in this, Tahira. Rahn has grown weary from the lack of 'favorable choices.' He may be a picky old sort, but he's a good man. I'd hate to get his hopes up for nothing."

"Trust me. He'll be taken by Rowan's grit and integrity." As Tahira had been.

Keld seemed to show a slight reservation before giving her a parting smile. "Till tomorrow then."

"I'VE RETURNED WITH GREAT NEWS!" TAHIRA ANNOUNCED, dashing into Rowan's room without knocking.

Rowan nearly jumped out of his skin, midway through dressing. A shockwave of pain ripped through his bruised ribs. "Burning skies," he huffed, gingerly donning his tunic, "must you barge in like a kalb in a hen house?"

"In this instance, yes," Tahira said, beaming. "I got us a meeting with Baron Myras."

Rowan's brows shot to his hairline. "Already? That was swift."

"The current mine captain at Iron Crossing is an old friend of my father's. I told him about you and your eagerness to meet with Myras, and he has arranged a time tomorrow afternoon for us to visit the baron's manor."

"Hm, just like that?" Rowan said, a smile tugging at his lips.

Tahira nodded with a proud grin and placed her hands on her hips. "Told you I'd prove useful."

"Sorry if I ever doubted." Rowan carefully slipped the tabard over his head, and then reached for the red sash.

Tahira stared at him, eyeing his clothes. "You going out?"

"Thought I'd leave the room and wander downstairs for dinner," Rowan said, tying the sash around his waist. "I'm done keeping to that bed." He wasn't accustomed to staying indoors for long stretches of time. After two full days in the same room, his restless soul wanted out.

"Well, then, you might want to use this on your face." Tahira removed an ointment jar from her ivory sash and tossed it to him. "I picked this up from an apothecary. It should help minimize the bruising. Wouldn't want Myras to think you're an uncivil brawler."

Rowan smirked, unscrewing the jar's lid. "You think of everything, don't you?"

"Just looking out for you and our interests," Tahira teased with a spirited smile.

Rowan shuffled to the mirror and applied the ointment to his bruises. The swelling around his right eye had lessened, though the color had deepened into a shade of purplish-red. It lent him a frightful appearance. He tapped an extra amount of balm upon the area before moving to his jaw.

"How're the ribs?" Tahira asked, maintaining distance.

"Still sore. Your sudden entrance didn't help."

Tahira shot him an apologetic look. "I'll remember to knock next time—save your ribs further pain."

He snorted, screwing the lid back on the jar. "Regardless of my many aches, I want to leave this room. Can't keep my face hidden indefinitely."

"Akaran isn't downstairs if that's what you're afraid of."

"I'm not," Rowan said, anger creasing his brow. "I only look like this because he drugged me—I couldn't fight back. The next time I see him, he won't be able to beat me as he pleases." He picked up Hal's knife and concealed it within the sash. "You joining me for dinner?"

Tahira's slender eyebrows lifted. "Is that allowed?"

Rowan rolled his eyes. "Of course it is. When I say keep your distance, I mean close proximity, not stay far away."

"Ah, very well, then. Thanks for the clarification." She edged several tentative steps closer. "So, what then is *too* close? Lips touching?"

Rowan's neck turned red. "Yes, *that* is much too close."

"Figured you'd say that," Tahira said with a pout, flinging her loose braid over her shoulder. "It sure puts a damper on things."

Rowan sighed and tromped toward the door. "It's my cursed life. The whole of it is one gloomy tale."

He half expected to hear a hope-filled rebuttal, but Tahira followed him in silence. She shuffled behind him until they reached the stairwell where the thrum from the bar reached their ears.

"Rowan, there's something I want to say."

Rowan turned to face Tahira in the dimness of the stairwell. "What is it?"

She lowered to his step, fiddling with her sleeve. "Look, I know you've experienced terrible losses, been abandoned time and time again by everyone close to you, but I . . ." Tahira met Rowan's gaze, and in her eyes brimmed the same stubborn persistence he'd witnessed early on. "I will be the first who doesn't leave you."

"You say that now, but you may change your mind. I wouldn't hold it against you." Rowan hopped down two steps to maintain the necessary distance between them. "I've borne this curse for seventeen years. I could harbor it for many more to come. Would you stick around that long, knowing we can't touch in the way we want?"

"We want?" Her eyes shimmered with ecstatic hope. "You just said '*we* want.'"

Burning skies! How did I let the confession slip out so casually?

Face aflush, Rowan forced his lips into a firm line, refusing to say another unbidden word.

"If you expect me to ever leave now, Rowan, you're dreaming." Tahira flitted past him, skirting her fingers across his sash, and bounded into the dining hall.

Rowan followed, reservation in his stride and in his mind. As Tahira ordered them meals and drinks, he agonized over whether to allow her to stay at his side. He didn't want her to leave. He'd grown fond of her playfulness, even her testiness. Surely they could remain companions with strict boundaries in place.

As long as we maintain distance, it should be fine.

Rowan claimed a corner table.

The curse won't latch on. I'll make certain of it.

CHAPTER 11
INFORMANT

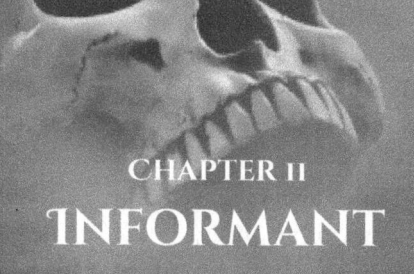

Inside The Red Canary, Akaran drummed his fingers upon the wooden table, waiting for his contact to arrive. He flagged the barmaid over for a pitcher of their stoutest ale. When his drink arrived, he took a satisfying sniff of the foaming froth and sipped away. His eyes hovered toward the stairwell, curious if his half-brother would venture downstairs. He'd learned Rowan had been staying here since the morning after his visit to the manor.

Akaran rubbed at his torn knuckles. Making a fist sent a surge of pain up his arm. The pain was worth it. For years, he imagined what he'd do if Zurie's bastard returned to Shandria. Playing the helpful friend to his half-brother only to knife him in the back fulfilled a long-held desire. He smirked remembering the horror in his half-brother's eyes as Rowan learned the truth—and the reason for Akaran's embittered hatred. The whole delicious reunion played out more perfectly than he'd ever imagined.

Sure, he would've enjoyed inflicting more pain, but there would be more chances to antagonize his half-brother. Akaran plotted the future encounters. It helped pass the time while he waited. After consuming a full mug, his informant, Klay, still hadn't appeared. An hour had passed since the agreed-upon time. Already the evening grew late, but Klay had sent word of an apparent urgency.

What urgency?

Akaran sniffed, pouring himself more to drink.

If Klay is this late, how urgent can it be?

Tired of waiting, Akaran rose from his seat right as Klay pushed through the inn door. Short and gangly, Klay's greased-back white hair hugged his long, scrawny neck. He toddled toward Akaran's table and plopped into a chair, rubbing his red-scabbed nostrils with jittery fingers.

Akaran offered the man a mug, and Klay chugged half the ale.

"What do you have for me, Klay?"

Klay swallowed in a rush before exposing his large, ugly teeth. "I got an update on your brother's—"

"Half-brother," Akaran corrected, irritated. Why was that so hard for people to remember? Did they say it simply to infuriate him?

"Er, right, uh, sorry—"

Akaran waved off the informant's fumbling apology. "Start over."

Klay collected himself with another swig and started again. "I've been tracking your half-brother's movements like you wanted, and I've learned what he's up to."

This sounds promising.

"Go on."

"He's only left his room once since you gave him that beating. Tells me he's scared stiff to show his face on the off chance he runs into you again."

Akaran smirked, enjoying the mental image of Rowan hiding away like a terrified rat. "Where'd he go when he left here?"

"Er, he didn't ever leave the inn. He came down here earlier this evening to eat, then went right back to his room."

Akaran frowned at the lack of sense in the informant's words. "Wait, back up a bit. If he's been holed up inside this inn, how do you know what his plan is?"

Klay's glazed eyes brightened with a sudden spark of sobriety. "He's got a companion—a young, pretty one too."

Akaran blinked, incredulous. "You mean a girl?"

Klay nodded before taking another gulp. "Yeah, she's been poking her nose around town for him, inquiring about mines."

How did Rowan manage to snag a girl, cursed the way he is?

Was she ignorant of it? If so, Akaran would gladly educate her on Rowan's shameful secret. He wanted nothing more than to deprive his half-brother of every comfort.

He let the thought pass for now. It wasn't important at the moment. "Why's he interested in mines?"

"All I know is the girl was mighty interested in only the closed mines."

Akaran scoffed. "Whatever good that does him. It's not like he has the prospects to purchase one."

Klay's brow creased, staring into his now-empty mug. "You sure about that, boss?"

"Dead sure," Akaran said, refilling Klay's mug. "Rowan came here from a backward village with nothing but the sack on his back. He couldn't possibly have capital or remotely enough in which to barter."

"Did you check his bag when he was at your manor?"

Akaran held his tongue. He hadn't checked. There'd been no reason to search. One quick look made it obvious the naïve whelp lacked anything of worth.

"Well, if he's got any capital, you'll soon find out, wont'cha?"

Akaran scowled at the amusement in Klay's tone. "Why's that?"

"He intends to visit Baron Myras tomorrow afternoon."

Akaran held in his alarm. "We're done here." He rose to leave.

Klay thrust out his pasty white hand, smacking his spindly knuckles on the table. "Hey, not so fast. Hand over my payment. I know ya got it."

Akaran withdrew a tiny pouch which held the white powdery substance Klay loved snorting so much. "Here's the usual amount. It should keep you fixed until next time." He flung the pouch toward Klay.

Klay snatched it and spied the contents. "You always manage to get the good stuff." He hid the pouch inside his soiled cloak and slinked away.

Akaran paid his tab and returned to Keliss House. He needed to speak with his uncle and devise a way to thwart Rowan's meeting with Myras at all costs. He marched through the manor's candlelit hallways to the ajar door to Adelkar's study.

Akaran pushed it forward. "Uncle, I need a word with you."

Adelkar paused from the earnest discussion he appeared to be having with his mine captain and glanced at Akaran. "I'm a bit busy at the moment preparing for the upcoming tribute—"

"It can't wait," Akaran interjected, not caring how impudent he sounded. "I've discovered something of vital importance."

Adelkar's brows scrunched as he gave Akaran a long stare. "Very well, Nephew. Let's hear what you have to say." His uncle gave their mine captain a dismissive nod.

Akaran waited until they were alone before speaking. "Rowan intends to visit Iron Crossing tomorrow afternoon. He's secured a meeting with Myras."

No further explanation was needed. They both knew where such a meeting could lead.

"Curses!" Adelkar hissed, swatting at his pile of papers, knocking them off his desk. "I've worked too hard for that upstart to show up and ruin my aims for Iron Crossing."

"Then we do something to stop him. It wouldn't be difficult. Have a few men go and rough him up so he can't make the meeting."

Adelkar drew his thin lips together, stroking his furrowed brow. "No, let him go."

"What? But think of what could—"

"I have another idea," Adelkar said with a shrewd grin. "I shall pay the magistrate a visit and inform him of the situation."

"I'll join you."

"That won't be necessary," Adelkar said, retreating to his desk chair and smoothing back his wavy hair. "While I'm with the magistrate, you will serve a better purpose by paying your half-brother a visit."

Akaran brusquely folded his arms. "And do what?"

"What you do best. Rattle him."

Akaran smiled devilishly. "That, I'll do gladly."

Adelkar sank back in his chair. "We play our cards right, and Rowan will be dealt with for us. Then I can continue my scheme of cutting Myras's legs out from under him. Iron Crossing will be mine."

"Along with the other closed mines," Akaran said.

"Yes, I shall secure them all."

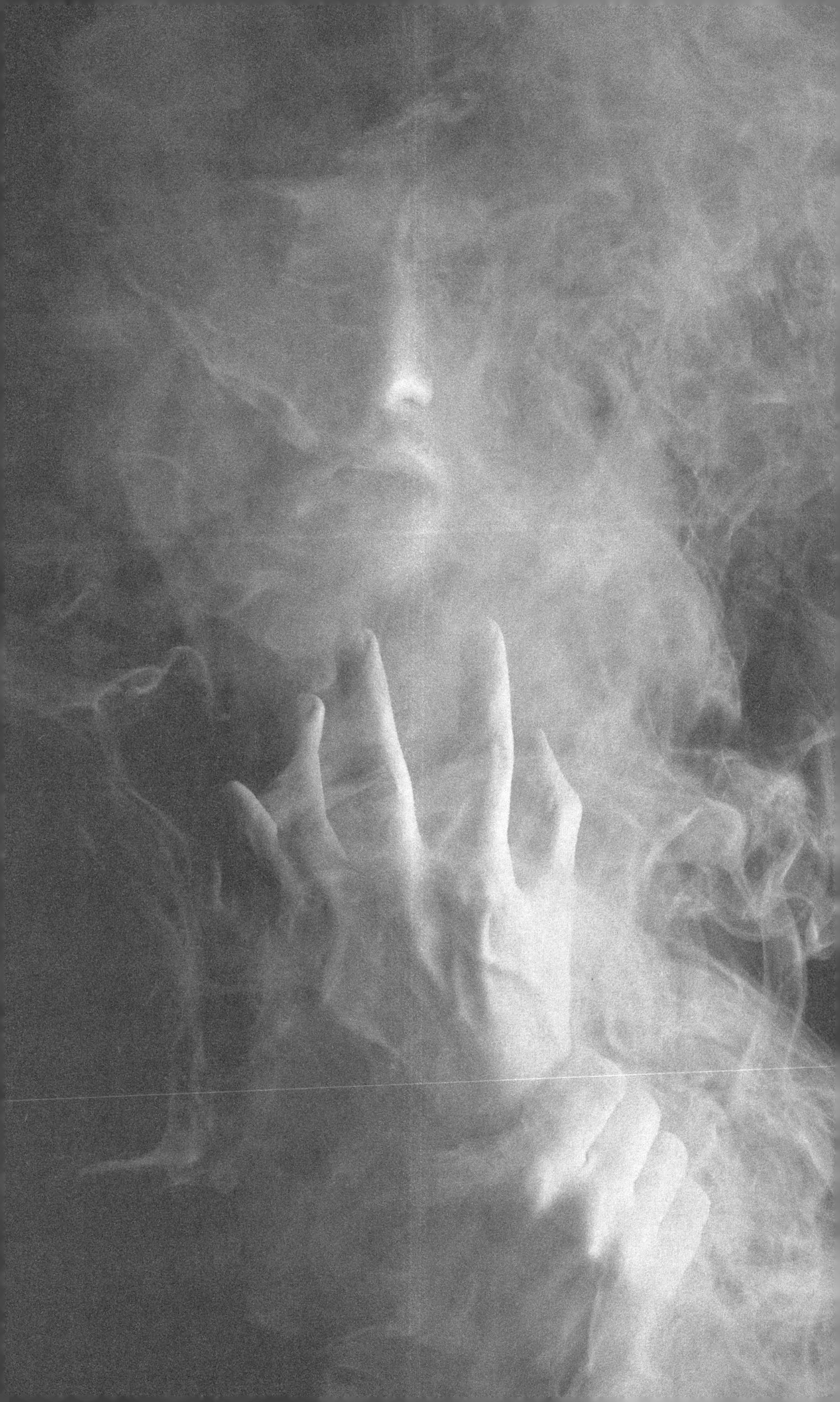

CHAPTER 12
A PEARL'S WORTH

The following morning, Rowan crept down the inn's quiet hallway to Tahira's room. After one knock, the door flew open, and Tahira bounded into the hall, the fringe from her emerald sash dancing like palm leaves around her leafy-green dress.

"You're in a good mood," Rowan said, shuffling backward until his shoulders struck the wall.

Tahira sashayed closer, grinning from ear to ear. "It's because I have a *good* feeling about today."

Her enthusiasm swirled around Rowan like a tropical wind. He felt his cheeks redden as Tahira strutted past him toward the stairwell. He stared after her, entranced, and the vow she made last night drifted through his thoughts.

"I'll be the first to never leave you."

The words seeped through the shame shrouding his soul. Rowan's heart thrummed, yearning to believe Tahira. But the curse had claimed the life of every person he ever loved — a fact he couldn't ignore. As much as he never wanted to suffer such heartbreak again, he could only hope Tahira didn't live to regret her promise.

"C'mon!" Tahira called with a giddy wave, snapping Rowan out of his thoughts. "I'm hungry. Aren't you?"

Rowan nodded with a smile and dashed after her.

They headed into the bar and ate breakfast long before their scheduled meeting with Rahn Myras. The baron's manor was a two-hour journey on foot, and Rowan wanted to arrive with ample time to spare.

Rowan and Tahira thanked Yorn for the eggs and biscuits, then scampered off to their rooms to gather their things. Rowan secured his black pearls inside his sack, strapped his spear to his back, and hurried to catch Tahira waiting at the inn's front door.

As soon as they stepped outside, a pompous figure swathed in black attire astride a dark stallion shot them a menacing glare.

Akaran.

A spike of alarm shot up Rowan's spine, reigniting the pain in his ribs. His feet jerked to a halt. "Burning skies," he muttered under his breath, clutching a fist to his chest.

"What is it?" Tahira asked, spinning around on her heels.

Rowan stood stock-still beneath the inn's awning. "It's Akaran," he said with a tight breath, "my half-brother."

Tahira's eyes widened as they veered toward Akaran. "Act casual," she whispered, drawing her shoulders back.

"Easy for you to say," Rowan grumbled, his clenched jaw aching. "You didn't get pummeled by him."

"Ignore him and keep moving." Tahira urged Rowan forward, and they moved onto the road.

Like an obnoxious bully, Akaran steered his horse to follow.

"I was wondering when you'd show your beaten face again." Akaran stooped his head, his mouth curling into a malicious grin as if admiring his handiwork. "Looks like the bruises are already healing. I should've hit you harder."

When Akaran's gaze beheld Tahira, a surprised smile warped his bow-shaped lips. "Now where'd a cursed wretch like you find a lovely creature like this?"

Tahira fixed Akaran with a coy smile. "A girl must be allowed her secrets."

"Ah, of course." Akaran's suave grin quickly soured. "But the bastard's secrets are known. Nothing escapes my uncle's ears or mine on this mountain."

Rowan scowled and kept walking. "Whatever you think you know—"

"Baron Myras," Akaran said in a knowing way. "Heading to our rival to try and gain a foothold against us?"

Rowan drew his brows together in surprise. "I must find work, and I'd rather try Iron Crossing than anywhere else."

Akaran scoffed. "You're wasting your time. No one will employ you with that curse. By nightfall, there won't be a single baron who doesn't know of it. The whispers have already begun. In a week's time, the mob will be clamoring to have you sent to Mount Maldere."

"The Mountain of the Damned . . ." Tahira whispered with a visible shudder.

Rowan frowned and stole a glance at Tahira, who bit her lip and stared down at the road, as if avoiding eye contact.

"Don't know of it?" Akaran leaned forward on his saddle, his dimpled chin smugly upturned. "I guess your pretty companion hasn't mentioned it then. It's where the accursed go to live in exile. Zurie is there."

The mention of his birth mother struck a chord with Rowan. "How do you know she's there?"

Akaran smirked. "My uncle orchestrated her imprisonment when she foolishly returned to Arjun. He made known her curse, and the mob all but clamored to have her imprisoned." Bitter hatred oozed from Akaran's lips. "I like to imagine her rotting there for all the misery she caused. You should join her. Save the people of Arjun the trouble and head there before things turn ugly. It's where you belong."

Rowan's blood boiled, and he curled his hands into fists. He wanted to swing the butt of his spear and whack his half-brother clear off his saddle. From there, pin him and drive fist after fist into his conceited face. The vengeful thought festered in his head, and a strange tingle developed in his fingers.

Rowan lowered his gaze. Black, illusory tendrils swirled around his fists. He blinked, convinced it had been a trick of the sun, but the wispy tendrils remained.

Is this what Hal had seen? Why am I only seeing it now?

Did it have something to do with the nature of this land? Or something more . . . internal? Maybe only once the curse's origins became known to him—that his curse was indeed *real*—his eyes were then opened to it?

"Don't let him get to you," Tahira whispered, gripping Rowan's wrist and pulling him out of his thoughts. "We're expected, remember?"

With a controlled exhale, Rowan let his anger pass from his head to his fingertips before increasing his pace and turning his back to Akaran.

"Hey, girl," Akaran said, with a forceful edge to his voice. "It isn't wise to stay near one who's accursed. He'll be the death of you."

"Who's to say I'm not also afflicted?" Tahira retorted, remaining close at Rowan's side. Her hand slid around his palm, gripping it firmly. "Perhaps I'm immune to Rowan's curse. If you fear its claws, then you'd do well to stay far from us. Otherwise, it may be the death of you."

Akaran glared with a look of astonishment. He clicked his tongue and steered his horse around, taking off in a trot.

With Akaran out of sight, Tahira released Rowan's hand. Had she only taken it to prove a point to Akaran?

"Akaran isn't wrong, you know," Rowan said, moving once more along the road.

Tahira's lips turned into a scowl. "I'd rather you didn't bring this up."

"Ignoring reality doesn't make my curse nonexistent."

"I understand its lethal claws, but I wasn't going to give Akaran the satisfaction of being right. I've dealt with his kind aplenty. A man like that revels in his bullying. My uncle was no different. I learned how to use his own twisted logic against him and shove it back in his face. Half the time it rendered him speechless."

"And the other half?"

"I'd get a slap to the face that left me dazed." Tahira's entire body seemed to bristle with the memory. "Either way, the conflict ended."

Rowan cringed at her harsh mistreatment. "I don't think I want to rely on your method. The odds aren't too favorable."

Tahira snorted. "How else would you suggest going about it, then?"

Rowan glanced at his hands, at the faint, swirling tendrils around his fingers. "I'd prefer to go one-on-one with Akaran. Solve it as men —fist to fist."

"You'll probably get your chance. If we talk Rahn into a deal, Akaran and his uncle will only hate you more."

"Ah, but at least it won't be solely due to the curse." One consolation he could think of. "I'll have stolen the mine right out from under their noses."

Hal and Curren would be proud.

"Akaran didn't seem worried by us going," Tahira said, her brow pensive. "He must be confident your curse will cast a negative shadow on our dealings."

Rowan stared straight ahead as the dirt road steepened, a wry grin curving his lips. "Well, we're going to prove him wrong."

THEY CAME UPON A SIMPLE TWO-STORY MANOR NESTLED ON THE windward side of the mountain. Unshaded by the surrounding crags, the entire stone exterior glistened like sunlit sand. Pockets of tilled land greeted them along the hillside as they traversed the road toward the manor. A group of men fell a grove of trees, clearing the land for a new field.

Not far from the manor stood a lone, double-peak crag shaped like a hound's head. At its base lay a wide, cave-like opening.

"There's Iron Crossing." Tahira pointed.

Dark like a Moonshade's mouth, the entrance didn't stretch into a tunnel as Rowan imagined, but instead dropped to a shaft set beneath the crag. He found it peculiar that people toiled underground, in relative darkness, all in the hopes of striking iron for a living.

"How deep do mines usually go?" he asked.

"It varies," Tahira said, sweeping the loose strands from her eyes. "Some can go a mile down. Then there are tunnels stretching just as wide. It can be quite the labyrinth."

A middle-aged man of average height and build emerged from the shaft. He removed his dirty cap and gave it a good shake before shoving it back over his sweaty, white curls.

Tahira waved to him with glee. "Keld, we're here!"

The man returned her wave and jogged over with a fond grin. "You are your father's daughter, no mistake." Keld's eyes shifted, and he gave Rowan a surprised frown. "And is this the potential buyer you mentioned?"

Tahira beamed. "He is indeed."

Keld paused for a moment, surveying Rowan. A measure of mirth twinkled in his red eyes. "You get in a brawl, young man?"

"Not one I picked."

"Ah! An unprovoked fight." Keld chuckled. "Happens to every man at least once in his life. Come, this way." He led them to the manor's carved front door and pounded his meaty fist against it.

A well-groomed manservant in his early-twenties with a lean build and closely shaved head answered the door. "Yes, Keld?" he asked in a studious manner.

"Shen, tell Myras his afternoon appointment has arrived."

Shen flicked his blinking gaze between Rowan and Tahira. "But they're early."

"I'm sure it won't disrupt your tightly-run schedule," Keld said, teasing the young man. "Loosen up a little and breathe."

The comment made Shen look even more uptight. "I'm breathing just fine."

"Don't mind Shen," Keld said to Rowan and Tahira—which earned the mine captain a prudish look from the manservant. "He makes a fuss about everything, especially the baron."

"Someone has to," Shen said with a sigh, as though the baron gave him nothing but trouble. "Well, come on in. I'll get you settled." He opened the door fully for Tahira and Rowan to enter.

"Good luck with negotiations." Keld tipped his hat to them and strutted back toward the mine.

Shen's disposition improved as he led Rowan and Tahira to a small circular table set in the center of a brightly lit parlor. "Wait here. The baron has just returned from the mine. He'll be with you shortly."

Rowan took a seat at the table and glanced about the room. One wall was composed entirely of windows overlooking the forested hillside. Beneath the windowsill, a host of leafy potted plants soaked in the sun's rays. Their verdant leaves and stalks reminded him of the Thulu Jungle's lush foliage and added a touch of life to their stone surroundings. The walls boasted a richly painted panorama of a valley surrounded by jagged mountains, and above the mantle was a depiction of a familiar spire upon a low-lying hill—the monument to the fallen.

Tahira appeared enraptured by the tastefulness of the room, her face beaming as her eyes roamed the panorama. She sat with comfortable ease, not displaying an ounce of nervousness. Rowan tapped his foot in restless agitation. He couldn't waste this opportunity Tahira had provided. She'd done her part. Now it fell to him to close the deal.

An old man entered, hobbling with a sleek, black cane. Tall despite his stooped back, the man wore a scarlet robe with a pleated collar and a long, silver necklace set with a large, iridescent gem. His sunken cheeks and high brow bore a map-work of wrinkles, and his short grayish-white hair frayed around his face like wispy clouds. It was little wonder why the baron sought to sell his lands. He couldn't be long for this world.

Rahn took the seat across from Rowan, clasping his knobby, veiny hands and placing them on the table. Once seated, the old man came alive with a vigor that belied his age. His eyes—deep crimson flecked with amber—gleamed like polished ocean pebbles. He aimed to do business.

"My mine captain tells me you're interested in my estate. Is this correct?"

"I'm more than interested, baron," Rowan said. "I'm here to purchase your lands and mine."

Rahn sniffed with a look of disbelief. "I'll admit I was intrigued when Keld informed me of a new buyer, but I never expected it to be someone so young." He stared at Rowan askance. "How does someone like you possess the means to purchase my property?"

Rowan pulled out one black pearl from his pouch and set it on the table. "Ever seen one of these?"

Rahn's eyes widened. He snatched up the pearl and gave it a thorough study, even testing its authenticity between his teeth. "Appears to be genuine."

"I guarantee you it is. I harvested the pearl myself."

Rahn redirected his attention back to Rowan. "So, you have more of them?"

"Much more," Rowan said. "I would be glad to show you when we come to an understanding on the purchase price."

"Of course." Rahn placed the pearl back on the table. The wrinkles on his temples tightened and his eyes narrowed. "It's curious you possess such a rare commodity. Permit me to ask where you come from?"

"Across the Ardruin Sea," Rowan said, "there lies a remote village at the southern tip of Luvaria. It's called Karahvel. No outsiders venture there as it's bordered by the savage Thulu Jungle." Rowan could say more, but he refrained. "Why do you ask?"

Rahn's expression grew quizzical. "Strange as it is, you seem familiar to me. I feel as if I know you somehow."

"I can assure you, baron, we've never met before. I've only been in Shandria for a few days."

"What of your parents? Did they ever live here in Arjun?"

Rowan's unease mushroomed in his stomach.

Why's he so curious? What does it have to do with these negotiations?

Tahira dipped her chin at Rowan, prodding him to answer the man's question.

"My mother Zurie lived here before I was born. She—"

"Zurie?" Rahn interrupted, his entire body jolting. "Do you mock me with that name?"

"Er, no, baron," Rowan said with haste, troubled by the baron's sudden, hostile tone. "She's my mother—"

"And what of your father?" Rahn pressed.

Rowan's composed posture melted. His stomach knotted with the fear of revealing any connections that would get him cast out again. "I couldn't tell you. I don't know who he was . . . only that he's dead."

Rahn leaned back, keeping his eyes on Rowan. The luster in the man's eyes seemed to shift from suspicion to something else that Rowan couldn't pinpoint.

"How old are you?" Rahn finally asked.

"Seventeen. Though, I'll be eighteen next month."

Rahn lifted a wrinkled hand to his thick beard. "Your pearls won't be necessary." He pushed the gemstone back toward Rowan. "My land shall be yours when I perish."

Rowan and Tahira locked eyes as their jaws dropped..

Rowan blinked, coming out of his stupor. "I don't understand. Why give me your wealth when I offer you payment? There's no sense in it."

"You cannot pay for what is rightfully yours." Rahn leaned forward, his dimly lit eyes awash with tears. "My son, Rorak, was your father. You have his bearing, his mannerisms, even the timbre of his voice."

Rowan wouldn't dare hope without certainty. "Wait . . . are you saying"—his voice caught—"*I'm* your grandson?"

Rahn's solemn expression reflected absolute certainty. "If you're cursed, then there can be no mistake. Do you bear the mark?"

Rowan hesitated for a moment before giving a grim nod. He tugged at his collar, revealing his cursemark.

Rahn stared at it long and hard. "So, it is true then: the Conjurer's cursemark. Tell me, what affliction were you cursed with?"

Rowan swallowed and met the baron's intense stare. "Death comes to those who remain close to me. Their life is shortened, dying well before their time." The crushing weight of the curse pressed against his heart. "Four women who cared for me as mothers have died from it."

Rahn's wizened face held a touch of sympathy. "I gather you wish to break the yoke of this curse?"

"More than anything," Rowan said, creeping forward in his seat. "If I am to have any hope in this life, I must break it."

"Hope has already arrived." Rahn's gaze shone with a warm, expectant light. "You brought it when you appeared at my door. This can only be the kind work of fate, bringing me an heir in my last days. You shall live here with me and learn how to govern my lands."

Rahn's offer was beyond anything Rowan ever dreamed possible, yet he couldn't ignore one deadly fact. "But, baron, what of my curse? It will kill you if I stay near."

Rahn shooed away Rowan's concerns with a raised hand. "It is a price I am content to pay. For you see, I would rather spend my remaining days getting to know my grandson than to face the darkness alone in the time to come. And, please, no more of this baron nonsense. You will call me grandfather. It will delight these old ears of mine."

Tears misted in Rowan's eyes. "All right . . . Grandfather."

Burning skies, that sounded strange.

Rahn looked toward Tahira, a genteel smile lifting his cheeks. "You must be Orman's daughter, yes?"

Tahira nodded.

"A real shame he left Iron Crossing. He knew the mine better than anyone. I was sorry to hear of his passing. But fate has brought you back, and here you shall stay."

"You mean, here, as in the manor?" Tahira asked.

"Yes, indeed!" Rahn chuckled. "You must stay with us. I insist. It has been far too many years since a woman has graced these stone halls."

Tahira beamed, perking up like she wanted to leap from her chair and hug the old man. "And how should I address you?"

"You shall do as my grandson and refer to me as grandfather. With my old age, I like to keep things simple."

"Simple works well for me," Tahira said. Her eyes glistened as she giggled, appearing just as astounded by this unexpected turn of events as Rowan felt.

Rahn stood with his cane, seeming quite pleased with himself, and dawdled toward his bureau. "Now that our business is concluded, we must make your claim legitimate. From now on, you shall wear this." He withdrew a simple ring from his desk and returned to the table. "This ring signifies you as my heir. Go ahead, put it on your finger."

Rowan accepted the ring, admiring the crest engraved upon its smooth surface, and placed it on his first finger. It resembled the hound-shaped crag he'd seen outside.

Again, Rowan's life had changed in an instant.

CHAPTER 13
OUTLAWED

The next day, Rowan joined his grandfather in a stroll around Iron Crossing. Tahira was lured away by the manor's small garden.

"Enjoy learning about mining," she teased with an infectious smile, then gamboled off.

Rowan watched her flit from plant to plant like a curious butterfly before tuning his ears to his grandfather's words.

"Mining is in our blood, like iron in the veins," Rahn said, toddling along with his cane outside the mine's entrance. "It's your daily sustenance. Eat, sleep, and breathe it. It's your salvation, and your nemesis. Makes you reckless, makes you bold." Rahn took up a piece of ironstone from the metal cart and tossed it to Rowan. "Take a good look at that, son. It's your fortune."

Rowan turned the cleaved hunk of uneven rock over in his hands. Its external surface held a richly russet-brown hue with bits of a grayish substance embedded in its cracks and crevices. When smelted, the sedimentary rock produced the iron used to make various weapons and welded crafts.

"Iron Crossing has been in our family for six generations," Rahn said, gazing at the hound-shaped crag with pride. "I inherited this land from my father, and I endeavored to make it more prosperous, doubling the levels, increasing our output. Rorak learned from me and eventually took over as I aged, continuing our prosperity."

Rahn's dim red eyes tinged with regret. "Rorak loved running the mine. Alas, he loved that infernal woman more."

Rahn drew in a deep breath, then expelled his sudden anger. "Forgive me, I do not mean to speak ill of your mother—but I cannot forgive her part in my son's death."

"I was told he died in a duel," Rowan said, returning the ironstone to the cart.

"Bah, that foolish duel!" Rahn barked, his lips twisting in a snarl. "I warned Rorak to stay away from Zurie—told him it would bring nothing but ruin—but the stubborn fool refused to listen. Love makes people do the foolhardiest of things."

"Like staying with someone who's cursed?" Rowan said with mild sarcasm.

"Well said." Rahn chuckled. "Guess that makes me as foolhardy as my son."

Several stocky miners finished loading the last of the ironstone into the wagon.

"We're ready to depart, baron," Keld announced from the wagon's driver seat.

"We'll follow in the carriage." Rahn signaled for Rowan to join him, and the two vehicles departed, traveling toward Arjun.

Rowan peered out the carriage window, spying the wagon's load. "Where is the ironstone taken?"

"To the smelters," Rahn said, leaning his wispy-haired head back.

"We don't smelt it ourselves?"

"Smelting the iron ore is done separately from the mining. The ore is sent to the smelters, who then refine it for use. Keld often handles the deliveries. He's a stickler for negotiating the best price for the ore. I used to enjoy haggling with the smelters, but as of late, I grow fatigued by the simplest of tasks."

"It must be good to have others you can rely upon, then."

"Keld has been a tremendous blessing," Rahn admitted, "and his loyalty is without question. He's become almost like a son to me. There's much you can learn from him regarding the mine. You'll need him when the time comes."

Rowan didn't want to think about the morbid eventuality. It pained his heart more to know death approached, slow and vicious, than for it to suddenly happen. With his guardian-mothers, he'd been oblivious to the curse's unseen strike. Now aware of how it worked, aware of how it teemed around his body, he would be more observant of even the slightest change in those around him.

Once they arrived in town, Keld drove his wagon down a different street as Rahn and Rowan's carriage continued toward the eastern edge of the city—the direction Rowan traveled with Akaran on his first day in Arjun.

Their carriage drew to a halt outside the Mestrian Garrison. Rowan stepped out, staring at the row of soldiers stationed on the ramparts. A nervous shudder passed through him. "What are we doing here?"

"Solidifying you as my heir," Rahn said, giving his old bones a careful stretch. "In the event of death, if a baron doesn't possess an heir, his lands are liable for seizure. And the last thing I want is some Mestrian lord, or worse, Adelkar to confiscate my family's legacy."

"That's why you needed someone to buy your land, wasn't it?"

"Yes, but not just anyone would appease me. It's why I held out for so long." Rahn placed an appreciative clasp on Rowan's shoulder. "You showing up couldn't have been better timed."

"Adelkar won't think so."

"Bah! That white crow can caw all he likes, but it'll do him no good now that I have a blood relation. There's no way to refute your claim."

Rowan trusted his grandfather was correct, but he wouldn't get his hopes up until the deed to the estate was in his name. His curse had proven time and time again to be the source of bad luck.

They approached the huge open gate, where two armored Mestrian soldiers stood rigid as poles. Rowan's throat tightened at the sight of the soldiers' chainmail gleaming beneath their cobalt tabards and the large hilts of their longswords swaying across their hips. A shiver of anxiety crawled up Rowan's spine, standing so close to these stern-faced, thickly muscled warriors.

"State your business," one of them ordered.

Rahn leaned on his cane with two hands, calm and composed. "I am here to meet with the magistrate upon a matter regarding the deed to my lands."

"Are you expected?"

"I sent word yesterday. Lord Ferron should be aware of my intent to visit."

"Very well, follow me." The soldier escorted them past the gate, across the wide, cobblestone courtyard, where dark-haired soldiers engaged in training exercises.

As they entered the fortress, Rowan glanced around, intrigued by the interior's dark wood-inlay instead of stone. The ceiling was gently arched and the hallways were lit by evenly spaced wrought iron sconces. Nothing suggested specific taste—no paintings, tapestries, or depictions of any kind hung from the walls. Then he remembered this was a military outpost, not a home. The soldiers stationed here served one function: keeping the townsfolk in line.

The soldier led them to a spacious room where the magistrate presided. Lord Ferron sat in a winged armchair behind a large desk resting atop an elaborately patterned rug. The middle-aged man stood only for the briefest of moments to motion Rahn and Rowan forward before settling back in his armchair. His high-collared tunic and richly embroidered surcoat, along with his sharp-featured face, gave him a proud, sophisticated air.

Ferron smoothed his coal-black hair and adopted a diplomatic smile. "I trust your journey into town was pleasant enough, Myras. It has been quite some time since you left your manor."

"The journey was fine," Rahn said once seated. "Uneventful."

"Uneventful is a word my ears strive to hear. Would you care for any refreshment?" Ferron indicated the jar and beverage glasses on his side table.

Rahn waved off the hospitality, getting straight to business. "I assume you've had a chance to review my letter."

"I did," Ferron said, his tone cool and curt. "And I took note of its urgency."

"Then I'd appreciate it if we didn't waste time and get the deed signed and transferred."

Ferron's eyes narrowed speculatively. "Are you in fear of your life, Myras?"

"I simply want this legitimized in the case of something unfortunate occurring."

"I understand your concerns well enough. Life isn't a guarantee, especially in your line of work."

"My mining days are long behind me." Rahn grunted, sounding fatigued. "Which is why I intend to leave everything to my grandson, Rowan."

Ferron turned a suspicious eye toward Rowan. "Now, you see, this is where we have a problem. I had a recent visit from Adelkar Keliss, who informed me of the stigma surrounding your late son's progeny—that he is accursed."

That slithery snake.

Already Adelkar went and involved the highest authority in the land. Rowan shifted in his seat. He shared a grave look with his grandfather and knew in Rahn's shaken gaze that Adelkar's shrewd maneuver caught him off-guard.

Ferron looked all the more menacing as he leaned forward, his prominent lips drawn in a solemn line. "Is Keliss's claim correct? Is the boy cursed?"

Rahn met the lord's measured stare. "He does have a curse."

"And does this curse infect people in his close proximity?"

"It does."

Ferron's expression stiffened. "Then you know the accustomed course of action is for him to be remanded to the Mountain of the Damned like the rest of his kind."

Rowan's stomach churned.

No, it can't end like this!

"This is Adelkar's plot," Rahn said with a snarl, gripping his cane as though he wanted to strangle the rival baron. "Just when my heir returns, he dares to interfere and deprive my grandson of his claim."

"I sympathize with you, Myras," Ferron said, "especially in light of your son's untimely demise. Duels are messy affairs, and they often bear needless consequences. Much like curses."

Ferron waved for the two guards in attendance to approach.

Rowan twisted in his seat, spying the soldiers. They would take him away—not only that, but cast him into a cursed prison.

Why does this keep happening to me?

"Things don't need to go this way," Rahn reasoned, seeming to struggle to keep a level voice. "Surely we can come to an arrangement which doesn't involve my grandson getting sent to that mountainous abyss."

Ferron feigned sympathy. "My hands are tied, Myras. You know the unspoken laws of your people when it comes to the accursed. I do not want trouble in my city." Ferron folded his hands upon the desk, straightening his posture. "My job is to maintain order in Arjun. I have seen what you Shandrians do to those who bear a cursemark, and frankly, I do not want a lynch mob executing their form of justice in my jurisdiction."

The guards stopped behind Rowan, towering over him, hands on their swords.

Ferron nodded to the guards. "Take this boy away."

Rowan shot to his feet, mind spiraling for a way out. A pair of hands gripped his forearms, yanking him backward. The tendrils spiraling around his arms snaked toward the guards, seeping into their skin. The soldiers took no notice, oblivious to the curse's infection. Only Rowan could see it. Could he stop it from spreading? Manipulate it somehow?

With only the mere thought, the tendrils retreated by a noticeable fraction. Yet in response, it created a backlash to Rowan's body, like a swarm of needles pricking his every pore. He hissed under his breath, abandoning the thought.

"Wait, lord," Rahn beseeched, struggling to rise from his chair. "I urge you to reconsider. The boy has brought no harm."

"As of yet, but I will not take chances with his curse." Ferron nodded once more to the guards. "Carry on—"

"I won't be a source of trouble, lord," Rowan interjected from the doorway, shackled between the guards. "If you fear a mob in the streets, then I won't enter Arjun again—not until I'm free of the curse."

"Your assurance means nothing to me—"

"Then what would?" Rowan said, his nerves rioting like a swarm of hornets. "What assurance do you require?"

A spark of intrigue glinted in Ferron's blue eyes. "You have something of value to offer me in exchange for your freedom?" he inquired, forestalling the guards with a raised hand.

"I do," Rowan replied without hesitation, keeping his voice firm.

"Show me then." Ferron beckoned to Rowan with a flick of his wrist.

Rowan shirked off the guards' grips and approached the magistrate. His gut clenched as he came beside Rahn, who stood rigid with his cane, looking as stressed as Rowan felt inside. Then his grandfather straightened his posture and fixed Rowan with an unwavering stare.

Rowan removed three black pearls from his purse and placed them on the magistrate's desk. "Consider this as assurance, lord."

Ferron ensnared the pearls between his ringed fingers. His face was an unreadable mask as he rolled the gems around on his palm.

Rowan held his breath as he waited for the magistrate's decision —a decision that would seal Rowan's fate.

A greedy smirk split Ferron's lips.

"These will do," the magistrate said, caging the pearls in his fist. His glittering gaze peered across the desk at Rowan. "In addition to your pearls, boy, you will sign a pledge to stay out of Arjun."

"I'll sign whatever you want," Rowan said, squaring back his shoulders, "so long as you don't deprive my grandfather of his request."

Ferron pulled out a parchment from his drawer and scribbled a series of adherents. When the magistrate finished, he melted red wax for a signet seal, slid the paper toward Rowan, and placed the feathered stylus beside it.

"Sign this and abide by its dictations," Ferron said. "If you step one foot inside Arjun proper, my soldiers will arrest you, whereupon you will be delivered to Mount Maldere. Understand in signing this, you will be deemed an outlaw."

"I understand." Rowan grasped the stylus, signing without hesitation, and pressed his signet ring into the wax.

"Now onto the deed transfer." Ferron withdrew another form and placed it before Rahn. "Inscribe the name of your heir and successor at the bottom."

Rahn wasted no time and did it while standing.

Ferron looked the parchment over before marking his seal of approval. He flashed a routine smile at Rahn. "Your lands shall pass to your grandson, so long as he adheres to this agreement. I would hate to see this visitation be for naught." The magistrate lifted his gaze to the two guards. "See that they leave the city directly. The boy's warrant begins the moment he leaves this garrison."

Rowan and his grandfather returned to the carriage and were on their way. Only then did Rowan's rattled mind slowly relax. He tilted his head back and shut his eyes, yet his heart still hammered inside his chest. He took deep breaths, repeating Naja's mantra over and over until his heart returned to a normal beat.

"Are you certain of the bargain you struck?" Rahn asked.

Rowan opened his eyes and gave a resigned shrug. "There was nothing to consider, Grandfather. You need an heir to protect Iron Crossing and all its tenants. Being outlawed from Arjun is a small sacrifice. If that's how it has to be, so be it."

Rowan turned his head and stared out the window.

Quiet tenements, firelit forges, peddler stalls, and rousey taverns raced past the carriage. Shandrians trekked up and down the lanes dressed in their layered tunics and colorful sashes. Several children kicked a leather-hide ball down an empty street, then chased after it, the sound of their laughter carrying through the window.

Rowan took his final glance at The Red Canary, as it too, passed out of sight. A sigh escaped his lips. He had held such hopes when he reached Shandria—to finally be accepted in his homeland—but the capital city had just been taken away.

Perhaps it was for the best.

Rowan feared how Adelkar and Akaran might retaliate. With their treacherous nature, they could make known his curse to the populace and stir up a mob against him. Adelkar had done it once already with Zurie.

"This predicament you face could be long-term, son," Rahn said. "Does it not bother you to be considered an outlaw?"

Rowan dipped his head, rubbing his cursemark. "I am already an outcast in my village. What could Arjun hold for me but growing animosity? I experienced it enough in Karahvel, and I don't wish to repeat it. The manor is the only world I need for the time being."

The tension eased from Rahn's face. "Then I best get you more familiarized with the world you are to inherit."

The carriage drew to a sudden halt, and the horses nickered. Rowan was thrown from his seat, and Rahn's cane thwacked against the other side of the carriage.

"Mighty Orthrin!" Rahn fumbled for his cane. "What's wrong with Gavan's driving?"

The driver hopped from his seat and appeared at the carriage window. He rubbed his trembling, callused hands together.

"Gavan, why have we stopped?" Rahn asked, securing his cane.

"W-w-we have a small p-problem, baron," Gavan stammered through plump, crooked lips. His speech was slow and slurred as though he wasn't sharp in the head. Rowan wondered if the dented groove on the shaven side of his skull had anything to do with his stutter.

"Oh, what now?" Rahn said, sounding a tad grumpy.

"A p-p-passel of men blocks the road. Adelkar is with them—so's his nephew."

Rahn furrowed his brow, tsking. "Come to make a spectacle of our exit, has he?"

Rowan grew uneasy. "You think he knows the arrangement we made with Lord Ferron?"

"Unlikely. He's here because you're not on your way to Mount Maldere."

Gavan flicked his big, shaky eyes toward their problem. "Baron, do you w-w . . . shall I handle this?"

"No, I'll handle this myself. Out, son. We have a confrontation on our hands."

Rahn shoved open the door and, despite his stiff, old bones, marched with a surprising amount of determined speed. Rowan scrambled after his grandfather. How did Rahn intend to handle Adelkar? Would Adelkar take measures into his own hands? A cluster of ten men stood with him—Rahn and Rowan were sorely outmatched.

Adelakr and Akaran dismounted from their well-groomed stallions. Akaran sported a confrontational glare; Adelkar did a better job at masking his emotions.

Just how much has Adelkar's quest for vengeance molded Akaran's blind hatred?

Rahn positioned his cane in front of him, standing tall and proud.

Rowan took his cue from his grandfather, pushing his shoulders back and holding his head high.

"Is there a reason for barring our way, Adelkar?" Rahn said, seeming to feign ignorance.

Adelkar cocked his head ever so slightly and narrowed his eyes. "I see the cursed mutt is still in your company."

"Despite your sordid attempt to interfere," Rahn said.

"He's cursed, Myras. You can't hide the obvious. So, why's he not on his way to Mount Maldere?"

"For the simple reason no order was given to have him sent there."

Adelkar frowned, apparently flummoxed. Akaran's face contorted into anger and disbelief, but Adelkar spoke first. "How is that possible?"

Rahn shot his rival a deeply grooved smirk. He drew himself up straighter, clearly enjoying this tête-à-tête. "We worked out our own arrangement with the magistrate. You can pay Lord Ferron another visit if you're so inclined."

Adelkar smirked. "Well played, Myras. I thought you'd grown senile after your prolonged years of isolation. But it appears you have more fight in you than anyone would've anticipated."

"Having two youngsters around the house has helped me feel more like my old self. So, here's what I'll tell you: My land is no longer for sale. It shall pass to Rowan upon my death. Didn't think I'd figure out he was my grandson, did you?"

Adelkar didn't seem to miss a beat. "On the contrary, Myras. I predicted you would, which is why I proceeded as I did. With his curse, he doesn't belong within the city. He will bring death to Arjun's citizens."

Rahn scoffed. "Oh, Adelkar, stop acting like you give an ironstone's worth about anyone other than yourself. You acted purely out of your own self-interest to brand my grandson as an outcast, but your scheme failed. We are within our rights to return to Iron Crossing. If you need convincing, ask our Mestrian escorts. They can answer your every question."

Adelkar's gaze shifted to the soldiers lingering a stone's throw away. "This isn't over, Myras," he snarled. "I'll see that boy is denied everything. Your days are numbered. With him in your company, I expect you'll be cold in your grave before the yearly tribute. How will he fare then, when everyone sees for themselves the death he brings?"

Rahn motioned Rowan to follow him back to the carriage. "Pay no heed to Adelkar's words. You belong here."

Belong?

The word awakened Rowan's deepest longing. He never thought he'd hear anyone utter such a thing. Could it truly be so? Had he finally found his home?

Rahn's eyes remained on him as they re-entered the carriage. "You don't believe me?"

Rowan hesitated. "I haven't ever belonged anywhere, so it's hard for me to accept all of a sudden."

"Well, accept it. Now that it's set in stone that Iron Crossing will pass to you, you officially have somewhere to belong." Rahn tapped the top of the roof with his cane. "Drive on."

The carriage lurched forward and Rahn settled back into his seat with a satisfied grin. "That little squabble seems to have renewed my energy. I haven't felt more alive in the past seventeen years."

Rowan smiled at his grandfather. He said nothing to dampen the old man's mood, keenly aware his vigor would soon wane. It was only a matter of time.

AKARAN SEETHED AS HE WATCHED THE CARRIAGE ROLL UP THE slope toward Iron Crossing. "Well, that didn't go as planned," he growled, stomping back toward his stallion. "I thought you dealt with Ferron. How could they have renegotiated a deal?"

"We'll know soon enough." Adelkar returned to his steed and walked the horse toward the Mestrian soldiers. "Excuse me, gentlemen. Might I have a word?"

"Be quick with it. We are here to make sure the cursed boy makes it back to the manor."

So they know he's cursed, and still they let him escape Mount Maldere.

Akaran couldn't understand it.

"You see, it's the boy I wish to inquire about," Adelkar continued. "What was the magistrate's ruling?"

"He made the boy an outlaw in Arjun city," one guard explained.

"It was the boy's idea," the other guard added. "He agreed to never enter the city again while cursed, so Lord Ferron saw no reason to deny Baron Myras's request to bequeath his lands to his grandson."

The soldiers exchanged a brief look, smirking as if there was more to the story.

"I think that explains the situation well enough," the first guard said, flicking the reins.

The soldiers continued on their way, leaving both Adelkar and Akaran to stew.

"What do we do now, Uncle?"

"We wait for Myras to die," Adelkar said. "I suspect it won't be long."

CHAPTER 14
RATE OF DECAY

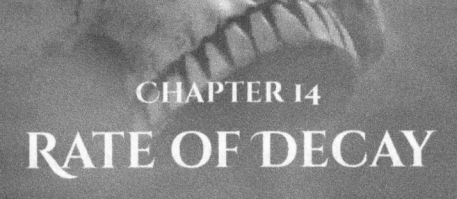

The next week, Rowan spent every work hour far beneath the grass, familiarizing himself with Iron Crossing's lengthy tunnels. Before he could set upon cleaving ironstone, Rahn tasked Rowan with observing the miners to better understand the demanding physical work. Even though Rowan had seen his share of difficult labor—harvesting barley and black pearls—mining required a bit more muscle and know-how.

All the miners he observed chiseled at the tunnel's interior in swift, careful strikes. Skin and clothes were covered in layers of grime, and sweat beaded on their ivory brows as their muscles swelled with each rhythmic swing. Carts rolled from one end of the mine to the other on rail tracks. Bits of cloven ironstone were piled into the carts, and once full, they were pushed to the mine's lower exit, where wagons awaited to haul the shipment to town.

The well-run system fascinated Rowan. It reminded him of his days in the barley fields. He didn't miss those long, grueling hours exposed to the harsh sun, but he did miss the simple act of working with his hands. He longed to assist and share in the mining. It was his fortune, after all, and he wanted a hand in achieving it.

"Rowan, over here." Keld and several brawny miners packed a few bladder sacs containing a mixture of oil and powdered firestone into sections of the rock face. "We're setting up to blow this area," Keld explained. "We concentrate the blast to blow only the portion of rock we need. Too much firestone and the ceiling could collapse."

Rowan shuddered, glancing up at the concave roof. "Does that happen often?"

"It's happened enough in my experience to be extra cautious. That's why precision is key." Keld grabbed a barrel of powdered firestone and poured out a thin trail, running it down the length of the tunnel. He then placed the lid back on the barrel and kept it in his hands. "I think we're ready to blow it. Everyone, behind me."

The miners gathered their tools and trekked to the front of the tunnel where Keld and Rowan stood. Keld knelt on one knee and struck the flintstone, igniting the powder. The spark sizzled, racing down the trail toward the oil sacs. Rowan tensed, his body squished between two bulky brothers in their late-thirties named Bashir and Bulan. A layer of dirt smeared their rugged faces.

"Wait for it," Bulan teased, exposing his crowded teeth with a wide, uneven grin. His short, wavy hair was unashamedly messy. "It'll steal your breath."

"Oh, and you might wanna cover your ears," Bashir added, who —unlike his brother—tamed his wooly hair in a braid woven along his scalp, ending in a bushy tail.

Rowan shoved his hands against his ears right before the explosion rocked his senses.

The thundering boom shook the entire tunnel. Rowan waved the billowing smoke from his eyes, along with everyone else. Once it settled, they ventured to the explosion site.

"Someone, get me a light," Keld hollered with a quick hand gesture.

Bashir retrieved a lantern for the mine captain. Keld studied the area for a quiet moment before his mouth spread into an ecstatic grin. "Mighty Orthrin! Look at this trail of ironstone!" He traced the natural gray line in the sedimentary rock. "Cast your eyes on this, Rowan."

In the flickering light, Rowan beheld spans of illuminated ironstone, sprawling out like dark vines. Dipping his head to a low section in the wall, he spied a rich seam of iridescent rock clumped in a small mass. He rubbed his fingers over it, unsure what it was.

"Find something?" Keld asked.

Rowan nodded, pointing at the bright, cerulean rock dotted with fiery speckles. "What is this?"

Keld squinted, then broke into a toothy grin. "Looks like fire opal."

"Is that valuable?" Rowan asked.

"It can be, depending on the quality. This bit of opal looks more like the precious variety, so it's worth quite a few marks. You'd be surprised by the vast amount of luminous treasures buried beneath the crags. I'll have Bulan chisel it out for you."

Rowan backed away as brawny-armed Bulan stepped in with his chisel and hammer. After a speedy excavation, the miner dislodged the opal deposit and dropped the pretty chunk of rock in Rowan's hand.

"If you ever wanna get gems out of this for a special lady," Bulan hinted with a wink, "I can arrange it. My wife, Kitra, is a splendid jeweler. Her work is sought after throughout Arjun and can bring to life anything you imagine."

Rowan blushed at the thought of crafting something special for Tahira. "Er, well, I may have an idea or two," he said, remembering the necklaces and bracelets Naja once wore.

"An idea or two is only the cusp of imagination," Bulan said, gesturing with his broad hands. "Think big, and the possibilities are endless!"

Keld flicked his finger at Bulan's large ear. "Bulan, stop talking the boy's ear off. You can boast about your wife's jewelry skills another time."

"Hah! I've been found out again!" Bulan released a booming laugh, which rumbled like thunder through the tunnel, then mouthed to Rowan, "We'll continue this later." He squared his shoulders and chiseled at the rock face with glee.

"We struck it rich with that blast," Bashir was saying to Keld, giving the mine captain's dusty shoulder a satisfied clasp. "There's more ironstone than I expected we'd find."

Keld smiled. "I had a feeling it'd be lurking behind this rock face if we blew it."

"Your gut was right," Bashir said, rubbing his large, bulbous nose bent like a knot from an old tree.

"Go topside and tell Myras. He'll be pleased to hear the news."

Keld surveyed the new hole, tapping his chin. "I bet if we continue this level here, it may lead us to more iron deposits. We're going to need more firestone powder."

He turned to Rowan. "I'll show you how to prepare the next batch. But first, we need to gather up the debris. There's bound to be chunks of ironstone we can salvage for smelting."

Bulan rolled an empty cart to the site. Rowan dove into the work, hefting rocks alongside the miners, the air thick with steaming sweat. Finally, a task he could perform. He positioned himself clear enough from the others to keep the curse from latching onto anyone. Even in the dimness of the tunnel, he could faintly see the curse's spiraling tendrils.

Right, it's time I investigate the true nature of this curse.

OVER THE COURSE OF SEVERAL EVENINGS, ROWAN WORKED ON fashioning a loom for weavescripting inside his bedchamber. He missed the craft and the heritage it represented: a way to remember his guardian-mothers. He worked on a new weave for several hours before heading outdoors to put his curse through a series of tests.

He tilted his head back, basking in the shaded sunlight. Shandria's comforting rays didn't burn his skin. The higher elevation and arid climate reduced the sun's overall harshness. With the sun at his back, Rowan ventured into the marshland far below the rear side of the mine.

The secluded spot provided the perfect place to perform his experiments, as it teemed with foliage—tanned sedges shooting up fuzzy spikelets and sprinkled with hardy wildflowers. After Rowan's encounters with those Mestrian guards, he wanted to see if he could manipulate the curse's reach and rate of decay.

Rowan dropped to his knees and swept his hands through the grass, watching the poisonous tendrils leap from blade to blade. The fleeting touch wasn't enough to infect the long stalks—not yet, at least. He snatched one of the thin blades, held it between his fingers, and waited for the curse to spread its toxins. The flaxen color drained from the grassy blade as a sickly black stain spread outward from his fingers. It took only a minute for the entire stalk to wither.

"Burning skies . . . This is how the curse kills . . ."

Did the blade wither quickly on account of its small size or due to its meager amount of stored life? Rowan glanced down, and the brush on which he knelt already showed signs of deadening. Ebony spots dotted the sedges nearest his body, while the grass three feet from him in every direction appeared unharmed. Would it remain that way? Or would the miasma spread farther?

Curious, he snapped off a flowering spikelet and held it in his palm. This time, he concentrated on the tendrils and, forming an image in his mind, coaxed them to swirl around the plant. Like a swarm of gnats, the miasma devoured the florets, reducing them to an ashy mound. Rowan blew a concentrated breath, and the ash dispersed into the air.

I really can affect the rate of decay.

The realization sparked a new question: Could he consciously prevent infection altogether?

He picked up another spikelet and attempted to keep the tendrils from latching onto the plant. Despite the pricking pain in his pores, the miasma spread, ignoring his mental pulls. He furrowed his brow, concentrating harder, but still the tendrils seeped into the spikelet. The plant did, however, decompose more slowly than the previous spikelet. Did that mean his resistant urges affected the rate of decay after all?

Rowan's hypothesis would need more testing.

Over the course of several weeks, he repeated his experiments, varying his mental pressure, observing how the tendrils reacted to his mental pushes and pulls. As if they possessed a mind of their own, the tendrils swirled with more dance-like glee when he urged them to kill more quickly, but they spun with sluggish twirls when he exerted resistance.

Why couldn't he prevent infection altogether? Did it have something to do with certain parameters the Conjurer might have embedded into the curse? That no matter what he tried, his curse would always endanger whoever he was with? His heart ached with a sense of crushing defeat.

Rowan heard someone calling his name and spotted Tahira

wading her way through the sedges. She wore a cream, knitted shawl over her shoulders, the fringe swaying in the dusk's breeze. Was it already that late? He viewed the sky—shades of deepening hues backlighted the dark blue mountains. Evening had come.

Rowan dusted off the ashy remains of his last experiment and rose to face Tahira.

Her eyes sparkled with curiosity. "What're you doing out here?"

"I've been experimenting."

Tahira hovered several feet away, scrutinizing the dead grass around him. "Looks more like you're killing plants."

Rowan chuckled. "It looks that way, doesn't it? I've discovered I can manipulate the curse's taint around me."

"How so?"

"Watch." He picked up a wildflower and coiled several tendrils around the stem. Then he applied a touch of pressure, and the tendrils drained all life from the petals. The flower withered and turned to ash. "Strange, isn't it?"

Tahira's hand went to her mouth, and she shivered. "It's a bit unsettling."

Of course, she's disturbed.

Rowan flushed with embarrassment. He'd just killed a healthy flower in front of Tahira as if it was a great accomplishment. "I realize this has a deadly application, but I may need this edge to kill the Conjurer, whoever she is."

"So, in the meantime, you're killing innocent flowers." Tahira smacked her lips together in mock disapproval.

Rowan folded his arms in playful defensiveness. "Do you have a better alternative? A less innocent plant I could kill?"

"As a matter of fact, I do." Tahira said with a grin. "This ability of yours could come in handy with the tree removal out in the grove. It would mean less work for the field hands, and more practice for you."

Rowan rolled his eyes. "You make it sound like I enjoy murdering plants."

"You did look quite engrossed," Tahira said.

"I was simply focusing on the task."

"Yes, of killing that poor flower," Tahira reminded him, her voice becoming more dramatic.

Rowan tossed his head back with laughter. "You're not going to let me off easy, are you?"

Tahira considered for a moment, swaying her hips like one of the wildflowers dancing in the breeze, then smiled as an idea formed. "If you help me out by eradicating weeds in the garden tomorrow, I just might."

Rowan grinned. "Then I'll get that out of the way first."

CHAPTER 15
KILLING TREES

Killing weeds brought far more satisfaction than flowers. Rowan's enjoyment multiplied with Tahira's exhilarated squeals every time a weed bit the dust.

"You're doing the vegetables a great service," Tahira said, beaming with delight.

"Hm, I could've sworn I was doing this so you didn't have to perform this menial task," Rowan said as a spiky weed shriveled between his fingers.

Tahira crouched beside Rowan, bringing her face in close. "And I thought you wanted more chances to practice. I call this a win-win exchange."

Rowan laughed. "Again, you think of everything." He stood and stretched his back, surveying the small, fenced-in garden. No weed had been left standing.

"Ready to head to the grove?" Tahira asked.

"Lead on."

They crossed through two narrow fields, teeming with long stalks of tanned wheat ready for harvesting. Rowan kept his thoughts centered on restraining the wispy tendrils flitting around his body; he didn't want to infect even a single stalk. The whole endeavor took more effort than he expected. By the time they reached the grove of trees adjacent to the field, Rowan was out of breath—in addition, every inch of his skin burned as though it had been singed by fire.

He released his control on the tendrils, collapsed to the dry brush, and sank his head against his knees.

Tahira gaped at Rowan. "How are you out of breath? We didn't walk that far."

Rowan swallowed a few more breaths before responding. "I was keeping the curse contained while we crossed the wheat fields. It's harder work than you realize and inflicts a painful toll on my body." He gripped his knees, groaning under his breath, and waited for the fiery, prickling pain to subside.

Tahira glanced at Rowan with concern. "Are you sure you're up for this?"

He flicked his head gently. "I want to give this a try. It's a good way to test the curse's strength. If I can kill a massive tree in a certain amount of time, it'll give me an indicator on how swiftly I could take a human life."

Tahira's eyes appeared to swirl with alarm. "I guess this'll be a good test then." She looked unnerved, and Rowan felt like an imbecile for casually talking about such morbid things. "Wait here and rest. I'm going to find the overseer."

Tahira headed toward the crowd of people chopping at the trunks of several trees. Their axes swung in turn, striking wood with a distinct *thunk*, *thunk*. Tahira flagged down one of the workers, who then pointed her to someone else—a bristly-haired man who possessed the height and width of a stout tree himself.

After a moment, Tahira ambled back to Rowan with a pleased expression. "Warin says we're free to do as we please."

"What did you tell him?" Rowan asked, looking toward the husky overseer.

"That we'd be in the grove scouting out a tree for making a garden bench."

Rowan cocked his eyebrow. "And he bought that?"

"You're the master here," Tahira reminded, like it was the most obvious fact. "Does he need more of an explanation?"

"When you put it like that, I guess not, no."

"C'mon, then, let's get started." Tahira wiggled her fingers, motioning for Rowan to get up.

He complied, shooting her a smile. "You're much too eager for this."

Tahira laughed nervously, twiddling with the ends of her hair. "It's so I keep from getting disturbed by the nature of your work."

"My work? Oh, is that what you call it now?" Rowan said with a chuckle.

"It's better than calling you a plant killer," Tahira teased.

Rowan sighed. "Fair enough."

Tahira spun around and trotted toward the shaded grove. "So, where shall we start?"

"Much farther in," Rowan said, strolling a safe distance behind Tahira. "Far away from the workers."

"They'll be finishing for the day in an hour as evening sets," Tahira said over her shoulder. "If you're worried, we can wait until then."

Rowan nodded. It was the sensible choice, and it gave Tahira plenty of time to scout out their first test subject.

After passing hundreds of tall trees, she touched her chin in thought. "How about you tackle that slim silver birch over there? It's not as big as the others."

They marched toward it and came to a stop beneath the tree's shade. The setting sunlight refracted through the wooded canopy. Rowan surveyed its many sleek limbs all intersecting from the short trunk.

"Stand back while I do this," he said with a cautioning wave. "There's no telling what could happen."

"Right—good idea." Tahira gulped and put several yards between them.

Rowan faced the tree, sucked in a breath, and placed both hands on the trunk. The tendrils shot from his fingertips and seeped their way into the smooth bark. He stood still, urging the curse to perform its infectious work. Minutes passed without a sign of decay, until Tahira broke the silence.

"The leaves—they're dying!" Her voice quivered. "Take a look, Rowan."

He turned to meet her wide-eyed gaze before glancing up at the branches. The once-green leaves turned a clayish brown, crisping and shriveling in various stages of death. A sweeping breeze shook some loose, and they tumbled to the ground, bearing tar-black veins.

Tahira picked up an infected leaf that had landed near her feet. "Is the tree dead?"

"No, not yet. I think the dying leaves are only the first stage. Unlike plants, trees have long lifespans, so it'll probably take a bit longer."

"In that case, I'm having a seat." Tahira stretched out her legs and started braiding her hair. "Let me know when you think it's dead."

Rowan shot her a look. "Sure, I'll just be working hard over here while you relax."

Tahira made a face. "Hey, you wanted to test yourself, so test away. Meanwhile, I'll enjoy the view."

Rowan shook his head and returned his attention to the birch. Imagining himself as a puppeteer, he guided the mass of tendrils up and down the slender tree. He pushed on them mentally, sending the miasma into the trunk's upper regions and around the branches.

The clearest indicator of decay centered around his hands where the silver bark darkened as if charred by fire. Even the texture felt more brittle, like charcoal. The blackness spread, encasing the tree from canopy to root, until not an element of color remained. The branches sagged with rot.

Rowan stepped back and surveyed the lifeless tree. "I think it's dead now."

"Incredible." Tahira's mouth hung agape. "How much time has passed, you think?"

Rowan shrugged. "Maybe fifteen minutes. The lumberers should have an easy time cutting this tree down."

Tahira stood and brushed off her emerald dress. "Well, onto the next?"

"Your choice."

Tahira picked another tree, one towering as a giant amidst the surrounding birches. "This should be a good challenge."

Rowan took a hard look at its thick trunk and tiered, interlocking branches and instantly regretted letting Tahira make the choice. He scowled. "Remind me why I let you choose?"

Tahira wrinkled her nose. "Um—"

"It was a rhetorical question." Rowan crossed his arms, staring up at all the sprawling limbs. "You had to make things more difficult."

"It's for your benefit," Tahira said, finding her spot in the brush once more. "Go on, kill the tree."

With a concentrated breath, Rowan thrust his hands toward the trunk and let the curse spread. He followed the same procedure as before, but this time he imparted more urgency to the tendrils.

Let's see if we can beat our previous time, eh?

In response, the tendrils whipped around his hands with tremendous speed, eager to demolish the first record. He executed commands like the chieftain of an army, dispatching groups of tendrils to different sections of the tree, waging his campaign of death. Branches creaked and snapped. One branch gave way, then another, plummeting to the grass with a tumbling *crack!*

Tahira released a startled yelp. "Branches are falling now? That didn't happen last time."

How to explain it?

"I gave the curse a challenge," Rowan said. "It's causing more devastating results."

"I'll say," Tahira said, her voice higher-pitched. "I wouldn't be surprised if the tree falls."

Rowan paused and considered. "For it to fall, its root system would need to weaken considerably. Given enough time, perhaps it will."

More branches cascaded from the heights, breaking off others in a violent descent. As the bark blackened, a storm of dead leaves rained down on Rowan's head. Even the tan grass around him wilted. The russet ferns lying at the base of the tree curled in on themselves, shriveling. The roots crumbled, and the tree itself groaned, its hold in the soil giving way.

"Um . . . Rowan?" Tahira called, shuffling toward him.

"What are you doing?" Rowan said with a sharp tone. "I told you to stay back. It isn't safe."

"I know, but there's a bit of a problem. We have company."

Rowan froze. He twisted his head. Several lumberers approached, including the overseer, Warin.

"I thought you said the workers would be gone?" Rowan whispered to Tahira.

"I did, and they *should be*." She chewed the corner of her lip. "Maybe we were making too much noise."

"Burning skies," Rowan hissed under his breath, dropping his hands to his sides. But the evidence of what he'd done stood out like a diseased blight for the four workers to see. "Don't be alarmed. I can explain..."

The dead birch leaned, groaning—as if a strong, invisible force pressed against the trunk.

The lumberers gasped, shock plastered on their faces.

"H-how's he done this?" a worker asked.

"The tree is completely dead!" another man shrieked in horror.

"It has to be his curse," Warin said. "I've heard the rumors from town—appears they're true."

"If he's cursed, why's he here?"

"Will his curse infect us?"

"Are we to become as dead as that tree?"

The workers cast Rowan wary glances, each one backing away with axes lifted.

It was happening again, exactly as in Karahvel—the stares, the whispers.

How could I let myself believe it would be any different here? I'm such a fool.

The truth would spread like wildfire, and before evening's end, every field hand, miner, and tenant would know what he was —cursed.

Rowan's insides churned like a storm-tossed sea.

There really is no place for me to belong.

Tahira stepped in front of Rowan. "You've got it wrong," she told the workers. "Rowan would never use this ability on any of you."

"Ability?" Warin scoffed, lifting his ax to indicate the dead tree. "You call killing a mighty birch an ability? It's a curse! Look at all the dead plants around him. That could be us, if we get too close."

Rowan said nothing in his own defense. Every word Warin spoke was irrefutable, which was only further punctuated by a prolonged, crackling groan. The lifeless tree crashed with a boom, a black scourge upon the golden landscape.

The lumberers broke out in a clamorous furor following the tree's fall.

"Leave this grove, boy!" Warin shouted, his command full of panic. "And take your deadly curse with you!"

Tahira pressed her lips together. "I'm sorry . . . I didn't think this would happen—"

"Of course you didn't think," Rowan snapped, before he could rein in his frustration. He jabbed his nails into his palms, immediately regretting his outburst. "But then, I should've exercised more caution. This isn't your fault. It's mine. I'm a walking, breathing curse. I was foolish to think everyone would treat me like you and Rahn do."

Rowan fled, leaving a trail of dead brush in his wake—mind too rattled to keep the curse at bay. He raced into the manor and shut himself inside his bedchamber. Finding his colorful cowl, he buried his face in its weaves and screamed.

His emotions unraveled, and the curse's tendrils swirled around him in a spidery torrent. He sank against the stone floor, staring numbly out the window. Dark shades of crimson and cobalt, a foreboding tapestry, blanketed the sky. This should be his world—viewing everything from afar, without the chance to curse and destroy a single life form.

"Rowan?" Rahn's voice carried deep concern. "Are you all right, son?" The door handle jostled.

"Don't come in here!" Rowan cried out, tucking himself into the corner. "It's not safe."

Despite his warning, the door thrust open, and his grandfather hobbled in. "What's happened? What's wrong?"

Rowan buried his face against his knees. "It's the curse."

Rahn sat on the stool beside the loom. "Has it killed someone?"

"No, but I used it to infect trees in the grove." Shame tied a noose around his neck, and with a sunken head, Rowan explained everything. "I only wanted to help. But I made things worse. The workers don't want me anywhere near them."

"They see the curse, and not the man."

"That in itself is another curse," Rowan grumbled, cradling his head.

"True . . ." Rahn paused. "But these curses need not define you. Isn't that so?"

Rowan lifted his head to meet Rahn's kind gaze. "I met a young man in Eldon who told me the same thing . . ."

Rahn curved his thin, bearded lips. "Hm, did he tell you anything else?"

Rowan thought back on what Mestria's Crown Prince had imparted to him. "He said the curse is merely an obstacle I must crush in order to alter my fate."

"I agree, so it must be wisdom." Rahn's lighthearted chuckle lifted Rowan's spirits. "There are other ways to lend a hand: inside the mine. Your curse can't corrupt stone. It's not a living thing."

Rowan sighed. "You're right. I just needed breaks from working underground."

"You get used to it. After all, it's only natural as a Shandrian. It's said the first Shandrians were carved from alabaster stone. The Mighty Craftsmith Orthrin breathed life into their mouths, and they awakened from their lifeless shells."

"Do you believe that, Grandfather?"

Rahn shrugged. "It's only a myth, but it would explain why we're different from other humans."

"Different, huh?" Rowan said with a quiet chuckle. "I'd gone all my life thinking I was the only one like me. It wasn't until I met Tahira that I realized I wasn't alone in this world."

Rahn's smile brimmed with tenderness. "I'm sure she wouldn't want to see you pitying yourself like this. Come, let's take a stroll outside. Show the tenants you have the right to be here. Besides, it's far too nice an evening to spend it holed up in this room."

Rahn rose from the stool, but a coughing fit sent him fumbling forward. His cane fell from his grip as his hands flew to his mouth.

Alarmed, Rowan leapt to his feet and steadied his grandfather. The coughing grew more violent.

"Shen!" Rowan yelled in a panic. "Come quick!"

Rahn slumped back onto the stool and pulled a handkerchief from his robe's pocket, covering his mouth. When the coughing subsided, a dark spot of blood stained the white cloth.

Rowan recoiled, flinging his hands through his hair in despair as the terrible truth sank in. The curse had begun wracking Rahn's body.

CHAPTER 16
ANOTHER JOURNEY

Shen came running, poking his worried face inside the room. "Is the baron all right?"

"He needs rest," Rowan said, guiding his grandfather with a shoulder for support. "He was coughing harshly a moment ago and is quite weak."

"Here, let me help." Shen offered his arm, and together they led a grumbling Rahn—who kept blathering he was fine and didn't need to be treated like an invalid—to his bed.

A pillow propped up Rahn's head, and the rest of the old man's form lay beneath several blankets, including a tricolored weaving Rowan had made as a gift for all his grandfather's kindness. Rahn appeared to treasure it more than any jewel or cherished plant he possessed. His knobby fingers clutched it, drawing it closer to his chest.

Shen left to retrieve nourishment for Rahn, whose complexion looked frightfully ashen. His breathing returned to normal, but a wheeze lingered.

Left alone with his grandfather, the shame of the curse tugged at Rowan's chest. He stood from his chair on unsteady legs. "I should go."

Rahn wrinkled his brow. "I haven't asked you to leave."

"It's unwise for me to remain so close." Rowan gripped the chair's seatback. "Look at what it's costing you."

Rahn's fatigued eyes brimmed with tears. "Closeness comes at a cost, son. To know you at this stage is to suffer death."

Tears spilled from Rowan's eyes. "I hate this curse—hate what it does to those I love. I fear another death will break me entirely."

"Regardless of curses, we all must experience death. It's the natural order of things. I am old. My time draws near. Curse or no curse, mind you." Rahn lifted a shaky hand, pointing to the vacant chair. "Sit a while longer. I wish to speak more."

Rowan swiped at his tears and slumped back into the chair. "What more do you wish to say?"

"There are things I wish you to know," Rahn said. "I hope it brings comfort. I, like you, have lost those most precious to me: my wife and my son. So, I can understand your heartbreak and your reservations."

Rowan didn't know anything about Rahn's wife and what had become of her. His grandfather had never mentioned her. "How did your wife die?"

A heavy sadness hovered over Rahn's countenance. "Hilda's spirit withered years ago. Much like a flower's ephemeral beauty, she let herself diminish. She couldn't reconcile the death of our son and the hope that could've been. You see, hope is a powerful thing. It allows us to move forward. Without it, one has no reason to live. Hilda lost hers and succumbed to death."

"But not you?" Rowan wondered aloud. "What made you not choose her path?"

A feisty fire flashed in Rahn's eyes. "I couldn't let the mine pass to Adelkar without a fight. I persevered out of sheer stubbornness, just to spite that scheming crow." Rahn coughed, then his face softened. "But, in my heart of hearts, I placed all my hope on a long shot: you. Now that you're here, I shall be able to die in peace."

Rowan rubbed the tip of his nose, needing some levity to ward off further tears. "Well, don't get any ideas of going yet. We haven't had nearly enough time together."

Rahn chuckled, then broke into another cough. "I'll muster more life to stave off death's claws for as long as I can. Though, seeing as the curse is taking its toll, now would be a good time for you to seek out your mother."

Rowan's gut twisted. "You mean visit Mount Maldere?"

Rahn nodded.

Rowan clenched his fists upon his knees. The thought of meeting his mother face-to-face shook him to his core. "Is she truly still alive?"

"No one can say for certain," Rahn said with a heavy sigh. "Mount Maldere is a dangerous place; it's not somewhere people come and go. They say the accursed folk interned there have grown savage from prolonged isolation and lack of nourishment."

Rowan gawked at his grandfather. "And you want me to venture inside?"

"Given the nature of your curse, I'd say you're more a threat to anyone residing within the mountain." His grandfather let his words sink in.

Rowan glanced at the tendrils swirling around his fingertips, remembering the way they'd drained life from those plants and trees. The curse was a weapon, but also a shield of protection. He could use it without caution in Mount Maldere.

Rowan leaned forward, fiddling with his hands. "Why must I see her?"

"Because she can tell you who cursed you." Rahn's gaze grew serious as did the timbre of his voice. "You both were cursed by the same individual, which means, if you kill the Conjurer who cursed you, you will break not only your own curse, but the curse upon your mother as well. This is the next step in your journey, son. You must move closer to breaking this curse while I'm still alive. Who knows what Adelkar will try once I'm gone?"

Rowan closed his eyes. His grandfather was right. He couldn't delay any longer.

"I understand," Rowan said, opening his eyes again. "I'll leave first thing tomorrow."

ROWAN GATHERED HIS SUPPLIES FOR THE JOURNEY AND VENTURED outside to the yard. The morning fog pooled like a soft cloud beneath the dawnlight, and the manor lay quiet. Gavan had the wagon ready.

He loomed like a large herron in the driver seat, conversing with Tahira and Bashir.

Rowan frowned at the brawny miner. "Why're you here?"

"I'm tagging along," Bashir replied. "It's to ensure no one tries to hassle you on the way."

Rowan didn't think his presence was necessary, but someone must've. "My grandfather put you up to this, didn't he?"

"That obvious, eh?" Bashir scratched the back of his thick, hairy neck. "Rahn means well, and frankly, I don't mind the wagon ride."

Rowan's gaze veered toward Tahira, who wore an amethyst, knee-high dress with dark leggings and boots—clothing more suited for travel. "And why're you dressed like that?"

"Because I'm coming with you." Tahira folded her arms, taking her usual stubborn stance. "You didn't imagine you'd go without me, did you?"

"It was the plan," Rowan said, throwing his sack and spear in the back of the wagon.

"We're traveling companions, remember?" Tahira said with a broad smile. "And that's all there's to say about it."

"Fine, you win. Let's get going." Rowan wasn't in the mood for her peppy games, not when Rahn's weakening condition weighed on his thoughts. Being away for a few days would be good for his grandfather.

He'll be free of my curse.

They set out as the other miners trekked toward Iron Crossing, hammers in their hands. Some gave Rowan strange looks. News of his curse had reached their ears. Those who knew tapped the shoulders of those who didn't and whispered the truth.

Rowan steered his attention to his lap, watching the tendrils flit around his palms. He concentrated for a moment, pulling at the tendrils, keeping them contained. Pain poked at his pores. He exhaled and let the curse swirl unhindered. He did it time and again, keeping his mind distracted, building endurance and increasing his pain tolerance.

"What're you doing in that wagon, Bash?" a short and grubby miner hollered. "Don't you know it isn't safe?"

"Baron's orders," Bashir replied.

"Glad it's you and not me," the miner said.

When they passed the long line of miners, Rowan lifted his gaze and stared at Bashir. He sat at the front of the wagon, his bulky frame blocking Gavan from sight. Only the top of the driver's tan cap was visible.

"Is my grandfather paying you extra to come along?" Rowan asked.

Bashir snorted. "I didn't need extra incentive. I volunteered."

"Why would you volunteer?" Rowan said, flabbergasted. "I'm cursed!"

Bashir rubbed at the stubble on his anvil chin. "You see, Bulan and I had an uncle who was cursed by a Conjurer, so we sympathize with your situation. We couldn't help him break his curse, but we'd like to help make things easier for you."

Rowan's face flushed, not knowing how to respond, so he simply gave an appreciative nod.

Gavan took a road leading away from town. Since Rowan couldn't travel through Arjun, they took an alternate route to circumvent the city. It extended the first leg of their journey by an hour.

Once they circled Arjun, the vast Valley of the Fallen sprawled before them.

"From here, it's a relatively straight shot across the valley toward the Vennor Mountains lying yonder." Gavan stretched out a hand, indicating the mountain range. "It'll take over a day to reach Mount Maldere."

"At least it's close," Rowan mumbled.

"The real journey will be the mountain itself," Gavan said, seeming to cringe. "I hope to Orthrin I never have to g-g-g . . . have to venture inside."

Rowan didn't dwell upon the fear he detected in Gavan's voice. However much he preferred avoiding this task, he *had* to enter Mount Maldere. Perhaps it wasn't as bad as people imagined. Rumors and stories could be exaggerated. Then again, they often stemmed from some measure of truth.

They soon neared the monument to the fallen, passing beneath its far-reaching shadow. Shaped like an obelisk, the silver spire rose high above the plains, its conical tip flashing blinding white light.

The wagon rolled along the road following the path of the babbling river, passing churning watermills and small farms with carved-out sections of flatlands growing various crops, including wheat.

"Are you nervous to meet your mother?" Tahira asked, elbows resting in her lap, hands tucked under her chin.

"I'm trying not to think about it," Rowan said, his eyes on some workers in a nearby field. "She's got information I need—it's all I'm letting occupy my thoughts."

"That can't be all? She left when you were a newborn. You must feel something?"

"I don't know what to think or feel," Rowan admitted. How should he view the mother he thought dead for eighteen years, only to learn she lived—but abandoned him? And not only that, she was cursed for having a scandalous affair, which led to him getting cursed as well? The whole situation was a dark, sticky web, with Rowan embroiled at its center.

Haraz withholding the truth about Zurie had been a kindness. Rowan could see that now.

"To me," Rowan continued, "she's simply the woman who gave birth to me. My guardian-mothers were my *true* mothers. Because of their nurturing care, I don't feel robbed of a mother's love." He paused, then sighed before meeting Tahira's gaze. "Not the answer you were expecting, was it?"

Tahira shrugged, drawing her knees against her chest. "I was expecting a little more emotion. I mean, have you ever wondered what she's like? Or what she looks like?"

Rowan rubbed at his cursemark. "In Karahvel, I was told she shared my features—nothing more. To them, a woman who abandons her child is known as a lynasi."

Tahira's brow creased. "What's that mean?"

"It's a creature that lives in the jungle. When in danger, the females are prone to forsake their cubs. They lack the maternal instinct to safeguard their young at the cost of their own lives."

Tahira rested her chin against her hand again. "Is this how you see Zurie then? As one of these creatures?"

Rowan nodded. "To an extent, yes. I want to hear from her lips the reason she left me. Only then can I form a true opinion." That maddening, gnawing thought alone would propel him into Mount

Maldere's depths to discover the truth. "I'll get it—and the name of the Conjurer."

THEY TOOK LODGING FOR THE NIGHT AT A FARMING RESIDENCE, then set out once more at morning's first light. The overcast sky—somber-gray with low-hanging clouds—obscured the road ahead. Leaving the river's path, they broke for the range of conical mountains jutting above the subdued horizon. The summit of the tallest peak—as well as their destination—was invisible behind a billowy mist.

By mid-morning, they reached Mount Maldere with a sheet of ghoulish fog creeping along its base. The wagon came to a halt.

Gavan set aside the reins and turned nervously in his seat. "This is as far as we dare approach."

"It's close enough." Rowan grabbed his spear, secured his knife, and leapt from the wagon.

Tahira hastened to join him, clutching at her forearm. "What an eerie mountain," she said with a shiver. "I've never been so close to it."

Mount Maldere possessed a gnarled, ominous peak and dramatic cliffs. Its tree-lined slopes and rocky screes lay steeped in shadow, as if even the sun dared not supply the mountain with a touch of warmth.

Rowan held in a shudder. "You're lucky this is as close as you need to come."

Tahira stepped in close and gave him a quick peck on his cheek. Worry filled her eyes. "Go in, find Zurie, get the name of the Conjurer, and get out," she said, fiddling with her sleeve. "Don't dawdle."

"Hey, this isn't the kind of place where I would choose to dawdle," Rowan said with a nervous grin.

"You know what I mean," she whispered.

Tahira appeared so anxious, Rowan yearned to reassure her. He pulled in the tendrils, clasping her hands. "I'll try to be as quick as I can."

"Just stay safe." Tahira's gaze wandered toward the shrouded peak, and her body shuddered once more. "And *please* . . . come back."

Tahira chewed her bottom lip, full and beautiful, and Rowan couldn't ignore its fearful quivering. His palms sweated the longer he held her hands. In that moment, he remembered their first kiss, and the strength of her spirit to meet him in the chasm of his shame. The desire to soothe her troubled mind as she had his was an impulse he couldn't contain. He wanted to answer—to give it life. And breath.

Rowan dipped his head and kissed her trembling lips. His heart pulsed as he held the caress, long enough for a surge of sublime warmth to flood his veins. For one shared breath, all cares vanished.

Burning skies, why have I denied us this wondrous touch?

The immediate answer pummeled his brain like a hammer pounding iron.

The curse, the curse, the curse!

Rowan quickly broke contact, and his throat tightened. He exhaled and found Tahira doing the same. Bashir and Gavan broke into snickers beside the wagon, then busied themselves watering the horses, acting as if they hadn't witnessed the moment.

Rowan's and Tahira's face reddened.

"I'll return," Rowan told Tahira, letting go of her hands. "I've got a curse to break, remember?"

Tahira's blush appeared to deepen. "You should drink some water and get a bite to eat before you go." She handed him the flask and several pieces of dried meat.

Rowan chewed in a rush and took sips often.

"Take no food or water with you," Bashir warned, all usual lightheartedness absent from his face. "It'll only make you a target."

Rowan took a final swig of water and finished off his last morsel of meat. It would have to tide him over until he returned.

"There's a path leading to the entrance where you'll find a small outpost guarded by Mestrian soldiers. It's the only way in or out of that mountain." Bashir indicated where the trailhead began. "Head straight as you can through the fog, and you'll find the path."

Squinting, Rowan perceived the sloped gradients and sharp

switchbacks—and those were only the ones unobscured by the fog. It was going to be an arduous trek.

"We'll make camp a mile from the mountain," Bashir told him. "If you're not back by sunrise on the second day, we'll assume you aren't coming back."

Tahira's eyes widened at Bashir's ultimatum. Rowan wouldn't fault him for his caution. Rahn forewarned that Mount Maldere was a dangerous place.

"I understand."

Rowan faced the mountain and traveled toward the trailhead. It lay a half-mile from where the wagon remained. Reaching the base, he spied the vertical slope ahead and started his ascent.

The path was a leisure climb at first. Birds chirped upon unseen perches, dry brush flitted in the wind, and leaves rustled on swaying branches. The rich notes of sugary sap and musky cedar wafted across Rowan's nostrils. It stirred memories of the Thulu Jungle and its lush foliage.

An hour into the climb, the path took on more drastic inclines, forcing Rowan to anchor his spear in the loose gravel as he hiked. He took short breaks, giving his legs a rest, but after another hour of relentless slopes, his muscles burned from fatigue. Sweat pooled beneath his collar, and he wiped his brow with his sleeve. His throat grew dry as desert sand; he wished to quench it with crisp, spring water.

Rowan came to another switchback, this one near the sharp edge of a cliff. He paused to stare out at the sprawling steppe. Pockets of fog, like tufts of wispy wool, drifted above the valley and along the lower screes. He'd traveled a long way—climbing for at least five hours well into the late afternoon—yet, he didn't know how much farther he had to go.

Turning, he trudged along the path, hoping the entrance was near. Another two hours passed before the trail leveled at last.

Rowan bent over and sucked in deep breaths. He lifted his head, venturing toward what looked to be a guard post. Smoke billowed from the cobblestone chimney. Through the windows, he noticed several broad figures moving about, yet, no one came through the door to investigate his arrival. Either the guards stationed here took a breezy approach to their posting, or they didn't get many visitors and no one was on the lookout. Why would they? Rowan couldn't imagine many people willfully visited this cursed mountain.

At the gated entrance, a young Mestrian guard lounged beside a fiery brazier, his trim, muscular frame unencumbered by armor. He chowed on his supper while gulping from a silver flask.

Rowan didn't feel a flicker of fear from this Mestrian soldier, who started humming a canty tune to himself. He seemed a far cry from the stringent guards stationed at the Mestrian Garrison.

The guard's lulling blue eyes veered in Rowan's direction, and he hopped to his feet, his dark ponytail flying over his shoulder. "What business have you in the mountain?" he asked, smoothing out his padded jerkin.

"There's someone I must find," Rowan replied, resting his spear against his shoulder. "She has information I need. Am I free to enter?"

"You are," the soldier said, giving Rowan a half-measured look-over. "So long as you know the mortal risk. Those interned here are accursed, plagued with all manner of ailments devouring flesh and mind. Most who enter of their own volition—like you—do not return. In light of this, do you still wish to proceed?"

Rowan gripped his spear more tightly and nodded. "I do."

"Then you are going to need this." The guard dipped a torch into the fire and handed it to Rowan. "Courage be with you, spearman," he said with a halfhearted tone, almost like he didn't expect to see Rowan's face again. He pulled the lever and the gate rolled open with a grating, nail-biting screech.

A cold, foreboding wind pierced Rowan's bones as he stared into the entrance's dark maw. He expelled a troubled breath, lifted his torch, and entered the Mountain of the Damned.

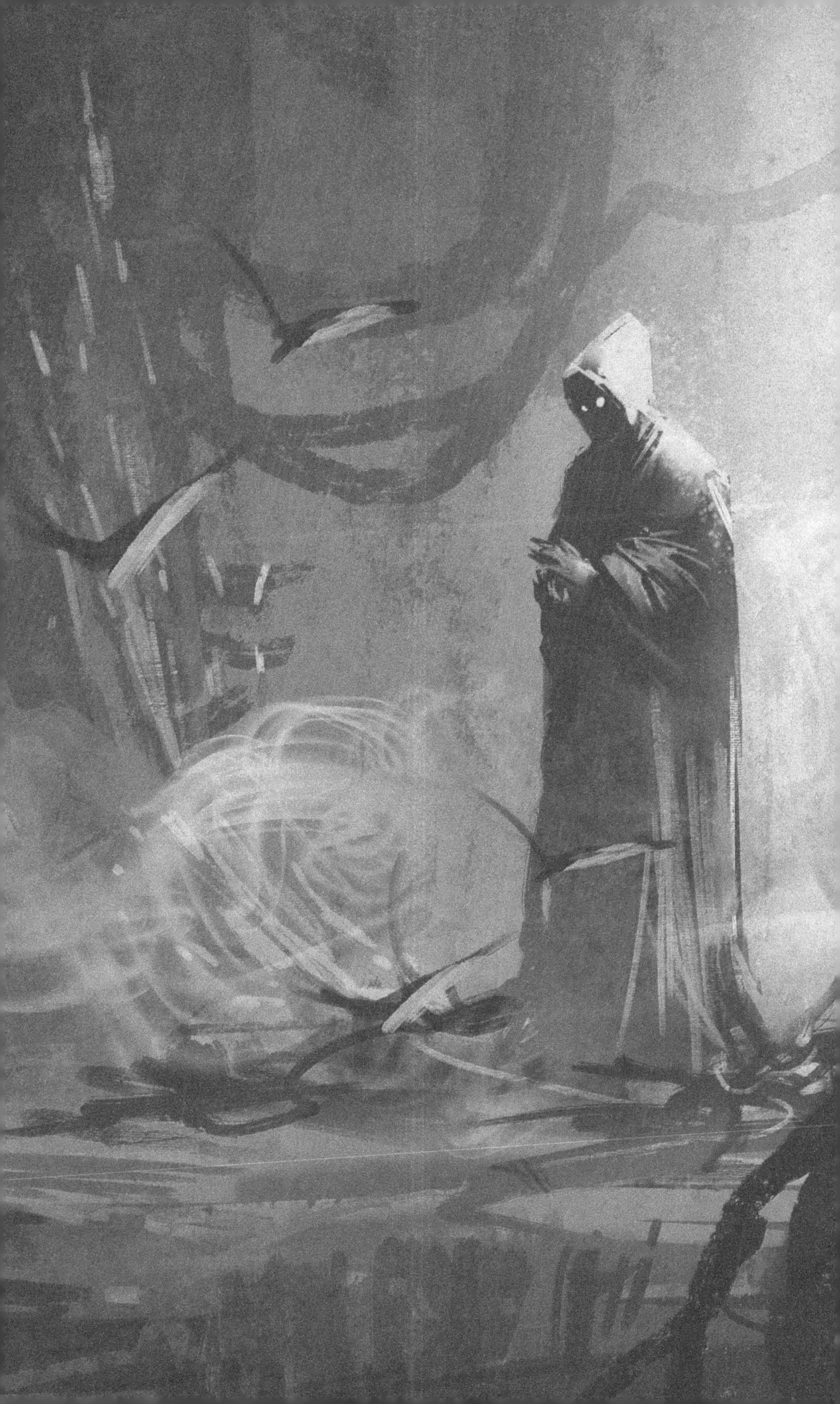

CHAPTER 17
MOUNTAIN OF THE DAMNED

Rowan crept inside the eerie mountain's cave-like passageway, breathing in the stale, damp air. A layer of musty undertones clung to the uneven rock face in the way wispy webs clung to the serrated ceiling. Within the tenebrous confines, the temperature plummeted, chilling Rowan's nose and cheeks. The torch supplied a meager amount of warmth and, thankfully, his cloak and tabard staved off much of the cold.

The utter silence unsettled Rowan's nerves. He squeezed his body between a tight grouping of stalagmites with spearhead peaks, his breathing as loud as drums in his ears. Quietness haunted him like a trailing shadow. His movement, his breaths, and the whirling of the torch offered the only din.

Rowan came to the end of the tunnel only to reach his first obstacle—a narrow gulf that sliced across the passageway. He hovered his torch over the chasm and peered down. The cliff appeared to fall sheer, and the faint sound of water trickled far below. On the other side of the gully loomed the jaws of another passage, its opening crowned with hanging rock-daggers, like a Moonshade's razor-sharp fangs.

Rowan drew in a chilled breath and leapt across the chasm.

As he landed, the torchlight illuminated the slick, uneven ground beneath his feet. He edged away from the ledge, exhaled a calming breath, and entered the tunnel.

Crazed shadows scurried across the cramped passageway, which soon split in two directions. Rowan proceeded along the gnarled path twisting left and came upon a small cavernous chamber where the blackness devoured the scant light of his torch. He took several cautious footsteps in before a malodorous stink blasted his nostrils. He tripped over something his torch failed to illuminate: a body lying bundled in tattered rags. And it wasn't alone. A half-dozen more bodies littered the cavern.

"Hello?" he called to them.

A series of moans answered.

Rowan held his torch aloft, getting a better view of the groaning individuals. Their limbs, hands, and feet were covered in bandages, tightly wrapped, and some appeared to be missing fingers and toes. The stench wafting from their bodies was like an animal carcass. They had to be stricken with disease.

Rowan recoiled, keeping his distance and continuing on through the passage.

Deeper and deeper, he crept into Mount Maldere's winding bowels. He encountered a down-sloping corridor in which he had to squirm on hands and knees, slinking with the torch outstretched in front of him. Reaching the other side, he came upon another chamber, this one more expansive than the one with the diseased people. Towering columns like unsculpted pillars spanned the entire width of the cavern. Rowan shimmied between two columns that had melded together at their base and peak; it left just enough of a gap for him to slide through.

Something was different about this chamber's gargantuan space. A light source existed other than the torch. Rowan turned toward the wall emitting a faint blue hue. Were those rocks glowing? He tiptoed closer and swung the torch in front of him. The striated rocks ceased their glow. When Rowan pulled the torch away, the gossamer light glowed once more.

Fascinating.

He spied more glimmering-blue rocks upon the jagged ceiling, and his mouth dropped in awe.

What a strange place to find such a marvelous wonder.

Loose rock crunched behind him, and Rowan spun, waving his torch.

"What do we have here—a wayward lamb?"

"Nah, looks more like a startled fawn."

From a shadowed alcove set in the nearby rock face appeared two men—one, disfigured with yellowed teeth, and the other, a hunchback with a lumbering gait.

"I can tell you've figured out our curse just by looking at us," the disfigured man said. His face resembled misshapen clay: eyes sunken, folds of skin drooping over his eyelids and lips, and a horribly crooked nose and sagging mouth. "So, what's your curse, runt?"

"I bring death wherever I step."

"Hm, sounds kinda like Zurie's curse," Hunchback said, scratching his patchy hair with a massive hand.

Rowan's eyes lit up. "You know her?"

"Everyone inside this mountain knows who she is," Hunchback said in a gruff voice.

"She's Maldere's Goddess of Death!" Clayface erupted into a raucous snicker.

It startled Rowan enough to cause him to shuffle backward. He stepped on something hard, a disturbing *crunch* beneath his boot. His torch illuminated a pile of bones, including a human skull.

"Whose bones are these?" Rowan asked, his skin crawling. "Friend of yours, perhaps?"

Clayface's droopy lips twisted into a capricious grin. "A friend for the night, he was, until an unfortunate accident occurred."

Rowan swallowed. "What kind of accident?"

Clayface's blood-red eyes glittered in the darkness. "The kind you don't see coming."

A phantom shadow pooled beneath Rowan, and a spike of warning ignited in his gut. Before he could twist around, something hard and sharp struck the back of his head. Pain exploded in his skull, and his vision swam. He staggered backward, disoriented, squinting at what hit him—a short and spindly old man with eyes whiter than his albino skin. The colorless eyes reminded Rowan of the Moonshade he fought near the Grimwood.

Is he blind?

The creepy, old man tweaked his head as if his ears caught every tiny sound.

"Nice hit, Bat!" Clayface touted, in a pitch dripping with insanity. "The fawn's dead meat now."

"He looks tasty." Hunchback drooled, his mouth opening like a cobra's. "Better than the last geezer we ate."

"Too bad you let that meaty mammoth escape your fat fingers," Clayface said. "This runt'll make up for it."

"Let's swarm him!" Hunchback howled.

Reality struck Rowan harder than the blow to his head.

Cannibals!

Rowan swung his spear and torch in a warning arc. "Stay back! All of you!" he yelled, a cascade of fear racing through his blood. "Come at me again, and it'll be your death."

Clayface withdrew a hiltless knife fashioned from obsidian. Hunchback picked up a pair of bludgeoning rocks. The one in Blindbat's hand already bore blood.

My blood.

"Go on, little fawn, run!" Clayface taunted, lifting his weapon. "See if you can escape." Clayface's wicked cackle echoed through the vast chamber, chilling Rowan's bones.

Rowan took off at a sprint, not caring which direction he fled. The path he chose sloped into a narrow tunnel, making him an easy target. Hunchback hurled a rock. It smacked Rowan square in the back, propelling him into the rock face.

Blindbat sprang quicker than a twin-tail's pounce onto Rowan's back. The man's arms snaked around Rowan's neck as he sank his jagged, rotting teeth into Rowan's shoulder.

Rowan howled and flung himself against the tunnel wall, hard enough to loosen Blindbat's grip. He drove a teeth-smashing kick into the man's frothing mouth and kept sprinting.

Hunchback, lumbering with loud, echoing footfalls, hurled another rock.

Rowan evaded it only to dash straight into a nest of bats. Their ear-splitting screeches scrambled his senses. He swatted at them with spear and torch, flinging them away from his face to no avail. Swathed in a horde of fluttering wings, the ground beneath him disappeared, and he lost his footing. His chin struck rock, and he bit into his tongue. The torch fell away from his grasp, and before he knew what was happening, he was sliding down a steep and bumpy slope.

Skin scraping against rock, he eventually rolled to a halt inside another chamber dimly illuminated by a smattering of ember-orange luminescent rocks. To Rowan's hazy eyes, they blazed like bonfires under a starless sky. He would be mesmerized if his mind wasn't submerged in panic. He crawled on hands and knees, every inch of his body screaming with pain.

A slithering sound raked his ears. Rowan twisted his head and caught Blindbat following his descent. Uttering unintelligible gibberish, the cannibal charged with reckless abandon, snarling like a ferocious Moonshade. Rowan snagged his spear and scrambled to his feet. He thrust the weapon forward, impaling Blindbat through the gut. The force of the old man's sprint sent the spearhead tearing clean though his stomach, driving Rowan to a knee. Blindbat snarled like a beast and careened into Rowan. The wild man's racing heart thundered in Rowan's ears before slowing to silence.

Rowan wiggled out from under Blindbat's corpse as Hunchback appeared at the base of the incline. The deranged man's back stooped so far forward, his long arms dangled in front of him like giant ropes. His large hands were a pair of panther paws dragging against the ground as he charged at Rowan.

A well-timed forward thrust wouldn't subdue this opponent, who had the eyes to see it coming. Hunchback swung his arms like clubs, slow but powerful—a direct hit would have Rowan seeing stars. He stayed on his toes, evading the swings, waiting for a moment to strike.

"Stay still, fawn, so I can make this quick," Hunchback growled.

Rowan ducked, then jumped back and scurried to his foe's flank. Hunchback flung a fist over his shoulder, covering his rear, thwarting an attack. Rowan wasn't aiming to strike yet. Hunchback may have looked as strong as an ox, but he likely lacked endurance and wouldn't be able to maintain his offensive for long. Rowan needed to hold out until Hunchback's energy wavered.

Rowan dashed left, then right, circling his opponent, wearing him down. Hunchback appeared to tire, his breathing heavy and raspy.

Now's my chance!

Rowan thrust high with his spear in a feint. Hunchback dodged it, and Rowan whipped the butt of his spear up in a flash, landing a hit under the man's protruding chin. Hunchback growled, falling back several steps. Rowan swung his spear in an arc and delivered the killing thrust.

Hunchback caught the staff right below the spearhead with his giant hand and yanked it from Rowan's grip.

Rowan leapt aside, seized his knife, and crammed it on the crest of Hunchback's shoulder. A guttural, outraged growl echoed through the chamber. Rowan looked to bury the knife again when Hunchback spun and swung his arm.

A well-driven palm to the side of Rowan's face sent him flying. He landed flat on his back, losing all air from his lungs—and the hold on his knife. He blinked away the fog right as Hunchback pinned him with the weight of a ship's anchor. His beefy mitts seized Rowan's throat.

Rowan flung his hands in desperation toward Hunchback's face, shooting out a wave of tendrils. Unbeknownst to his foe, they seeped into his ears, eyes, and through his nostrils, slithering toward the brain.

Kill it, kill it, kill it!

Rowan prayed they reached his attacker's organ—before Rowan ran out of air or his neck snapped.

Rowan's sight darkened within Hunchback's strangling grip. In his spotting vision, the mass of tendrils snaked in and around Hunchback's maniacal face. Still, the cannibal remained clueless.

Death lurked over their heads, coming for one of them. It all depended on whose attack killed more swiftly.

Rowan choked under the pressure on his throat. His fingernails dug into Hunchback's skin, uselessly drawing blood.

As light faded from Rowan's eyes, Hunchback groaned and released his grip. His eyes sank into his skull, his facial skin grayed, and his entire body convulsed. Then all movement seized as though he'd gone stiff from fright. Rowan pried Hunchback's hands from his throat and rolled away. He refilled his lungs with air and climbed to his feet, staring down at Hunchback's motionless form.

His head had shrunk, caving in on itself, as though all bone and tissue had melted away. Rowan clasped his hand over his mouth to keep from retching. He stumbled around on shaky legs, searching for his spear and knife. He laid hold of his weapons right when a voice boomed above him.

"Where are you, fawn?" Clayface's taunt floated down. The cannibal stood at the top of the slope, cackling, dark and demented.

Holding in a groan, Rowan shook off his disgust and searched for an exit. The slope was too steep to climb, but that wouldn't stop Clayface from finding a way down to come after him.

"Did you fall down this slope, I wonder?"

The sound of a sliding body drew Rowan's attention. He was soon to face another fight.

Burning skies! There's nowhere to run.

At least not a way he could find without more illumination.

Find a place to hide.

Rowan dashed behind a thick, rocky column and readied his spear.

"Looks like you got the others," Clayface said, clicking his tongue. "Clever fawn—but you aren't out of the woods yet."

Rowan couldn't see the last cannibal's face, but from the sound of his demented voice, he was closing in on Rowan's hiding spot.

I won't wait to be cornered.

Rowan held the advantage with his spear's reach. He recited Naja's mantra in his head and slowed his breathing, keeping his spearhead level with his eyes. Clayface's footsteps indicated he'd drawn even closer. Rowan waited a moment longer, readying to leap out.

A sudden commotion froze him in place.

"No, wait! Don't hurt me!" Clayface cried in terror. "Don't—"

A horrifying scream filled the chamber, echoing off every craggy surface.

Rowan thrust his head around the column and lost his breath. Clayface doubled over, writhing in agony upon the orange-ember rocks—thrashing as though on fire, yet, no flames consumed him. Something unknown assailed him.

Rowan watched in horror as Clayface's skin decayed, aging and blackening in a span of seconds. Bits of his flesh and muscle detached from his bones, rapidly decomposing. His mouth hung open in a crazed scream, stealing all moisture from Rowan's throat.

Clayface's droopy jawbone sank away from his head, shattering into a pile of dust.

An eerie silence descended.

The rest of the cannibal's body continued to deteriorate as footsteps approached.

"Stay where you are," Rowan said, raising his spear. "Don't take another step."

"Or what, boy?" a bossy alto voice taunted. "You'll kill me with that measly spear of yours?"

"I have other weapons," Rowan threatened, summoning the tendrils to form a cloud around him. "Like the one you used on Clayface."

Silence followed his claim. It lasted only a moment. The footsteps continued.

Out of the darkness appeared a middle-aged woman, stern of face, with ferocious curls dangling to her slender waist. Garbed in a black-wool dress and a tattered-sleeved shawl, her lithe frame blended in with the darkness. She carried no weapon in her thin hands, but her feral eyes shone fiercely like the glowing amber rocks.

At that moment, Rowan remembered what Clayface had said. *"She's Maldere's Goddess of Death."*

Rowan lowered his spear. *"Mother?"*

CHAPTER 18
ZURIE

T he woman went stock-still. She tilted her head, parting her ghostly pale lips. "Akaran?"

"No, it's me, Rowan."

"Rowan?" Zurie invoked his name like it was impossible. She squared her diminutive shoulders and regarded him for a silent moment, then drew close, her face brimming with suspicion. "Show me your neck."

Burning skies, will this always be my defining feature?

Rowan pulled back his cloak and revealed his cursemark. "Recognize me now?"

"The cursemark is a giveaway." Zurie paused. "Yet, even without it, I can see Rorak's features in yours." She flicked her gaze around warily. "Let's not talk here. Follow me to my sanctum."

Rowan followed with anxious steps. They rounded a dark alcove and came before a long fissure in the rock face. Inside lay a narrow passageway he never would've found on his own.

"Stay close," Zurie instructed, slinking inside the passage. "There are multiple junctures that lead to chasms. One wrong step, and you'll plummet to your death."

Rowan shuddered and did as Zurie instructed, wedging his body into the black passageway that was barely wide enough for his shoulders. His hands felt the way ahead as he shimmied alongside his mother. No glowing rocks existed within to light their way. The cold, serrated walls and the absolute darkness pressed against Rowan like a phantom weight. An urge to get to open space gnawed at him. His heartbeat pounded in his ears, his body surging with adrenaline.

"How much farther?" he asked, refusing to let his voice quiver.

"Not far. Remain calm."

Rowan sucked in a deep breath, swallowing his misgivings. "Still water, steady heart," he whispered to himself.

He repeated the mantra until a blue light shone at the end of the passage. Could it be the sky? His mind and heart wished it so. After being deep underground for what felt like weeks, he wanted nothing more than to see the vast blue above him.

At the passage's exit, he beheld no sky, but a cavernous space where moisture dripped from stalactites clinging to the concave ceiling like inverted stalks of barley.

"This is my sanctum," Zurie said, ushering Rowan inside. "You're safe here."

Rowan staggered into the cavern, and his breath hitched.

Zurie's sanctum teemed with bioluminescent plants in vibrant sheens of viridian, amber, and amethyst. Somehow—and to Rowan's profound wonderment—the foliage thrived in this sunless environment with hardy leaves and stalks. Succulents with chunky florets clung to the stalagmites like dark-shelled sea muscles, whilst other plants attained the heights of trees, their tips kissing the domed roof. Even their exposed roots, white and veiny, glowed along the cavern's floor.

Luminescent rocks radiating soft cerulean hues mimicked the brilliant luster of the sea. For a brief moment, Rowan believed the crystalline ocean surrounded him, lulling his mind. He'd only ever seen these bright, vivid colors inhabiting the seafloor. How then could such wondrous creations exist in a hellish environment reserved only for the damned?

The sound of babbling water drew his gaze to a mountain spring trickling into a clear pool. Rowan rushed for it and used his hands as cups, inhaling the water. To his parched mouth, it was the crispest, most refreshing thing he'd ever tasted.

After drinking his fill, he lifted his wetted hands and cooled his forehead and neck.

"How are you here?" Zurie asked, snapping off a large leaf and submerging it in the pool. "I left you on the other side of the sea."

"I journeyed to Shandria to break my curse."

Zurie held out the drenched leaf. "For your shoulder. Clean the wound so it doesn't get infected."

Rowan pulled back his collar and hissed at the abrasions. He soaked the wound—a mild relief.

Zurie broke off several leaves from two different luminous plants and rubbed them between her palms. "When you've cleaned the wound, wad this into the cuts. It will prevent infection."

Rowan finished cleaning his shoulder, then took the crumpled leaves from his mother. Zurie gave him space to tend to his wounds, sitting upon a smooth rock shaped like a natural stone bench. Her gaze stayed on him like a cagey cat's, tracking every movement. Rowan pressed the leaves into his cuts, rubbing the remains around the swollen area. His eyes drifted toward a twisty vine crawling along the concave wall surrounding the pool. It grew small clumps of fruit.

Zurie noticed Rowan's wandering gaze. "Help yourself to the berries. They're quite sweet."

Rowan pulled off a cluster and stuffed them in his mouth. His taste buds awakened, drenched in the fruit's tangy nectar. He consumed another handful, only to then grow puzzled. "How do all these plants grow in your, uh, company?"

"I keep the curse contained, and oddly enough, the plants aren't all that affected. To survive in relative darkness, they're of much hardier stock." Zurie pointed to one of the giant plants with fan-like leaves. "Break off a piece of that one's root. It's edible and abundant in protein."

Rowan crouched before the violet-glowing plant. "Do you ever eat meat?"

"Occasionally—when I'm in the mood for bat," Zurie said with a quiet laugh.

Rowan broke off a piece of the gleaming root and took a bite. It didn't have much taste, but it crunched like jicama between his teeth. "So this is how you've survived down here . . . . How long has it been?"

She tilted her head at him. "Well, how old are you?"

"I'll be eighteen in a few days."

"Then it's been nearly eighteen years." Zurie grew quiet for a time, her eyes glazing over as if lost in a swirl of thoughts.

Rowan left her to her silence while he studied more of the bizarre plant life. If Rahn could see these bioluminescent mysteries, he would probably never want to leave—or at least take clippings of every plant to propagate. His grandfather had a fondness for peculiar flora. Every room in his manor housed at least five plants, save for Rowan's, which regrettably had none.

An idea came to him.

Having these plants to nurture may rouse Rahn's spirit.

Rowan collected a floret leaf from a fiery-red succulent and a phosphorous root and shoved them in his pocket.

"Where've you been staying in Shandria?" Zurie asked, breaking the silence.

"At Grandfather Rahn's manor," Rowan said, chomping on another root.

Zurie's overgrown eyebrows twitched. "I'm surprised Rahn's keeping you around with your curse. He must be desperate."

A stab of sadness struck Rowan's heart, and his shoulders drooped. "Rahn isn't faring well. He doesn't have long."

"Do you expect me to harbor compassion for that old curmudgeon?" Zurie said with a calloused grunt. "He showed no compassion toward me."

"Can you blame him?" Rowan shot back. "Your affair led to his son's death. He holds you to blame for the part you played in it."

"Yes, well, so does everyone," Zurie grumbled, folding her arms against her chest. "Even my parents wanted nothing to do with me. There was no place for me but here." She idly roamed the small cavern. "I've established a name here. No one dares enter this sanctum I've made for myself. They know the penalty is a death that kills them from the inside out."

Rowan lifted an eyebrow. "You mean in the way you used the curse to kill Clayface?"

"I learned I could manipulate it once I was committed here." Zurie turned her palms upright, showing off the tendrils she hosted within her body. "It became a necessity for my survival. You've learned how, then?"

"Only recently," Rowan said, holding out his hands, watching the tendrils perform their flitting maneuvers. "I've been testing the curse on plants and trees, figuring out my measure of control. It wasn't until I faced the hunchbacked cannibal that I intentionally killed someone with it." He shuddered, remembering the sight of the cannibal's caved-in skull.

"It's a marvelous curse, isn't it?" Zurie's eyes glistened like the ember rocks in the previous chamber. "I doubt Zamara intended for us to learn how to wield it as a weapon."

Rowan's brow creased. "Who's Zamara?"

"She's Adelkar's aunt, and the matron of the Keliss family. She's the one who cursed us."

Rowan's heart thrummed. "She's the Conjurer?"

Zurie nodded with a grim scowl. "Vengeful hag. She never liked me—nor most women, for that matter. I think she despised women who didn't share her skill for the dark arts."

"Tell me how it happened," Rowan said, moving to sit cross-legged at the pool's edge. "I want to hear from you the events that led to us being cursed. I've heard two versions so far."

Zurie's eyes narrowed. "Whose versions?"

"Rahn's and Adelkar's." Rowan paused, catching his distorted reflection in the pool. "Akaran bears much hatred toward you—and me. He beat me harshly the first day we met."

"I would imagine he's angry," Zurie said, tinkering with her outgrown nails. "He grew up without a father. But then, so did you, and you don't seem to be consumed by hate."

"I only recently learned the truth," Rowan said, putting his back to the pool. "But for Akaran, who's been force-fed Adelkar's version for many years, it twisted and corrupted his heart."

"There's nothing I can do about that," Zurie said, her dull tone lacking remorse. "My life is here."

"And how did it come to be this way?" Rowan pressed, getting back to his earlier question. "It's why I came—to hear the truth from you."

"You want *my* truth?"

Rowan nodded. "I do, yes."

"Hm. I'll tell you, then, since you came all this way." Zurie lowered to the ground before him, her face diffused in cobalt shadows. "My parents held close ties to the Keliss family, as they were mining partners, and so they arranged for me to marry Kainan even though he wasn't the man I favored."

"Who did you favor?" Rowan asked.

"Rorak," Zurie confessed, her cool countenance shifting to one of fondness. "We spent much time together in our youth, same as I did with Kainan—who was handsome and audacious—but Rorak had an unassuming, yet daring way about him that lured me in. He took great zeal in running his father's mine, working side-by-side with the miners. I admired his bold approach and often stole away to Iron Crossing to pass the time in his embrace. But it wasn't meant to last. The Myras family was rivals of ours, and my parents would never have let me be united with Rorak. Even though they said it was a love doomed from the start, their disapproval only spurred me to spend more and more time with Rorak."

Zurie sighed, drawing her shawl close against her chest. "My parents soon put a stop to it and had their way. Kainan and I were married. It wasn't a cheerful marriage by any means, simply one that benefited our families. Kainan was pleased to have a beautiful wife to show off at social gatherings, but emotionally, he was indifferent toward me. Once we had Akaran, the child was all he cared about. I was forgotten, as my duty had been done. But I craved more. Adelkar took notice and often gave me his lingering eye—when he thought I wasn't looking—but he was quick to correct his gaze when his brother, Kainan, was near.

"Rorak soon learned of my neglect, and we rekindled our youthful love. I conceived, and it led to my undoing. Kainan was furious and confronted Rorak. A duel with twin daggers ensued, and both died with blades embedded in their chests." Zurie hung her head, only to rear it a moment later with her lips drawn into a bitter line. "Zamara was outraged. Then and there, she cursed me and the child within my womb. I had no recourse but to flee the country and find somewhere unknown to deliver you. I left the continent and sailed east to Luvaria. But a violent storm blew us off-course, and we wrecked against a reef not far from land. I managed to swim ashore, and that's when I arrived in Karahvel.

"At first, the villagers were horrified and confused by my white skin and thought I was a ghost. The chieftain alleviated their fear by suggesting I'd been swallowed by a whale, which resulted in me having bleached skin." Zurie broke into a laugh at the memory. "So little they knew of the vast world. The chieftain only realized my white skin was natural when you were born. But then I beheld your cursemark, and the truth of Zamara's curse became real to me."

Zurie's unfeeling gaze fell on Rowan. "If only you never happened. You were a mistake."

Rowan's emotions churned, lending fire to his words. "You made a choice that created me. I didn't ask to be born, nor did I deserve this curse. I was a day old, and you left me in the hands of strangers in a foreign land!"

"I knew there were plenty of women who could care for you," Zurie countered, her voice cold and apathetic.

"Yes, there were, and four of them died because of the curse." Rowan clutched his chest, the sting of their losses still fresh. "Kialla. Telula. Sylda. Naja. Those were their names. They raised me in your place."

"Would you have preferred this as your home?" Zurie motioned to the space around them, a hard look in her eyes. "Living in the shadows, afraid some cursed soul would try to eat you for a meal?"

Rowan held his tongue. "Living here would've been hell."

"A hell I spared you from. Don't ever forget that."

Rowan bit his bottom lip. "Is that your way of saying I should be grateful that you abandoned me?"

Zurie expelled a flustered breath. "Hate me for it if you like—"

"I don't hate you," Rowan interjected, firm and direct. "I don't want to hate anyone. I only seek to understand."

"What else is there to understand? I've told you everything."

"Not everything. There's something I need to know." Rowan hesitated, quieting the emotions raging in his heart. "After I was born and you left, why did you come back here?"

"Shandria is all I'd ever known. I couldn't exist anywhere but here." Zurie's shoulders slumped, and the pitch in her voice turned more somber. "Had I lived elsewhere—tried to find a man to share a life with—my curse would've become known, and I'd very likely been outcast from every city across Tarcia."

An outcome Rowan knew firsthand. "And what if you'd never been cursed? Would that have changed your decision?" It was fruitless to think what might've been, but he had to ask, if only to have it resolved in his mind.

Zurie clacked her nails together in an agitated rhythm. "Which decision? The one to return or the one to leave you behind?"

"The latter."

"So, that's what gnaws at you the most—if I would've kept you had I not been cursed?" Zurie only took a brief moment to consider. She smacked her lips together. "The simple answer is no, I wouldn't have. How could I when I'd been caught in an affair? Even if we'd never been discovered, Kainan never would've believed the child was his. I would've had to get rid of you somehow to cover my deed."

Rowan swallowed a hard lump, seeing his mother in a cold, dismal light. The cool-blue glow reflecting off her shoulders and face only made her appear more austere. Her eyes and tongue lacked the warmth and tenderness of a loving mother. Did it stem from the lack of care her own parents had shown her? Or was she just selfish to the core?

"Not what you wanted to hear, was it?" Zurie said.

Rowan's face and voice hardened. "No, but if that's your truth, I'll bear it in the way I've borne your curse. I suffer under no fault of mine, but yours. And you don't even seem to care."

Zurie squared her shoulders back, chin held high. "I've accepted my fate, as should you. I've grown fond of my title as the Goddess of Death. It rings of power and fear. Have you not realized it is I who rules this mountain?"

"You may rule it," Rowan said, scoffing, growing more and more irked by his mother's apparent callousness, "but you're just like everyone else who's cursed here. You're not free to leave."

"I can leave whenever I want," she declared, rising to her feet in a swift motion. "Do you honestly think the guards stationed at the entrance could stop me before I infected their insides?"

"Then why haven't you?" Rowan demanded, matching his mother's hostile stance. "Better yet, why haven't you confronted Zamara? Surely with the way I saw you kill Clayface, you could easily challenge her."

Zurie's confrontational demeanor suddenly altered. She ran a hesitant tongue over her lips.

Rowan pressed on a hunch. "Or do you fear confronting Zamara because she could strip you of your powers?"

Zurie gave no reply, and Rowan sensed that he had hit upon her selfish truth.

A dark sickness swirled in his gut. "That's it, isn't it? Admit it—"

"You're right," she said, a begrudging confession. "It's been my greatest fear. I'm not brave like you. My curse is my sword, as well as my shield."

"And yet you've used it to make everyone interned here fear you as a goddess of death. Well done, Mother," he sneered, his aversion toward her actions alighting his tongue. "I'll not do as you've done. I'll not revel in the curse of death. I don't want this power. Now that I know who cursed me, I'll put an end to Zamara. Say farewell to your dark powers. You won't have them much longer."

Zurie snatched his forearm quicker than a twin-tail's strike, her gaze deadly. "Taking away my curse will leave me defenseless. I could die here without it."

"You might as well be dead," Rowan snarled, his heart swathed in anger. "Your life is a ruinous waste."

Zurie's eyes flashed with rage. "Watch your tongue, boy." The snaky tendrils spiraled around her forearms. "I have the power to turn you to ash."

Rowan shot his mother a dangerous glare. "You'd kill me just to hold onto the curse's power?"

"I could ask you the same thing: Would you kill me just to leave this place alive?" Zurie's claw-like nails dug into his skin, all reason gone from her eyes.

Rowan didn't flinch. "I don't want to kill anyone," he hissed through clenched teeth, "least of all, you. I simply want a life not dictated by this curse."

"Then you better stop me!" Zurie's tendrils whirled from her fingers, circling around his arm in a rope-like coil. Dark insanity shrouded her face as she unleashed her curse's full arsenal.

Rowan summoned his tendrils to thwart her attack. His heartbeats thundered in his ears.

She's really doing this! She's really trying to kill me!

Like two storm clouds clashing, their spiraling mass of black tendrils swarmed around them in a riotous tangle. Rowan twisted his wrist and seized his mother's forearm as Zurie's grip strangled his sleeve. His tendrils grappled with hers, twisting and slithering like a pit of snakes. The lambent roots near their feet quickly withered, the brightness of their effulgent sheen dimming with each passing second.

The curse's field of death expanded, spreading toward the towering amethyst stalks. If Zurie feared destroying her food supply, she showed no sign of it. Only a desperate madness contorted her countenance—all focus centered on destroying him.

Rowan summoned a host of tendrils to encase his skin in a protective cocoon against her attack. Zurie didn't think to do the same. Her tendrils seethed against his skin, swirling rapidly. The more they spun, the more he feared his skin was decaying. But as seconds passed, no sign of infection entered his body. Even Zurie's skin showed no evidence of a taint.

How can this be?

Zurie snarled with frustration, digging her nails deeper into his forearm as if the tendrils could seep into the broken skin. Nothing happened. His skin wouldn't decay.

Realization struck Rowan sooner than his mother: Neither of their tendrils could infect the other. They were at an impasse. Not knowing if Zurie would attack with another weapon, Rowan acted to ensure his life.

He shook off her grip and withdrew his knife from his sash, warding it in front of him. Zurie's shaking eyes fell on the knife in fright. With their curse's ability rendered inert, he held the advantage in their current position, and she knew it.

So much for being the Goddess of Death.

Rowan leveled his knife at her. "Stay back, and I won't harm you."

Zurie lifted her hands, her cagey gaze fixed on his knife.

Rowan hated resorting to it, but his mother wasn't entirely sane. He blamed it on this accursed place. She'd spent too long in isolation with only herself for company. But even that didn't excuse her heartless self-preservation before she came to Mount Maldere.

"All these years you've stayed here in hiding instead of doing what you should've done." A tight clamp formed around Rowan's throat. "So much pain and heartache you could have spared me

—*your son*—perhaps even preventing my guardian-mothers' deaths. To see you enthralled by the curse enrages my heart."

"Go on, despise me," Zurie said, her chin lifted high, "but it changes nothing."

"No, the only way to change things is to end the curse."

"Then go do it!" she screamed, the tendrils around her arms billowing from her outburst. "Or die trying. I'll know one way or another whether you succeed or not."

"*When* I succeed," Rowan said, "I'll return and get you out." Despite his anger, he couldn't abide abandoning her here, defenseless, to be eaten by cannibals.

The wild fire in Zurie's eyes calmed. Her facial muscles slowly relaxed, and she appeared more herself. "You would really do that?" she said, taken aback. "You'd come back for me?"

"It's one kindness I'll show to the woman who birthed me." Rowan grabbed his spear and donned his cloak, staring hard into her eyes. "But know this: You aren't my mother, and you never will be."

He picked up a luminous stone, pocketed it, and marched back to the narrow fissure, leaving Zurie to dwell alone in her sanctum.

CHAPTER 19
ZAMARA

Akaran vied for something to alleviate his boredom. Waiting for Rahn to die was a tiresome drag. A month had passed and all fared annoyingly well at Iron Crossing.

Akaran needed Rowan to make an appearance, do something warranting arrest—curses! Or give Akaran the chance to expend another beating. It infuriated him to the depths of his core to know that his half-brother freely wandered Rahn's lands. The cursed runt *belonged* in that infernal mountain along with the rest of the damned.

One uneventful evening while Akaran stewed over his supper, news arrived via messenger that his informant Klay had pertinent information. Akaran could've kissed the greasy scumbag. He snarfed down his meal and told the attending manservant to ready his horse.

Akaran raced up the winding stone staircase to the tower where his great aunt worked on her spellcraft—and all manner of drugs and potions. The long, narrow room boasted a wrap-around window-pane wall. Dried leaves and herbal bundles tied with string hung from the rafters along with three circular chandeliers providing ample illumination. His aunt's shelves—crammed full—stored jars containing strange liquids, mixtures, herbs, seeds, and other oddities Akaran couldn't begin to determine, including the age of the old woman occupying the room.

Zamara sat on her rickety stool in a skin-tight black dress with a crimson-lace wrap covering her bony shoulders. She hunched over her worktable like an egret, her long, crinkled snout buried in some dead amphibian's guts. Akaran liked to think she was a hundred, but he'd thought that for the last decade, so her true age was anyone's guess. And Zamara—being an insufferable bag of tricks—saw no reason to offer clarification on her actual age.

Akaran stomped into the room, and acrid aromas assaulted his nostrils. "Auntie's lair," as he liked to call it, had long been a melting pot of scents either delighting the senses or repelling them. A punch of pungent formaldehyde churned his stomach, and he nearly lost his dinner.

"Curses, it reeks in here," Akaran complained, shielding his nose and mouth. "Would it kill you to crack a window?"

"I've warned you about coming up here after you've had a meal," Zamara said with a scratchy voice that grated Akaran's ears. "Don't blame me if you lose it again."

"It couldn't be helped," Akaran grumbled, annoyed by her I-told-you-so attitude. "I have somewhere to be, and I need a pouchful of caine powder."

Zamara lifted a wrinkled finger with a wickedly curvy nail and pointed to a pile of white powder at the end of her workstation. "Help yourself. It's there for the taking."

Akaran found a small, leather pouch and scooped a fair amount of powder into it.

"Who's the lucky sot who gets my mind-numbing creation?" Zamara said with a cackle.

"Your regular customer—Klay," Akaran said, tying the pouch's strings. "He has information for me."

"On your brother?" Zamara said, without turning her head.

Again with the incorrect term.

Akaran scowled. "More than likely, yes."

"Hm. And what are you hoping to gain by having him tailed?" Zamara asked, making an incision with her scalpel.

Akaran toyed with a dangling bundle of herbs, picking off leaves and flicking them with his fingers. "I'm just keeping tabs, making sure he doesn't thwart our endeavors."

Zamara removed something gray and stringy from the amphibian and placed it on a porcelain dish. "Did Adelkar ask you to do this?"

"No, I'm doing this on my own."

"In other words, you're obsessing."

"So what if I am?" Akaran smashed the leaves under his boot, grinding them to dust. "I want to hurt my half-brother where it hurts most. He recovered from my beating without a hitch in his step."

His great-aunt paused from her work and spun on her stool. Despite her old age, her face lacked the expected amount of wrinkles. Her taut cheeks belied her true age.

Zamara's scarlet eyes harbored a stern admonishment. "Rowan has been cursed. There's nothing worse for him than that."

"You're wrong," Akaran said, clenching his fists. "His suffering can increase. The curse hasn't removed all comfort or relationships from his life. Rahn has been giving him shelter. And then there's that impudent girl, clinging to his side like he can actually give her a happy life. She's a fool—they're both fools."

"Yes, much like Zurie and Rorak." Zamara left her stool and rummaged through her shelves. "You should know what happens to fools like that. Love and allure may thrive for a fleeting moment, but eventually, misery descends. If Rowan is anything like his parents, we shall have nothing to fear from him."

"So, you're not worried he may come and try to kill you?"

Zamara sniffed. "That ignorant tot has no idea I exist." She snatched several jars containing oozy substances. "I've done well to live in secret. Not even our household staff knows my true existence."

Only Akaran and Adelkar knew she was a Conjurer. But then, so did Zurie.

Akaran surveyed his aunt's worktable, running his finger along the weathered edge. "For the sake of argument, what if he was to learn of your existence?"

"Then I shall lay another curse upon him," Zurie said matter-of-factly, slinking back onto her stool. "One that'll give him no place to be a threat."

"Curses, you sound like Uncle." Akaran pulled at his hair, flinging it from his eyes. "Why not simply end him? I don't understand why you and Uncle won't just deal with the problem."

Zamara shot Akaran a disapproving glare. "Are you so blind, you can't see the obvious reason? It's the very same reason *you* wish to increase your brother's suffering. The best revenge is a living nightmare. It's what I did to Zurie, that flouncy trollop." Zamara poked again at the dissected frog. "Do you know how many people I've cursed?"

Akaran shook his head. "I'm guessing it's up there."

"Hundreds." The word oozed from Zamara's mouth like sap weed. "Some for my own purposes and some at the behest of others." She lifted her scalpel as she spoke, wiggling it like a wand. "When I throw a curse, I consider how it shall best impact the target. With Zurie, I made it so no other man would ever dare touch her again. I strike at a soul's vanity—letting it be the tightening noose around the neck."

"Why didn't you take her beauty as well?"

"That would be too obvious. Men would see her ugliness and recoil." Zamara's colored lips creased into a heartless curve. "No, I wanted Zurie to know she herself would be the cause of death for any man she dared love again. It's a far more befitting curse."

Akaran blew out a slow, marveled breath. "You are relentless, Aunt. Now I see where Uncle gets his deviousness." He leaned over and kissed her cheek, snagged the drug pouch, and stomped down the steps, wondering what news Klay had for him.

Akaran rode to The Red Canary, secured his preferred table, and waited for his informant to arrive. The man was once again tardy, but at least within reason. He launched into his news, drinking long sips of ale between sentences.

"He left the manor, you say?" Akaran repeated, snapping his fingers to keep Klay's attention. "Well, where did he go?"

"All I know is, I saw the wagon head into the Valley of the Fallen. I followed at a distance to the monument before turning back. They kept on heading west, toward the Vennor Mountains."

"Anyone with him?"

"A big miner." Klay puffed out his chest, mimicking the aforementioned man. "And the pretty girl I've seen him with before."

Akaran tapped his forefinger on the table. "And when was this?"

"Yesterday morn, they left—haven't returned yet." Klay leaned his head closer, his breath foul. "You don't suppose he'd be heading to Mount Maldere, eh?"

Akaran dropped his chin into his hand, his elbow propped on the table. "They'd be fools to venture in there."

Klay sniffed, his nose sounding clogged. "Then he oughta have a crazy good reason for it."

"More like a desperate one."

Finding Zurie.

Akaran didn't reveal his suspicion. There was no telling if Zurie was even alive at this point. If Mount Maldere truly was Rowan's destination, then perhaps fate would favor Akaran, and his half-brother wouldn't return.

A man can hope.

It would save Akaran, his uncle, and his aunt a heap of trouble.

"I don't see why you care what he does and where he goes so much," Klay mumbled, scratching at his scabby nostrils. "Tells me you need to find a hobby, or do like me, and numb the mind for a time. Speaking of numbing the mind, give me my pay." He reached out his grubby hand, wiggling his greedy fingers.

Akaran threw him the pouch. "Don't use it all in one sitting."

"SOULS ABOVE, THE SPEARMAN HAS RETURNED!" THE MESTRIAN guard guffawed in bafflement, his opal-blue eyes twinkling. "I was certain you would have been devoured."

Rowan gripped the bars of the gate, his legs shaking, on the verge of collapsing. "Can you please let me out?"

The guard kept on laughing and pulled the lever. Rowan labored forward, free of the darkness's hold, and he breathed in the clean, crisp air. Daylight assaulted his face. The brightness turned his vision white. He lifted his hood and shielded his watering eyes. All those hours spent in darkness, he'd only had the soft glow of the luminous stone to guide him back.

Rowan let the rock slip from his grasp as he dropped to the dirt, craving rest.

A firm grip clutched his shoulder. "You all right there, spearman?"

Rowan flinched at the guard's touch and scooted away. "I'll be fine—just need time for my eyes to adjust."

The guard hovered beside the brazier, eyeing Rowan with stunned curiosity. "Did you find the person you were looking for?"

"Met her and got what I needed." Rowan felt for the speckled rock and returned it to his pocket—a memento for what he'd faced inside the mountain. He dug the butt of his spear into the ground and climbed to his feet once more. His legs wobbled.

"Leaving already?" the guard asked with a touch of concern in his voice.

"I must get back."

"Hold up, spearman. You look like you could faint while standing." The guard bent by the fire and retrieved a fistful of jerky, then offered it to Rowan. "This should help recover your strength."

Rowan's mouth watered. He stared at the thick strips of meat, confused by the Mestrian's generosity.

The guard's chapped lips curved into a friendly smile. "Go on, I am not hungry. Besides, you still have a ways to go yet."

Right, the others waited on his return. Rowan wasn't sure how long he'd been inside the mountain, but Bash said they'd leave without him if he wasn't back by the second morning.

Rowan accepted the jerky and tore into the meatiest strip. "How long was I inside?"

"Two nights. I swore I would never see you again." The guard looked Rowan up and down, his fair face warming with another smile. "You are stronger than you look."

"Hey, Gowin!" a snappy voice hollered from inside the guard post. "Who the flames is with you?"

"Just a Shandrian. He returned from inside Mount Maldere. Can you believe it?"

A window opened and a churlish-faced guard thrust his head out along with a shooing hand. "Well, make haste and send him on his way. He could be riddled with disease. I shall have none of that at my outpost, got it?"

"Loud and clear, lord." Gowin's laid-back expression didn't show a mite of concern.

The window slammed shut, and the urgent need to disappear from this outpost pressed against Rowan.

"He is always so flaming uptight in the morning," Gowin muttered under his breath. He sighed, then gave Rowan a friendly, yet cautionary, look. "Best get a move on, if you want no trouble from us."

Rowan thanked Gowin for the food and left as quietly as he came. At least the remainder of his journey was downhill. He feared one more uphill slope would spell his defeat.

The morning hours dwindled along, and Rowan passed the time in deep thought, oblivious to the passing trees. He at last had attained the name of the Conjurer who cursed him.

Zamara.

With that mystery solved, came the next: How would he get to her? Also, where did she live? Did she live in Adelkar's manor? Rowan hadn't seen an older woman there...

His mind lurched with a sudden recollection. No, but he had *heard* an older woman's voice.

What did she say again? She'd barked an angry admonishment at Adelkar and Akaran.

"Don't stand there in his midst. Cast him out! His curse could infect us all."

Rowan bet his black pearls it was Zamara's voice.

She must reside in Adelkar's manor.

Unfortunately, therein laid the problem. Rowan wouldn't be allowed entry again. Zamara would know he aimed to kill her.

So, how can I secretly gain access?

Switchback after switchback, Rowan thought long and hard on a way, considering different possibilities, none plausible, save for one. He chalked it out initially on account of it requiring help from the most unthinkable person. Even if it was a long shot, it might be his only option.

Nearing the trailhead, Rowan glanced out at the expansive steppe. Had Tahira, Bashir, and Gavan waited for him? If they adhered to Bash's promise, they would've left soon after dawn.

Rowan shielded the sunlight, spying something in the distance. He quickened his stride, attaining a clearer view.

The wagon was still there, resting beneath the shade of a tall arbor. They hadn't left.

Rowan's spirit soared, and he pushed his feet into a beleaguered run. A ways off, Tahira scrambled out of the wagon and raced toward him. Rowan forced the curse to retreat into his skin, flinching from the backlash for but a breath.

Tahira sprang with open arms and buried her face against Rowan's chest. "Don't even think of telling me to keep my distance."

The forceful cheekiness in her tone brought a soft smile to Rowan's lips. "I hadn't planned on it." After the horrors Rowan had faced, he welcomed her embrace. The fresh scent of her hair, like sweet rainwater, flooded his mind with peace, grounding him in the present.

"You've no idea how relieved I am you've returned," Tahira whispered, her arms snug around his waist. "Bash was making ready for us to leave, but I convinced him to wait until noonday. I just knew you'd come back."

Rowan dropped his spear and took hold of her arms, pulling them to his sides. "It wasn't without difficulty," he said, heart and mind withdrawn. So much had happened in the two days he'd spent on Mount Maldere. The return trek wasn't long enough to reframe his rattled mind.

Tahira's gaze lifted, staring intently at him. "What is it? You seem . . . *changed*." Her concerned gaze searched his face. "What happened in there?"

"I grew up."

Tahira's eyes flickered with confusion. "What do you mean?"

"I killed men," Rowan said, his breath hitching. "They'd gone savage—devolved into cannibals—but still, I killed them."

"Wait—cannibals!" Tahira pounced on the word, her eyes affright. "Did they try to eat you?"

"They tried. I have the bite mark to prove it. Want to see?" Rowan went to pull away his collar when Tahira's face paled.

"No, I don't want to see!" she shrieked, cupping a hand to her mouth.

"Um, all right then, moving on." Rowan retrieved his spear and strolled toward the wagon. "I met my mother and learned the truth of how I came to be." He left it there so his anger didn't boil to the surface.

Tahira shuddered as if fighting off her queasiness, and with a noticeable swallow, she asked, "And what of the Conjurer? Did you learn the name?"

"Zamara," Rowan said as a cold shiver snaked through his body. "She's the matron of the Keliss family—Adelkar's aunt."

"A whole family affair, huh? Who would've guessed?" Tahira tilted her head in conspiratorial interest. "So, how do you go about ending her?"

"I have an idea . . . but it's going to require outside help."

"Who's?"

"Akaran's."

Tahira stopped short and stared at him, her mouth agape.

Rowan had predicted this reaction.

Here it comes.

"Tell me you're joking."

"I'm serious," Rowan said. "I think I can make an appeal to him."

Tahira's eyes shook in disbelief. "You think you can appeal to the colossal brute who pounded your face into meat? I'd very much like to know how?"

"By relying on our newfound connection."

Tahira looked even more floored. "And what connection is that?"

"Our abandonment." Rowan forced the tendrils to retreat once more and held out his hand to Tahira—a gesture he knew she wouldn't be able to resist. "Come on, I'll fill you in on the way back home."

Tahira's expression softened, and she grasped his hand with an eager grin. "Spare no details."

Rowan smiled. "I wouldn't dream of it."

CHAPTER 20
LEGACY

They arrived back at Iron Crossing shortly before dusk. An unexpected sight greeted Rowan—Rahn strolling the manor's yard with his cane.

Rowan's heart surged. "Grandfather!" He leaped from the wagon and hastened toward the old man. "You're looking much better."

"And feeling it as well, my boy." A warm smile lifted Rahn's bearded cheeks. "Shen tried to keep me on bed rest one more day, and I told him to quit his fussing and switch places with me. After much squabbling, he finally agreed and has been sleeping all afternoon, in fact."

Rowan tossed his head back with raucous laughter. "He probably needed the rest with all the fuss you gave him."

"I'm afraid I'm a lousy patient," Rahn said with a cheeky chuckle. "Well, enough about Shen. I want to hear all about your travels." He trekked the short distance to the garden and lowered onto a stone bench. Tahira stayed near, tending to the herbs and vegetables, which appeared to have been starved for attention in her absence.

"Were you successful in finding Zurie?" Rahn asked, turning his gaze toward the darkening mountains.

"I was. She lives in a secluded cavern filled with glowing plants." Rowan pulled out the ruby-tinted succulent and the plant root, placing them in Rahn's hands. "They only grow in darkness. It's when they reveal their brilliant glow."

"Then I shall find a dark place for them to thrive." Rahn smiled like a child receiving the task of caring for his first pet and tucked the items away in his pocket. "I gather Zurie gave you the information you needed?"

"Yes, along with her version of the past." Emotion clogged Rowan's throat as he shared Zurie's story, and the calloused reasons why she'd abandoned him. "Even though I now know the truth, I'm confused by her actions—and angry." He gripped his head. "She told me, even if she hadn't been cursed, she still would've given me up— just to cover up her mistake."

How could she be so heartless? So selfish?

Rowan's guardian-mothers lost their lives raising him. But the mother who birthed him—the one who *should've* kept him safe from harm—ignored her responsibility to preserve herself.

Just like a lynasi.

Rahn rested his hand on Rowan's shoulder. "You have every right to be angry, son. I wrestle with my anger every day."

Rowan expelled a tight breath. "How do you not let it consume you?"

"By focusing on the blessings around me, especially you." Rahn's crinkled lips curved into a smile. "Since you've been here, my heart holds far more love than it does anger for Zurie."

"There's more I haven't shared." Rowan relayed the vital information Zurie conveyed: the Conjurer's identity. "When Zurie realized I intended to kill Zamara, she tried to kill me with the power of our curse. But, as fate would have it, our curse is unable to infect each other." His skin turned cold, and he took a shuddering breath as the clash with his mother flooded in his head. "I can't shake the madness I witnessed in her eyes. Her sanity has splintered from years spent in that horrible mountain."

"I'm not surprised. Prolonged isolation—unending darkness— can wreak havoc on a person's grasp with reality."

Rowan nodded, dispelling a heavy breath. "It's why I told Zurie I would return to free her from Mount Maldere once I break the curse. Despite all the grief and strife she's caused me, it didn't sit right in my soul to abandon her as she did me."

Rahn regarded him like a proud parent. "You're a good lad, Rowan. Your guardian-mothers raised you well. Perhaps there's a silver lining in that. Had you been born elsewhere, you may have had a harsher upbringing."

Rowan sighed, a heaviness settling over his shoulders. "You're right. I could've been born in Mount Maldere, knowing only a world of darkness."

"Then all is as it should've been." Rahn took hold of Rowan's hand and gave it a firm clasp. "You are where you belong. And I'll keep saying it until you believe it."

Rowan held back the tendrils from flitting around his grandfather's hand. "What about the tenants?"

"That's not for you to fret about. It's been handled. Keld spoke with the miners and the workers, apprising them of your curse. Regardless of their qualms, you are the master here after I'm gone. If anyone gives you trouble, they'll answer to Bashir and Bulan. Those two have a soft spot for you."

"It's only because they had an uncle who was cursed, and they feel sorry for me."

"Oh, it's more than that, son." Rahn's eyes twinkled with secretive information. "They see qualities of Rorak in you, much as I do. You have his noble, daring spirit, and his willingness to tackle hard endeavors. It's why I know you will keep these lands prospering."

"You put much faith in me, Grandfather. I'm young and new to this land. There's much I don't understand about my people."

"But you understand legacy. Your guardian-mothers who taught you weavescript understood they were passing on a precious gift, something that would far outlive them. I have done the same with bequeathing you my land." Rahn paused, and his gaze panned Iron Crossing's twin peaks. "This place is our ancestral birthright. A Myras shall always be baron here. I know you will find yourself right at home."

Rahn's kind smile granted all the reassurance Rowan needed.

THE NEXT MORNING, ROWAN BLAZED FORWARD WITH HIS PLAN TO reach out to Akaran. He found Gavan brushing one of the horses in the stable, the dent in his skull acutely visible. According to Rahn, the young wagon driver had been kicked by a horse as a child and developed a stutter thereafter. He suffered his share of mocking from the hillside kids, which led him to gravitate toward handling animals — hence how he came to be in Rahn's employment.

An orange-and-white tabby groomed itself beneath the short wooden stool beside Gavan's splotchy boots. As Rowan wandered in, the strong odor of hay and dust bombarded his nostrils. He sneezed, and Gavan shot up with a start. The cat's ears twitched in alarm, narrowing its golden eyes at Rowan.

"Shush, Sato," Gavan chided before glancing at Rowan. He fumbled with the brush in his hands, standing awkwardly with his shoulders slumped. "Y-y-you, uh, here for the horse?"

Rowan shook his head. "Can't ride, remember?"

"W-w-we can change that, if you w-want," Gavan said, straining to make his crooked lips work more swiftly. "Though I'm better at riding, I'm pretty good with teaching, and the horses trust my lead."

"The day I'm free of the curse, I'll take you up on the offer. As it stands, I'd hate to be the cause for killing one of the horses."

A cloud of grim understanding passed over Gavan's face. "Uh, right—the curse . . . forgot about that." He cleared his throat. "Well, uh, if y-y-you don't need a ride, why're y-y-you here?"

Rowan revealed the letter in his hand. "Will you deliver this for me?"

Gavan set the brush on his stool and dusted off his hands on his pants. "Who's it for?"

"My brother, Akaran Keliss." Rowan handed Gavan the letter and several copper marks.

"I'll head t-t-to Keliss House right away." Gavan saddled the horse he'd been grooming, hopped on, and trotted down the hill.

Rowan left the stable with his sinuses still under siege. Sato frolicked at his feet before prancing ahead. Rowan sneezed several times before he could breathe something other than the musty hay.

Tahira, who'd been idling by the garden's stone fence, wandered up to Rowan. She picked up the fluffy cat, cradled it in her arms, and stroked its white chin. Memories flickered at the simple sight. Of when Rowan had slept alongside his friendly kalbs, holding them close—ignorantly killing them, slowly, day after day.

"Do you think Akaran will come?" Tahira's question pulled him out of his dour thoughts.

Rowan placed his hands on his hips. "I do."

Tahira huffed. "You're optimistic."

"I think his obsession will get the better of him."

"Oh, on that we can agree," she said with a sarcastic tone. "But don't blame me if he breaks your nose as soon as he sees your face."

Rowan chuckled. "That's a risk I'm willing to take."

A FAST FIST TO THE NOSE SENT AKARAN REELING BACKWARD. He steadied himself against the wall to keep from falling. He swiped the trickle of blood from his nostrils and shot his boxing opponent a miffed glare. "Lucky cross, Rav."

"Luck had nothing to do with it," Ravel Grise—Akaran's longtime friend and fellow pugilist—gibed. He had a snide voice, murky-red eyes, short hair tousled in a sweaty mop, and manners as flippant as Akaran's. Suffice it to say, they made taking potshots at one another a competitive sport. "Your guard was abysmal, and your jabs were all over the place. Curses, Aka, where's your head at?"

"I've got my half-brother on my mind." Akaran had learned from Klay that Rowan had returned to Iron Crossing. Where he'd gone for certain or what he'd done remained a mystery, but Akaran had every intention of uncovering the answers.

Ravel blew an exasperated-sounding sigh and moved to the bench. "I'm done for today. Reach out again when you're in the mood for a more serious match."

Akaran scowled. "I was taking it seriously enough."

"You weren't focusing. That's the problem." His friend unraveled the leather wrappings covering his hands. "Normally, you know to focus while you fight. But once you lose your cool, it all goes to waste. Losing your temper—throwing your jabs without thought—is how an idiot fights. There's no beauty in it."

Akaran rolled his eyes. "Thanks for the usual bluntness."

"Certainly. You're off your rhythm," Ravel continued without pause. "Even a blind novice could tell."

Akaran unwound his wrappings and flung them to the floor. "Look, my half-brother showing up and swindling Iron Crossing has gotten under my skin, all right?"

"Again, you're proving my point: He has you off your rhythm. It isn't like you to get so worked up over anyone in particular."

Akaran shot his friend a testy glare. "Rowan isn't just anyone. He's the troublemaker who could ruin everything."

"I think you're exaggerating there, Aka."

"It's the truth. With Myras's assets, he could move against the mines we've pressured into closing."

Ravel's eyebrow lifted and touched his sweaty bangs. "You certain that is what's carting your ore? Sounds more like your uncle's concerns."

"His concerns are my concerns," Akaran said, tapping his forefinger against his chest.

Ravel stared back with a doubting glint in his eyes. "You're not convincing me with that line."

"Fine." Akaran growled, folding his arms. "Here's how it is: I hate his guts and wish him dead. There. You satisfied?"

Ravel clicked his tongue. "Curses, I had no idea you had it so bad."

"Have what so bad?" Akaran asked with a sneer.

"Mother issues."

Akaran's eyes flashed, and an angry fire surged up his throat. "What does she have to do with what I just said?"

"Oh, everything." Ravel stood and smugly crept toward Akaran like he was the bearer of a profound secret. "Your half-brother's been here a month and all of a sudden, you act like his existence is the bane of yours. Your antipathy is noted, maybe even warranted, but perhaps displaced. I mean, it's your mother whom you *truly* hate."

Ravel circled Akaran with an air of indifference. "But by all means, if it makes you feel better, give Rowan a pounding. Isn't that how you prefer to solve things—with your fists?" His friend displayed a knowing smirk, his eyes as dark as wine. "Take out your hatred for your mother on her bastard. It's quite the ingenious solution, Aka, and should put your mind right. When you've got it sorted, I'll return for a rematch."

Ravel flung his leafy-green tabard over his shoulder and left the manor, leaving Akaran in a swirl of emotions. He could've used another match if only to clear his head.

Drenched in sweat, Akaran hurried to wash and joined Adelkar in the dining hall. The vigorous boxing session left him with a ravenous appetite.

"Slow down, Nephew. You're not a pauper who hasn't had a meal in weeks." Adelkar was always one for maintaining appearances, even if no one was watching.

Akaran took another bite of the roasted pork, chewing more leisurely to placate his uncle.

Horace, their bug-eyed manservant, toddled into the dining hall and halted by Akaran's chair. "You've received a letter."

"From who?"

"Someone from Iron Crossing," Horace said

Akaran frowned, as did his uncle from across the table. "Well, let me see it," Akaran said, setting down his fork.

Horace handed over the letter. Sure enough the seal showed the image of Iron Crossing's hound-shaped crag. Akaran tore open the seal with his cutting knife and read the brief message.

Brother,
I think we should meet. I have news you will be interested to hear. Come alone to the crossroads on Kaklin Hill at noon tomorrow.

"What's it say?" Adelkar inquired.

"My half-brother wants to meet."

"That's a peculiar move." Adelkar cupped his chin. "I wonder what the upstart is thinking. You must go and discover his plan."

"Of course, I'll go. I'm curious to see what he has to say. It must be important if he's brazen enough to reach out in light of our past encounters." Akaran sank back in his chair, tapping the letter against the edge of the table. He'd been waiting for this — a chance to square off with his half-brother. If it turned out to be a complete waste of time, he'd make Rowan pay for it in a way he wouldn't forget.

Akaran resumed his meal with a smirk, anticipating tomorrow.

Chapter 21
Brother to Brother

Rowan arrived at Kaklin's crossroads early and enjoyed taking in the sights of the city. Smoke rose from the forges, metal clanged against anvils. To think, only a month had passed since he rode into Arjun on Kirani's wagon, ignorant of his race. It felt like a lifetime ago.

So much had happened. He'd learned the truth of his existence, why he'd been cursed, who cursed him, and gained control over his curse's terrible ability. And now he sought to build a bridge with the enemy—perhaps, the hardest task of all.

Akaran was the surest way into Keliss House. Rowan had no intention of wantonly using his curse to kill men Adelkar could assemble against him. Although he would if he had no other option. Hopefully, Akaran would provide it.

A lone rider ascended the hill. Akaran had come.

His brother arrived dressed in a richly-woven charcoal tunic and tabard, his jaw-length hair flapping behind him. He slowed his dark stallion to a walk, dismounted, and led his steed by the reins. Akaran stopped several feet away, his eyebrows arched and confrontational. Despite his obvious disdain, his brother was here.

Perhaps hope existed after all.

"You really came?" Rowan said, letting his genuine surprise show.

"I was simply curious." Akaran remained in front of his horse, his arms folded across his muscular chest. "So, get on with it. What's this about?"

"I met our mother. I went inside Mount Maldere, found her, and spoke with her."

Akaran didn't shield his shock. His mouth hung open for a moment. "*You* went inside that accursed place?" Akaran's tone shifted from marvel to contempt. "My, that was impetuous. And what did that trull have to say for herself?"

"The truth. At least, her version of it."

Akaran's eyes narrowed. "You don't sound entirely convinced by it."

"I'm not the one who needs to be convinced. It's you."

"Me?" The prominent cleft in Akaran's chin tightened. "What truth do I need to be convinced of?"

"Our connected past."

Akaran balked at the very notion. "There's nothing connecting us save for having the same deplorable mother."

"And she abandoned us—me as a newborn, you as a child. But what recourse did she have? Your great-aunt cursed her, drove her from the family." Rowan didn't like defending Zurie's actions, but he needed to drive a wedge in Akaran's relationship with his uncle and aunt. "Zurie couldn't be your mother even if she wanted to. Zamara ensured that, and you suffered."

Akaran gave a start at the mention of his aunt, then his brows bristled. "Don't shift the blame. The fault is Zurie's!"

"And your uncle didn't help matters," Rowan said, a brazen edge to his voice. "He made certain you hated her as much as he did. And in so doing, you became his tool. But you don't have to go along with his schemes any longer. We can be free of their meddling, if we work together."

Akaran's lips curled into a snarl. "I can't be hearing you right. You want me to ignore everything I believe, shove aside all my hatred, and join you—in what? Ending *your* curse?"

"Yes."

Akaran stomped forward. "I think the stale air inside Mount Maldere has addled your brain if you think I'll ever help you destroy my family."

"I don't want to destroy your family," Rowan said. "Only your aunt must pay for the curse she placed upon me."

"I'm glad she did it," Akaran snapped. "I'm glad she cursed you both—"

"No, you're not," Rowan challenged. "Your hate is misplaced. You've been misguided to direct your hatred upon me and our mother. What Zurie did was wrong. But your father and mine also bear responsibility."

Akaran's nostrils flared. "My father was betrayed by *her*! How dare you suggest he is culpable in this?"

"Had Kainan not neglected our mother, she may have never been drawn toward Rorak, and I never would've been born." Rowan paused, only then realizing how it would've altered Akaran's life. "Your family would still be intact, and no one would have suffered a needless death. All I ask is you consider these variables."

Akaran's jaw unclenched as his eyes flickered with confusion. "Why spare a thought for me, huh?"

"Because we're brothers," Rowan answered with all the sincerity he could muster. "If you change your mind, you know where to find me."

Akaran scoffed. "You're quite deluded, if you think I'll ever assist you."

"Maybe you're right. I hoped you'd listen to reason."

"Reason?" Akaran shook his head in apparent bafflement. "I don't get you. You should hate me."

"Why? Because you hate me? Or I should hate you because your first act as a brother was to show me the savagery of your fists?" Rowan shook his head. He had ample cause to despise his brother, but hate was like a liquid poison eating a person alive. Akaran's heart festered with it. "How does hating you benefit me? I can see what it's done to you; I won't live in such misery."

Rowan braced himself as Akaran's face shifted from confusion to antipathy.

"Misery, you say?" Akaran seized Rowan by the collar, pulling him close beneath his chin. "Just where do you get off taking the moral high ground?"

"I had mothers who taught me both kindness and strength," Rowan said, holding his brother's hate-filled gaze, "which is why I'm keeping the curse from infecting you." The tendrils retreated into his skin, pricking every pore, yet stayed away from Akaran's flesh.

His brother's eyes flickered for the briefest of seconds, before growing even more volatile. "Showing me kindness?" Akaran sneered, spitting in Rowan's face. "You think you're better than me, do you? You're an illegitimate bastard. You are nothing!"

Akaran clamped his fist at his side, his other hand still clutching Rowan's collar.

"Is this the part where you feed your fury and beat me to your liking?" Rowan asked.

"I'm considering it!" Akaran said. "Maybe you'll put up more of a fight this time. You've grown quite the iron pair since returning from Mount Maldere. So, come on, bastard. Hit me!"

Rowan didn't rise to his brother's bait. "Call me that all you like," he hissed through clenched teeth, "but it won't change the fact my grandfather has recognized me as his legitimate heir. What has Adelkar given you? A mine of your own? Land in your name to cultivate? Or a stipend to pursue other business ventures?"

Rowan paused, giving Akaran a chance to refute his words. When his brother didn't, he planted more seeds of doubt. "If he hasn't, you might want to start wondering why that is. He may even be cheating you out of assets." Rowan couldn't give verity to his suspicions, but sowing doubt into Akaran's mind could be the path to winning him over.

Akaran's grip slackened, and his brows twitched. "You know nothing of our relationship. He raised me after my father's death."

"Then you should have no trouble asking him outright," Rowan said, using sensible words Akaran couldn't ignore. "See for yourself the truth behind your uncle's dealings."

Akaran flung Rowan back roughly, saying nothing. He fumbled for the reins and mounted his horse. "I'll investigate what you've said," he finally responded. "One way or another, you'll be hearing from me."

DURING THE RIDE HOME, AKARAN'S MIND BESIEGED HIM.

His half-brother's words sank in like quicksand. Akaran despised Rowan for rehashing the events of the past. Just this hint of "supposed" truth cast doubt on everything he knew and believed. Rowan had to be wrong.

There's no cursed way Adelkar is hoarding wealth from me.

Akaran would discover the truth.

Arriving at the manor, he stabled his horse and searched for his uncle. After checking his quarters and the dining hall, he stomped his way to Adelkar's study. The door was shut, but unlocked, and so Akaran flung it open and marched inside. A blazing hearth diffused orangish hues upon the stone floor and his uncle's face.

Adelkar lifted his gaze. Akaran's fiery entry warped his thin lips into a testy glower. "Is there something you need?"

Akaran leaned forward and pressed his fists onto his uncle's mahogany desk. "I want my father's inheritance."

"What brought this on?" Adelkar sat back in his armchair with a tiresome stare. "Rowan said something to you, didn't he?"

Akaran tsked sharply. "He has nothing to do with this."

"Oh, and I'm expected to believe that nonsense when the instant you return from meeting with him, you spring this demand on me?" Adelkar stood, and a sternness overtook his insouciant expression. He rounded the desk, pointing an admonishing finger at Akaran. "You marched in here as if I've been withholding something from you. Can't you see what that upstart is doing? He's trying to muddy the waters, sowing doubt and mistrust. Have I not looked after you these past eighteen years, giving you anything and everything you've ever wanted?"

"You have," Akaran acknowledged without contest, "which is why you shouldn't be bothered by me asking for what is rightfully mine."

"Kainan entrusted me to manage your income —"

"Yes, but I'm sure he didn't mean indefinitely," Akaran interrupted, miffed by his uncle's repeated avoidance. "I'm twenty years old, in case that's escaped your notice. I'm a man. I think it's high time I managed my own wealth."

"Are you certain that is wise, Nephew?" Adelkar scrutinized him like a flaw in one of his ledgers. "Given your consistent lack of interest in mining and business management altogether, I didn't think you craved ownership this vigorously."

"My attitude has changed."

"And quite at the drop of a mark, I'd say."

"I've given it thought," Akaran said, arms folded, "and I want to be my own man. I can learn to mine, and while I do, a good mine captain can oversee the day-to-day operations."

Adelkar considered for a moment, tapping his fingers against his left hand. "Well, if this is what you truly desire, I see no reason to impede you. All you had to do was ask." Adelkar stepped in close and gripped the back of Akaran's neck. The timbre of his voice changed as his lips curved into a smile. "We're family, after all. Your good fortune is mine. Let's proceed together, as partners, as I'm sure Kainan would've wanted."

A sliver of disingenuousness seemed to lurk in Adelkar's tone. Though his smile denoted sincerity, the glint in his eyes sparked suspicion.

"I appreciate you doing this, Uncle," Akaran said, swallowing a lump of misgiving.

"Of course, Nephew." Adelkar tightened his grip by a slim degree. "I only want the best for my brother's son." He wandered back to his armchair and clasped his hands together on his desk. "Tomorrow, I'll show you what assets Kainan left you. You may then begin breaking ground on your endeavors. May your riches flow like veins of iron ore."

As Akaran departed from his uncle's study, the hair on his neck refused to lie still. Why were his nerves so unsettled? Adelkar agreed to his demands. That was a good sign, wasn't it?

So why do I feel the strangest sense of disquiet?

It was the doubt Rowan sowed. Akaran couldn't shake it. If there was truth to it, he would keep a careful watch. For the first time in his life, he wouldn't so blindly abide by his uncle's decisions.

TAHIRA PACED AT THE BASE OF THE HILL BETWEEN TWO

cobblestoned homes, mind and body restless. Her fingers tapped her forearm in an anxious rhythm. Her stomach somersaulted with agitated nerves. She hated the long wait and dreaded the possible grisly aftermath.

Out of her peripheral vision, she caught movement down the road. Rowan trudged up the path. Her heart flooded with elation. She hastened toward him and swept her arms around him in a fast embrace. Neither his high cheekbones nor sculpted mouth bore any dark blemishes.

She expelled a great sigh of relief. "I see your nose isn't broken."

"Akaran didn't throw a single punch."

"Oh?" Tahira lifted her eyebrows. "Then the meeting was successful?"

"Yes, in the sense that I've gotten Akaran's mind entrenched." A confident gleam brightened the flecks of amber in Rowan's red eyes. "He'll begin to doubt Adelkar, and with enough doubt turning to truth, Akaran might be swayed."

Tahira couldn't help but harbor caution. She wasn't optimistic about Rowan's plan, but she forced herself to remain supportive. "What do we do in the meantime?"

"Live." Rowan smiled with determination and walked with her up the hill. "I'll be heading into the mine, learning more from Keld. I need to understand this business and all it entails. Rahn tells me mining iron is in my blood. I want to know if it's really true."

When they reached the entrance to Iron Crossing, Rowan turned, and his alluring smile caused Tahira's heart to flutter. "Were you really worried I'd return with a broken nose?"

Tahira snorted, vexed by the mere thought. "Need I remind you the last time you were alone with Akaran, he beat you so severely, I attended to you for three days."

"Three days I know you didn't mind at all," he said with a wry grin.

Tahira blushed beneath his teasing smile. "Then next time, I won't worry." She curled her lips. "If you should come back beaten, I can attend to you without having to hear you say, 'Keep your distance.'"

Rowan laughed, and the loose strands of his silvery-white hair slid across his brow. "You're touchy when it comes to that phrase, aren't you?"

"I'm anticipating the day when it shall never cross your lips again."

"You're not alone in that wish." Rowan surprised her with a quick, blushing kiss.

The warmth of his breath sent shivers down Tahira's spine. But as before, the kiss ended as quickly as the snap of a finger. The rapturous touch left her heart aching for infinitely more.

Tahira quieted the urge, winding her fingers in her shawl. "After you come up from the mine, we'll have a little celebratory dinner for your eighteenth birthday. I hope you didn't think I'd forget."

"I didn't." Rowan laughed again. "I've learned there's very little that escapes your mind." He turned away and disappeared into the twisting tunnels beneath the crag.

Tahira ambled to the garden and hoed the rough soil for planting lavender. Her hands needed something new to cultivate while time lagged like a boat on stagnant water. Her listless mind took solace in the confidence in Rowan's deep-set gaze. She hoped with all her heart that his gutsy plan bore fruit. Only time would tell if any seeds of doubt rooted in Akaran's head.

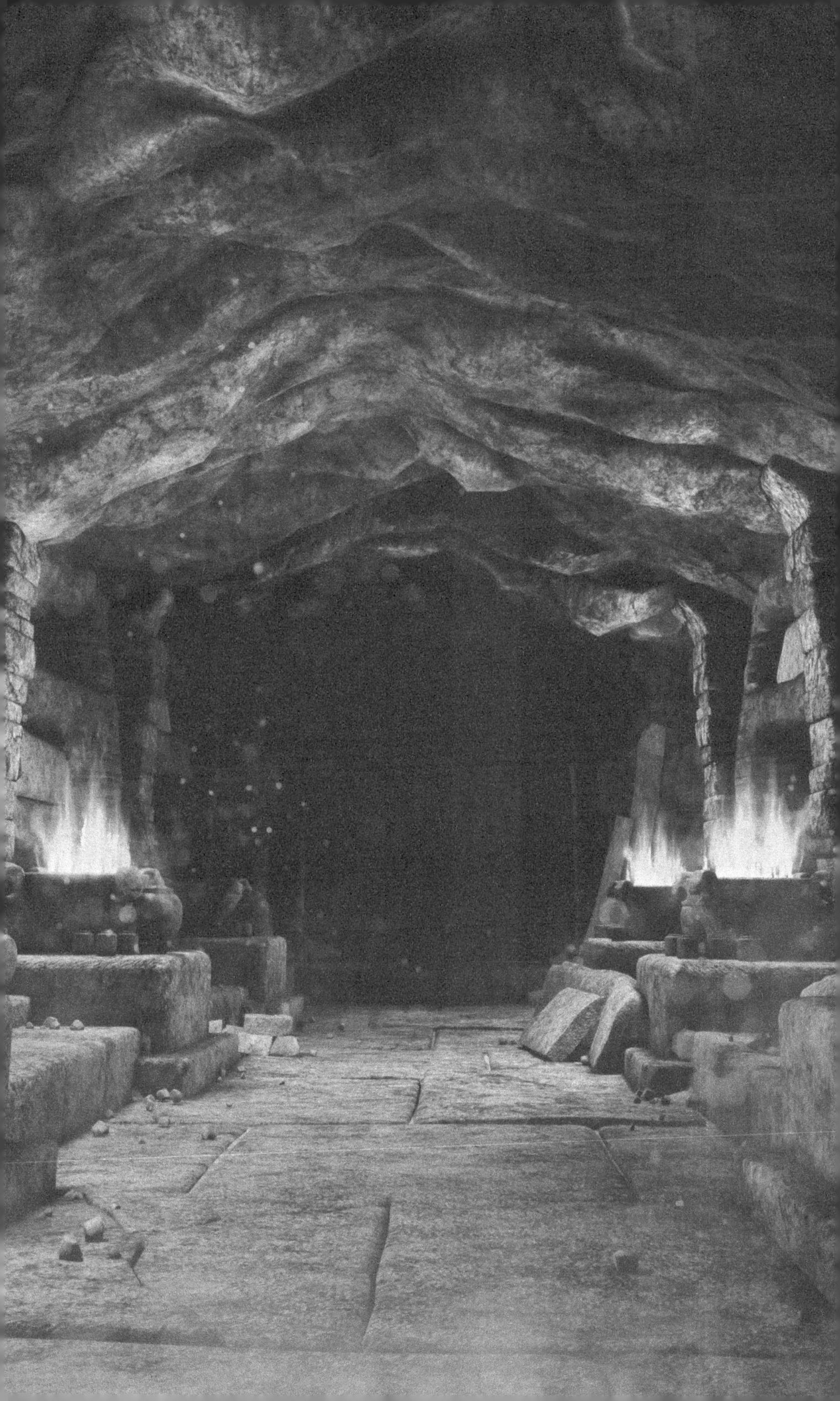

CHAPTER 22
INTO THE MINES

"Here's the deed to Castle Crag." Adelkar slid the parchment across his desk toward Akaran. "I'll visit Ferron today and transfer it to your name. This mine once belonged to Zurie's parents, which should please you. The shame of having a cursed, scandalous daughter circulated among the barons and drove them to close the mine."

"How then did you acquire it?" Akaran asked, giving the deed a brief scan.

"Val Kamand sold it to me after I applied pressure."

Akaran smirked. "So, you forced him to sell."

"I encouraged him." Adelkar's lips curved in a crafty smirk. "The sale allowed him and his wife to quit Arjun and reside in another country. I doubt they shall ever return."

"A boon for me," Akaran said with a callous grin. He was their grandchild, after all. It was only fitting he received their mine.

"The mine is yours to resurrect if you so choose."

"I'll give it a look over." Akaran returned the deed to the desk, pleased by his uncle's show of goodwill. He didn't feel the same misgivings from yesterday when in Adelkar's company. Either he caught his uncle in a more agreeable mood this morning, or Adelkar was keeping a lock on his true emotions. Whatever the case, Akaran wouldn't be foolish and dismiss the peculiar behavior.

Adelkar tucked the deed safely into a leather sleeve along with several other documents. "Shall I give you an expert's tour of the mine tomorrow afternoon?"

"That won't be needed, Uncle. I'd hate to hoard your time when I have someone else who can do the job."

"Suit yourself. My knowledge in these matters is yours if you so choose."

Akaran gave his uncle a cordial nod. "Now about my other assets . . . I'm sure my father left me a cache of marks. I'll need a portion of it to get the mine up and running."

"Of course, Nephew. I'll make it available to you by tomorrow morning. Will that satisfy you?"

"It will." Akaran showed a false smile. "I appreciate your willingness to aid me in these matters, and for keeping my wealth secure all these years. It must've been done out of great love for my father." Akaran fished for a visual signal, anything, to suggest Adelkar wasn't as agreeable as he appeared.

Adelkar revealed only a flicker of surprise. "How eloquent you are today. Has the prospect of being your own man added honey to your customary crassness?"

"Who can say? I do feel much changed since yesterday. And it's all thanks to you." Akaran left Adelkar's company and passed a letter off to Horace. "See that this is delivered promptly."

Akaran clasped his hands behind him, a daring pleasure surging within him. Onto the next step in his new business ventures. His half-brother wasn't the only one who could learn to govern a mine. Akaran endeavored to educate himself, and lucky for him, he had just the person to show him how.

"When you said you wanted to meet at Castle Crag," Ravel said from atop his sable horse, staring at the high-rising mine shaped like a wide plateau with two prominent peaks, "I thought a joke lay in store—not a business opportunity."

Akaran looked upon his new property with great pride.

It really does resemble a castle. How fitting for me.

"I wanted someone I can trust to give me an honest opinion."

"Curses, I'm touched. I'd no idea I ranked so high on your trust ladder."

Akaran laughed. "Don't get excited. The list isn't long."

"Ah, well then, I'll temper my enthusiasm. Though, I think your uncle could've given you better assistance. When it comes to mines, he has decades of experience on us."

"I don't want to rely on him for everything." Akaran had done it enough in his adolescence. And besides, if Rowan could blast his own ore, then so could Akaran—and do it better. "It's time I handled my own affairs without my uncle's input or permission."

"You said it, Aka. You're finally beginning to sound like a man."

"Oh, and what did I sound like before?" Akaran quipped.

Ravel didn't pull his punches. "A whiny, pubescent prick."

Akaran rolled his eyes. "Leave it to you to give me brutal honesty."

"You can always count on it," Ravel gibed. "Now, let's see what this mine has to offer. Shall we go below grass?"

"By all means. I believe after today, my fortunes will be broadening."

They dismounted and wandered into the derelict mine. Akaran lit two torches, and they traveled from one level to the next, investigating for signs of metalliferous ore. Ravel remained silent as they roamed the tunnels, his brow scrunched in thought. Akaran was pleased to have his friend along for his expertise. He oversaw much work at Griselode—his family's mine. Though only a year Akaran's senior, Ravel was not only adept in boxing, but in the broad aspects of running a mine.

Ravel stopped in the middle of a dead-end passageway, surveying the fissures. "There are marks to be made in this mine."

"How can you tell?"

"My gut says so." Ravel pointed to a series of cracks, illuminating the crevices with the torchlight. "These lodes in particular show signs of previous iron veins. If we were to continue blasting, I think we'll hit even more, perhaps striking an untapped champion lode."

"That's what I wanted to hear," Akaran said, racing his fingers along the rough fissures. "I'll need to hire my own miners and a mine captain. How many men should I employ?"

Ravel rubbed his jaw. "I'd say around fifty. When would you like to begin work?"

"Within the week."

"That shouldn't be too hard. Many miners are out of work. When they hear you're reopening Castle Crag, you'll have every male from age fifteen to fifty lining up at the entrance."

"Which will allow me to be selective." Akaran imagined these passages bustling with workers and his lips widened into a smile. "I only want the healthiest working my mine. Let's spread the word and see who comes. And who knows, maybe I'll even steal workers from Iron Crossing."

They returned topside and mounted their horses. Akaran stole one more glance at Castle Crag—*my mine*. With a satisfied smirk, he nudged his horse onto the path. They spurred their steeds to crest the hill, then settled into a leisurely walk across the treeless steppe. Wind teased the high grass. Sunlight polished the passing crags, burnishing brighter than silver.

"So, tell me why Adelkar granted you this particular mine?" Ravel inquired, his voice colored with suspicion.

Akaran whipped the hair out of his eyes and stared at his friend. "What's with the suspicious tone?"

"I'm suspicious of everyone."

"Even me?"

"I make no exceptions."

Akaran grunted. "Nice to know where I stand."

"So, the mine," Ravel pressed.

Akaran indulged his friend's dogged curiosity. He explained what transpired between him and his uncle over the past several days.

Ravel listened with cynical intrigue. "I doubt Kamand wanted to sell. The mine must've been prosperous if your uncle sought to acquire it. Yet, why then leave it idle? Why keep it closed when it could increase his coffers?"

Akaran shrugged. "Perhaps he was simply waiting for me to take an interest."

Ravel narrowed his eyes. "Or something else is amiss, and you're blind to it."

Akaran gave a low growl. "There you go again with your conspiracies. Must you see sordid plots wherever you look?"

"I don't trust people—it's my habit," Ravel said with a flippant wave of his hand. "It makes little sense to me for a lucrative mine to remain closed unless your uncle wanted it that way." He paused, his brows drawn together. "What is his relationship with the Kamands?"

"There is none, at least not anymore. Val Kamand and his wife forfeited this land after their daughter was committed to Mount Maldere. Adelkar said the shame of Zurie's actions drove them to leave."

Ravel stared at him, his eyes glinting for further elaboration. To say nothing would only fuel his friend's conspiratorial digging.

"All right, Adelkar pressured them to sell," Akaran admitted. "That's all I know. Happy now?"

"Aha!" Ravel touted. "The piece of information I've been waiting for." He grinned like a smug know-it-all. "I'm sure threats were involved. He could've threatened to have them cursed by a Conjurer. Anyone would concede their land if faced with getting cursed."

Akaran mulled it over. Adelkar did have a Conjurer he could deploy whenever he wanted. Zamara must've cursed numerous folk on his behest alone. "He has employed Conjurers in the past," Akaran said, revealing nothing about his aunt. "So, I wouldn't put it past him."

"Hm." Ravel paused for a moment, his fingers tapping against the saddle's pommel. "Wait, weren't your families business associates, though?"

"A long time ago, they were."

"Then if you ask me, it reeks of spiteful intention."

"How do you mean?"

Ravel turned his face, which held all the markers of one who was about to launch into a discovery. "Look, it's no secret you hate your mother, but who taught you to despise her in the first place? Even I know it was Adelkar. So, isn't it probable Adelkar's hatred for Zurie drove him to ruin her family?"

"I suppose it could, yes," Akaran said, navigating his horse past a pile of stout boulders. "Adelkar would've wanted them to pay for Zurie's treachery against his brother—my father. Still, I don't see how this is of particular interest to me. I don't care how he acquired the mine—it belongs to me now. The Kamands' wealth will become mine."

Ravel snorted. "You're missing the point."

"Which is?"

"Your uncle is a shrewd business hound. This mine he's given you may appear as a gift, but more than likely, it's to keep you off the scent of what he's really doing."

"Which would be?"

Ravel's expression turned grave. "Keeping your inheritance for himself."

Akaran exhaled, unable to hide his surprise. "Curses, Rav, I hadn't realized you distrusted my uncle so much."

"I can spot a crafty blackguard when I see one," Ravel said with a shrug. "My father is too similar. All I'm saying is you might want to look into your uncle's business ledgers. You never know where he could be cheating you."

Akaran glowered. "You're beginning to sound like my half-brother. Even he thinks Adelkar is cheating me."

"Does he indeed? How interesting." Ravel smirked before tossing back his head and guffawing. The wind flung his moppy hair in every direction. "Looks like you have two well-wishers watching out for your better interests. You should count yourself fortunate."

Akaran tsked. "Annoying prick."

"Thickheaded prat," Ravel jabbed back in jest. "But in all seriousness, do yourself a favor and check your uncle's records. Better yet, have a look at your father's will. You may learn all the truth you need right there."

"I'll look into it, Rav," Akaran said, if only to get his friend off his back.

Akaran couldn't admit to Ravel that he'd never actually seen his father's will. There'd been no need—not with Adelkar handling his finances. Admitting he hadn't seen it would give Ravel all the ammunition to call him a "foolish idiot who lacked a brain," or something coarser to that effect. Adelkar faithfully handled the distribution of any funds Akaran required, and Akaran—in his cavalierness—never bothered to understand his own inheritance. The chance Adelkar could still be keeping assets from him awakened his misgivings once more.

Now his irksome friend was feeding his mind with doubt. When

Akaran got the chance, he would dig into his uncle's finances and find the truth for himself.

A WEEK HAD PASSED SINCE ROWAN MET WITH AKARAN, AND HE hadn't received any further contact. He didn't expect a letter, but he did wonder if his brother had heeded his caution. For now, it remained a mystery that only time would reveal.

Rowan pushed the issue out of his mind and concentrated on his work at Iron Crossing. He entered the premier shaft and lowered down the ladder, dropping into the first level. There, Keld waited for him alongside Bashir and Bulan, who flashed broad, welcoming grins.

"What's the work for today?" Rowan asked.

"Blasting in the twenty level." Keld's love of explosives was evident by his earnest smile. "The powder has been set. We're ready to blow it if you are."

Rowan nodded. "Let's get it done."

They ventured to the mines' lower levels and arrived at the blasting site. The oil pouches had been stuffed in the fissures, the firestone powder prepared.

Keld handed Rowan the flintstone. "Wanna do the honors?"

"Happily." Rowan took it and ignited the powder trail. "Here's to iron."

The blast rocked the tunnels, and after the dust settled, the awaiting miners scrambled to hammer and collect the abundant ore. Rowan did the same work as everyone else, toiling, sweating, and hefting ore from bucket to mine cart. He may have been their superior by title, but those around him held superior knowledge. He worked closely with Keld, Bashir, and Bulan, who treated him as a fellow miner.

After a time, Keld increased Rowan's responsibilities, allowing him to make orders for coal, timber, wax candles, and the like — whatever they required to keep the mine in peak operation.

"We're going to need timber to reinforce the new shaft we made last week," Keld mentioned.

"Let me know the amount," Rowan said, jotting a note on his charcoal slate, "and I'll see Warin receives our request. There's plenty of timber we can use now that the long field has been cleared."

Bashir and Bulan traded wary looks.

"Best let one of us take the request to him, Row," Bulan advised. "He and the lumber workers still harbor distrust toward you. Let's not give them reason to express complaints."

Bulan's words cast a shadow on Rowan's enthusiasm. He pursed his lips. "I understand. I'll leave it to you then, Bulan."

"Don't look so glum," Bashir said with an encouraging twinkle in his garnet eyes. "We're pleased to have you down here with us. Gives you the chance to get some meat on your bones."

"Those small wrists," Bulan said, shaking his messy-haired head in jest. "Don't know how you can even swing a hammer."

"This again?" Rowan grunted with amusement. "Will you ever stop teasing me for my leaner build? I'm by no means a twig." The brothers were three times as broad and had him beat in height.

Bashir folded his thick arms across his impressive chest, where a nest of coiled hairs pushed past his open collar. "I will when you've got a bit more muscle on your flesh."

"I'm working on it," Rowan said with a chuckle. "With the ore I've been hauling daily, I expect I'll be as big as you soon enough."

Pleased by Rowan's response, the brothers turned their attention to Keld.

"Don't even give me that look," the mine captain warned. "I'm afraid this average build is all I'll ever muster, which suits me fine. Not everyone can become muscleheads like you both."

The three miners roared with laughter before getting back to their tasks.

Learning the ropes, Rowan found himself taking great pleasure in mining. He worked underground daily, while he spent the evenings with Rahn and Tahira, regaling them with the mine's progress. Rahn took those moments to share his many exploits as a miner. Rowan gleaned much from his stories, especially the ones including his father.

"Rorak didn't rest until he'd rescued every soul trapped in the shaft after its terrible collapse," Rahn said, lounging in his comfy, pillowed chair as he pruned a spider-like plant bearing numerous spiderettes.

Tahira sat beside him at the parlor table, watching closely. Rahn handed her one of the spiderettes to plant in her own pot. "We were lucky to have lost only three lives during that accident. It could've been far worse."

"Keld often reminds me that blasting can be dangerous," Rowan said, relieved that nothing so devastating had happened on his watch.

"My son's swift actions saved over a dozen lives that day." Rahn tilted his gaze to peer at Tahira. "Including your father's."

Tahira's face glowed with wonder. "I never knew that happened!" She looked at Rowan with fond affection. "Now I see where your knack for rushing into danger comes from."

"I hardly rush." Rowan said. "I assess, and then I rush." His comment drew laughter from Rahn and Tahira.

Shen walked in, and upon seeing the state of the table spattered with dirt clumps, his hands shot to his face with horror. "What a mess! Couldn't you have done this propagating in the morning—and *outside*?"

"There's no need to fuss," Rahn chided, his fingers frolicking in the soil. "It's just a bit of late-night planting. Which reminds me: Can you bring in my glowing plants from the cellar? They're in need of pruning. Might as well do it now while I have the energy."

Shen's brow tightened and his lips squirmed. "Those'll be the last you prune tonight, baron. Then it's time you get yourself to bed." Shen marched out of the parlor to retrieve Rahn's favorite plants.

Tahira giggled, pressing the soil around her newly planted spiderette. "Must you make things hard on Shen, Grandfather?"

Rahn rubbed his long nose, and a blot of dirt clung to its crinkled tip. "It's my way of teaching him to loosen up. Just because he likes to keep me on a tight schedule for my health, doesn't mean we all have to abide by it. Remember that, you two."

Shen returned with the silver-white root and the ruby-red succulent. Both had doubled in size since Rowan had given them to his grandfather.

Rahn set aside his spidery plant, and with a vermillion sheen upon his face, he worked on removing the succulent's dead leaves. "Who's up for another story?"

"Keep it short, for Shen's sake," Rowan said with mild amusement.

"Let's hear one where you're the chief character," Tahira insisted.

"Ah, I have a humorous one—and it includes Rorak when he was a boy." Rahn continued, making a mound with the dead leaves. "One year on Tribute Day, Rorak and I were on our way to the Mestrian Garrison when the unthinkable happened. Our front wheel axle broke while descending Kaklin Hill."

Tahira gasped in shock. "What did you do?"

"The only thing I could do in that situation. I sprang from the wagon and wrangled the horses before we lost our load."

"Did that work?" Tahira asked, on the edge of her seat.

"Er, not exactly. I saved the load but lost my grip on the reins. The wagon continued speeding down the hill—me chasing after it—with Rorak bobbing along, clutching the driver seat and screaming at the top of his lungs. By the time it reached the bottom of the hill, all the wheels were busted. It seemed impossible we'd make the tributary delivery in time—which, mind you, would result in immediate imprisonment."

Rowan leaned his shoulders against his chair's seatback, enjoying the deep timbre of his grandfather's storytelling voice.

"With that looming over our heads," Rahn went on, using his pile of dead leaves to represent the cart's load and two separate leaves as the horses, "we scrambled to find a way to rig the wheel-less cart to the horses, which resulted in dragging it behind us like a sled. The loud, scraping sound it made when we entered the city drew every eye and ear. Laughter broke out amongst the populace, dispelling the usual gloominess."

"I bet the magistrate didn't like that," Tahira said with delicious satisfaction.

"He gave us the oddest scowl when he saw the peculiar state of our delivery."

"But you made it in time," Rowan said with a laugh. "So, it all must've worked out in the end?"

Rahn snickered. "All the magistrate could do was give us a lengthy reprimand for arriving at the last possible second."

Rahn's stories never got old. Rowan loved them, as much as he loved the man who told them. They connected him to his heritage and instilled him with a sense of belonging. He was part of a long legacy—one that would continue, even after Rahn departed this world.

Rowan pushed the unhappy thought from his mind, hoping they would have many more evenings like this one.

At the start of the new work week, Rowan overheard a group of miners discussing another mine—one he was unfamiliar with.

"Did you hear about Castle Crag? It's reopened."

"No, can't be," one miner said in disbelief. "That mine's been closed for seventeen years, ever since the Kamands sold it."

"It's the truth, I tell you. Castle Crag has been resurrected."

"Well, then, who's opened it?" another asked.

"I heard from folk in Arjun that the new owner is Akaran Keliss. He's hiring miners. It could be our chance to work elsewhere, far from the cursed master."

They discreetly glanced Rowan's way.

Rowan kept his eyes on his work, filling his bucket with chunks of ore. When he had a full load, he hefted his bucket and walked toward the miners. The men clamped their lips and backed away from him as he deposited his ore in the mine cart.

Rowan flashed a kind smile. "Though I'm cursed, I'm not your master. You're free to seek employment at Castle Crag if you so choose."

Surprise spread across the miners' shadowed faces. The men held their tongues. Rowan said nothing more and wandered back to his secluded work area.

Keld chiseled out ore nearby, having watched Rowan's exchange with the miners. "So, you've heard of Castle Crag, then?"

"Just now," Rowan said, wiping his brow and lowering his bucket. "If men want to work there, I'll not stop them."

"You can't let them go without contest," Keld said, his eyes igniting like firestone. Rowan had never seen such a heated expression from the mild-mannered mine captain. "This is Akaran we're talking about, remember? He's aiming to deprive you of workers in the hopes your mine fails. I know it."

"That may be," Rowan said, exhaling, "but I'm not in competition with my brother. I'm pleased he's opened the mine. It'll give him something to craft with his own hands. It may even reshape his mindset." Rowan crouched and piled more ore into his bucket. "But I hear what you're saying, Keld, and I understand your concerns. I'll give the workers an incentive to stay by increasing their wages."

Keld gnawed on his chapped lower lip. "Even with monetary incentive, you're likely to lose miners."

"It's fine. I won't force men to hammer and chisel alongside me if they're in fear for their lives." Rowan lifted his bucket, bracing it over his shoulder. "Tell the miners my offer."

He trekked back to the mine cart. Halfway down the passage, Bashir pushed people aside, trotting toward Rowan.

"Row, come quick!"

"What is it, Bash?"

"It's the baron. He's had another spell. Shen says it doesn't look good."

Rowan dropped his bucket with a tumbling clatter and raced out of the mine.

CHAPTER 23
LOSING SOMETHING GOOD

Rowan found Shen and Tahira in Rahn's dimly lit quarters. His grandfather lay in bed, appearing more ashen and frail than ever. His wispy hair, gray and brittle, hung limp around his head. Even his eyes no longer held their once-warm luster. Tahira's delicate face showed strain and the telltale tracks of tears.

Rowan came close and took Rahn's hand. The curse's dark stain coursed through his grandfather's veins.

Rowan's heart plummeted. The stark, black veins mirrored the same infection the dying birch leaves exhibited before they turned to ash. Rowan understood with terrible certainty that the end was near. He caught Tahira's watery eyes, realizing she, too, was keenly aware of it.

Rowan sagged in the chair, regret and guilt washing over him. "Grandfather, I'm not ready for you to go. I thought we'd have more time."

"So did I, my boy," Rahn whispered, his breathing shallow. "But do not despair. I have known only joy these past several months. I wouldn't take them back for all the iron beneath the crags."

His grandfather's words burrowed into Rowan's heart and soul. Tears welled in Rowan's eyes.

"Now, there is something that would ease me," Rahn said.

Rowan stifled his tears. "What, Grandfather?"

"I'd like you and this lovely lady here to handfast."

"What is that?" Rowan asked.

Rahn gave a weak smile. "It's a betrothal of sorts—a union that ties you together for a year until formal vows are made. I was your age when Hilda and I handfasted."

Rowan's face flushed. "You want us to be betrothed?"

"You love each other, yes?" Rahn gave them each a knowing look, as if this was the simplest of questions—and most obvious to him.

Rowan's neck heated. "It's moving in that direction . . . I care for Tahira deeply."

"And I him," Tahira said with a blush, meeting Rowan's eyes from across the bed. "I'll not break the vow I made to you, Rowan. No matter what the future holds."

Rowan's heart fluttered. Burning skies, her adamant resolve enraptured him. She was all he knew—all he ever wanted to know. He loved her sweet, playful persistence, and admired her courageous spirit. She captured the deepest part of his soul by remaining steadfast at his side amidst his dismal circumstances. He wanted no one else but her as a lifelong companion—this petite and lovely miner's daughter who possessed a heart more precious than pearls.

"Then grant this old man a cheerful sight before the end." Rahn squeezed their hands with his weak grip. "I'd go easier knowing you pledged a vow of commitment to each other."

His hope-filled plea tugged at Rowan's heart. He didn't need time to contemplate.

"We'll do it, Grandfather. For you." Rowan didn't see the harm in indulging this innocent request. He blushed when he met Tahira's coy gaze. "How do we handfast?"

"Take each other's hand," Rahn said, his voice a raspy wheeze.

Tahira crossed to Rowan's side, and they clasped hands. Rowan sucked in an anxious breath and forced the tendrils to retreat inside his skin. "What comes next, Grandfather?"

"We wrap your hands together. Your weaving will be fine." Rahn indicated with a subtle head tilt for Shen to assist in this intimate ceremony.

Shen pulled the woven blanket from the bed, loosely draped it over their clasped hands, and tied it in a bulky knot.

Rahn placed his trembling hands above and below theirs. "Grow in love," he said. "Abide in strength and mind, working together as partners who share a common goal. Let love deepen until your vows of steadfast ardor are exchanged from the depths of your hearts. Will you keep to this vow?"

"We will, Grandfather," they said in unison.

"Then you are handfasted, my dear ones."

A wistful smile bloomed upon Tahira's face as she gazed at Rowan. He smiled back at her, embracing the bittersweet joy of the moment. It was how Rahn wanted to go, beholding hope, knowing his legacy would continue. His pallid arms—resembling withered branches—slackened and slipped to his sides.

And with a peaceful grin on his face, Rahn breathed his last.

SHEN HANDLED THE FUNERAL ARRANGEMENTS. ON THE EAST SIDE of Iron Crossing, out on the grassy steppe, stood a burial tomb shaped like a giant earthen mound. Flaxen brush with small violet wildflowers carpeted the oval hill. The landscape boasted a half-dozen of these mounds.

Rowan stared at his ancestral burial grounds, transfixed. Today, this place held only a hollow wonder.

He, along with Bulan, Bashir, and Keld, carried the casket to the mound's entrance, which was flanked by two thick stone slabs. They entered the torchlit tomb, the ceiling braced with stone columns and timber beams. Everyone in attendance placed a small stone upon the casket—a Shandrian burial custom. Rowan removed the luminous stone from his pocket he'd taken from Mount Maldere and laid it to rest with the others. It added a touch of cool, blue light to the tomb —a light that would never go out.

A moment of silence was held for all to recount their appreciation for the baron and bid him farewell. Rowan's own memories brought tears to his eyes. Tahira took his hand in those short minutes before letting her fingers slip away.

Shen ushered everyone out of the tomb and gave the nod for Bulan and Bashir to close the slabs. They shut the stone slabs with a cold, grinding thud. All the mourners then trekked back to the manor, where food and drink had been prepared. People grew livelier as they relayed tales of Rahn's life.

"Rahn's death is a great loss to us all," Keld said to the group at his table, drink in hand. "He was a man of the stoutest degree with good sense and conviction. Possessed the common touch and lived a simple life. We who knew him best would do well to follow his example."

"Lucky for us we have his heir to guide us into the next era here at Iron Crossing," Bashir said, lifting his mug aloft. "Our future will be as bright as glittering gems. Ain't that right, Row?"

Rowan flashed a humble smile at the beefy miner. "I think you'll all be guiding me a while still."

"True," Bash said with a chortle, "but you're learning quick."

"Indeed," Bulan agreed. "Must be 'cause it's in your blood."

Rowan hid from their rousing praise behind his mug. It pleased him seeing everyone with mirthful spirits, even if his heart experienced this loss more deeply than anyone present. He'd found a friendly familial relation and lost him in two months. All because of the Conjurer's curse.

"Excuse me," he said, standing and leaving his drink behind. "Please enjoy yourselves."

"You all right, Row?" Bashir asked.

Rowan nodded. "I'm fine—just need some time alone."

He slipped away from the gathering hall. Once inside his bedchamber, he closed the door and dropped onto the stool before his loom. He forced his fingers to weave, fighting the grief blooming within him. The activity stilled his soul yet stirred his mind with somber reflections. Rahn's death tore open a gaping wound in his heart, and the sting of his absence brought with it the loss of Naja. Rowan had never fully processed her death—breaking his curse and working the mine kept his mind occupied and his heart distracted. But as he weaved, Naja's death swirled anew in his thoughts.

Had her body withered like Rahn's? Become infected with those inky-black veins? The end had come too swiftly, without any warning signs. Nothing to tell him her death was imminent.

His heart wrenched as his fingers spoke in weavescript—of how much he missed Naja. He composed words of blue and silver thread along the tapestry. His tale of their time in the Thulu Jungle showed only somber shades.

Rowan swallowed a painful lump. His nimble fingers trembled. All at once, tears flooded his eyes, cascading out of him in a pool of his repressed memories. His head dropped into his hands, his exhausted body wracked with sobs, as time seemed to screech to a standstill. Light from the windows waned, and his loom remained untouched.

A quiet knock snapped Rowan out of his melancholy. He swiped at his tears and picked up where he left off on his weaving.

Tahira entered, holding a candle. "Weaving at this hour? My, you're diligent."

Rowan ran his fingers across the colored threads. "Weaving reminds me of my guardian-mothers. Their loss feels tenfold after Rahn's passing. There's so much more I wanted to say to him—to them, especially Naja. This is the only way I know how to free the words from my mind."

"I understand how you feel. More than you know." Tahira brushed a hand upon his shoulder, then brought it to her lap as she slumped into a chair two feet away. "My parents are gone . . . being back here at Iron Crossing brings with it many memories. Like the miners, I used to live down the hill with my parents. A day doesn't pass when I don't think of them and suffer the sting of their loss."

Rowan lifted his head to look at Tahira through his misty eyes. "You've shown no signs of it."

"Because I've found joy that eclipses the grief. When you lose something good, it shakes you enough so when you find it again, you don't let go." She held his gaze, love and adoration alight in her eyes. "You are something good, Rowan. And I'm going to hold on as tightly as I can so I don't lose you too." She leaned toward him, tilted her chin, and kissed his lips.

At her touch, Rowan's tears stopped. The immediate thought to pull back at once entered his mind, but in that emotional moment, he lacked the will to resist. His broken heart got the better of him, and he strengthened the kiss, weaving his fingers through her lush hair.

As if drawn by the magic of their touch, Tahira eased into his caress, wrapping her arms about his neck. Her breath was a nourishing draught, like the crisp spring water he consumed in Zurie's sanctum. That water replenished his body; Tahira's kiss awakened his soul from despair. He desired nothing more than to drown in her balmy waves and sail away from the grip of every lost life the curse had taken.

Rowan broke contact only to catch his breath. When he leaned again to press his lips against hers, his eyes widened with alarm, and he almost toppled off the stool. All thoughts governed by impulse vanished in a seized breath. He unslung her arms from around his neck and yanked his face and body away.

"What's wrong?" Tahira asked.

Rowan sat there, frozen yet *angry*—angry at himself. "Your lips have lost pigment."

Tahira lifted her quivering fingers to her mouth and rose to stand before the mirror. She pressed the back of her hand to her trembling lips, looking as if she might be sick. Then her hand lowered, resting against her heart. "So they have."

The weight of the curse crashed upon Rowan, pinning him in place. He clenched his fists, grinding his knuckles against his knees. Even with reining in the tendrils, the curse had sucked away the living color from Tahira's lips, turning them as gray as stone.

What was I thinking? Have I learned nothing from the past?

Rahn—the curse's latest victim—was just entombed! Would he wantonly let Tahira be next?

Burning skies, I hate this curse!

Rowan raked his hands through his unbound hair. He hung his head, ashamed of his lack of restraint. "Forgive me. I knew better than to kiss you like that—"

"Well, I'm not sorry," Tahira interrupted, her voice as stubborn as ever, "and you're forgetting I started it."

"Then I should've had the sense to not give in."

Her eyes gleamed, as if challenging him. "As if our kissing could've been so easily prevented. Sense had nothing to do with it."

"And still I should've restrained myself." Rowan gulped. "I can't afford to be reckless. Your safety must always outweigh my wants."

Tahira's chin came up a notch. "You're determined to take the blame, aren't you?"

"I'm cursed. It comes with the territory." A defensive wall fortified around his heart. He shook his head with abject self-loathing.

"You don't know what it's been like for me. Living with the shame of having caused the deaths of the four women who raised me, and now Rahn." His voice caught. "Don't you see? It's unbearable."

"It's not your shame to carry, Row," Tahira said, her voice soft and empathetic. "It's Zurie's."

Rowan scoffed, dropping his head to avoid her eyes. "Zurie hardly spares a thought for the lives she's destroyed."

"And so you feel you must?"

The dead faces of his guardian-mothers flashed in his mind, blotting his vision like dark clouds. Rowan's voice hardened. "I've had to suffer the curse's cruel aftermath . . . the deaths of the people I've loved. It's a crushing weight that hardly lessens. It's why I don't want anyone else to die because of my curse."

Tahira pursed her colorless lips, not backing down. "I know you think the curse only steals life, but it also reveals it."

Rowan cocked his head back. "I don't know what you mean."

"Then I'll make this simple. You gave me a taste of your passion—the thrilling life teeming inside you. It's something the curse couldn't prevent, and I'm glad for it. So, wipe the guilty apology from your face. I knew what I agreed to when we handfasted—to live together as betrothed partners until the day of our union."

They hadn't spoken of their handfast since Rahn's death three days ago. And honestly, being betrothed baffled Rowan. He understood its wonderful implications, but an undeniable cruelty still existed: He couldn't truly enjoy Tahira's company without fear of the curse's reprisals.

Tahira turned back toward the mirror, scrutinizing her lips. "The pigment may return in time."

"Provided we refrain from kissing."

Tahira's smile faded. "If we must."

Rowan shot her a stern frown. "Of course we must. The effects of the curse aren't matters we can ignore. Do you want your lips to turn black? Or, worse, your entire mouth to decay?"

Tahira hesitated. "I'd say it's worth the risk, but in the end, it's ultimately foolish." She pulled back her shoulders with another resolute smile. "The memory will suffice for now."

Does her persistent smile ever waver?

"Nothing keeps you down for long," Rowan said with a quiet sniff.

"I have my heart fixed on the future. It helps bypass my laboring frustrations."

Rowan needed a way to abate his own rising concerns. He spooled red and gold thread around his fingers, occupying his hands with a necessary distraction, and weaved a braided cord.

"This curse is torturous for me. How it could be shortening your life even now . . . the thought of it tears me up inside. I have lost too many people I've loved . . . I don't want to lose you also."

Rowan's honest confession drew Tahira back to the stool. She regarded him with firm resolve. "You won't lose me, Row," she said, hands listless in her lap. "I made you a promise, remember?"

He did, and it tugged at his heart to trust in her conviction. He couldn't conceive of a life without Tahira's companionship. She had become his one constant—much as Naja had been in his younger years. But this risk she took to remain steadfast at his side could end in ruin.

"This curse could drain more life from you," he said, his stomach turning at the possibility. "I don't know if my heart could endure another blow. Could yours?"

"Even if my heart breaks, I'll never abandon you." Tahira blushed, and a sincere truth glistened in her eyes. "I love you far too much."

Her tender confession soothed Rowan's soul like a warm, ocean breeze.

Moved by her resiliency, Rowan summoned the will to do likewise. He tied off the woven cord and placed it in her palm. "This is a braided cord, a weaving together of people and memory. Wear it so you know, without a doubt, you never have to be alone again."

Tahira admired the braided thread. "What's it say?"

"I love you"—his face and neck surged with heat as he spoke those pivotal words—"and, um, other things."

"Other things?" Her ardent smile illuminated his darkening room. "Won't you tell me?"

Rowan grinned. "I'll leave the rest for you to imagine."

Rowan rose from his stool, feeling far less guilty and ragged. He splashed water on his face from the bowl on the end table, dried off, then moved with renewed determination from his bedchamber and into the night. Tahira wove the token of love into her hair and joined him. Despite the scare back in his room, her face didn't reveal a flicker of misgivings.

Burning skies, she is steadfast to a fault.

They stood beneath the stars, which twinkled like lodes of opals. The full moon cast silver light upon their faces.

Rowan scanned the moonlit fields and crags, thinking back upon Tahira's earlier statement.

"When you lose something good, it shakes you enough so when you find it again, you don't let go."

In that moment, he fully grasped his many blessings. Despite Zamara's intention for his curse, he was surrounded by all manner of good—his grandfather's legacy, a prosperous mine, loyal workers, and an unwavering companion who had every reason to stay far from his reach yet remained by his side.

Tahira peered up at him. "What's on your mind?"

"You mean, beyond the curse siphoning life from your body?"

Her teasing gaze eased his mind. "Yes, beyond that."

Rowan smiled and let himself relax. "You said when you find something good, you don't let go."

Tahira nodded. "I think I phrased it differently, but yes—and?"

"This place is something good as well," Rowan said, admiring the landscape given to him. "This land Rahn cultivated, I'll not relinquish it for generations to come."

"Generations, huh?" Hope glimmered as starlight through Tahira's eyes. An earnest wish Rowan read like weavescript. She seemed to dream of the future already—their future. The one free of the curse, when their love and friendship could truly blossom.

"Yes, generations," he said, desiring to take hold of her hands. After what happened in his room, he reined in the impulse and clasped his hands behind his back. "All that stands in our way is my curse."

"Not for long." Her eyes held a determined fire—one that ignited his belief. "I've every hope your detestable curse will be vanquished by the year's end."

"Does that include having hope in Akaran?"

Tahira's silver brow furrowed. "You just had to bring him up."

"Well, my plan does depend on him," Rowan reminded.

She sighed. "Then I suppose I can muster a meager amount of hope in that reptile, but only if it makes you happy."

"I'm already happy," he answered with a smile. "I have you."

Now, if only Akaran would come through for him. Everything depended on his brother having a miraculous paradigm shift. Not the brightest of hope, but even the dimmest could result in a breakthrough.

CHAPTER 24
BURIED SECRETS

Akaran's mining exploits were well underway. Workers flooded to the mine, with many turned away. Akaran hired the miners who came from Iron Crossing on the spot, and from them, he learned valuable information. Rahn Myras had died, months earlier than Adelkar predicted. Akaran informed his uncle of Myras's demise at their next shared meal.

Adelkar's jubilation was written all over his face. "At last, we're rid of that thorn in our side. Your little brother must be quite forlorn. His curse has claimed another soul. And I hear you've acquired quite a number of his workers."

"Myras's death was certainly the catalyst. Again, a boon for me."

"Seems you're having all the luck, Nephew," Adelkar said, with the barest hint of envy.

Akaran pretended he detected no avarice in his uncle's statement. "You still mean to seize Iron Crossing from Rowan, yes?"

"All in good time. I have a notion or two. Though, with Myras having made his grandson his legal heir, I'll have to rely on intimidation."

In other words, Zamara would get involved.

"Is there anyone special in his life?" Adelkar asked with an earnest smile.

"Just a foolish girl," Akaran said, remembering the way she'd mouthed off to him.

"A girl, eh? Very interesting." Adelkar sank back into his chair, fingers tented together against his thin lips. "That could be useful indeed."

Akaran stood from the table and chugged the last bit of his beverage. "Enjoy your plotting, Uncle. I have work at the mine to keep me occupied."

With all the labor it took to get Castle Crag operational, Akaran hadn't given his half-brother's offer any consideration. He hadn't even told Ravel about it either. Keeping the matter close to his chest ensured no stray word reached his uncle's or aunt's ears, not until he could ascertain the real story for himself.

Of course, his delay in the venture didn't prevent Ravel from turning into an irksome pest.

"Have you checked those records yet?" Ravel asked for the thirtieth time.

"No, I haven't," Akaran snarled, scribbling his signature at the bottom of a purchase order for more coal and firestone. He handed the form off to his mine captain before whirling on his friend. "Your constant pestering isn't going to make it happen any faster. Rummaging through my uncle's things takes planning and forethought—"

"Which you aren't an expert at."

Akaran scowled. "My usual impulsive way would likely get me caught. It's why I'm waiting on a safe clearing. Uncle Adelkar has been keeping more and more to his study, almost as if he's onto me."

Ravel cocked his brow. "Are you sure you're not being paranoid?"

Akaran grabbed his forehead, massaging the tension lines. "Curses, I don't know. I feel like the atmosphere has shifted ever since I received my inheritance."

"Ah, now that does sound like a troubling piece of information. And it tells me one thing: Your uncle is waiting for you to make a move—to see whether or not you'll be satisfied with this bone he has thrown you. If you decide to press deeper, who knows what could happen."

Akaran forced out a nervous breath. "You're not swaying me to investigate by saying that."

"What's the worst that could happen?"

"I could get cursed—that's what!"

"Hm, I suppose there's that to consider." Ravel shrugged. "Only you can decide if the truth is worth the risk or not."

His ever-direct-and-blunt friend was right, and it gnawed at Akaran day and night. There was only one thing to be done. He had to look.

The day Akaran had set his mind to investigate, a note came for him from Castle Crag, bidding him to come at once. Hopefully, there hadn't been another collapse of one of the shafts. It had happened on their opening week, injuring several miners. New timber had been ordered to replace the rotten wood.

The mine captain would've mentioned if there was an accident. So, what could be so urgent? Maybe they struck a more keenly lode in the lower levels. Akaran left in a hurry, forgoing breakfast. He swung by Ravel's home and insisted his grumbling friend accompany him.

As soon as they arrived, they saw the mine captain, Joah, pacing back and forth outside the entrance. He nervously combed his large worker hands through his thick, curly hair, then squeezed his linen cap between his palms.

This can't be good, Akaran thought, nearing the unusually jittery mine captain.

"Baron, there's something you need to see," Joah said, his voice tense and troubled.

"Is it the lode?" Akaran asked.

"No, it isn't that." Joah scratched his dirty scalp before shoving his cap back on his frizzy head. "We, uh, found two dead bodies..."

Akaran's brows rose. He never expected news of that nature. "How dead are we talking here?" he asked the mine captain. "Dead, as in recently deceased, or dead for years?"

"Dead for years, I'd have to say."

"Now, isn't this exciting?" Ravel said with an amusing glint in his red eyes. "I'm thrilled you forced me to skip breakfast for this. Who knew your mine also doubled as a tomb?"

"Apparently, mining brings with it many strange surprises," Akaran retorted, folding his arms.

"Come see for yourselves," Joah said, moving toward the entrance. "I'll warn you—it's not a pretty sight."

Akaran and Ravel followed at once to a deep level, where a fissure was carved out of the rock face. Crammed within was a pair of skeletal bodies with limbs twisted together like aged vines. Tattered and dusty clothes hung loosely over brittle bones.

"We were hammering in this area when the wall crumbled, exposing these remains," Joah explained. "Spooked two of the miners pretty bad."

"I'll bet," crowed Ravel, who didn't appear to be revolted in the least by the grotesque find. He stepped closer to the fissure and ran his hand over the soft rock. He rubbed his fingers together, scrutinizing the substance. "No wonder the rock gave way. This is far denser sediment than the surrounding rock."

The mine captain stared with astonishment. "Are you suggesting this was a fake wall?"

"Yes, precisely." Ravel flicked the dust from his fingertips. His eyes glinted with conspiracy. "My guess is these bodies were purposely concealed here in the hopes they'd never be found."

Akaran stared at the remains, his fingers cupped over his mouth. The sight of their weathered bones, nonexistent noses, and empty eye sockets turned his stomach. "Any idea who they were?"

"We thought you might know, as this is your land." The mine captain turned and pointed. "Although, this could be helpful: The male there is wearing a signet ring."

Had no one thought to remove it beforehand? All eyes turned to Akaran, as if this task ought to fall to him.

Akaran swallowed his revulsion and approached the body. Cringing, he broke off the brittle finger and pulled the ring free. He held it up close, studying the ring's crest: two obelisks flanking a triangular crag. In a way, the image reminded him of a castle silhouette.

"Recognize it?" Joah asked.

Akaran shook his head. "No, but I've got a sinking suspicion that'll need confirming. Cease all hammering in this vicinity until I say otherwise. And tell no one about these bodies. I want it kept quiet. Conceal the fissure with an iron slate if you have to."

"How do I keep something like this quiet?" Joah asked, his tone testy. "Word of the bodies is already spreading through the mine!"

Akaran stepped up to his distressed mine captain and gave him a stern look. "As the mine captain, you'll think of something. But if you need an idea, here's mine: I'll cut wages if this story gets out, starting with yours."

Joah composed himself, then nodded. "That'll work fine, baron."

Akaran turned to his friend. "Ravel, we're leaving."

They raced out of the mine, and when they were alone by their horses, only then did Ravel open his mouth to speak. "Are we going where I think we're going?"

"If you're thinking Kamand House, then yes." Akaran glanced at the ring once more before securing it in his pocket. Driving a kick to his horse's flank, he raced to his grandparents' abandoned manor.

AKARAN AND RAVEL DISMOUNTED BENEATH THE MANOR'S LONG, angular shadow. The stone-crafted home was a dreary sight. Neglected for nearly two decades, the stone was cracked in structural places, and the filmy windows were as black as tar. The yard's vegetation grew and coiled as it pleased. Savage brambles and twisted vines clawed their way against and up the walls. The nearby stable had a dilapidated roof, and the old hay inside exuded a pungent, musty odor.

Akaran's nostrils recoiled at the stench as he moved toward the manor's heavy wooden doors.

"Ah, so this is the infamous place where your whoring mother lived, eh?" Ravel reached for the handle and gave it a pull, but the doors didn't budge. "Hm, so, how do we get in, Aka?"

"We break the doors down if we must."

"Always resorting to violence before common sense," Ravel chided, before asking the obvious question. "Your uncle didn't give you the key to this place?"

Akaran shook his head. "No, it didn't come with ownership of the mine, which means there must be something inside he doesn't want me to see."

Ravel's grin was mocking. "Good to see you finally using that brain of yours."

Akaran rolled his eyes. "Shut your mouth and help me find a beam to ram these doors."

"Before we go that taxing route, let's see where a bit of tinkering gets us." Ravel returned to his horse and retrieved a small, woven bundle from the saddle.

"What is that?" Akaran asked, doubting whatever his friend had in mind.

"Hopefully, our way inside." Ravel unwrapped the bundle, revealing a pair of slender instruments. "Step aside, Aka, and watch me work."

With an irritated growl, Akaran moved out of his friend's way. Ravel stooped and inserted the two slender prongs into the keyhole. He tilted them at various angles, his brows knitted.

Akaran watched his friend, huffing. "I had no idea you'd learned the art of lockpicking, Rav."

"I'm by no means an artist in this skill," Ravel said with pride, "but I did break into my father's lockbox on occasion. Ah, as well as stealing into my sister's room just to give her a good scare when she was locking lips with the manservant. Curses, did I ever hold that one against her. The things I could get her to do for me to ensure my silence."

Akaran grunted with amusement. "Why doesn't that surprise me?"

"Like I always say: People are prone to secrets and schemes. Where something is locked, you'll often find the hidden truth." A quiet click came from the keyhole. "Ah, wonderful." Ravel straightened and threw open the door, gesturing with a flick of his wrist. "After you, Aka."

Akaran moved into the dark entryway. Faint light pooled from the windows, hardly enough illumination for them to sleuth their way around. Ravel took out a flint tool and lit a pair of tarnished candelabras. He kept one and handed the other to Akaran. The warm light revealed the layers of dust on every piece of furniture and the cobwebs clinging to the corners of the stone ceiling.

"If you find an image of the Kamand Crest," Akaran said, his squeaky steps echoing in the silent house, "give a holler."

Ravel stepped into a separate room, while Akaran approached the zigzagging staircase. He studied the various images painted on the stone, searching for the crest. After passing several depictions of historical battles, he came across a painting of a man and a woman holding a young girl on her lap—Zurie more than likely. The man's left hand rested on the woman's shoulder, and there he caught sight of the familiar ring.

He pulled it from his pocket and rested it against its painted copy. "Ravel, come to the staircase. I found the ring."

Ravel dashed up to Akaran, and he took a comparative look for himself. "They're one in the same, no mistake. I saw the same crest down in the dining hall above the hearth." He shot Akaran one of his famous conspiratorial looks. "You know what this means, don't you?"

Akaran sucked in a quick breath. "That someone killed Zurie's parents and had their bodies concealed in their mine."

"If I recall correctly," Ravel said, leaning against the stair rail, "that isn't the story Adelkar fed you."

Akaran shook his head. "He told me he'd pressured them into selling the mine—that it'd been in their best interest—in light of Zurie's scandalous affair."

"A convenient story, albeit steeped in a dark lie." Ravel's expression showed unwavering conviction. "Now that we've discovered the bodies of your grandparents, wouldn't it be fair to say Adelkar had them murdered instead?"

Akaran didn't want to even consider it. Adelkar was a shrewd iron monger, quick to pounce on any opportunity to widen his purse and influence, but murdering Zurie's parents? Why go through the hassle when a simple curse or actually buying their land would have sufficed? He was missing a key component.

Ravel's pushy eyes were on him. "I see you aren't biting at my conspiracy. You know what will give you the answers you seek."

Yes. Adelkar's records.

"Now's the time to have a look, Aka. Without delay."

Akaran couldn't put it off a day longer, not after discovering the Kamands' remains. "There's just one thing I need before I do," Akaran said. "Show me that trick with the lockpicks."

AKARAN WAITED UNTIL THE WEE HOURS OF THE NIGHT—WHEN even his nighthawk uncle surrendered to bed—to creep from his room. He ventured through the quiet hall and down into Adelkar's study without the aid of candlelight. A smoldering fire with glowing embers still burned in the hearth. He struck a flintstone, lighting the candlesticks on his uncle's desk, and set to digging.

He didn't waste his time with the unlocked drawers. Anything secretive would be locked safe and secure. Crouching on his knees, he removed the lockpicking tools from his robe's pocket and inserted the ends into the keyhole. He tweaked and angled the two prongs for several anxious minutes. Clearly, Ravel made this look far easier than it was, but his instruction gave Akaran a much better chance at gaining entry.

After another long, frustrating moment, the locking mechanism finally sprang loose, and Akaran pulled open the drawer. He found parchments lying within and seized hold of them, flipping from one to the next. Most were deeds or purchase agreements to the mines Adelkar acquired, and the prices he paid for them. Not entirely secretive information; Akaran was privy to the more recent deals. Yet none revealed the purchase transaction for Castle Crag, as Adelkar alleged. Akaran was growing more and more convinced it never took place—hence the murders.

Getting to the bottom of the stack, the parchments held nothing applying to his inheritance.

This can't be all there is!

He gnawed on his bottom lip and shoved the parchments back in their slot. As he did so, his knuckles banged against the wood, creating a hollow knock. His spike of frustration lifted, replaced with curious suspicion. He studied the drawer's bottom, tapping it again, then pressed his fingers firmly against one of the corners. The wooden slat dipped.

A false bottom? Of course! Just like in the mine with the false wall. More smoke and mirrors to conceal Uncle's secrets.

Akaran removed the slat and "struck iron." A leather sleeve held a small stack of old, yellowed parchments. He combed through them, finding two different wills. One named Akaran as inheritor of Keliss House and it's adjoining mine; the other named Adelkar. Another discrepancy emerged—the dates on the wills. They showed a three-year separation—one before Akaran's birth, the other two years after, occurring not long before his father's death.

Adelkar must have learned Kainan changed his will and hated the idea of losing out on everything he hoped to possess. When Kainan died, Adelkar must have switched the wills and presented only the older one to the magistrate. Why then keep the will naming Akaran? As a precaution? In case he needed to rely on it in the future to make a forgery? Whatever the reason, the documents proved Ravel's suspicions.

Uncle, you lying, thieving snake! You stole what belonged to me.

Adelkar had taken advantage of Kainan's death, deviously inserting his control over all the Keliss property. The only ones who could have contested his actions were the Kamands and Zamara. Why didn't his aunt stop Adelkar? And what of the Kamands? Did they contest the will's legitimacy, giving Adelkar cause to murder them?

That has to be it.

Akaran's body shook, as did the parchments in his hands. He released his breath in a slow exhale, wrestling with this undeniable truth. Though his mind fought it, his heart and body knew without a doubt. His uncle had betrayed him with the lowest form of treachery.

"What are you doing snooping in Adelkar's desk?"

Akaran froze. His aunt stood in the door's shadow. Her menacing eyes were two glowing embers in the dark study. Her wiry hair resembled a nest of spider webs.

Akaran didn't bother concealing his actions; his aunt wouldn't believe any lie he told. And so, he held up the wills. "Did you know about this?"

Zamara grunted. "I may be a Conjurer, but even I can't read that scribble from this distance."

Glowering, Akaran closed the gap between them and thrust the wills in front of Zamara's face. "Take a good look, Aunt. This one names me as heir, not Adelkar; while this older one—dated before I was born—names him. Uncle switched the wills! He made it so he could have Keliss House. All of this belongs to me, not him!"

Zamara flicked her eyes between the two parchments. "Well, isn't he a sneaky devil."

Akaran paused. "So, you didn't know?" He found that hard to believe.

Zarama sniffed, thrusting the pages away from her face. "It didn't concern me. So long as I have a roof over my head, I'm content."

He gave his great aunt a cold, hard glare. "You may be, but I'm not."

Zamara whirled on the challenge in his tone. "What are you going to do, Akaran? Confront Adelkar? Force him to amend the will in your favor?"

Akaran fought against the unease crawling up his throat. "You make it sound like I shouldn't."

Zamara shrugged her bony shoulders. "It all depends on how great a fight you want on your hands."

Akaran leaned his head in close. "That doesn't frighten me, Aunt. I'm adept at fighting with my hands. If Uncle wants to fight me for it, I'll take on the match."

Zamara ran her tongue deviously over her wicked lips. "And what if he asks me to curse you instead?"

Akaran froze, a jolt of fear spearing his gut. "You wouldn't."

"Wouldn't I?" Her taut, wizened face held an indifferent mask. "A curse is a curse to me. It doesn't matter to me who receives my spellcraft."

"You heartless hag!" Akaran spat. For a fleeting moment, he thought of wringing her scrawny neck. "Curses, I'm your nephew!"

Zamara's eyes narrowed, sending chills through Akaran's spine.

"Don't forget: Half of your blood belongs to that conniving trollop," she said. "A fact that has never once escaped me."

Akaran was taken aback by the venom in her voice—the disdain evident in her dark gaze. "If you loathed Zurie's blood so much, why didn't you curse me along with her and my half-brother?"

"Because Adelkar bid me not to."

Akaran didn't understand. "Why would he protect me from you, if all along he planned to deny me my full inheritance?"

"That is a question you'll have to ask him. But I would be very careful if I were you. You've only begun to unearth a dark secret. Tread wisely."

Akaran tightened his fists. "Is that a threat, Aunt?"

"Take it as you think most prudent." Zamara took her leave leisurely, like a snake slithering back into the shadows.

Zamara's demeanor—and her words—left Akaran in a troubled stupor. He needed to unravel what he'd discovered from the one person who'd tell it to him straight.

CHAPTER 25
PARTNERS

At dawn, Akaran rode to Ravel's home. He'd left Adelkar's study only a few hours prior, not bothering with sleep. With his agitation, it would've been a losing match. Eager to avoid his uncle and aunt, he made himself scarce, leaving the manor without a soul taking notice.

As a regular at the Grise home, Akaran was freely admitted. He hastened his way to Ravel's bedchamber and gave the door a most urgent knock. A cranky voice within hurled expletives.

Ravel opened the door, his brows bent in a perturbed slant, his moppy hair in wild disarray. "What's with this gross intrusion?"

"Good, you're awake. I have news to share."

Ravel's sleepy eyes fully adjusted, widening with recollection. "Curses, if you're at my door this early, it must be terrible."

"I'll tell you all about it over our match."

"Oh, great, because who doesn't love waking up to a boxing match?" Ravel stifled a yawn and slapped his cheeks in an apparent attempt to further rouse himself. "Let me get my hand wrappings. I'll meet you in the sporting hall."

Akaran marched to the western-most room in the house. The sporting hall boasted plenty of window light, and the Grise collection of ancient weapons and armor. A fitting setting for dueling and pugilism. Akaran removed his tabard and prepared his leather wrappings, winding them over each of his hands. He readied a stance and loosened his arms with a series of jabs and crosses.

Ravel strolled into the hall, wearing a loose sleeved V-collared tunic and trim-fitting black pants with a fluttering blue sash around his waist. "So, let's hear it, Aka." He put his hands up in a right arm forward guard—the opposite of Akaran's stance. "What did you uncover?"

Akaran told his friend everything, sparing no detail. No longer loyal to his family, he unveiled the truth of his aunt's background as a Conjurer, which Ravel found highly amusing.

"I always knew there was something creepy about that old crone. Curses, no wonder you came to me in need of a match." Ravel guffawed behind his raised guard. "Family. Who would we be without them?"

Akaran grunted. "Someone we wouldn't recognize."

The match went on, each choosing their moments to advance against the other. Thinking only of his current opponent, Akaran let his uncle's conspiracy against him fall away. If he confronted Adelkar, he couldn't behave like an irrational youth. He needed to be steely, focused, and uncompromising, as he would be in a serious match.

Ravel, on the other hand, wore a most unserious expression.

No doubt reveling in his conspiracies having been proven true.

Ravel kept his smug grin plastered to his face, even when Akaran landed a flurry of punches.

"Your aim is much improved, Aka. It's been months since you fought this well."

"I've found my focus."

"And all it took was for your world to be inverted," Ravel said with apparent sarcasm before his tone turned grave. "If your aunt and uncle could do this to you—not to mention kill your grandparents—I think it's fair to say you're in mortal danger."

There he goes with his worst-case imaginings.

"As long as I continue to reflect gratitude, I don't think they'll move against me." Akaran said. "Besides, they don't know I've learned of my grandparents' murders."

Ravel shrugged, rolling his shoulder with one of Akaran's jabs. "Well, it's your funeral—I mean your life to risk."

"Look, I'll be careful," Akaran said, bringing his arms in close. "I'll be my usual self in person—ingratiating myself to Adelkar, however galling it may be—while in secret, I'll be forging my own plot."

"To do what?"

"Get rid of them both. It's time I paid my half-brother another visit." Akaran lowered his fists and unfurled his hand wrappings. He'd spent the three hours before dawn coming to his decision. Once he met with Rowan, there was no going back.

"Is that on today's agenda?" Ravel asked, fetching glasses of water.

"Yes. I'm heading to Iron Crossing after I leave here." Akaran chugged the water in one long gulp, and then slipped his black tabard over his scarlet tunic.

"Well, since you'll have your hands full," Ravel said between measured sips, "I'll head to the mine and make sure Joah did as told and concealed those hideous bodies away from spying eyes."

"Mind your tongue, Rav. Those are my grandparents you're talking about."

Imagining their deaths disturbed Akaran. Did they die together? Facing death wrapped in each other's arms, as their corpses revealed? The ghastly sight burned in his mind. Their bodies belonged in a burial mound within the Kamands' ancestral grounds, not stuffed in a fissure and forgotten.

Adelkar would pay for their desecration—and not only that, but for eighteen years of deceit and thievery.

AKARAN RODE UP THE HILL TO IRON CROSSING SHORTLY BEFORE noonday. He caught many of the tenants entrenched in their laborious tasks. Rowan's pert companion hoed a furrow in the garden. A lavender headband kept her hair from her face. When she spotted him, her face flashed with shock. She dropped her hoe in haste and approached, wiping her hands on her waist apron.

"You there, girl. Find my half-brother for me," Akaran ordered. "I need to speak with him."

The girl didn't budge. "I'm the mistress here, so don't command me as if I were *your* maidservant."

Akaran glared at her, not hiding his irritation. "I'd apologize, *girl*, if I thought it would soften your bite."

"Go on and give it a try, *reptile*," she retorted, folding her arms across her chest. "You'd do well to show some civility—that is, if you want to see Rowan."

Where did this girl get off telling him what to do? She was all fire and quips today, showing none of the coy behavior he remembered from their first meeting.

Akaran flattened his lips, putting a latch on his anger. "Forgive my rudeness, *mistress*. May I see my half-brother?"

The girl mulled it over, tapping her finger against the corner of her lips—lips which lacked a pink hue. "I'll send for him on one condition: you vow not to start an altercation."

Akaran dropped from his horse and took a moment to size up the feisty specimen before him. "You're quite protective of Rowan, aren't you?"

"Only when there's a cold-hearted reptile on the prowl." Despite her petite frame, she didn't cower before him.

For some strange reason, he *liked* the gumption in her spirit. "You think me a reptile?"

Her gutsy red eyes affirmed her accusation. "I've yet to see you behave otherwise."

"Then let this be a start," Akaran said, forcing a smile. "I won't harm Rowan. I only came to talk."

She searched his face for an awkward length of time. "Wait here."

She disappeared into the mine and returned above ground some time later with Rowan. She hovered nearby, arms folded, on guard, and she wasn't alone. Two other miners—whose behemoth frames made her look like a child—came topside to flank her, and keep a steady eye on Akaran. A clear indication everyone knew of the beating he'd given their new baron.

A rugged Rowan, with hair pulled back in a low ponytail and tunic slick with sweat, parted from the three and approached.

Akaran started the mood off light. "Your girl has an agile tongue."

"In more ways than one," Rowan said with a wry smile.

Akaran smirked in amusement. "Securing such a rare girl—curses, you're a lucky devil. I'll give you that. Know any other girls like her?"

"I'm afraid she's one of a kind." Rowan broke into a laugh. "Despite my curse, I'm a fortunate man."

"Yes, along with inheriting Myras's lands right before his untimely death." Akaran offered no condolences; it would hardly appear sincere from his lips. "I trust there are no hard feelings over your loss of miners. It was simply business. I needed all the good miners I could hire to get Castle Crag operating on a swift schedule."

"As you say, it's only business," Rowan said without hostility. "Our daily intake may have lessened, but at least I know the miners working for me are men I can trust to not harvest in greener pastures. But surely you didn't come here simply to rub your success in my face?"

"No, indeed not."

"So, why have you come?" Rowan's gaze was a gritty one.

Akaran worked his jaw before clearing his throat. "I've decided to help you break your curse. And before you get all excited, know this isn't out of brotherly compassion or anything of the like." Akaran squared his shoulders. "By helping you, you're, in a sense, helping me."

"What's changed?"

"Pretty much everything." Akaran blew a sharp breath. "My uncle and aunt have orchestrated things to keep me under their thumb—a place I despise now that I'm in possession of the facts."

"Which are?"

Akaran paced away from Rowan, diving into the information he gleaned. "Adelkar stole my inheritance from me after my father's death, using an old version of his will. He then seized control of the Kamands' property by 'supposedly' forcing them to sell. But there's no record of the sale anywhere in Adelkar's records. All I ever saw was the estate's deed, which my uncle had in his name. He told me Zurie's parents desired to leave due to their daughter's scandal. But yesterday, I found their bodies buried behind a false wall inside

Castle Crag. Adelkar must've had them sign over the deed before killing them."

The gold flecks in Rowan's eyes brightened, as if dawning with revelation. "Wait, Zurie's parents—but that would make them . . . *my* grandparents?" He put a hand to his forehead, and a troubled sadness crossed his face. "They're dead? I had hoped they were alive somewhere, that one day I'd have the chance to meet them."

"A chance Adelkar robbed us both of." Akaran paced with fists at his sides. "Adelkar killed them—I know it was him. He killed our grandparents and swiftly took ownership of their land without contest. My uncle's well-convincing lie kept anyone from investigating their disappearance. He could then do whatever he wanted with Castle Crag."

"But now you're in possession of it," Rowan said, rubbing his temple, slow and pensive.

Akaran sniffed in contempt. "He gifted me the mine as a ruse to keep me from discovering the real truth of what's rightfully mine."

"You think he killed them solely because they could've contested the will?"

Akaran nodded. "It's my speculation, but it would have given him additional incentive—getting back at Zurie for her treachery against my father."

"There might be even more reason than that." Rowan's brows knitted, seeming to be deep in thought. "Our mother said a peculiar thing. I didn't think anything of it until now. She mentioned Adelkar often gave her 'his lingering eye' when Kainan wasn't around. It's possible your uncle had unrequited love toward our mother and harbored jealousy, coveting what his brother possessed. You wouldn't suppose Adelkar kept your inheritance from you out of spite toward his brother?"

Akaran's jaw dropped. "Curses, I don't know what to think anymore." His whole world had gone mad. All of this secretive scheming taxed his mind. "I'd always believed my father and uncle had a close relationship, but if Adelkar fancied Zurie, and my father was neglectful, as you say, then it would give him even more motive to do what he did. Adelkar must've both loved and despised Zurie and my father."

Rowan shook his head. "Sounds tormenting."

Akaran wouldn't go so far to say that. He himself had never met a girl worth pining over like a sick hound. But he could at least grasp his uncle's motives.

"I will help you seize back what is yours," Rowan said, an obvious fire in his eyes. "All you have to do is get me inside Adelkar's manor. From there, I'll handle Zamara."

"And I'll deal with Adelkar." Akaran would ensure their day of reckoning came swiftly.

"Do you have a plan for going about this?" Rowan asked.

"Haven't gotten that far yet," Akaran admitted, scratching at his temple. "Frankly, it took everything in me to sidestep my hatred of you and make this trip over here. I've given no thought to the next step."

"Then we better hash out a plan." Rowan smiled and turned his face toward the manor. "You're welcome to come inside, brother."

Akaran hesitated, taken aback by the offer. His gaze flicked toward the girl and the two large miners. "Wouldn't your pretty guard dog mind?"

"She might, but seeing as we're now partners, she'll have to set aside her prejudices as you've done."

"I haven't set them aside," Akaran said, keeping his voice terse. "I still intend to beat you up when this is all over."

Rowan frowned. "For what reason?"

"Don't have one at the moment, but I'm sure you'll give me one."

Rowan shook his head before breaking into a boisterous laugh. "That sounds like the dumbest thing I've ever heard."

Akaran glared at his half-brother. "Shall I beat you up right here and now?"

Rowan held his hands up in mock surrender. "No, thank you. I'd rather you didn't. I doubt I could rein in the curse if your fists started flying. You'd likely end up dead with your skull caved in and your brains turned to mush. But, of course, it's your choice when you'd like to extend my beating."

Akaran shuddered from head to toe. "You're right. Waiting until after your curse is gone is the sensible choice."

CHAPTER 26
HATCHING A PLOT

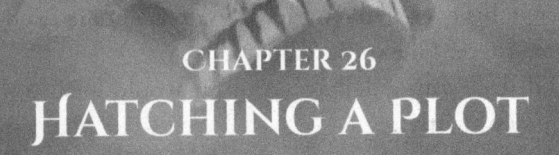

Inside the plant-teeming parlor, Rowan and Akaran chiseled out the details to remove Adelkar and Zamara from their lives.

Beforehand, Shen fussed for several minutes against showing Akaran any hospitality but finally relented his disapproval only after Rowan stressed multiple times this alliance was temporary and for the good of ending his curse. Then—without another word—Shen prepared a light nourishing fare for them to enjoy, as well as keep their minds fully engaged in their plotting.

Rowan chomped on bread and goat cheese, staring at the miracle before him. His brother was really here—a long hope coming to fruition. Though he couldn't ignore the reason it came about. Zurie's parents' murder was a traumatic shock. Yet, despite its horrible nature, their deaths played a significant role in switching his brother's allegiance. Another connection to cement their partnership.

Akaran ran his hands through his hair, breathing out a deep sigh. "I'm not one for plans. Spur-of-the-moment suits me best."

Rowan raised his brow. "Was beating me with your fists a spur-of-the-moment decision?"

Akaran made light of his brutality with a guiltless chuckle. "Er, no. I put the drug in your drink knowing I'd beat you once it took effect."

Rowan wetted his lips, finding that telling. "Ah, well then, it appears you can plot a sordid scheme after all. So, tap into your devious mind and figure out a way to stop your uncle and aunt. You know their habits, their routines—"

"Right, right, I know." Akaran nodded with a mouthful of freshly baked bread. "Zamara usually keeps to her lair in the tower. It's not hard to find. I'll draw a map of the manor's layout so you know where to head." He snagged parchment and stylus from the table and started drawing.

"What am I to expect with her?" Rowan asked, watching his brother draw rudimentary lines.

"Well, she's a crafty hag who likes to rely on tricks. Her entire lair is filled with spells, elixirs, and oozy substances I've made a point to stay away from." On his diagram, Akaran drew a circle around the tower's upper room, indicating her location.

"So, you don't truly know what she's capable of?"

"I know she's cursed hundreds of people in her lifetime," Akaran said, continuing his rendering. "She may be as ancient as bedrock, but she doesn't move like a cripple. Think of her as a serpent and attack accordingly. Strike first, before she can strike you."

Akaran finished his diagram of Keliss House and slid it forward. Rowan lifted the crude rendering and made note of the main rooms Akaran had labeled, including the room marked as Adelkar's study. It resided on the opposite side of the house from the tower. They could attack each of their targets without either hearing a sound.

"If you give Zamara the chance to speak," his brother said, "she'll throw curses or conjure spells. Either way, you'll be in for a hellish fight."

Rowan swallowed. "If Zamara uses tricks, I'll have to think of some myself." An idea sprang to mind almost immediately. "Who's a blacksmith you'd recommend?"

"That would be Garm," Akaran said, sinking his teeth into a chunk of cheese. "I've used him for the ironworks I've needed for Castle Crag. Why? You have something in mind?"

"I'm wondering if he can craft me a modified shortspear."

"I don't see why not," Akaran mumbled, engrossed in his bite like a cheese fiend. He'd consumed most of the platter on his own. "Visit his forge next time you're in Arjun."

Rowan lowered the diagram to the table and gave his brother a pointed stare. "I can't, remember? I'm outlawed."

"Curses, I forgot about that." Akaran dusted off his cheesy fingers on a cloth napkin. "Well, then, tell me what you want done, and I'll see it's made."

Rowan's brows lifted with surprise. "You're willing to do that for me?"

Akaran sneered—making it clear this was no act of kindness. "I'll help you out this one time. Don't get used to it. When it's completed, you can send one of your own people to retrieve it."

Rowan took a moment to explain what he wanted. He composed his own drawing so his brother would have an accurate representation to take to the blacksmith. As he drew, Akaran continued to feast.

Burning skies, could he eat!

Did Akaran not have a meal before this? Or maybe something else had worked up his humongous appetite? Several blemishes colored his face, signs of a possible brawl. Perhaps fighting was simply a frequent recreation of his.

Rowan finished the drawing and held it toward Akaran to admire.

His brother's lips split into a wicked grin. "This could definitely catch Aunt Zamara by surprise." Akaran took the drawing and folded it into his pocket. "Seems I'm not the only one in the family with a devious mind, eh?"

Rowan chuckled, if only to indulge his brother's jest. It was odd seeing him interact so casually without hatred marring his face or voice. It reminded Rowan of the friendly attitude Akaran displayed when they'd first met in The Red Canary. Stripped of his hatred, he wasn't such a bad person. Yes, he was still a brash and conceited hothead, but already his behavior was leaps and bounds improved from their last interaction.

"So, what's your plan for Adelkar?" Rowan asked. "Do you mean to kill him?"

"Absolutely," Akaran said without pause. "Especially if he killed our grandparents just to take their lands for himself—lands we would've inherited without his meddling." Akaran rubbed his jaw. "But there are things I need to know for certain before he dies: the *real* reason why he killed our grandparents and stole my inheritance."

"I hope you get your answers." Answers Rowan also wanted to know, though not with as much fervor as his brother. "So, you'll go in, confront him, and keep him distracted while I ascend the tower and kill Zamara."

"Sounds simple enough."

"So, are we agreed on this plan?"

Akaran nodded. "Yes, indeed."

Rowan took a deep breath. "Now all that remains is to decide when to strike."

"Soon," Akaran said, rising from his seat. "With what I learned from the wills, my uncle and aunt are probably growing suspicious of me. If we let several weeks pass without any visible threat, they may lower their guards. That's when we strike."

Rowan sighed, not liking that answer. "Don't make me wait long without a word."

"Eager to be free of that curse, huh?"

"Every day is a torture you can't imagine."

"I wouldn't want to even try." Akaran snagged one more handful of cheese, then took his leave.

Tahira entered the parlor only seconds afterward, holding a pitcher of water in her hands. She moved toward the row of plants, giving them a modest watering. Ever since Rahn's death, she and Shen steadfastly cared for the house plants he'd adored.

About her shoulders, she wore the colorful wrap Rowan recently weaved for her as a handfast gift. Woven with threads of teal, coral, and ivory spaced in varying lengths, it expressed his fond desire for her in weavescript. Even though Tahira couldn't read it, he made known its message—his way of embracing her when his arms could not.

"How was the scheming?" she asked, tilting her head in his direction.

"Productive." Rowan remained at the table, studying Akaran's drawing. "We established a plan to get rid of Adelkar and Zamara."

Tahira moved to the spider plant, brushing back its long, spindly leaves. "When will this plan occur?"

"In a few weeks."

Tahira frowned. "Why the delay?"

He gave her Akaran's reasoning, but from the flutter of her white eyelashes, Tahira wasn't pleased. She set the empty pitcher on the table and released a quiet, disheartened sigh.

"I know it's not what you wanted to hear," he said. "I'm disappointed as well."

She folded her arms, drawing the shawl in more tightly. "This past month has been a struggle, you know. Most nights, I can hardly sleep. I lie in bed sick at heart. I toil in the garden daily to give my mind a distraction. It may seem like I'm keeping a composed spirit, but I fear what the curse could rob us of if it's not soon broken."

"It's not been easy for me either," he admitted, setting the drawing aside. "With fewer workers in the mine, the additional workload has given my restless mind a distraction also. Yet, in those toiling hours, my thoughts often turn toward you and the future we want together. We both suffer from this." He dug his fingers into his palms, wrestling with the yearning in his chest. "Not knowing how the curse is affecting your life is the cruelest agony my heart knows."

Her eyes misted. "When will this end, Row?"

"Soon. I promise. As hard as it seems, take joy in today. Akaran aiding me is what we've long hoped for."

She sniffled, giving her petite, ivory nose a rub. "I deemed it a fool's hope to ever expect that reptile to have a heart."

"I wouldn't say he's there yet," Rowan said.

"And do you trust him?"

Rowan paused. "I trust in his vengeful desire to take back what's his. Though selfishly motivated, his mind is in the right place, which is good enough for me. We're that much closer to breaking the curse than we were yesterday."

"You're right. This is a big moment for us." Tahira smiled. "Can I help in some way with your plot?"

"There's one thing you could do, yes." Rowan grinned, and Tahira's demeanor lightened like the morning sun. "I'm having a new spear made that I hope will give me an edge against Zamara. Akaran is taking the order to his blacksmith in Arjun. When it's completed, will you retrieve it for me?"

Tahira's smile broadened. "Of course!"

Unable to embrace, they had to make do with these shared smiles. He ached to hold Tahira close—to experience the warm embrace they shared in his room. He remembered the thrilling surge in his blood from their last kiss. The way his spirit soared away from grief. But the consequence from that wondrous connection put a dark damper on ever being so close again.

They needed this obstacle removed from their lives. Akaran's appearance today was the hope they needed to keep their spirits high.

Tahira retrieved the pitcher, and with budding curiosity asked, "What'll be special about your new spear?"

"I'll show you when I have it."

"Mm, it must possess quite the clever trick."

He grinned. "If it's crafted as I designed, it certainly will."

AKARAN ENTERED GARM'S WORKSHOP AND FOUND THE BURLY blacksmith hammering away on a hot slab of steel. A trail of billowy smoke from the forge's burning coals filtered up to the rafters. On Forge Row, the clang of iron clashing with steel was a near deafening sound. It took Akaran yelling Garm's name three times before the blacksmith lifted his head. He sported a thick goatee around his jutting chin and wore his grizzled hair tied in a topknot, mimicking the warriors of old. A long burn scar blemished the right side of his cheek.

"Well, if it isn't the new iron baron paying me a call," Garm called out over the surrounding clamor. "Need more ironworks?"

"Actually, I need you to forge something entirely different—a weapon. I have a drawing of the specifications."

Garm's singed brows lifted. He set down his hammer and wiggled his blackened fingers. "Well, let's see it."

Akaran removed the folded drawing from his pocket and handed it over.

Garm gave it a dubious once-over. "This is what you want made?" He rubbed his bristly goatee, then gave Akaran a befuddled stare. "I didn't peg you as a spear wielder."

"Oh, I'm not. The spear is for an associate of mine."

Garm's face grew even more perplexed. "I didn't think you were the sort to run errands for other people, even business associates."

Akaran folded his arms, irritated by Garm's nosiness. "This is a special case."

"It must be," Garm said gruffly.

"Well, can you make it?"

"Of course, I can make it," Garm snapped. "Don't doubt my skills." He scrutinized the drawing once more, scratching at his scar. "It'll be tricky to hollow out this section of the staff to conceal the hidden spearhead, in addition to allowing it to separate and still be sturdy enough to wield effectively. But to the eyes, it'll look like any ol' shortspear—that's the genius of it." His eyes gleamed. "It truly is cleverly designed, and it'll take time. I have a number of orders before I can set to work on it. Who do I notify when it's ready?"

"Send a notice to Iron Crossing. Someone there will retrieve it and give you payment."

Garm set the drawing on his soot-covered stool and picked up his hammer. "I have to say this is rather unorthodox. Yet, in light of our solid work history, I'll forgo the usual prepayment requirements."

"I appreciate that, and your discretion, of course."

"Discretion?" Garm repeated, as if he hadn't heard clearly enough over the noise. "This spear supposed to be a secret?"

"Let's just say I don't want anyone in my family to know about it."

"If that's how you want it. Anything else you need?"

"Well, since you're asking," Akaran said, throwing his thumb over his shoulder, "you have time to reshoe my horse? I've been running him ragged over the past month."

Garm spied the stallion and flicked his head in a nod. "For you, I'll make time." He led the horse to the trough and set to work.

Akaran took a seat outside the workshop. Noise droned about him as his mind turned toward the complex conspiracy he uncovered. He grew nervous at the thought of returning to Keliss House. How did one behave whilst in the company of someone who'd committed so egregious a crime? There was only one way: pretend like he knew nothing of the dark secret. But how long could he mask it before he wanted to claw the truth from Adelkar's deceitful mouth? A day was hard enough. Could he truly wait weeks to exact his plans? He remembered Rowan's downcast expression before their parting. It confirmed what he figured—the waiting would be aggravating.

As much as they desired to eliminate Adelkar and Zamara, great risks were involved. What if Rowan failed to kill her? Would she then curse Akaran for betraying the family? He shuddered in his chair.

Why have I only now thought of this possibility?

The answer was obvious. His desire to get revenge against his uncle and aunt for their treachery prevented him from stopping and considering the possibility of failure.

This was a fisticuff match he couldn't afford to lose, or else he'd wind up like his dead grandparents—his corpse buried behind a wall of sediment.

"Well, curses, how lucky is this!" a greasy voice hollered. "It's a chance meeting!"

Akaran darted his eyes and found Klay slithering over to him, his body more jittery than ever.

Must've run out of caine powder days ago.

"What're you doing here?" Klay asked with an intrusive eye. His snooping, scabby nose turned up as he scrutinized the forge.

"Relax, Klay. I'm only getting my horse reshod. Not everything is a tale for your lips to relay."

Klay sniffed, his listless fingers twiddling. "Least you remembered to reshod 'em in good timing. Unfortunately, you missed our meeting."

Akaran's brain scrounged to remember. "Did I?"

"Was set for last night. I waited at The Red Canary for over an hour, but you never showed."

Last night, he was hunkered inside his room waiting to raid Adelkar's desk—a far more important task than hearing the latest prattle from his informant. "I had my hands busy with more pressing matters, Klay."

The twitchy informant scratched his oily scalp. "I thought information on your half-brother was always the most pressing."

"You'd be surprised what else could take its place," Akaran mumbled under his breath.

Oh, how the world could shift so dramatically in one day. The half-brother he once loathed and wished dead was now an allied partner in the revenge plot against his family. Could the irony get any more laughable? Fate was certainly having a good guffaw at his expense.

"Well, I can give you what I learned now, boss."

"That's really not necessary." Akaran waved his hand. "I'm not—"

Klay mistook his gesture—either that, or he didn't hear Akaran—and broadcasted his news. "Word from Iron Crossing is your half-brother has got himself handfasted to the fair maiden residing at the manor."

Interesting. Rowan hadn't mentioned a word about it. Before yesterday, such news would've irked Akaran. He would've droned on for hours about what utter fools they were to handfast whilst Rowan remained cursed. But his outlook had altered. Now he understood why the girl insisted he address her as mistress. Being handfasted to the baron essentially made her the matron of the manor.

Curses, I really shoved my fist in my mouth with her.

"How long have they been handfasted?" Akaran asked, feigning eager interest.

"Going on about a month now. Happened right around Rahn Myras's death. If you ask me, she's the surefire way to get back at your half-brother. It's the kind of delicious details you've been waiting on—right, boss?"

"I have, haven't I?" Now that he heard it from Klay's warped lips, his obsessive loathing sounded ridiculously juvenile.

"Job's done," Garm announced, walking the horse over to Akaran. "This feller is all shod and ready for riding."

Akaran took the reins from Garm, paid him, and made to mount, when Klay snagged at his sleeve.

"Hey, I told you what I knew. Now give me my caine powder."

Akaran shook Klay's hand free. "I don't have any on me."

Klay's limbs squirmed in fitful agitation. "I'm out and need it bad, boss."

"Look, I'll see you get some. But it isn't a priority of mine." Akaran mounted his horse, eager to be rid of the slimy worm. "Oh, and you can stop spying on my half-brother for the foreseeable future."

Klay's brows twitched. "Why's that?"

"I'm moving on with my life and growing up."

Klay snickered at the statement. "Mining making a man out of you, eh?"

"That and more, Klay." Akaran clicked his teeth and rode off.

That and more.

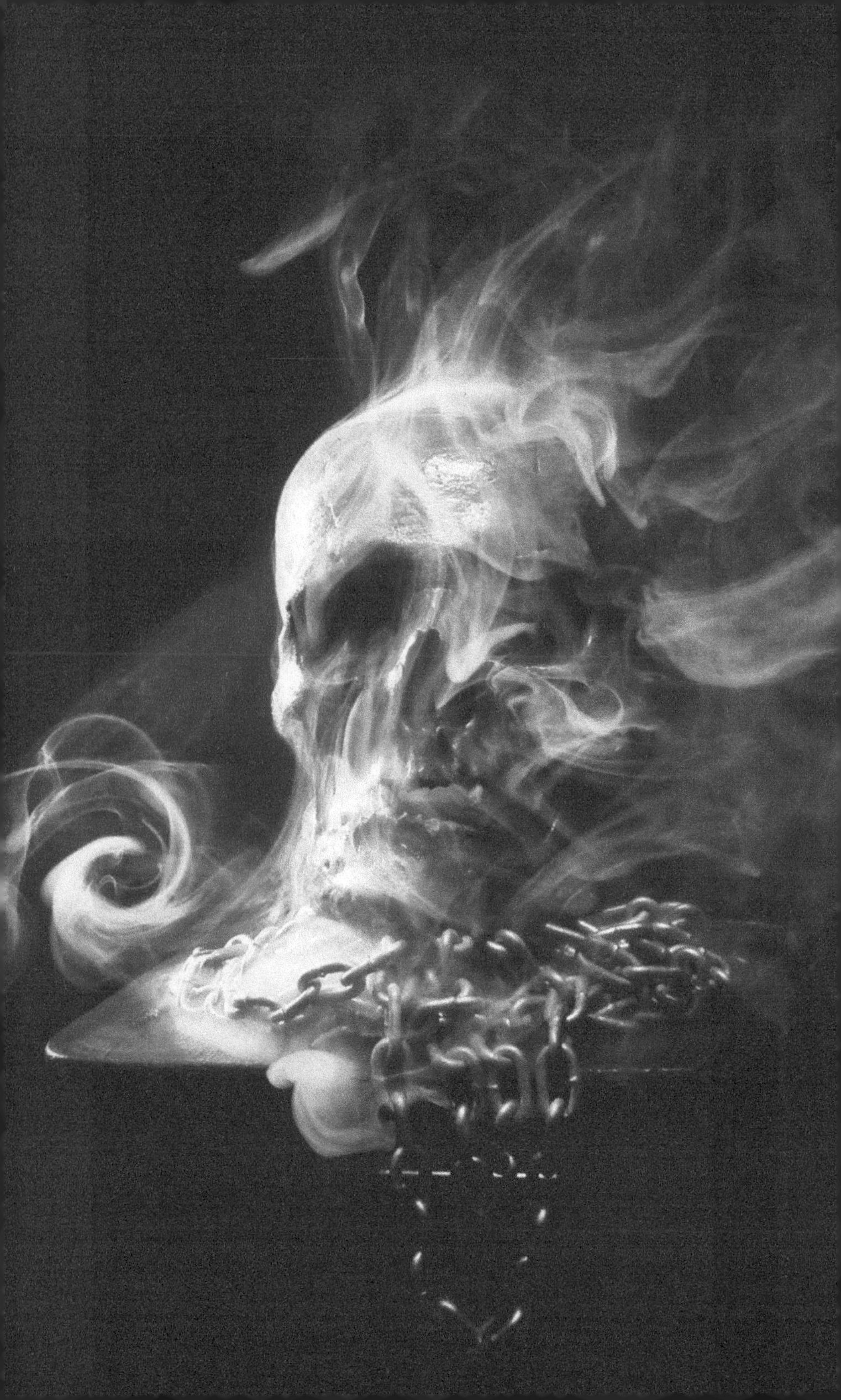

CHAPTER 27
INGRATIATING SYCOPHANT

Akaran didn't know what to expect when he returned to Keliss House as evening set. He crept into the main hall, anticipating an ambush. Instead, his uncle bent at the dining table having supper. Aunt Zamara wasn't around—normal behavior for her. She so rarely dined downstairs with them, preferring to eat her meals in her lair, where she wouldn't be interrupted.

Adelkar spotted him and waved Akaran over. "Come, join me, Nephew. You look wearied by the day's toils." He called for the scullery maid to bring a plate of food for Akaran.

This should be interesting.

Akaran approached without a show of reservation. He couldn't afford to give his uncle any cause for suspicion. "I'm weary indeed, Uncle," he said, taking a seat.

"Here, have some wine. It'll ease your mind." Adelkar filled the silver goblet and slid it toward Akaran. "It's your favorite vintage."

Akaran's suspicion soared. If Adelkar was serving Akaran's preferred drink, did that mean he suspected something? Zamara must've told him about the wills, but knowing Adelkar, he wasn't about to show his hand.

Akaran lifted the goblet to his lips, pretending to drink, but didn't swallow an ounce. He wasn't about to drink anything offered by Adelkar. There was no telling if it'd been drugged.

The maid brought his meal, and despite his riled nerves, Akaran couldn't refuse to eat. That would be far too suspicious, as Akaran never skipped meals if he could help it. Since the maid brought him the plate, he doubted she'd tampered with it.

Adelkar cut a piece of his half-eaten pork and forked it into his mouth. "How are things progressing at the mine?"

"Very well, Uncle. I think you'd be impressed by our recent haul."

"The lode shows no sign of petering, then?"

"Not at all." Akaran sliced into the tender pork, taking a meaty bite. "We've embarked upon a new level in hopes of increasing our intake from last month."

"That's excellent to hear." Adelkar's praise lacked gusto. "Who knew that derelict mine would prove so prosperous?"

"Well, surely you knew it was prosperous already, Uncle. I mean, why else would you have purchased it from the Kamands in the first place? You wouldn't waste marks on a sinking mine, even to get rid of Zurie's parents."

Adelkar ceased his chewing and stared at him. He held the unflinching stare for a long moment, then continued chewing once more. He sipped from his wine. "What do you mean by 'get rid of'?"

Akaran took another bite, chewing casually, like he meant nothing sinister by it. "Well, it's no secret you hated Zurie. You forcing the Kamands to sell was simply a way to get revenge against her parents. With them quitting the country, you were able to revel in your shrewd victory. Quite the genius scheme, Uncle."

"Hm, you think so?" Adelkar held his goblet gingerly between his fingers. "Well, now that you have the mine firmly underway, I'd love to come and take a look at your operation."

Akaran almost choked on his pork. "You would?"

Curses, this is bad.

He couldn't let Adelkar visit the mine. If he saw the false wall exposed, he'd know Akaran was onto him. "Now isn't exactly the best time, Uncle. We had a tunnel collapse the other day, and so the lowest levels aren't accessible."

Adelkar's eyes narrowed. "I thought you said everything was going well at the mine?"

"It is. The collapse was only a small setback. It hasn't halted our production."

"When might you have this tunnel cleared?"

"I'll have to ask my mine captain."

"He didn't give you an estimated timetable?"

"I didn't ask."

Adelkar made a chiding noise with his teeth. "Nephew, as the Iron Baron, you should've inquired. It's only obvious—"

"Give me a break, Uncle," Akaran grumbled, clanging his fork down against his plate. "I'm new at managing a mine. I can't think of everything."

"Of course. You're quite right." Adelkar's voice turned smugly condescending. "How careless of me to hound you like an informant. I thought you were more equipped to handle such obstacles than I gave you credit. My mistake."

Akaran scowled inwardly at the slight in Adelkar's words.

He's trying to diminish my confidence in my abilities.

"I'll get a report from Joah and let you know the verdict."

"Please do. I've not stepped foot in that mine for eighteen years. I'm dying to see what you've done with it."

His uncle's curious choice in words unsettled Akaran. Each bite of food was harder to chew. Tomorrow, he would visit Castle Crag and make sure his grandparents' murder remained secret.

EARLY THE NEXT MORNING, AKARAN RODE ONCE AGAIN TO Ravel's home and made his way to his friend's bedchamber. This time when he rapped at the door, Ravel hurled something against it, uttering, "Curses, not again."

Footsteps tramped toward the door, and the door flew open. Ravel tied his robe around himself as he kicked a boot with his bare foot. "For the love of iron, what is it this time?"

"We have a problem," Akaran said, placing his hand against the doorframe. "My uncle wants to visit the mine."

Ravel's eyes widened with alarm. "That's not a problem, Aka. That's a *big* problem. He sees the slate covering that wall, and he'll know in an instant his murderous secret is out."

"You don't think I know that?" Akaran snapped. His nerves in a riot, he wiped at a layer of sweat beneath his collar. "But I'm not an utter fool. I concocted a lie that should stall him off for a week."

"What was the lie?"

"That a tunnel collapsed."

Ravel smacked his palm against his forehead. "Curses! You had to say something drastic like that."

Akaran glowered. "Oh, I'm sorry I couldn't have been cleverer with my lie. It was the only thing I could think of on the spot."

Ravel pressed his fingertips to his forehead, deliberating. "Then there's only one way to handle this: We'll have to make it true."

Akaran cursed. "I was afraid you'd say that. Joah isn't going to like this." The mine captain was an uncompromising stickler for procedure and would need convincing.

"Shall I come with you to soften the blow?" Ravel said with a smirk.

"How truly useful that would be," Akaran said.

Ravel threw on his clothes, and they left at once for Castle Crag.

They arrived at the entrance with the morning's golden light still hovering along the crests of the mountains. Workers pushed several full mine carts upon the tracks to the loading zone, where a group of miners awaited to transition the ore to the wagons. Akaran surveyed the large load for the smelters to appraise and experienced a momentary rise in pleasure. But then, he remembered what needed to be done, and his spirits deflated.

Joah wasn't overseeing the loaders. It left the mine's deep belly as the only alternative. Akaran asked one of the miners on which level Joah was last seen, and he and Ravel ventured to his location. They found him working in the thirty level, not far from the false wall—keeping an ever-watchful eye. After receiving a positive production report from the mine captain, Akaran revealed his bizarre demand.

Joah blinked, like he'd misheard. "You want me to collapse a tunnel on purpose? Have you lost your mind?"

"I assure you, it's in perfect working order," Akaran said, annoyed. "I realize doing this will block us off from having access to our champion lode, but I need to take more drastic measures to ensure those bodies remain hidden."

"What's so important about them?" Joah demanded, scratching his sweaty hairline.

Akaran hesitated, trading a look with Ravel, who mouthed, *"Don't look at me."* With no help from his friend, Akaran returned his attention to the mine captain and evoked a solemn warning. "If I tell you, Joah, you'll be involved in the conspiracy."

Joah stood straighter, his hammer against his chest. "Look, I've toiled harder than any man here to get this mine turning a profit, and if I'm going to blow a hole in a perfectly good tunnel—which might I add, goes against every rule I adhere to as a mine captain—I certainly want to know why."

Ravel's lips creased into a highly amused smile. "Well, after that adamant speech, I say let him join the conspiracy."

Akaran wouldn't be so cavalier about it. This was his neck, after all. "Tell a soul about this, and I'll see you're ruined. You'll never work as a mine captain again."

Joah rolled his eyes like he heard such threats all too often. "The threat isn't necessary, baron, but I understand your need for it."

Akaran lowered his voice. "Those bodies are my grandparents. Adelkar murdered them to claim this land for himself—among other reasons. So, think what he'll do to any of us if he learns we know about it."

Joah kept silent for a moment, long enough for the information to sink in like wet sediment. "How big of a collapse do you want?"

Akaran stated the unthinkable. "Big enough so it takes weeks to clear."

Joah clicked his tongue. "I'll prepare the firestone powder right away."

JOAH DID EXACTLY AS AKARAN ASKED. HE COLLAPSED THE tunnel and prevented access to the burial site, yet paranoia plagued Akaran. He was, after all, living under the same roof as a murderer and a crafty Conjurer, who both—at any moment—could turn on him.

Sleep was elusive with dark imaginings of beating Adlekar to death only to then find Zamara lurking in wait and casting a wicked curse upon him. Routinely, Akaran woke to regard the door, making certain no dark apparition entered his room. The heightened vigilance and constant stress encroached upon his appetite, which displeased Akaran greatly as food and boxing were his only true loves.

Akaran threw on his black hooded tabard, vacated his room, and hastened down the stairs. He hoped to exit the manor without being seen. Yet, as he rounded the stairwell's bend, Adelkar stepped into view, loitering beside the front door.

Curses!

Adelkar's shrewd, red eyes pinned him in place. "I hope you weren't trying to sneak out before we could have the chance to speak."

After taking a quick composing breath, Akaran continued forward. "Of course not, Uncle. I only wanted to get a head start at the mine."

Suspicion brimmed in Adelkar's scrutinizing gaze. "Skipping breakfast again?"

"I'm not hungry."

"You're usually ravenous in the morning."

Akaran rolled his shoulders. "What can I say, Uncle? Perhaps my body is simply undergoing a change."

"Hm, perhaps." Adelkar tilted his head to the side. "But there is something different about you."

"Is there?" Hopefully it wasn't the shadows under his eyes from lack of sleep.

"It's your newfound drive for mining. I was convinced you'd throw off the leather wrappings and forfeit a month into the endeavor. But your gumption has surprised me. In fact, I don't think I've ever seen you display more diligence in anything other than pugilism."

"I'm redirecting my focus to something more productive in the long term," Akaran said, as if his redirection wasn't anything deserving praise. "You should be pleased. My success will only further the Keliss name. Isn't that what you wanted?"

Adelkar's nod was a measured one. His thin lips broke into an agreeable yet forced smile.

Akaran reached for the door handle. "So, was there something you wanted, Uncle?" he asked, pulling the door open.

"Ah, yes, I wanted to let you know I'm visiting your mine today. We'll ride there together." Adelkar strolled outside, his hands neatly clasped behind his back.

A rush of panic stole over Akaran. He dashed to follow Adelkar, who headed straight for the stable. "We haven't cleared the tunnel yet—"

"No matter. I'm sure there's plenty to see. It's a large mine, as I recall, with many sprawling levels. Show me how it's thriving." From the forceful insistence in Adelkar's voice, there was no denying him.

Ingratiate, ingratiate, ingratiate, Akaran repeated in his mind. *That ought to be my mantra.*

Akaran flashed a businesslike smile. "Certainly, Uncle. Nothing would please me more."

They retrieved their horses from the stable and set out for Castle Crag. When they arrived, Ravel stood within the loading zone alongside Joah, surrounded by mining carts ready for shipment. When his friend noticed Adelkar was with Akaran, he spun away and concealed himself behind a mining cart before he could be recognized. Joah stayed in place, gave Adelkar a quick nod, and continued on with his managerial role.

No one wanted to be near Adelkar. Akaran couldn't blame them. The less interaction with him, the better. It lessened the chance for a careless slip of the tongue.

"Looks like you have a good haul in the works," Adelkar noted, marching along the path to the entrance.

"The miners have been chiseling ore at a steady pace. I'm fortunate to have employed an experienced group."

Adelkar nodded along, half-interested. His gaze remained fixed on the mine's premier shaft. He entered, keeping hands resting at the small of his back, like he was only out for a stroll. If Adelkar endeavored to remain exempt from suspicion, Akaran would act to match.

They traveled from level to level, wandering the old, petered lodes. His uncle strolled as he pleased, a silent hawk on the prowl. Journeying to the thirty level brought them to the champion lode. The excavation remained on hold due to the tunnel's deliberate collapse. A group of miners shoveled away the debris, loading it in buckets for the slag heap.

Adelkar's disappointed glower was a telltale sign that he hadn't accomplished his one true quarry—ascertaining whether or not the Kamands' bodies were discovered. It put Akaran ill at ease.

He strangled his qualms and continued the charade. "As you can see, Uncle, we're still in the process of clearing away the rubble."

Adelkar lifted hand to chin. "What happened?"

"A miscalculation with the firestone powder brought the ceiling down. We were hoping to begin a new tunnel, branching off from this one, and then this unfortunate accident occurred."

"I trust no one was injured." Adelkar's voice feigned concern.

"Thankfully, everyone was clear of the blast."

Adelkar hovered in front of the pile of rock for a long pause. "A pity this tunnel collapsed. I would've loved to see the deeper levels."

"I don't see how they're any different from the higher levels," Akaran muttered.

"Every level has its buried treasure, Nephew. You simply have to know where to look."

"Then perhaps when the tunnel is cleared, you could lend me your expertise," Akaran said with a fixed smile. "I'm certain I could benefit from your expansive knowledge."

His uncle finally pulled his eyes from the rubble and looked at Akaran with a stoic stare. "Finally being sensible and taking me up on my offer?"

Inwardly, Akaran scowled; outwardly, he continued playing the part of a sycophant. "If I intend to be a prosperous Iron Baron, I'd do well to seek guidance from the best."

"Then you're beginning to make the right moves." Adelkar put his back to the rubble. "I've seen enough."

Akaran traveled with his uncle back to the entrance, walking alongside him until they reached their horses. Adelkar mounted his steed and took another long look at the mine in its entirety. "You've done well here, Nephew. Your father would've been proud to see you finally making something of yourself."

"And what of you, Uncle? Are you proud?" Akaran didn't even know why he asked the question. It launched unbidden from his mouth. He convinced himself he said it to take Adelkar off-guard. His uncle's eyes flickered as if it did. Yet Akaran feared the question came from a place more deeply rooted. Despite Adelkar's treachery, his uncle was the only paternal figure he'd ever known. Akaran didn't remember his father; and so, for eighteen years, Adelkar was the man to emulate. Somewhere hunkered in his masked heart, he vied to know if his uncle held any regard for him at all.

"I am proud, yes. Very proud indeed." His matter-of-fact tone held no sincerity, no truth. The words were perfunctory, as if the man was compelled to utter the praise if only to shield his indifference.

Adelkar clicked his lips and steered his horse up the path.

Once he was far from sight, Ravel wandered from the loading area to Akaran's side. "Now that he's left, I can finally breathe again."

Akaran shared the feeling. "It's a good thing we were proactive and collapsed the tunnel."

Ravel nodded in grim agreement, smoothing his floppy hair from his eyes. "It allowed us to dodge your uncle's iron fist. What happens the next time?"

"There won't be a next time, Rav. My uncle will be dead by the time the tunnel is cleared."

CHAPTER 28
AS FATE WOULD HAVE IT

The days crept on, and Rowan didn't hear a word from Akaran. The prolonged silence hung like a heavy cloud over him and Tahira. Every day, they waited for a note, a message, even a glimpse of Akaran riding up the hill. But nothing came. It was dangerous to send notes back and forth—a fact Rowan understood. The risk of it falling into the wrong hands was too great.

And so, Rowan continued the listless idling—albeit, well spent with mining, weaving, and mastering his curse.

Several days ago while Rowan toiled in the mine, chiseling loose veins of iron, he'd stumbled upon an unexpected discovery. After filling his bucket, he left his pickaxe behind, dumped the ore in the cart, and when he returned, several tendrils swirled around the helve. His jaw dropped as he stared at the wayward tentacles.

How are they doing this?

Rowan called the tendrils to him, and they scurried off the helve, rejoining the smoky wisps around his body. He didn't know how it happened or if the phenomenon was only a chance occurrence. So, of course, a flood of experiments ensued.

He spent that evening and the next lassoing the tendrils on nonliving items in the manor. And sure enough, the tendrils latched on and remained in place without his constant mental command. Even as he sat at the parlor table, the tendrils swirled around his fork, bound to the object. The peppery aroma of sizzling meat wafted from the kitchen into the parlor.

Tahira had something special planned for breakfast. Rowan smiled at the things they did to show affection to each other. The shawl and braided cord he weaved for her were such tokens. He planned to have more items crafted: jewelry was his next venture, including a significant ring.

It's what you gave a girl you fancied, Bulan had informed him yesterday evening after a long workday.

"My wife is more than happy to create such a gift when you so choose," Bulan offered when they came topside. "Just say the word! Kitra can craft whatever you want."

Rowan had put off the miner's offer long enough. "All right, Bulan, I'm saying the word. I'll hire your wife."

"Splendid!" Bulan whooped.

"Keep quiet," Rowan quickly scolded. "I don't want Tahira to get wind of this."

In the distance, Tahira toiled in the garden like usual. Bulan's ecstatic outburst drew her gaze. She tilted her head in their direction, squinting.

"Now look what you did," Rowan chided under his breath. "She suspects something."

Bulan rolled his massive shoulders, showing no concern. "Just continue on as before, and her curiosity will ease."

"You don't know her like I do. She's a persistent fish."

"Then don't give her a reason to be one," Bulan answered, again, far too simply.

Rowan didn't give Tahira an invitational glance as he strolled into the house. He retrieved the cerulean opal from the small chest on his nightstand and brought it back to the miner. Bulan slipped it inconspicuously into his pocket, whistling like he carried nothing special.

"Use that to make a ring and a set of earrings," Rowan whispered. "Oh, and a necklace as well."

Bulan let out a boisterous laugh. "Anything else for the budding romantic?"

Rowan's face reddened. He'd never done anything like this before. Weavings were the only gifts he'd ever conceived. Jewelry was outside his scope of knowledge. "Well, not unless you have other ideas?"

"My mind is an endless lode of ideas," Bulan boasted, tapping a chunky finger against his tousled head.

"Then I'll leave it to you."

Bulan gave him a dispirited look. "You sure you wanna leave the designing up to me and Kitra?"

Rowan passed his dirty fingernails through his sweaty hair with an overwhelmed breath. "I know my strengths, and jewelry isn't one of them. I'd rather let the artist work her magic."

Bulan's sunset-red eyes twinkled. "I'll let my wife know."

As Bulan scampered down the hill like an eager kalb, Tahira hung up her apron, snagged her shawl, and wandered over. Her eyes held an inquisitive gleam. "What's Bulan all excited about?"

Rowan squirmed for a vague response. "He's helping me with a project."

"It must be quite the thrill by the sounds of Bulan's roaring laughter."

"Bulan gets a thrill out of most things."

"Yes, especially when it comes to his wife. Does she factor into this project of yours?"

Rowan found no words to counter the question. Luckily for him, his stomach rumbled, and they shared a gut-aching laugh. "I'm starved." He moved toward the manor door. "Let's head in for supper."

Tahira smacked her lips, eyeing him sideways. "I know what you're doing, Row."

Rowan played coy. "What am I doing?"

"Distracting me with food."

"Is it working?"

"Currently, yes." She smiled knowingly at him. "The secret of your special project can keep until later."

She didn't press him further, and hopefully, if he was even luckier, it would slip her mind entirely.

As Rowan waited in the parlor, he slouched in his chair and fooled around with Hal's knife. The tendrils spiraled from his hand to the blade. His thoughts drifted back to when the red-haired prince gave it to him.

"Something tells me you will have need of a knife."

It was almost as if Hal had possessed a keen awareness of the dangers Rowan would face.

Rowan set the knife on the table, mentally ordering the tendrils to stay latched to the blade. They remained in place, spiraling end-over-end with glee, like they enjoyed inhabiting their new host. Of course, the curse couldn't infect the knife, but it could infect anything organic claiming hold of the knife. Another useful trick in his arsenal.

Tahira entered, holding two steaming plates of eggs scrambled with sausage and garnished with herbs from the garden. Rowan moved the knife aside, making room for the plate.

Tahira took a seat, smiling from ear to ear. "Remember the first time I brought you this meal?"

"Fondly." He smiled, taking a bite. The spice of the sausage delighted his taste buds. "Though, I think I'll enjoy this one better. I can actually chew without my jaw aching."

"Dare I forget Akaran's handiwork?" Tahira's lashes fluttered with irritation. "I've not forgiven him for beating you so severely."

"I haven't either. I'm only overlooking it in light of our partnership. It won't help us stay unified if we hold grudges."

"Speak for yourself, Row. I'll need to witness much more civility from Akaran before I give him a pass."

"Another long hope, then," he teased with a smile.

Tahira swallowed a small bite, her expression warmed by a reminiscent smile—much better than the scowl she displayed when speaking of Akaran.

"What's on your mind?" Rowan asked, scooping up another mouthful.

"Just thinking of how far we've come." Her eyes gleamed, her voice one of sweet fondness. "You know what I miss most? Those early days, when we journeyed together, and you were less hesitant with making contact. You shielded me in the sandstorm—stayed close beside me all night nestled within those boulders."

"Where I woke to you drooling on my shoulder," Rowan added, and Tahira's face colored. "But I didn't fully understand the curse then. I wasn't aware of how it spread its infection."

"Had you, would you have acted differently?"

Rowan sighed, knowing she'd be saddened by his answer. "I think so, yes."

Tahira's countenance grew more somber. "What a morose soul you would've been."

"Morose enough for you not to take interest in me?"

"Who can say?" Tahira started to avert her eyes, but instead held his gaze. "I like to think everything happened as it should've."

Rowan smiled. "Rahn said the same thing to me once. Being raised by my guardian-mothers instead of Zurie, having this curse, and getting outcast from my village—it all transpired as fate would have it, bringing me here, where I belong." He stared into Tahira's eyes, his heart swelling with love. "Without you, I wouldn't be here. I may have never been reunited with my grandfather. You made this possible."

Tahira's cheeks blushed, and she smiled all the more boldly. "I told you I'd be useful."

"You're far more than useful, Tahira. You're indispensable. Irreplaceable."

Her shoulders quivered at his words. She parted her lips, and burning skies, did he ever want to claim them against his. Their hands crept toward one another, the need for contact an astronomical pull. The tips of their fingers touched, and a spark of sensation shot through Rowan's body. He could lose himself with one kiss. And therein lay the doom of their predicament. One kiss would lead to more, and another part of Tahira's body would lose its luster. Her lips had yet to regain their color, and with the long stretch of time since their last kiss, it became clear they never would.

"We're allowed this," she said with yearning. "Surely we are, Row."

"It will lead to us wanting more—much more." He slid his hand back to his lap, restraining his amorous impulses.

Tahira lowered her eyes to her plate. "The food's getting cold." She picked up her fork and continued eating, yet remained unable to hide the tear streaming down her cheek.

Rowan swallowed the pained lump in his throat and returned his attention to his meal. The kindness and care she took to make this for him broke his heart.

Shen dashed into the parlor, disrupting the sullen mood. "A note has been delivered." He hurried to Rowan's side and handed him the letter.

Rowan braced himself and read it.

Tahira lowered her fork, waiting tensely. "What's it say?"

"It's from Garm. My spear is ready."

Tahira patted her lips with her napkin and rose from her chair. "Then I'll be heading into the city."

"I'll join you, mistress," Shen said, moving her chair aside. "There are items in the storehouse in need of replenishing. I'll have Gavan drive us."

Shen rushed out of the parlor.

"Well, this'll be it, won't it?" Tahira wrapped her shawl around her shoulders, hovering as closely as she could. "Once you have the spear, you'll be ready to confront Zamara."

"Provided Akaran gives us the go ahead, yes," Rowan said, retrieving his knife.

The barest hint of a scowl crossed Tahira's face. "If he doesn't give it by the end of this week, I'll vex him until he does," she said in her pert way.

They left the parlor and headed outdoors to the stable. Gavan prepared the wagon and maneuvered it out to the yard, waiting on Shen to compile his grocery list. While they waited, a figure on a resplendent stallion trotted up the path.

Judging by his dark clothes, muscular build, and his mid-length, swaying hair, Rowan recognized him as his brother. "We have company," he told Tahira, indicating with a flick of his head.

Tahira's eyes narrowed for all but a moment. "Why's he come, you suppose?"

"Perhaps he's come to tell us it's time to strike."

Her countenance softened. "All the more reason to make haste and get your spear."

Akaran dismounted and led his horse to the trough. "You making a journey?" he asked.

"Only me," Tahira answered. "Rowan's spear is ready, so there'll be no further reason to delay, yes?"

Akaran's smirk brimmed with amusement. "You're hasty, mistress."

"For reasons I know you can guess."

Akaran's lips curved into a sly smile as his eyes roamed her comely figure. "Indeed I can, mistress."

Rowan cleared his throat, earning Akaran's attention. "Why've you come, brother? I know this isn't simply a social call—"

"And why can't it be?" Akaran planted his hands on his hips and launched into a debonair laugh. "Perhaps I only wanted to come see my half-brother and his charming mistress."

Tahira's face was blank, apparently not duped by his flattery.

"Cut the act, and tell us what happened," Rowan demanded.

All the jesting in Akaran's voice fell away. "Adelkar visited my mine this morning."

A spike of alarm lanced Rowan's gut. "Did he discover—?"

Akaran shook his head. "He saw nothing, but even still, it presents a problem." He took a brief moment to explain what countermeasures they took to forestall Adelkar. "He can't know with certainty I've learned of the Kamands' murders. If anything, I think his suspicion is rising. We need to act sooner than planned."

"You'll get no complaints from us." Rowan faced Tahira and helped her into the wagon, bidding her a safe journey.

"I won't be gone long." She settled into her seat, eyeing them. "Don't fight with each other while I'm away."

"No chance at that, mistress," Akaran promised with an innocent grin.

Shen arrived, fumbling with his sack as he unceremoniously plopped onto his lower-than-expected seat. Gavan held back a chuckle before smacking the reins. The wagon pulled away, and Tahira waved before facing forward.

"Don't be so casual with her," Rowan warned, giving his brother a firm stare.

"Oh, don't give me that look," Akaran said, folding his arms. "I need the practice. How else am I going to win the hand of a willful maid if I don't show myself civil toward yours?"

"You have a strange way of sense, brother." At least he'd made an attempt to be friendlier. "You sticking around?" Rowan asked.

"If that's acceptable to you and your miners?"

"It is."

"Good, because I'm eager to see this spear I had a hand in bringing into creation—see if it holds up to the test."

"I can test it on you," Rowan said, playful yet serious. "You'll have first-hand experience that way."

Akaran broke out in laughter. "I walked right into that jab." He cupped his hands around his neck, stretching his upper back. "Well, until it arrives, how should we pass the time?"

"I can think of a few things. I'll show you my training grounds." Rowan pointed, indicating the marshland far below the rear side of the mine.

Akaran grinned and followed him down the path. "Is this where you practice with your spear?"

"No, it's where I kill plant life with the curse." Rowan pulled the knife free from its place of concealment. Tendrils swarmed around it like a mass of gnats. How well would the tendrils work in tandem with the blade? Curiosity brimmed within him, eager to attain the results.

Akaran gave it a glance. "Interesting knife. The crossguard looks Mestrian. Where'd you get it?"

"From a friend in Eldon." Rowan still couldn't believe he'd gotten it from Mestria's Crown Prince.

"Mind if I see it?" Akaran reached for the hilt without reservation.

"That wouldn't be wise," Rowan said, moving the knife out of his brother's reach. "It's been infused with the curse."

Akaran whipped his hand to his side, incredulous. "Wait, your curse can inhabit objects?"

"If it's in close proximity to me, then yes, it can, when I consciously direct it. With lifeforms, it's different. The curse will latch on and slowly siphon life without any input from me." Something he wished he would've known years ago. "I can restrain it for short increments, but it's exhausting. It's like trying to hold back a crashing wave with only my mind. The curse still manages to slip its tendrils past my reins."

Akaran's brow lifted. "What else can it do?"

"How much time do you have?"

Akaran smirked. "All afternoon."

Rowan led his brother out on the curse-scarred marshland below Iron Crossing's steep crag. There, he displayed the full deadly nature of the curse—killing sedge, brush, and tree. Knife in hand, he let the tendrils spiral at its tip as he sheared the surrounding reeds. The tendrils leapt from the knife, latching onto every fallen blade of grass. The ground beneath his feet browned, and sliding his feet forward—continuing his slashes—the trail of death followed his every step.

Akaran kept a wide berth, matching pace with his stride. "Are you sure you want to relinquish this ability? I could make great use of such a deadly skill."

"You sound like our mother." Rowan hurled the knife into a clump of tall reeds, tasking the tendrils to abandon the weapon and infect the surrounding plants. The sickness spread at once. They consumed the reeds like a swarm of crop-devouring locusts. "Zurie became enthralled by the curse's power, using it as her sword and shield. But ultimately, it corrupted her mind."

Akaran tilted his head left, then right, surveying the dead foliage all around. "All I'm saying is, it has many useful applications."

"Yet comes with a cost I detest," Rowan said, marching toward the dead reeds. "It kills and infects those around me. I can't even embrace the girl I cherish."

Akaran tapped the corner of his mouth. "I noticed her lips have grayed—your doing, I assume?"

Rowan nodded glumly, then retrieved the knife from atop an ash mound. "I haven't touched her since. It's been a deep pain for us. My heart aches for her in a way I can't explain. Know what I mean?"

Akaran shrugged, shaking his head. "Not in the slightest. I've never loved anyone. Frankly, I don't understand it. I've dabbled here and there just to have a thrill. What you have with Tahira is rare, I think." He paused, and a sliver of compassion entered his voice. "I'm sorry you were cursed like this."

Rowan stared at his brother. He never expected him to utter such sympathetic words, let alone an apology. "Let's return to the manor. Tahira should be back from Arjun soon."

They left the marsh, eager for refreshment and further discussion. As they made their way up the hill, the wagon trickled along the road toward the manor, but only Shen and Gavan were visible.

Tahira was nowhere in sight.

CHAPTER 29
WHAT BLOOD REVEALS

"Something's wrong." Rowan dashed toward the wagon as it came to a halt.

Gavan's and Shen's faces were bruised and bleeding. Rowan gasped.

"Gavan, what's happened?" Rowan asked. "Where's Tahira?"

Both men lumbered from the wagon, their stances stiff and pained. Shen held Tahira's shawl in his hands; Gavan held the custom-made spear. A somber shroud of shame etched their battered faces.

"Forgive us, baron, we were jumped by a g-g . . . by a group of ruffians," Gavan said, his hand covering the mass of bruises on the right side of his face. "They bludgeoned me and Shen in the head, then seized Tahira. We were powerless to stop them."

"They took her?" Rowan's face blanched. He regretted in an instant letting her go, but then, how could he have known this would happen? She wasn't known to Adelkar or Zamara. "Who could've done this?"

Shen shook his head, eyes downcast. "We don't know."

"I might have an idea." Akaran narrowed his eyes. "Was there a slippery-faced fella among them? Greasy hair, gangly frame—a bit jittery?"

Shen blinked with recollection. "Yes, he's the one who struck me. How did you know?"

"I think I know who's behind this." Akaran half-turned to Rowan, his expression one of grim certainty. "Adelkar."

Rowan's face hardened with suspicion. "How would Adelkar even know about Tahira?"

Akaran hesitated, clamping his lips. His silence was a swallowing abyss. A moment passed before he divulged the answer. "I may have told him about her connection to you."

"May have?" Rowan's gaze and tone sharpened. "Did you, or didn't you?"

Akaran's face betrayed him. "All right, I did," he admitted, then quickly added, "but this was weeks ago, before we started working together."

Rowan stormed away from his brother. Anger clawed at his insides in a way it never had before. He flung his hands in his hair, reeling with inexplicable rage. His mind swirled with thoughts of retaliation. He felt betrayed all over again. Just when he and his brother formed a bond, this withheld information reignited Rowan's distrust.

His fingers clenched, forming a fist. Rowan spun around and crashed his knuckles against Akaran's mouth. His brother grunted in surprise and stumbled backward. Rowan's rage shunted the explosive pain in his hand—but not the one burning in his heart.

Fire flashed in Akaran's eyes. His bloodied lips twisted into a heated glare. "Is that how you want to solve this?" He threw up his fists, protecting his face. "Come on, then, little brother. Let's have our rematch."

This time, Rowan wouldn't avoid the fight. He needed it to expel his fury. Well aware Akaran was a studied pugilist with a height and size advantage and a longer reach, Rowan still didn't back down. Fists weren't everything. He'd fought spear-to-claw with the fiercest twin-tails. Akaran was just another beast Rowan would subdue.

Rowan fell into a ready stance, dodging his brother's quick jabs. He executed his own swift punches to Akaran's gut, like driving thrusts with the butt of his spear. It earned him several lucky blows before Akaran sent out an angry, forceful kick. His boot smashed against Rowan's pelvis, knocking him flat on his back.

In a flash, Akaran hovered above him, bearing down with another fist. Pain exploded in Rowan's skull as the first two punches landed, ripping open skin. Rowan moved his head before the third blow connected and swung his legs between his brother's ankles, dropping him on his chin. Both on the ground, their fist fight devolved into a wrestling slog, each taking knees to the gut and elbows to the ribs. Teeth clenched and faces bloodied, the brothers grappled, rolling down the hill.

Shen and Gavan hovered at the hill's crest, nursing their own aches and staying clear of the fight. It was just as well. This rematch between brothers was long overdue.

Akaran scored a series of hits to Rowan's face before landing a blow to his jaw.

Rowan's vision spotted as Akaran dove in with more flying fists. Rowan's mind flooded with the bitter rage of being at Akaran's mercy during that first beating. In that visceral moment, he didn't see Akaran as he was now but as the two-faced bully who had tricked him and spiked his drink. Every pounding fist and battering kick flashed in his mind—each one a painful reminder to repay his brother for his flagrant cruelty.

A vengeful voice emerged in Rowan's head.

Teach him a lesson like he taught you. A beating isn't good enough. Seep the lesson into his soul.

It became the only desire in his mind.

Make him pay, make him pay.

Rowan's hands thrust forward, seizing hold of his brother's forearm, and in a quick snapping rotation, he yanked the arm behind Akaran's back. Wrestling for a firm hold, Rowan forced his brother's face into the dying grass, driving a knee to his back. He tightened his hold, entangling his legs around his brother's hips in a secure lock. Akaran thrashed to break loose. His one free hand tugged at Rowan's hair.

All of a sudden, Akaran's body seized as if he'd lost all breath. His fingers loosened their grip, and his head bucked against the ground. Had he conceded the fight? Or was this a desperate trick to get Rowan to break his hold? He wouldn't budge until Akaran ceased movement altogether.

His brother's sudden, strained plea shattered Rowan's merciless thought.

"Stop this . . . brother!" Akaran wheezed, as if some invisible noose cinched his throat. "You're—*killing me!*"

His brother's shout snapped Rowan out of his trance-like fury. He froze. The curse's tendrils bound Akaran in a choke hold. With a forceful command, Rowan ordered them back to his body. They retreated, but in their place, a dark taint lingered around Akaran's neck—a veiny band of grayed skin.

Akaran's face blanched with horror. "Curses, get off me!"

Rowan released his hold, and Akaran scrambled away from him. Each stared at the other, heaving for air. Akaran's complexion slowly returned to a healthier shade, yet the circular mark remained fast.

Burning skies, I almost killed him.

"What was . . . with you . . . just now?" Akaran demanded between breaths.

Shame at giving into his rage—at feeding the curse's desire—crept through Rowan. He shuddered. "For a moment, my mind was . . . subsumed with pure rage. Hatred took control of my thoughts, blinding me from my own actions. Rage, it's—"

"Terrifying." Akaran swallowed. His voice wasn't judgmental, but laced with deep understanding.

They'd given into it, exacting the same vicious judgment upon one another. The rage may have vanished, but anger harbored on the surface. Rowan couldn't banish it, not when he didn't have all the answers.

"Why, brother?" he hissed through his teeth, tasting blood in his mouth. "Why would you even mention Tahira to Adelkar?"

Akaran rubbed at his throat, unaware of the mark. "He wanted a way to intimidate you into selling Iron Crossing."

"And you gave it to him without the slightest hesitation, didn't you?" Anger blazed through Rowan, drawing him closer to Akaran. He fought back the urge to strike his brother again. "Was getting close to me just another one of your tricks?"

Akaran sniffed through bloodied nostrils. "I wouldn't waste my time tricking you—"

"You've done it before," Rowan said.

"I promise you this isn't a trick." Akaran swiped the blood from his nostrils; it smeared across his cut knuckles. "I need you to help me move against my uncle and aunt."

"Then how could you not tell me about Adelkar's plotting?"

"It wasn't on my mind," Akaran snapped. "I've thought of nothing else beyond getting rid of my uncle."

Rowan scoffed in his brother's face. "Oh, so it was only an honest mistake that you forgot to tell me your uncle was plotting to take Iron Crossing from me?" His heart surged with mistrust. "I can't think of anything more vital. Your carelessness has allowed Adelkar to exploit my relationship with Tahira. This changes everything we planned."

Akaran grew defensive. "Look, I've had a lot to process lately. This entire conspiracy has fogged my brain to the breaking point."

"Don't give me excuses." They were the last things Rowan wanted to hear. "We've wasted enough time bickering." He bolted to his feet and labored back up the hill. "Tahira is in danger. We go now."

Akaran swished after him. "But that's what my uncle's expecting. There's no telling what he has lying in wait for us if we go now, and that goes for Zamara as well. We'll be losing our element of surprise."

"And whose fault is that?" Rowan struck his palm against his brother's chest. "This is happening because of your original desire to see me ruined."

Akaran sighed. "Look, I'm sorry, all right? I was a spiteful prick before our partnership."

"And Tahira's paying the price. Who knows if Zamara has already cast a curse upon her?" Rowan's heart hitched at the horrible thought. "This ends today."

He reached Gavan and Shen, and without a word, seized hold of his new spear. He untwisted the iron shaft, revealing the sleek, hidden spearhead, then cinched it back together. "Let's go, brother."

They dashed for Akaran's horse, and only then did his brother realize Rowan meant for them to ride together.

"Um, what of your curse?"

"I'll rein it in as long as I can. Any other concerns?" Rowan shot his brother his most severe glare, daring him to voice a contentious word.

Akaran grabbed the reins and shook his head. "No, that covers it."

VICIOUS HANDS PULLED TAHIRA UP A LONG SET OF WINDING stairs, then thrust her into a stuffy room. It smelled foul—no, make that worse than foul. It reeked as though a host of plants had either wilted from rot or festered with decay.

"Let me go, you filthy fiends!" Tahira squirmed to no avail, her arms ensnared in the two brutes' grips. They shoved her to the floorboards right before a small pair of black, pointy shoes. Tahira's breath caught in her chest.

"Excellent, you've brought her like I asked," an older woman's voice slithered above her ears. "Wait outside the door until I call for you."

The two ruffians unshackled their callused mitts from Tahira's arms and turned around. Tahira whipped her gaze up and took in the earnest smile on the old crone's menacing face.

Tahira swallowed. "Are you Zamara?"

The woman's twisted smile was all the confirmation Tahira needed. "You're well informed, girl." She stooped over and snagged a strand of hair from Tahira's head.

Tahira recoiled. She shuffled backward toward the open door. Zamara breathed out a murmurous stream of words, and the door slammed shut as if blasted by a forceful wind. Tahira tugged at the handle, repeatedly, but it held fast.

"Foolish girl, there's no escape for you here." Zamara's tone spoke a clear message: No amount of struggling would free her from this situation.

Tahira spun to face the evil Conjurer. Back against the wooden door, her heart squeezed in her chest, vying for a calming breath. "What do you want from me, witch?"

"A drop of blood will do at present." As quick as reins snapping, Zamara snatched Tahira's hand and stabbed the tip of her curved fingernail into skin.

The sharp prick to the center of her palm sent a shiver down Tahira's spine. She winced and tugged her hand back. Zamara let it go, content with what she got. Fear flooded Tahira's veins as the Conjurer sucked the beads of blood drenching her fingernail.

Zamara's eyes gleamed with discovery, and every bone in Tahira's body quaked. She wanted far away from this wicked woman and to be back at Rowan's side. Hopefully, Shen and Gavan had returned to Iron Crossing and delivered Rowan's spear. She imagined Rowan would abandon all sense and rush to find her.

Stall for time. It's the only thing you can do.

Tahira raised her chin. "Do all Conjurer's enjoy ingesting blood, or just the *really* depraved?"

Zamara smirked at Tahira's bold slight. "Blood reveals the truth of things hidden. The experienced know how to decipher its messages."

Tahira scoffed to keep from cringing. "That's a nice way of making what you did sound less creepy."

Zamara gave her a piercing stare, her red eyes even redder after ingesting blood. "I know your blood," she revealed, smacking her lips with curious insight. "Answer me this: Are you a descendant of Durene's?"

Tahira flinched. She never expected hearing her ancestor's name uttered from the Conjurer's lips. "What's it to you, hag?"

"She was my teacher before the battle that claimed her life."

"A pity you didn't die with her."

"Watch your tongue, brat. You know nothing of that war, nor my relationship to Durene." Zamara's voice stewed with long-held bitterness. "I lost much in those battles against the Mestrians—my fellow sisters, our esteemed position in society, even our young acolytes didn't escape the enemy's sword. Our order never recovered."

Tahira knew the terrible stories from her childhood. Her mother hadn't left out the bloody details. "Sounds to me like a stroke of fate."

"As is our meeting." Zamara rubbed the strand of hair she'd plucked between her palms, dousing it within the remaining blood. "I taste similar properties in your blood as Durene's. Had I known one of her descendants remained, I would've taken you under my tutelage."

Tahira snorted, folding her arms against her pounding heart. "You would've been wasting your time as I don't have *the gift*."

Zamara's eyes glittered. "Oh, but you do. Your blood reveals the truth. It teems with energy and potential."

Tahira's jaw slackened. That couldn't be true.

Mother would've said something. Unless she didn't know . . .

"Blood never lies. You don't believe me?"

"Why should I believe the words of a Conjurer like you?"

"Because when it comes to dealing with my own kind, I'd never utter a lie." The cruelty in Zamara's expression waned for the briefest of moments before a look of disapproval hardened her gaze. "Unfortunately, you fell in love with that upstart. Such a shame. What I have planned for you will torture the boy's soul."

Tahira's gut clenched. Her stalling had come to an end.

Zamara's lips twisted into a heartless snarl. She invoked an incantation as she flicked the bloodied hair away from her palm.

Tahira's heart beat out of her chest. She veered away from the door in panicked desperation. The move was futile, but the unyielding persistence within her wouldn't give Zamara the satisfaction of standing there helpless, waiting for some spell or curse to ensnare her soul.

An invisible, paralyzing force struck her body. It pinned her in place as a surging chill swept through her veins. All at once, her mind was sucked into a black void, and all thought disappeared.

CHAPTER 30
DAY OF RECKONING

Evening closed in as Akaran led his horse up the final stretch to Keliss House. Deafened silence accompanied the ride from Iron Crossing all the way toward the jutting crags surrounding his home. Akaran feared any utterance would only be met with short jabs. He never considered his half-brother could become so enraged—but then, Akaran had given him ample reason.

He rubbed his fingers over his throat and discovered a band of skin less smooth than the rest. Something happened when Rowan almost killed him. The curse left a mark. And like Tahira's grayed lips, he suspected the blemish wouldn't fade. If he lived past today, the mark would serve as a visible reminder of how close he came to losing his life by Rowan's curse.

"We stick to the initial plan," Akaran said, nearing the hill's crest. "Here's where you get off. Go the rest of the way by foot, then wait to approach the manor until I draw away any hired men my uncle might have lurking around."

"Where should I hide?" Rowan asked.

"The stable. At this hour, no one is likely to be inside."

Rowan slid from the saddle and dashed off the road, his spear snug against his torso. He turned to give Akaran a lingering glance. His half-brother's gaze held no malice. Only what appeared to be a wishful, good-luck sentiment.

The fight had settled things between them. What emotions they buried for the sake of their partnership resurfaced in that explosive clash, but in its wake, a newfound bond formed. After tonight, they would be family.

"Don't die, brother," Rowan said, his jaw swollen from their brawl.

Akaran grinned with split lips. "Is that your way of wishing me luck?"

"Take it how you want."

"Well, then, don't you die either. You've got a curse to break and a girl to find."

Rowan's eyes turned steely. He dipped his chin in a nod, then scurried off.

Akaran continued onward at a trot. He steered his horse across the manor's yard toward the stable. A cluster of burly henchmen approached him from every side. They said nothing as he dismounted, yet they loitered—their presence a firm message. Akaran tucked his horse into the first stall and made for the manor's entrance. The men followed.

The door opened before Akaran reached it. Horace, the full-eyed, pointy-nosed manservant, greeted him. "Your uncle wants to see you."

"How convenient," Akaran said with a cheeky smirk. "I want to see him as well."

Horace didn't budge from the doorway. He narrowed his large eyes and peered past Akaran in a conspiratorial way, like he expected another person to be present.

"Well, are you going to let me in?" Akaran pressed, making a move forward. "This is my home. I'm allowed to come and go as I please. Unless something's changed that I'm unaware of?"

"Uh, not at all, young baron." Horace pushed the door fully open and stepped aside. "Do come in."

Akaran entered, as did the four men hovering at his back.

Adelkar isn't taking any chances, is he?

Horace stared at him, his grizzly brows drawn in a stringent slant. "See that he carries no weapons." Two of Adelkar's henchmen gruffly seized Akaran as the other pair patted him down.

Akaran outstretched his arms in annoyance. "Has my uncle grown paranoid all of a sudden?" he asked Horace, playing ignorant.

"He should know I don't carry weapons other than these." He clenched his fists, making a visual statement.

"It's only a precaution he tasked me with," Horace said, like thoroughness was his chief virtue.

"He's clean," one of the henchmen said.

Akaran held his hands in front of the manservant's face. "See, Horace? Nothing to fear from me, so you can go about your business."

Horace vacated the entryway without another word.

Akaran turned and faced the henchmen. "And as for you thugs, I gather you're here to deliver me to my uncle—which isn't necessary. I know where to find him at this hour."

"Again, baron," a shady-faced henchman uttered, "this is a precaution we were tasked with."

"Suit yourselves." Akaran moved to close the door. Before he did, he motioned with two fingers close at his side for Rowan to approach, then faced Adelkar's lackeys once more. "Let's get this over with, shall we?"

The henchmen escorted Akaran into Adelkar's study. His uncle lounged upon his preferred cushioned chair beside the hearth. Adelkar lowered his ledger on the small side table and gave Akaran a scrutinizing stare.

"Get in another scrape, Nephew?"

"Only the usual tussle."

"Your face is rather battered; it must've been a vigorous match."

"Nothing I couldn't handle."

Adelkar's eyes narrowed on his throat. "And the strange blemish around your neck? Was that also nothing you couldn't handle?"

Akaran paused, then offered a comeback jab. "It almost did me in, but I found a way to break free."

Adelkar gave a measured sigh. "Ever the fighter, taking on matches even you would do best to avoid."

"Every match is worth the fight, Uncle. The harder the fight, the sweeter the victory—and its reward."

Adelkar smirked. "Well said, Nephew. Let us speak plainly, then."

"Oh?" Akaran blurted, a pointed stare fixed on his uncle. "You have something to confess?"

"Stop playing coy." Adelkar eyed him sharply, all levity from his previous questioning gone. "I know all about your partnership with your accursed half-brother. You're not the only one who can employ Klay. A promise of caine powder was all it took to turn his spying eyes on you."

Adelkar flicked his head to the room's darkest corner. Klay surfaced from the shadows, a large pouch of caine powder gripped within his fist.

Klay had played a key part in this whole scheme—kidnapping Tahira for one—but seeing his slithery face in Adelkar's study wearing a sly smirk was an assault Akaran took personally.

His jaw came unhinged. "You traitorous snitch! You sold me out for a grip of caine!"

"It wasn't personal, boss. Just business." Klay's eyes glazed, a side effect from ingesting his mind-freeing drug. "You never sent the amount you promised. And your uncle was more than willing to give me double, provided I spy for him."

"You lousy snake," Akaran growled, thrusting a finger in Klay's direction. "You won't live to enjoy it. I'll make certain of that."

"A bold threat, boss, 'specially as you're grossly outnumbered," Klay jeered, gleefully fingering his pouch like it was his greatest love.

Adelkar snickered from his chair. "All right, boys," he crowed, flicking his wrist. "Rough him up."

Akaran moved in a flash. He leapt toward the hearth and knocked an armchair into the henchmen's path, curbing their advance. He lunged for the fire iron, snagged it in his grip, and rushed Klay. The greasy informant scrambled backward like a stray cat. His frightful pleas fell on deaf ears. Klay would pay for his treachery, as would Adelkar.

Akaran flung the iron poker down upon Klay's head, driving the sharp prong deep into the top of his skull. The drugged-up informant cried out in terror and staggered behind Adelkar's desk. Akaran didn't leave it there—one blow wasn't good enough. He wouldn't stop until this despicable creature was a miserable, dead wreck. As quick as thrown fists, he struck the fire iron five vicious times against Klay's head. Blood spattered on Akaran's face.

A strong grip arrested his arm, preventing another bludgeoning blow. Two of the henchmen wrestled Akaran off Klay's body and yanked him toward the center of the room. Akaran thrashed, kicking at their legs until another thug joined in and pinned him to the ground. Someone flung their boot against Akaran's head.

The blow knocked him senseless. He spat out a wad of blood, fighting off the daze.

"My nephew knows how to take a hit," Adelkar said over the sound of the beating. His fingers moved smoothly across his lips. "Make sure to be severe."

Rowan stayed crouched behind the stable's thick beams as his brother went inside with the gruff-looking men. A minute later, Akaran gave the signal to move, and the door closed.

Rowan sucked in a breath and dashed for the entrance. The double doors were unlocked. Perfect. He slipped inside without letting the door creak, then scurried for a place of concealment. His racing heart steadied as he spied his surroundings. A corridor lay to his right, the main dining hall to his left—the study beyond, where Akaran was at the moment. Those four brutes weren't loitering in Rowan's vicinity—a great relief—yet a savage commotion rumbled from the study.

Akaran must be giving someone a beating.

Rowan turned down a hall, his brother's drawn map at the forefront of his mind, and crept his way to Zamara's lair. He tiptoed up the dark stairwell and reached an open door. A punch of stomach-churning odors accosted his nostrils. He shoved a palm over his nose, forcing back a sneeze. Slowly, he released a breath and peered past the doorway. An older woman stooped over a worktable. Her ratty hair was wound into a braided bun, and her fingernails—wickedly curved like talons—picked at the intestines of a stout bird.

Rowan held in a shudder. *Still water, steady heart. Strike before she strikes you.*

When a serene calm stilled his nerves, Rowan poised his spear for action. He sprang into an attack, shooting out the tendrils and seizing Zamara's neck. Firmly arrested, he thrust his spear directly into her heart. Her body sagged forward against her worktable, her arms slumping dully to her sides.

A long moment passed before Rowan dared to believe it was over.

Then suddenly, Zamara's impaled form deconstructed into a pile of bones, cascading to the floor in a spine-tingling clatter.

Rowan recoiled in horror. A trick? A conjuring? He steadied his spear before him, glancing to and fro. A diabolical laugh emerged, bouncing off every wall, chilling Rowan to the marrow. The Conjurer was here somewhere, lurking unseen, now possessing the advantage.

A shadow dropped from the rafters and lunged straight for him. Rowan barely reacted in time. He shifted his head as a handful of sharp, curved nails scratched a groove across the side of his neck, slicing clean through his cursemark. He whirled on his swift attacker. The form of a short, old woman wearing a slim-fitting ebony dress stood before him. As Akaran had said, her face lacked the trove of haggard wrinkles one should possess at her age. The tautness of her cheeks and the plumpness of her lips held an unnatural allure. It twisted Rowan's insides.

Zamara grinned wickedly at him, her blood-tipped nails held close to her face. "You know, this is a rare treat for me. Those I've cursed have never returned to try and kill me. Their fear gets the better of them, and they stay far away."

"I'm not like them."

"Oh? Because you possess courage where they did not?" She cackled, running her tongue over her blood-soaked fingernails. Her red eyes flared as if discovering a mystery. "You're afraid. I can taste it in your blood. You fear for the safety of your beloved."

"Tell me where she is!" Rowan redirected his spear and whipped it toward Zamara's head. It shimmered and faded, along with the rest of her body.

Burning skies, another apparition.

Behind him, Zamara made a chiding sound with her lips. "Aiming for my head? Don't want to be doing that, boy."

"Oh, I think I do." He spun and shot out his spear. It slid down his grip, extending his reach. The spearhead buried itself inside her breast once more. Blood bloomed upon the shapely chest of a young woman wearing an emerald dress and a woven shawl around her delicate shoulders.

Rowan's gaze lifted in horror. Tahira peered at him through stunned eyes.

"Rowan?" Her hands reached for the spear's iron shaft, cradling it through pale, shaky fingertips. "Why would you kill me? I thought you loved me?" Her body slumped forward, and her misting eyes rolled back into her head.

Rowan's heart froze.

Burning skies, what have I done?

AKARAN GRITTED HIS TEETH AS A BARRAGE OF FISTS CRASHED against his body. After a dozen or more blows, he ceased resisting, conserving his energy. This wasn't the moment to put his all into the fight.

Let Adelkar think he has me beat. Bide my time and wait to deliver the knockout blows.

Two henchmen stayed their assault yet kept their hands firmly gripped around Akaran's arms. They yanked him to his knees and tugged at his hair, keeping his head lifted.

One thug rounded the desk to determine Klay's condition. "He's dead, baron."

"It's no matter. He served his purpose in bringing me the information I needed." Adelkar at last rose from his chair. He smoothed out his tabard and surveyed the wreckage done to Klay's skull. "A bit of overkill, don't you think, Nephew?"

"Not in the least." Akaran snarled, squirming against the hands binding him. "That shifty snake betrayed me. I only gave him what was coming to him."

"Hm, as I should with you? Shall I have you killed in the same manner?" Adelkar picked up the blood-soaked fire iron and strolled toward him, his gaze dark and lethal. "You turned against your family and joined forces with your accursed brother. What utter madness possessed you to do such a thing?"

"You turned against me first," Akaran snapped, his words dripping with derision. "You stole what my father intended for me—not you!"

Adelkar ignored his outburst. "You know what I hate?" He whacked the fire iron across Akaran's face, splitting skin. "Ingratitude." He swung the iron a second time. "Disloyalty." And a third time. "I took you in, raised you when you had no one else."

Despite the newly made gashes to his face and the ringing in his ears, Akaran managed to direct a brazen smirk at Adelkar. "Now, that isn't true, is it, Uncle? I had my grandparents, the Kamands, didn't I?"

Adelkar pulled his next swing up short. He studied the blood seeping into his fingernails. "I told you what happened to them. They wanted to leave Arjun because of the scandal."

"Another one of your lies." Akaran lifted his chin. "I found my grandparents' bodies crammed behind a false wall my miners excavated. You didn't expect that little secret to ever be uncovered, did you? That's why you pressed me to visit the mine. You wanted to make sure your secret was still safe."

Adelkar scoffed. "Come now, Nephew. You really think I murdered them?"

"Don't be coy, Uncle. I know you did. The evidence I found is compelling. You failed to remove Val's signet ring when you stashed his body inside the fissure. It made identifying him possible. You're the only person who had something to gain from the Kamands' deaths."

Adelkar's lips stretched to a thin line. He let the moment linger before a wicked sneer contorted his face. "Yes, I killed them. They were old and frail, so it was easily done."

"Why did you do it?" Akaran demanded, hot and hateful. "Did they contest the will you showed to the magistrate? Learn you planned to deny me my inheritance? What was it—?"

"They wanted you!" Adelkar spat with malice, banging the fire iron on his desk. "With Kainan's death and your mother cursed, they wanted you as their ward—be raised in their keeping at Kamand House. Knowing Kainan would've left his property to you, they would've taken the Keliss lands under their control, forcing me and Zamara out, leaving us with nothing. Well, I couldn't let that happen, so I did the only thing one could in my position."

"You murdered them," Akaran interjected, his hatred amassing, "all so you wouldn't lose the chance to steal *my* inheritance."

"Don't interrupt me!" Adelkar snarled, striking Akaran's cheek with his hand. "I met with Val Kamand and told him to sign over the deed to his land. Otherwise, Zamara would curse him and his wife. With her standing in their midst, you can imagine how swiftly they signed. Of course, at that juncture, they still had the hope of living in another land, with you amongst them."

So, Zamara was involved in the scheme after all. That deceitful hag.

"Then came the dagger to their chests," Adelkar said, his tone cruel and succinct.

"You did it yourself?"

"Naturally," Adelkar said with a dark, reminiscing smile. "They never saw it coming. Not when they were paralyzed with fear from the Conjurer standing in their midst. The shock that stole over their faces was a hot brand stroking my vengeance." Adelkar sounded so pleased with himself, so smug, like he was the most cunning of men. "So, you see, Nephew, I struck first, before they could strike me. Isn't that what I've always taught you? You've approached every fight in the same manner. It's what you did to your unsuspecting brother. You bludgeoned his body before you knew of his intentions."

Akaran hated Adelkar for infecting him with his devious logic. "You don't know the Kamands would have driven you out. Just like I didn't know my brother never wished me ill. Hate clouds everything. Your desire for revenge drove you to murder two innocent people. And then you had the gall to cover it up with a lie everyone would believe."

Akaran kept speaking, raising his voice, so his uncle couldn't sneak in another defensive word. "And so you got your revenge on everyone. Zurie. My father. The Kamands. All so you could sit on a crag of wealth."

"I loved their daughter," Adelkar hissed, his confession a violent outburst, "and she didn't care about me, or Kainan, and certainly not you. She chose to throw everything away in a doomed romance."

"That's what really irks you, isn't it, Uncle? You couldn't stand the fact she denied your advances and chased after Rorak instead. Her choice to betray my father was wrong and deceitful, but so was yours to murder her parents and ignore my father's wishes. Zurie bears much blame, but her sins are far less egregious than yours."

Adelkar bristled. "I tire of this." He straightened, and the indifference in his gaze confirmed he was ready to cover up another sordid deed. "You are not my problem anymore, Nephew." He flicked his head to his henchmen. "Take him and dispense with him. Your death will be simple to explain. A tragic mining accident claims the life of an inexperienced baron. A story everyone will believe."

Chapter 31
Conjured Horrors

Rowan's heart shrieked within him. His lips contorted, hissing out a keening cry. Blood pooled from Tahira's wound—*where I stabbed her.*

Her face went slack, and a dribble of blood seeped out of the corner of her pale, silver mouth. Rowan's breath caught, and he couldn't move. His entire body trembled, legs paralyzed. His eyes quivered as they beheld the dying face of the girl he loved.

Burning skies, no! NO!

Rowan thrust off his shock with a stifled scream and withdrew the spearhead. His feet staggered forward in a rush. He reached out to pull Tahira against him.

His hand grasped nothing but air.

Heart and gut colliding, he stared into her fading, lifeless gaze as Zamara struck him from behind. Her claw-like nails raked deeply into his side.

"You have to be sharp to outwit me, boy," she hissed in his ear, thrusting him face-first against the glass wall.

His temple smacked against the glass. A spider web of fractures sliced into his skin and skull. His vision spotted as frantic breaths escaped his lips. He stepped forward only to sway from dizziness. Rowan dropped the butt of his spear against the floor, steadying his footing. Three Zamaras stood before him, each one illusory and distorted. Was this another one of her tricks, or a result of his hazy vision?

Rowan grunted at the pain in his side. "Where's Tahira?" he yelled, leveling his spear at the Conjurer.

"Your girl?" all three Zamaras said, each one echoing the other. "Oh, she's somewhere you'll never find without me."

The middle Zamara studied the blood on her fingernails. She brought them to her lips and gave him an evil glare. "Kill me, and she's as good as dead."

"Kill me," the second Zamara threatened, "and you lose the one you love."

"Kill me," the third Zamara purred, "and you'll regret it all your days."

The threats enraged Rowan's heart. How crafty and clever Zamara was setting this contest in her favor. Weaving Tahira's life thread to her own was the wickedest scheme Rowan could imagine.

The first Zamara's smile twisted more nefariously. "What will you do now, boy?"

"Take my chances." He unraveled the tendrils from around his arms and sent them scurrying across the length of his spear. With every swing of his weapon, the curse would scatter—having a better chance at infecting the real Zamara. He would use every trick at his disposal.

Zamara's eyes went from reflecting surprise to untold bewilderment. "I never imagined the curse would take on a life of its own.... How marvelous! I'm going to enjoy studying your corpse."

Each Zamara scattered a handful of bones upon the floor, invoking a guttural incantation. The bones rattled and reattached themselves, growing sinew and forming into a trio of bloodthirsty wolves. Dark violet gas swirled about their mangy bodies as they frothed at the mouths, their eyes darkly crimson.

"Kill him," Zamara commanded.

The three wolves charged at once.

Cornered against the glass, Rowan had no ground to concede. His fingers felt for the middle of the shaft, the place where it separated. The wolves swarmed and smashed against him, shattering glass. The wall behind him fractured in an explosive crash, and he fell into the night amidst a hail of glass.

AKARAN JERKED AT THE SOUND OF GLASS SHATTERING—THE DIN faint to his ears—yet it could've been his imagination. The beating he received, not to mention those blows from the fire iron, submerged his head in woozy depths.

Curses, he groaned; his head smarted.

Fresh night air slipped through his nostrils, rousing his mind. Adelkar's henchmen dragged him past the stable. Two clutched him by the arms, and the other two walked farther ahead. They veered toward the looming crag with every intention of taking him into the Keliss mine and hurling him down a shaft.

Now was the time to summon his strength and fight back.

Akaran planted his feet and yanked his arms free. Before either opponent could retaliate, he hurled a powerful fist to the shorter man's skull. It sent the thug staggering forward in an unconscious heap. The other man—thicker, broader, and slower—called out for aid from his cohorts. Akaran sprang at him, swinging his elbow right into the path of his bulbous nose, breaking it with an audible *crunch*. The man cried out in an angered howl but didn't lose the will to fight. He lunged clumsily with a fist. Akaran sidestepped it, threw out his foot, and tripped the henchman. As the man fell, Akaran knocked him in the back of the head with a flurry of hits before silencing him for good with a fiercely driven elbow to the apex of the man's skull. The cranium bones cracked beneath the blow.

With two henchmen dispensed in rapid succession, the other pair charged Akaran together. One came in low in a grappling maneuver, securing his arms around Akaran's waist, ramming him hard against the cobblestone well. The shock to his back destabilized his footing. He would've plummeted to his knees, if he had not been still pinned against the well. Gritting his teeth, Akaran formed his hands together and pounded them against the henchman's upper spine, then he quickly slugged a fist against the thug's temple. Before Akaran could stumble free, the other thug snagged him around the neck and whipped him to the ground.

The henchman kicked Akaran in the diaphragm, stealing his breath. He labored on hands and knees, fighting to rise, but he was tackled once more, and a rain of punches and kicks tore at his body.

The haze swept in again. The stars above blurred and dimmed.

AMIDST HIS FALLING, ROWAN SEPARATED THE STAFF AND DUG both spearheads against the tower. They lodged inside the seams between the stones, halting his fall. The wolves, having fallen with him, continued their plummet, crashing against the stable's roof in a cacophonous ruckus. Rowan's fingers coiled around the shafts, just below the spearheads, the rest of his body dangling against the tower. He took a steadying breath, his shoulders straining. He was too high to drop and make a safe landing. It left only one way to proceed.

Be quick.

Bracing his feet against the wall, he removed one spearhead at a time, cramming it into a secure lower groove, before proceeding with the next spear tip. In a tedious fashion, he labored his way down the tower, descending to the stable's roof. His heart raced as his arms labored. The wolves snarled far below. The fall hadn't shattered their bones.

He neared the bottom, and the wolves took turns springing up the wall, snapping at Rowan's heels. One finally reached him, its fangs seizing him by his boot. The additional weight, and the relentless tugging, proved too much for him.

The spearheads dislodged, and Rowan fell flat against the stable's straw roof. He lay there stunned for a split second before three glowing pairs of eyes dashed toward him in ravenous pursuit. Rowan sprang to his feet and spun away in a frantic scamper. The wolves gave chase across the rooftop. The lead wolf snapped at his ankles, and a flicker of pain tore at Rowan's heel. He twisted, readying a counterstrike. Rejoining the spear into one shaft, he arced it toward the wolf, slamming the spearhead flush against the beast's head, knocking it clear off the roof.

Rowan took a steady step backward, and the straw beneath him gave way. He sank into a horse stall, landing upon a musty pile of hay. The dust and straw tickled his nostrils, and he sneezed multiple times racing for the exit. Two wolves barred the way, their gaseous bodies a pair of smoking bonfires.

Rowan flung his knife at one, striking the beast between the eyes. The tendrils inhabiting the object swarmed the conjured creation.

Devour the bones, he commanded the tendrils. They spiraled with sea-churning speed, and within a handspan of breaths, the curse stripped away the wolf's head.

One down, two to go.

Rowan ignored the infected beast and concentrated on the one bolting toward him.

His weapon surging with a host of tendrils, Rowan thrust his spear at the wolf. The beast evaded, digging its freakish paws in the dirt. It flashed its fangs and sprang in a monstrous leap. Rowan timed his swing and struck the creature square in its ribs, knocking it into an empty stall. It rebounded in a flash, lunging with a snapping bite. Rowan redirected his spear's thrust, piercing the creature clean through its glowing red eye. The tendrils leapt from the spear tip and overtook the creature like a swallowing tidal wave.

Rowan kept his spear buried in the wolf's cranium, cramming it deeper. The conjured creation howled and squirmed in a fit of rage. The legs on which it stood were swiftly eaten away, and the wolf's trunk dropped to the ground on its belly. The remainder of its bones grew brittle and splintered, turning to dust. Without them as a binding object, the conjuring dispersed into a gaseous mist.

Rowan seized his knife from the pile of ash and almost made it out of the stable when something snagged him from behind. A ravenous snarl pounded his eardrums.

The third wolf!

It tore at his left shoulder with savage tenacity.

Rowan hissed in pain. He sent out a furious shockwave of tendrils, blasting the wolf full in the mouth. It staggered backward, but only for a moment before it sprang at Rowan once again, slamming its body against his. Knocked on his back, he flung his spear across his chest right as the wolf pounced on top of him. Rowan pressed the shaft against the wolf's throat, keeping its razored fangs at bay. It snarled and thrashed. The froth from its nebulous mouth dripped upon Rowan's face. Its fangs gnashed, vying for flesh.

One more time, he urged the tendrils. *Devour!*

The curse spread, and as it surged, the wolf lunged its head forward. Its claws ripped into Rowan's skin. It wasn't about to yield like the others.

"See the beast as an equal, and be fearless in your strike."

Naja's words strengthened Rowan's focus. He evoked a fearless yell, growling his own fury at the creature. The tendrils swirled more fiercely, biting away at the wolf's bones. Its snarling snout snapped forward. Its fangs broke into Rowan's skin, then its head unraveled in a gaseous explosion, along with the rest of its body.

Rowan sank his head against the dirt and gasped. He dusted off the wolf's ashy remains and labored to his feet, panting. His body sagged from exhaustion, and he hadn't even killed Zamara yet. In facing her again, what other nightmares would she hurl in his face? He didn't let the thought waylay him. He took another moment to still his galloping heart, then sprinted out of the stable.

A scuffling noise arrested him. The sound came from down the path leading to the Keliss mine. Fearing Tahira could be involved, he crept toward the mine's entrance. As he neared, he detected two burly men dragging a thrashed Akaran. His face was a bloodied mess. He didn't struggle, his body limp — unconscious.

Rowan panted, labored from his skirmish with the wolves. Becoming entangled in another slog fest was the last thing he needed.

One of the henchmen lit a lantern before seizing Akaran's arm. They continued on with their business, yanking his brother past the entrance — toward the shaft. Rowan grasped their deadly intentions, and he quickened his steps.

Both men heard his footsteps and spun in a lurch to face him.

Rowan freed his knife and hurled it in warning at their feet. "Back away from him, or I'll kill you." Rowan poised his spear forward. The tendrils inhabiting his two weapons whipped around the metal, waiting to be unleashed. Though the men couldn't see the curse, they could see the spear. Hopefully, it offered enough of a deterrent.

"Even with that spear, you're outnumbered, boy."

"Looks a bit wobbly on the legs, too," his partner gibed. His gaze lowered, noticing the knife. "And his aim is terrible."

Rowan strengthened his stance. "This is your last warning. I can kill you both from here."

The two men guffawed. "He's bluffing. We'll deal with him, then take care of the Keliss brat."

The one eyeing the cursed knife picked it up. At Rowan's mental nudge, the tendrils snaked up the man's arm. *Kill quickly,* he commanded.

The other man reached for an ax lying at the entrance. Weapons snug in their grips, the thugs lumbered toward Rowan.

Rowan swung his spear in a high arc, shooting out a mob of tendrils at the ax wielder. Their slithery, gaseous coils adhered to the henchman's throat and commenced their silent infiltration.

Both men snickered.

"Was that it?" the one holding the knife jeered. "'Cause, you missed us by a mile."

They grinned with assured victory and lunged with their weapons. Their feet didn't make it one step forward. The curse's toxins had long since infiltrated skin, and by now, invaded the brain. Their bodies paralyzed, the men froze, their eyes widening with stock-still fright, horrid screams erupting from their gaping mouths.

Rowan hurried past them. He dragged his brother away from their midst so the tendrils didn't latch onto him as well. The henchmen's eyeballs bulged then sank into the depths of their skulls. The flesh on their faces tore away in strips as if assailed by a ravaging sandstorm. In a span of seconds, their dreadful screams ceased and their bodies dropped into heaps. The curse continued consuming the flesh of the dead henchmen.

A disturbed shiver rocked Rowan. He wrangled his knife from the dead man's grip, then put his back to the carnage. He crouched two feet from his brother and used the butt of his spear to tap Akaran awake. His brother roused with a start, his hands fisted before his bloodied face.

"Relax, it's me. I took care of those henchmen."

Akaran's face contorted with anguish; his eyes blinked furtively. "What are you doing out here?"

"Zamara sicced her conjured wolves on me, and I fell from the tower. You?"

Akaran spewed a guttural grunt. "Those lackeys thought they'd bury me in the mine. Guess they didn't expect to run into you."

Rowan grimaced. Yes, he'd employed the curse against those men, but they gave him no choice. "I take it Adelkar is still alive, then?"

Akaran gave a sluggish nod. "Same with Zamara, huh?"

Rowan sighed, nodding. "You weren't joking about her tricks. She's put my mind and heart through every torment."

"It's her way." Akaran tilted his head back, staring at the mine's domed ceiling. "This night is far from over. Back to it, eh?"

Rowan surveyed his brother's battered condition. "You don't look like you're in any state to keep fighting."

Akaran waved off Rowan's concern, his knuckles torn on both hands. "Trust me, I've got plenty of fight left in me. Besides, Ravel hits harder than those chumps. I'll shake this off, no problem. Just need a moment to convince my body."

"Need help with that?" Rowan offered an arm, reining in the tendrils with a low hiss.

Akaran took hold only long enough to climb to his feet. He rested against the entrance's interior wall, cradling a hand over his ribs. "Have you learned where your girl is?"

Rowan glumly shook his head. "Zamara has her hidden somewhere. She said if I killed her, I'd never find Tahira."

Akaran grunted with noticeable contempt. "Don't let that stop you from killing the devious hag. We'll find the little mistress even if we have to search every inch of this estate. Do what you came here to do, as will I." His gaze hardened, his expression brimming with vengeance.

"Then you might need this." Rowan held out his knife, drawing the tendrils away.

Akaran eyed it suspiciously. "I thought that thing was cursed."

"I drew the curse from the blade, so it's no longer a cursed object."

"Ah, well, in that case, I'll happily take it off your hands." Akaran took hold of the knife. His eyes glinted. "Uncle won't expect this. He knows I prefer to settle matters with my fists." With a pained hiss, he tucked the knife at the small of his back. "Ready to end this clash?" Despite hosting a plethora of scrapes, gashes, and bruises, his brother looked more determined than when they first arrived.

Rowan steeled his nerves. "Lead on, brother."

THEY SEPARATED IN THE FIRST HALL. AKARAN LUMBERED PAST THE dining area, back toward Adelkar's study. His uncle reclined in his chair, facing the hearth, his feet lifted upon the cushioned ottoman.

Well, isn't this a pleasant scene?

Adelkar looked far too comfortable after calling for the death of his nephew. The wish to see him dead raked at Akaran's heart. His hand crept for the knife, but he didn't grab hold, not yet.

Akaran entered the room, his footsteps loud enough for his uncle to detect.

"Is it done?" Adelkar asked, not turning in his chair.

"By done, if you mean I dispatched your hired goons, then yes, it's done."

Adelkar's head whipped around. "How are you still alive?"

Akaran savored the sight of Adelkar's bafflement. "You should've known your thugs wouldn't have been enough to stop me." He stepped forward. "If you want me dead, you'll have to do the job yourself. Like you did with my grandparents."

Adelkar's angry scowl tightened every muscle on his face. "Very well, Nephew. I'll rise to this undertaking. Besides, you look halfway dead already."

"Before you try, Uncle, answer me this one last thing: Why didn't you let Zamara curse me? I know it's what she intended. So why not let her, especially as you despised my father for altering his will and for securing the woman you loved?"

"That's your last request?" Adelkar scoffed, turning his body to fully face Akaran. The fire iron idled close by his hand. "Very well. It was simply to keep appearances. I needed to play the part of a well-meaning uncle who was taking in my brother's son to rear as ward and heir. I hope you didn't think it was for more compassionate reasons."

"No, of course not, Uncle." Akaran freed the knife, keeping his hand low and unseen. "That would suggest you had a heart other than iron."

Adelkar didn't misinterpret the deadly ice in Akaran's tone. His hand, which already had the fire iron, lifted in a swift maneuver.

Akaran shifted his body and stuck the knife to the hilt in Adelkar's chest. His uncle's pupils expanded, and his breath seized. Akaran eased him back into the chair as he panted for breath. Adelkar tried raising the fire iron once more, but Akaran caught the weapon and pried it from his fingers. He tossed the poker aside and took a seat across from his uncle.

"As you taught, Uncle, I struck first."

"A knife to the heart . . ." Adelkar sputtered.

"It's fitting, isn't it? It's what you used against my grandparents. I only returned the gesture."

"Is that what also . . . awaits—burial inside my own mine?"

"It's what you deserve. However, I won't tuck you away like some dark secret. No, you'll have a funeral, so everyone will know your dirty deeds against me." Akaran leaned forward, resting a firm hand on Adelkar's shoulder. "Fret not, Uncle. The estate is in good hands. I've learned much from you. It will keep me prosperous until the end of my days. A pity you won't be there to share in my triumph."

Adelkar's chest heaved. "The pity's mine . . . for taking in a . . . brat like you."

"Well, you won't have to regret your decision much longer. You'll be dead in a minute." Akaran leaned back and flipped his feet upon the ottoman, settling into the armchair. "Enjoy the view, Uncle. Staring at a fire is a pleasant scene. Take rest in its mesmerizing embrace."

A minute passed with shared silence between them; the crackling flames and Adelkar's labored breaths the only sound. Then in a quiet motion, his uncle's head slumped to the side and his breathing stilled.

Akaran nestled his head back against his chair, basking in the fulfillment of his hard-fought revenge and welcoming his well-deserved rest.

When Rowan reached Zamara's lair a second time, a filmy apparition of her stood in the doorway, expelling a disturbing cackle. It chilled the blood in his veins.

"Defeated my wolves, eh?" She circled him like a ghost, surveying his wounds. "And not without difficulty. Came back for more punishment?"

"You know why I've returned—to see you dead."

"I like your resolve, boy. I haven't had this much fun in decades. Now make this easy for an old woman." She swung her nails at his face, evoking another incantation.

Rowan ducked and rolled past her, scrambling into the lair, then spun on his heels, keeping low. Something swift and sleek whizzed through the air, grappling at his face. He yelped as a tangle of black feathers blurred his vision. Somehow the raven Zamara had dissected earlier returned to life.

Burning skies, her incantation must've done it.

Its talons raked at his scalp, then clawed for his eyes. Rowan warded it off with a stroke of his spear, swatting the revived raven against the bookshelf. It flopped several times before lying still. He'd had enough of her devilish tricks. Dashing forward, he drove his spear toward her head, vying to slice off her evil grin.

Suddenly, her face shimmered, transforming into a dark-skinned woman he knew and loved.

Rowan gasped, stopping his spear short. "Naja?"

"Don't stab me, Rowan!" Her frightened plea shackled his bones, but more than that, it was the fear etched on her bronzed face—a face he never thought he'd see again. Her expression softened, and her dark lips turned into a gentle smile. "That's not what I taught you to do with a spear. Be a good son and put it down."

Her strong alto voice—just as he remembered—reverberated through his skull. He hesitated, his spear poised at her face.

"You've always heeded my words. Won't you do so again?" Her

words were bewitching, hypnotizing. It took everything in him to push against them.

No, it's not her! It's not her.

Even though his mind knew it, Rowan's heart was slower to believe. It couldn't relive killing another person he loved. And so, he forced his eyes shut at the last second and thrust the spear forward, burying the tip in Naja's chest.

In the same breath, he uncinched the center of the shaft, revealing the hidden spear tip, and flung it backward. The blade struck flesh, and Rowan spun to behold a shocked Zamara. A small pooling of blood emerged from her stomach. At this juncture once before, he made certain her death was real. Whipping his longer spear in an arc, he crammed it through her chest. The tendrils surged upon her like a pall of black smoke.

The trick was on her this time. He predicted she'd move in close and attack while he concentrated on striking her conjured apparition. As much as it pained him to impale an image of Naja, it set the trap for the crafty Conjurer. And she walked into it perfectly.

Zamara's wiry hair was the first thing to shrivel, followed by her crinkled nose and her taut cheeks. The veiny infection spread like wildfire across every inch of her skin. In hoarse gasps and growls, she stumbled toward the shattered hole in the glass wall—the curse relentless in its assault. Amidst the churning tendrils, her seething gaze narrowed at him. For the first time, he witnessed acute fear in her eyes—the realization that someone as renowned as she could be outwitted.

"You never expected a curse you cast to bite back, did you?" Rowan said, holding her gaze. "You should've known one day it could end like this."

He withdrew his spears, and her body staggered backward—out the window. As if sucked by a vacuum, the host of tendrils teeming around Rowan's body fled and chased after Zamara's plummeting form. He watched her fall with hollowed emotions, her flesh flying away like withering leaves. By the time she hit the stable, nothing was left of her but dust and cloth.

Rowan released a sullen breath.

It's done.

Zamara's demise slowly sank in, and as it did, Rowan checked his hands and limbs for signs of the curse. Not a tendril remained. He recombined his spear, then lifted a shaky hand to the cursemark. He didn't feel the slightest bulge. It, too, had vanished.

I'm finally free.

Overcome with emotion, he succumbed to his knees and let the tears fall.

CHAPTER 32
MORE TRICKS

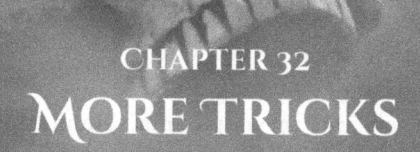

Rowan wandered back down the stairwell. Relief and heaviness stole over him. The curse was gone. The tendrils had disappeared from his body, and though he wanted to find joy in accomplishing his goal, he couldn't feel an ounce of elation with Tahira still missing.

He made his way to Adelkar's study and found his brother lounging by the hearth. His feet were kicked up, his head tilted at an awkward angle, and his eyes shut. Had he fallen asleep in that position? Rowan approached and gave his shoulder a firm nudge.

Akaran jolted awake, then relaxed when noticing Rowan. "Kill the old hag, eh?"

Rowan nodded. He separated the spear and revealed the blood on the small, hidden blade. "I tricked her with this. She never saw it coming."

"Looks like we both gave our targets a crafty slip. That knife of yours came in handy. If you'd like it back, it's buried in my uncle's chest."

Rowan turned and beheld a dead Adelkar seated stiffly in the other armchair. If not for the knife embedded in his chest, he would've appeared to be sleeping.

"Can't you pull it free?" Rowan asked, disturbed by his brother's suggestion.

Akaran grinned. "Fine, I'll do it, but only when I'm ready to stand, which isn't at the moment." He groaned, holding a hand to his ribs. "I'm feeling utterly wracked."

"You got your vengeance," Rowan said, staring into the fire. "How do you feel about that?"

Akaran shrugged. "I thought I'd feel elated. Instead, I don't feel much of anything. Strange, isn't it?"

Rowan gave an understanding nod. "Killing Adelkar and Zamara doesn't bring back our grandparents, Rahn, or my guardian-mothers."

"No, but it does give us a future we can carve without their meddling. They've paid for their treachery. That's all I need to soothe my mind."

Rowan knew of only one way to resolve the burden weighing upon his mind and heart. "Help me find Tahira."

Akaran tilted his head up at him. "Zamara didn't give you a clue, huh?"

Rowan shook his head. "She took the secret to her grave."

"Nasty hag. Well, I know a good place to start looking—the mine. It's a hunch, but considering what Adelkar and Zamara did to the Kamands, we should check the mine for false walls."

Rowan's breaths hitched, and a wave of fear surged through his chest. "You're saying they may have buried her already?"

"It's worth checking." Akaran lowered his feet to the floor and braced a hand on the seatback, steadying his rise. He approached Adelkar's body, hesitating for a moment, and then pulled the knife free. He cleared the blood off with his sleeve, then held the hilt toward Rowan. "All yours."

Rowan returned the knife to his sash and followed his brother from the study.

"Wait by the door," Akaran said, heading to another room. "I'll get us lanterns."

THEY CLIMBED DOWN THE LONG ENTRY SHAFT IN SLOW FASHION, each nursing their own aches. At the bottom, light from their lanterns warmed the roughly hewn walls.

"We'll split up to cover more ground," Akaran said, the candle-flame intensifying the bloody gashes on his face.

"What am I looking for?" Rowan asked, as he'd no idea what constituted a false wall.

"Look for sedimentary walls that don't feel like rock to the touch. Also, keep an eye out for tools that seem out of place, perhaps even vats of plaster—anything that could be used to build a hasty facade."

Rowan nodded and ventured down the first level, his brother taking the following. Each time they cleared a level, they reconvened before delving deeper. The hours slipped away, and with it, the disquiet amassing in Rowan's heart. Mines had become a place of wonder and legacy; tonight, it was an underground bastion of fear and dread. And it had swallowed his love somewhere inside its depths.

Where could she be stashed? Rowan's mind reeled in perpetual torment, scouring every jagged surface he passed. If she was buried behind layers of rock, and with little to no source for air to breathe, was there any chance to find her alive?

They made their way down to the twenty level, and this time when they met up, Akaran was wearing a grim scowl. "I know you don't want to hear this, but it's beginning to look hope—"

"Don't say it. There's hope yet."

Akaran sighed with a fatigued, sincere look. "Face it, we may never find her. Sometimes a man has to know when a fight is finished."

Rowan whirled on his brother. "And what if it was you trapped somewhere down here, huh? Running out of air every passing hour? Wouldn't you want me to explore every crevice to find you?"

Akaran chewed his split lip. "I don't have to answer that. I'm not the one missing."

"Oh, don't give me that heartless answer," Rowan grumbled, brushing past his brother. "You'd want to be found. There are more levels we haven't searched yet."

"A half-dozen more, yes." Akaran's droopy stance and dull voice showed every indication that he was at his limit. Fatigue and frustration swathed him like a waterlogged cloak. "Don't get your hopes up. If Zamara said you'd not find Tahira without her, she wasn't joking."

"You're the one who told me not to let that stop me from killing her," Rowan reminded him. "Why would you say that if you knew this could happen?"

"Because I knew she would never come clean. It was all part of her trickery—her scheme to bind your hands and safeguard her life."

Rowan's insides twisted, hating the rationale in his brother's answer.

They split company once again, and Rowan had to consciously keep Akaran's words from rooting in his mind. His brother might be ready to concede the search, but Rowan would never stop looking. Tahira was only taken as leverage in Adelkar's scheme—and Zamara hadn't wasted a moment in using it to her own advantage. He refused to let Tahira pay the price for their evil whims.

He entered another level, this one glittering with veins of ore yet to be excavated, which meant this had to be one of the final tunnels. He continued roaming a hand over the walls, poking his head through crevices, holding his lantern over unlit shafts—hoping something would stand out.

Rowan took several steps toward a narrow fissure, stepping on ground that didn't feel quite like rock. He shuffled backward and held his lantern over the odd surface. He tapped his foot against the ground and grew more puzzled. It resembled rock yet gave off a hollower sound. Could there be space beneath the ground?

Rowan set aside the lantern and clawed his fingers against the ground. A stiff substance gathered beneath his fingernails. He sniffed at it and smelled plaster. The substance had various uses miners relied upon in forging equipment and repairs. But using it in the ground like this was strangely amiss.

Could Tahira be buried underneath? Hope sailed within him at the small chance.

He pulled out his knife and used it to tear away more and more of the hardened material. Someone had done an exceptional job of coloring this plaster exactly like rock. It would've worked if not for the distinctly different sound it created. After prying most of the plaster away, another obstacle faced him. A slatted slab of metal.

Why was there an iron grate in the middle of the walkway? Had the ground beneath recently caved and required stronger reinforcement? Then another more nefarious thought came to him—that it was placed there to cover a purposely dug hole.

Rowan dug furiously with his knife and exposed the edges of the grate. It was roughly six-by-three feet—the width and height necessary to conceal a petite woman's body. When he finally dislodged the grate from all the surrounding rock and dirt, he muscled it aside and peered into the cramped hole.

There, he found Tahira lying on her back, half of her body buried, with her hands folded upon her chest. A shallow basket concealed by a cloth covered her head.

"Tahira!" he cried, flinging the basket away from her face. Her eyes were closed, and the deathlike pallor of her skin froze his heart. Fear spiked his gut.

Tell me she's not dead...

He lowered his ear to her chest, and heard the swift yet muted beat of her heart.

She's alive!

He shoveled the dirt away from her legs and hoisted her free. He cradled her head against his chest, tears welling in his eyes. "Wake up, Tahira. Come on, wake up!" He tapped her cheeks and gently shook her shoulders. Her head slackened, and her arms hung limp.

Burning skies, what's happened to her?

"Akaran!" Rowan screamed for his brother. "I found her! Come quick!"

Akaran raced up the tunnel a minute later. When he caught sight of the hole in the ground, his eyes widened. "Huh, I didn't think to inspect the ground. Luckily you did."

Rowan sank his head against Tahira's. His body numbed. To have come this far and still be at the mercy of Zamara's tricks riled every emotion within him.

Akaran came close, standing above him. "Is she alive?"

"I don't know!" Rowan couldn't restrain the hysteria from coloring his voice. "I think she is, but she's stiff as stone."

"You sure it's not from the cold?"

Rowan gave his brother a sharp glare for the lack of concern in his voice. "Yes, I'm sure. Her heart still beats."

Akaran lowered his lantern and crouched beside him. "Then that's a good sign. Means she's not dead."

"Then what's wrong with her? I killed Zamara, so if she did something to Tahira, why won't she wake?"

Akaran scratched at the tender gash on his jaw. "She must be under an enchantment."

Rowan's frown deepened, and his heart grew more riled. "I don't understand. My curse is broken because Zamara is dead."

"Yes, but enchantments work differently than curses. Your curse was tied to Zamara's life. An enchantment isn't. It lingers after a Conjurer's death."

It was the worst news Rowan could have received. "Then how do we break it?"

"By finding the right spellbreaker." Akaran used Rowan's wounded shoulder to help himself rise. "Let's head to Zamara's lair. I'm sure there's a spellbook or two that will give us ideas."

Rowan gathered Tahira into his arms and trudged after his brother, his mind in torment. If Tahira remained in this death-trance state, he'd never forgive himself. It was a price he never would have paid.

ROWAN LOWERED TAHIRA ON THE LAIR'S FLOOR. COOL WIND blew through the shattered glass wall as he stared dully at her sweet yet deathlike countenance. "How do you know so much about enchantments, brother?"

Akaran pulled out several spellbooks from the shelf, dropped them on the worktable, and rifled through the pages. "Aunt Zamara thought it amusing to enchant my horse whenever I mouthed off—which happened quite often. Oh, the hours I spent wracking my brain to discover the cure. I learned to start with the obvious, and then move on to the most bizarre."

Rowan caressed a hand to Tahira's cold cheek. "And what's the obvious spellbreaker for this enchantment?"

"That would be a kiss."

Rowan frowned, pulling back his hand. "Why's that obvious?"

Akaran held up a page from the spellbook, indicating its depiction of a man kissing a sleeping maiden. "It's a common enchantment Conjurers invoke when they wish to punish lovers. The aim is to have one member killed, so the other remains asleep for all time." Akaran smirked. "Perhaps that's the reason I never considered securing a girl's heart. Zamara could've employed her spellcraft on the poor maiden just to vex me."

Rowan suspected that wasn't the main reason at all. Akaran didn't understand matters of the heart, plain and simple. Regardless, he'd seen the prudence in keeping himself romantically unattached.

"Anyhow," Akaran said, getting back to his point, "such an enchantment is often broken by a lover's kiss, much like in the old fables, you know."

Rowan shook his head. "No, I don't know. I'm not familiar with any Shandrian fables."

"Oh. Right. I forgot you were raised by tribal Luvarians." Akaran set the book upon the worktable and put his hands on his hips. "Trust me, just try it."

Since Rowan was now rid of the curse, he could touch Tahira without fear. Yet, this wasn't how he ever imagined their reunited kiss to be—with her life hanging in the balance.

"What are you waiting for—an invitation?" Akaran prodded. "Kiss her."

Rowan tuned out his brother and dipped his head, kissing Tahira's cold, pallid lips.

"Anything?" Akaran voiced.

Rowan waited several breaths. Her eyelids didn't stir. He sighed in frustration. "There's no change."

Akaran pinched his jaw. "Strange. I thought for certain that would've been it." He returned to the spellbook and kept flipping through more pages. "All right, here's a chant that might do the trick." He cleared his voice and uttered a long, jumbling stream of deep vowel sounds. "How about now?"

Rowan shook his head. "Still nothing."

"Perhaps I didn't get the tones right." Akaran repeated the phrase, and to Rowan's ears, it sounded worse than the first time.

"Try something else," Rowan hissed, unable to hold back his rising frustration.

"Hey, don't bite my head off. I'm only trying to help." Akaran moved to the second book. "Hm, we don't have one of those lying around . . . The wrong moon is in the sky for this one . . . Oh! Maybe this—er, no. Wait—I have an idea!"

"What?" Rowan asked, surprised by his brother's sudden elation.

Akaran paused and turned his head. "Perhaps I should give it a try and kiss her."

"You?" Rowan went from being surprised to dumbfounded. "If it didn't work for me, why would it work for you?"

"Ever heard of a 'kiss from an enemy'?" Akaran asked, wearing a mischievous grin. "It would be just like Aunt Zamara to put a tricky twist on the old enchantment."

"But you're not my enemy anymore."

"I may not be yours, but I'm no friend of your feisty mistress. I've seen the askance looks she's given me. In her mind, I'm every bit the reptile she dislikes. So, it's worth a shot, isn't it?"

Rowan couldn't refute the reasoning. At this desperate hour, he would try the smallest chance to see her awaken. "Make it quick."

"Of course." Akaran's expression turned smugly roguish. "I wouldn't dream of leaving a lasting impression as you have." He lowered to his knees, stooped his face in close, and kissed Tahira.

Rowan bumped his brother's shoulder immediately after. "That's good enough, now move back."

"All right, all right, I'm moving." With laughter alight in his eyes, Akaran lifted his head away.

They waited several tense seconds. Rowan scooped up Tahira's hand, willing her to wake.

Please, come back to me. Open your eyes.

Tahira's eyelids quivered. Her lips parted, and she gasped in a panicked fright, as if reemerging from underwater. Her eyes opened, full and wide, and her chest rose in frantic heaves.

Rowan's jaw dropped in astonishment. "Burning skies, it worked!"

"You're welcome." Akaran stood, giving the couple space.

"Rowan?" Tahira's eyes focused on him, her body shivering.

"I'm here. You're safe." Rowan caressed her face, giving her a joyous kiss. He couldn't restrain himself, and Tahira didn't mind at all. Her fingers tangled in his hair, tugging on the strands to keep him from pulling away.

Easing back, he had the joy of seeing a blissful smile illuminating her face.

"If you're kissing me, then the curse is broken?"

"Yes. Finally."

Akaran cleared his throat and dipped his head into view. "Just so you know, mistress, it was my kiss that broke your enchantment."

Tahira's face blanched. She gave Rowan a pointed stare. "You let him kiss me?"

"I kissed you first," Rowan said in his defense, "but it didn't wake you. Apparently, the kiss of an enemy did the trick." For which he had the feeling Akaran would never let them forget.

Tahira remained quiet for a moment. Her lips quirked, repeatedly, a clear sign she was coming to terms with her distaste for Akaran. "I suppose I should thank you."

Akaran broke into a smug grin. "It would be the civil thing to do in your case, mistress."

She chuckled. "Well, then, in all civility, thank you."

"It was the least I could do for my brother's betrothed," Akaran said in an over-the-top, ingratiating manner. "I do hope this means I'll receive an invitation to the wedding—when the time comes, of course."

"It will be considered," Tahira said with a noncommittal smile. Her eyes drifted back to Rowan's. She placed a hand against his chest, taking in his countenance. "You look sorely battered. Was the fight as terrible as you feared?"

"It had its frightful moments." Rowan shivered just remembering the conjurings and apparitions Zamara had used against him. He doubted he'd ever cleanse from his mind the sight of stabbing Tahira. Having her awake and alive within his arms was a balm to his heart.

"I think it's fair to say, we were both put through the smelter," Akaran said with a tired huff. "I'm ready to sleep and not wake for days."

The tension surrounding Tahira's enchantment departed, and the adrenaline flooding Rowan's body dissipated. His wounds smarted more acutely. "I feel the same, brother."

Tahira nudged him. "Then can we please leave this creepy place?"

Rowan gently took her hand and nodded. "Yes, let's head home."

CHAPTER 33
BELONGING

Scrapes treated and wounds tended, Rowan slumped on the parlor's low-cushioned couch beside the hearth. Tahira joined him once she'd bathed and changed into a slimming celadon dress. Lulled to sleep by the fire's gentle thrum, they spent what was left of the night nestled in each other's arms. When sunlight touched their eyelids, they stirred to sweet wakefulness.

Rowan dipped his head and kissed her smiling lips.

"A girl could get used to this." Tahira giggled, her eyes as bright as dawnlight.

"So could I." Rowan stroked the curve of Tahira's shoulder, and his fingertips tingled with sensation. Burning skies, he could scarcely believe he could touch her without fear of repercussions.

She twiddled with the fringe around her shawl. "Shall we celebrate with a feast for abolishing the curse? It would be a splendid way to commemorate our handfasting."

Rowan smiled, warmed by the idea. "Make the arrangements to your liking. I only ask that you push the festivities back a fortnight. I need time to take care of a certain task."

"Freeing your mother, yes?"

He nodded, holding in a shudder. The mere thought of visiting Mount Maldere again disturbed him to the marrow. But he wouldn't go back on his word. "I promised I'd return as soon as the curse was broken."

Worry crawled over Tahira's face. "But you'll not have the curse to protect you this time."

"Which is why I'm going to see if Akaran will join me."

Tahira snorted loudly. "Good luck convincing him to help. He'll likely put up a fuss."

"Then I'll have to be extra persuasive and appeal to his heart."

Tahira gave him a flummoxed stare. "You sure he has one?"

"Oh, he does, whether he wants to admit it or not."

Tahira sidled in closer, caressing Rowan's bruised cheek. "I know the curse is gone, but I can't help but think what a toll it took on you. How are you?"

"Shaken," Rowan admitted. A cold shiver passed through his body. "All night long I kept seeing Zamara's face. The fearful way she looked at me just before she died. I can't help but wonder how many people looked upon her in the same manner before she cursed them."

It was yet another wicked trick—to attain freedom only by taking the life of the one who'd cursed him. To know his soul had to be tainted to have a future.

Tahira stroked his arm. "Killing Zamara and ending her evil doesn't make you like her. Conjurers must know to throw a curse is to court repercussions."

"So, you're saying she got what she deserved?"

"In a manner of speaking, yes. Don't you think the same?"

"Oh, I do." Rowan sighed. "But it's one thing to think it, and another to believe it in one's heart. A life should never be idly taken on a whim—even one as vile as Zamara's."

"The mere fact you're sparing a thought for the Conjurer who cursed you, reveals the depth of who you are. You are good, Rowan, and it's your goodness that won my heart at our first encounter." Tahira lifted her hand to caress his chin. "Do me a favor and think no more of her. We survived her designs for us, so let's live in the way we couldn't before. It's been my deepest hope."

The persistent longing in her voice and gaze eased the disquiet in Rowan's heart. He put thoughts of Zamara aside and chose instead to dwell on thoughts of hope for their future. "I've longed for this day as well." He scooped his arms around Tahira and brought her in for a lengthy kiss.

A thrilling spark coursed through him, setting a torch to every nerve in his body. His lips warmed at her touch, and the sweetness of her aroma pervaded his senses. All he wanted forevermore was to know her completely. She was an ocean, vast and unknown. All he'd perceived was the shoreline. Even in a lifetime, he doubted he'd understand her in entirety, but he was eager to try.

"When will you visit Akaran?" she asked.

"In a couple of days. We each could use some time to recover from our wounds."

Tahira smiled, running her fingers through his hair. "Good. Until then, I'm keeping you all to myself."

"No complaints here." He sank his lips against hers, getting lost in the joy of having her close at his side. Snuggled with his love in his arms, Rowan couldn't think of a more sublime way to pass the hours.

AKARAN HELPED HIMSELF TO A FOUR-COURSE MEAL HE'D TASKED the scullery maid to prepare, consisting of all of his favorite foods: roasted pork, scalloped potatoes, savory stew, and stout bread. He couldn't think of a better way to commemorate his victory. The chewing was slow and tiresome, and he regretted getting hit in the face so many times. He swigged his wine. It helped the meatier bites go down.

When he was halfway through his second course, Ravel strode in with a jubilant grin. Clearly, he'd heard the gossip buzzing around Arjun of Adelkar's treacherous demise.

"I'm gratified to see you alive, Aka, yet I don't think I've ever seen you look quite so ugly. You offed your uncle and got your body bludgeoned in the process. A fight I fear you could've handled better."

"If that's what you think, you should've seen my contenders," Akaran said, fighting back a chuckle to keep his ribs from smarting. "I can't chew so well right now, and my ears keep ringing. Then there are these relentless headaches."

"That shouldn't affect what I brought for you to enjoy." Ravel unveiled a squat wine bottle and plopped it on the table. "Your favorite vintage. I nabbed it from my father's cellar."

Akaran smiled broadly, despite the ache it elicited. "An elixir to numb the pains wracking my body."

"Indeed! So let's celebrate this auspicious occasion." Ravel poured their goblets, then raised his and clunked it against Akaran's. "Cheers to you, Aka. You claimed back your lands and are now the wealthiest Iron Baron in all of Arjun. You must be enjoying this triumph."

Akaran took a long and pleasurable swill of the wine. "I'll enjoy it better when my head isn't so mired."

Ravel gave him a blunt stare. "Frankly, you should be resting."

"This is me resting."

"Have you slept?" his friend asked.

"My mind fights it."

"I can knock you out if you'd like?" Ravel suggested with a straight face. "That'll solve your problem."

"No, thanks. Sleep will come when my mind is good and ready."

"What's eating at it?"

"The silence." Akaran swirled the wine in his goblet, peering around the hall. "My mind is having a hard time grasping that my uncle and aunt are gone. Every room I enter, I expect to find Adelkar, but there's nothing there. Only silence."

"You'll get used to it. This house is yours now and everything in it. It's what your father wanted. It's the legacy he left you. Think of how you can master it."

Akaran lowered his goblet and chortled. "Curses, Rav, I didn't know you could be so sentimental."

"It's only because it's weird seeing you so internalized. I'd challenge you to a match and throng you out of this, but your face doesn't look like it can handle another blow."

Akaran chuckled again, then winced in pain. "Come back in a week, and I'll be ready for whatever you throw at me."

Ravel's face flashed with a competitive grin. "I'm holding you to it, Aka."

Their conversation turned toward mining, which brought on another headache. Yes, he was thrilled to be the owner of two lucrative mines, but he would need to grow in character to be a successful administrator of his wealth. Luckily, he had a savvy friend who would keep him doggedly poised in the right direction.

Ravel bid him farewell. As soon as he left, another visitor arrived, one who looked as haggard as Akaran. They shared a long understanding stare before breaking into smiles.

"Well, this is a surprise." Akaran waved his brother closer. "Have a seat. Enjoy some wine. We both deserve it."

"Offering me wine, brother?" Rowan said with a genuine smile.

Akaran snorted. "Think I might drug you again?"

"I wouldn't rule it out." Rowan pulled up a chair but didn't reach to pour himself a drink. To refuse such an exceptional vintage indicated something heavy weighed on his brother's mind.

Great, and just when I was ready to be unburdened with weighty cares.

"There's a matter I want to discuss with you."

Akaran tsked. "How troublesome."

"You don't even know what it concerns."

"No, but I have the feeling I'm not going to like it. The first time you proposed something requiring my assistance, it was about breaking your curse, and I ended up looking like this." Akaran gestured to his swollen and stitched-up face. "I can only imagine what daring escapade you want me to join next."

Rowan hesitated, the silence stretching between them.

"Well, are you going to tell me or sit there like a mute?"

Rowan eased his hands in front of him in a placating gesture. "I made a promise to Zurie to free her from Mount Maldere after I broke the curse, and I want you to back me up. Two of us have a better chance of getting her out of there safely than one."

Akaran thrust his goblet upon the table. "Curses, why'd you make her a promise like that? For us to risk our necks for the likes of her—it's asinine."

"To you, perhaps," Rowan conceded, "but if you'd seen her as I did in her fractured state, even you might've doled out a compassionate promise."

Akaran highly doubted it. He harbored no kindness toward his mother whatsoever. "Don't assume you know what I would've done. I'm not the forgiving type." He shot his brother a hard look. "Don't tell me you've forgiven her for abandoning us."

"I haven't yet . . ." A flicker of emotion warped Rowan's tired countenance; it faded with a steadying breath. "Freeing her doesn't excuse what she did to us. She'll have much to atone for, especially when she learns what befell her parents."

Akaran gave a sardonic grunt. "That should go over well." He sipped more of his wine, reveling in its woodsy notes. "Has it occurred to you that I don't care what happens to Zurie?"

"It has."

"And yet, you still thought to come here and make this appeal? Why?"

"Because she doesn't belong in that cursed mountain."

Akaran sniffed and poured himself another drink. "And where does she belong? Certainly not with either of us."

"No, but we can return her to her childhood home at Kamand House."

It belonged to Akaran now, but he wasn't stoked by the idea of restoring its luster. "That place is run down and has been neglected for years."

"I doubt Zurie will mind. She's been living in a dark, secluded cavern for eighteen years. To be above grass in her old home might help remedy her mental state. She no longer has the curse to protect her, and she will become easy prey for the more savage minds interned inside that mountain."

Akaran stared at his brother, reluctant to give in. What did he owe Zurie? Nothing. "We're finally unbound to anyone. We have our lands passed down by our fathers, and you want to bring Zurie back into the fold? I'll not be bound by any more ties."

"You forget we're bound as brothers. Do you aim to sever that?"

Akaran narrowed his eyes but recovered quickly. "It's the only one I shall allow. Consider yourself fortunate."

"I do," Rowan said with a short laugh. "Not every familial relationship is an affliction to one's self. I think we've made good strides to disprove that. So will you not go with me?"

If Akaran did, it would only be to help his brother—he did, after all, owe Rowan for saving his life from Adelkar's henchmen.

He huffed. "Fine, I'll go with you, but only to have this matter settled. Rescuing Zurie from her own folly changes nothing between her and me. I still hate her."

"The fact you hate her, indicates at one point, you loved her as any child would their mother."

Akaran was quick to jab back at the statement. "Don't analyze me." He'd gotten enough of it from Ravel; he didn't need it from his brother. "Any more of that kind of talk, and I'll punch you. Then you'll find yourself going alone."

Rowan's sigh was a resigned one. "All right, I'll give it a rest."

Akaran eased from his seat so as not to provoke another headache. "Let's go before I change my mind. We'll take my carriage."

"SOULS ABOVE, I CAN SCARCELY BELIEVE IT!" THE MESTRIAN guard stationed at the entrance to Mount Maldere bellowed a hearty and bewildered laugh. "The spearman has returned! You must be a glutton for punishment."

"Actually, Gowin, that would be my brother here," Rowan said, indicating Akaran.

Gowin took one look at the discolorations and stitches marring Akaran's face and broke out in laughter once more. His lazy blue eyes rested back on Rowan. "Discounting the glutton, you look like you've had your share of troubles already, so why come back here?"

"There's a woman interned within we're here to free. I broke her curse by killing the Conjurer who cursed her long ago."

With the conversation taking on a more serious note, the young soldier's demeanor straightened to match it. "Do you have a witness to corroborate this?"

"That would be me," Akaran replied.

Yet another reason why Rowan must've wanted me on this daring crusade.

"The Conjurer is dead."

"Then by all means—proceed." The guard moved to open the iron gate. "I would wish you luck, spearman, but I am beginning to believe you already have it."

Akaran dipped his head and whispered to his brother, "He's far too friendly for a Mestrian soldier."

"We have a history."

"So, you're the reason for his civility? What exactly did you do to earn it?"

"I came back alive. To him, it's an impressive feat, which earned me a meal."

"He treated you to a meal?"

Rowan nodded. "I'd been in desperate need at the time."

"Hm, I wonder if he'll be in a sharing mood when we return," Akaran said aloud, more to himself.

The gate swung aside, and Gowin handed them a pair of torches. The cold maw awaited.

Curses, why did I agree to come along?

If Akaran had remained at home, he could've been supping his favorite wine and enjoying a savory meal.

Rowan moved toward the dark opening and divulged a solemn warning. "Be on your guard. The last time I came here, I was attacked by a trio of cannibals."

Akaran gripped his brother's shoulder in the next breath. "And you're just telling me this now—right before we enter this abyss?"

"You might have backed out if I had."

Akaran scowled. "How tricky you are. I fear Aunt Zamara has rubbed off on you."

Rowan grimaced. "Don't even joke about that."

"Why? Afraid it might be true?"

"No, I'm not. Can we forget about her and enter the mountain?"

"Sure, brother. Right after you."

Akaran took full advantage of Rowan's weapon and remained safely tucked behind his brother as they wandered inside Mount Maldere's cavernous depths. He removed his leather wrappings and wound them over his fists and wrists. He aimed to be ready for anything.

At the start, the mountain's interior was much like a mine: deep, dark, cold, and damp. But as they delved deeper, the differences soon widened when they reached the first cavern. The vast serrated ceiling loomed above their heads with spiked stalactites dripping like fangs. It was as if they were inside the jowls of a colossal creature.

A straining, rumbling moan encompassed the chamber, and Akaran thought for certain the mountain had come alive.

"What are those moans?" Akaran whispered to his brother. "Tell me it's just the wind."

"Sadly, no. It's people afflicted by a skin-devouring curse. Their bodies are littered all around. Keep your distance."

"You don't have to tell me twice. I'm staying far away from any of the accursed in this—"

Something snagged Akaran by the ankle, and a spine-chilling jolt brought his fist into action. He swung it right into a man's diseased face that possessed neither nose nor eyeballs. The body dropped in a heap without a fight.

Rowan whirled to his side, holding his torch to inspect the unmoving form. "Burning skies, did you have to hit him so hard?"

"I thought it was a cannibal."

"If there are any, they'll be farther down."

"Oh. Great. Thanks for the information."

The sickened moans quieted, and once again the only din came from the whirling torches and the scraping of their boots against rock. Their path got trickier when the roof sloped so drastically, they were forced to shimmy on hands and knees to reach the next chamber, and what a wonder it was.

Akaran beheld heavenly blue rocks glittering like deposits of opals upon the walls. Though their light emanated only a faint glow, the expansive rock roof twinkling above his head gave the illusion of a night sky.

His brother noticed his awe. "Beautiful, isn't it?"

Akaran shrugged. "Remarkable is the word I'd choose."

"It was home to the cannibals I encountered."

"Perhaps they had an eye for the cosmic."

"They're dead, but others could've chosen this place to dwell. Let's carry on." Rowan grew visibly more wary as he approached a downward slope.

A cauldron of bats, clinging to the slanted roof, dropped like a scatter of rainfall and swarmed in their direction. Akaran swung at a passel of bats screeching their teeth in his face. Rowan swung his spear, clipping wings and flinging several of the flying rodents against the rock face.

"Annoying pests," Akaran growled through his teeth.

"Press on toward the slope," Rowan hollered, dashing forward.

Through the shroud of fluttering wings, a scrawny form slithered out from the darkness. It rushed for his brother.

Akaran struck another bat with his fist, and shouted, "Behind you!"

Rowan spun just in time and flung the butt of his spear directly into the gut of a raving madman. The accursed denizen dropped on all fours, skittering like a beast, hungry for flesh.

Akaran charged from behind and grappled the crazed man by the throat. The man thrashed and snarled like he had no mind at all. His teeth were filed into a row of sharp points, and they sank their way into Akaran's hand wrappings.

Akaran hissed a fiery growl and cinched his arm all the more tightly around the beastly man's thin neck, squeezing with all his strength. The man's outgrown nails clawed into Akaran's skin. For a gangly person, the man possessed more fight than Akaran thought possible.

"Stab him!" Akaran yelled at his brother. "Before he breaks loose!"

Rowan pushed his spear forward but waited for an opening. Akaran repositioned his body and exposed the man's chest. In a flash, Rowan speared him, and the fight in the madman abated. Akaran unshackled his arms and flung the body aside.

Rowan approached and took a hard look at the dead man. "Now this was a cannibal."

"Say it isn't so," Akaran said with a huff, grimacing at the state of his hand. "Crazed wretch bit clear through the leather."

Rowan cringed. "You're lucky he didn't get you by the throat."

"Well, let's not stick around for another one to try."

After descending the steep slope, they arrived at a chamber where stones emitting ember-orange hues mottled the broad floor. Akaran didn't let any sort of fascination steal into his mind. He'd had enough of this place.

"We're almost there," Rowan said, scuttling across the chamber to a dark and obscenely narrow fissure. "Through this passage, we'll come to Zurie's sanctum."

Akaran lifted his brow. "Her sanctum?"

"It's her word for it, not mine."

Rowan slid inside the fissure, and Akaran gave a not-so-thrilled grunt before entering. With his broader build, he feared getting stuck. His brother didn't have such a worry. He shimmied with annoying ease, quick on his toes, unlike Akaran. The jagged interior scraped against his back and chest, tearing at his clothes.

Blue light touched his eyes, and Akaran took solace in the fact that the way out of this skinny passage lay just ahead. When he peered into the sanctum, he was met with the last thing he ever imagined: a thriving, bioluminescent ecosystem miles beneath the mountain.

Well, isn't this a pretty scene?

Zurie washed her face in a small pool nestled beneath an array of vine-like flora growing curious fruit. Her teeming head of silver curls covered her shoulders and most of her slim torso.

Akaran hung back, concealing himself in the shadows. He preferred letting his brother make the initial overture.

Rowan stepped into the illuminated sanctum and greeted their mother.

Shock filled her eyes. "You came back for me?"

"I said I'd return. I'm not one to betray an oath, or abandon you to die in this cursed place."

Akaran scoffed under his breath.

She abandoned us easily enough.

Zurie's curly head dipped in shame. "I don't deserve this kindness."

Her admonition provoked Akaran, and a stern rebuttal launched from his tongue. "We didn't come here out of kindness," he said, marching out from the dark corridor. "We're only here because Rowan made you a promise he couldn't break."

Zurie's gaze fixed on Akaran, and her entire countenance shifted. Her eyes widened with recognition, and her quivering lips parted. "Akaran . . . I didn't expect you'd come with your brother."

"Don't take it to mean anything," Akaran interjected, before she jumped to any heartfelt conclusions. "I did it for him, not you. You're nothing to me, as I suspect I'm nothing to you."

"Such a harsh exterior," she chided, dodging his accusation, "but it's expected from someone raised by Adelkar and Zamara."

"And whose fault was that, huh?" Akaran snapped, his entire body bristling. "Because of you, I grew up without my father."

"I wronged you, and likely, you'll never forgive me."

"You've got that right." He had the mind to persist biting back, but one mediating look from Rowan curbed his rant.

"Let's get out of here," Rowan urged. "More can be said when we're free of this place."

Curses, why did he always have to sound so sensible?

"Fine. Let's go." Akaran returned to the passageway, inching his way back to the cavern brimming with the orange, glowing stones. When he was free of the dark and jagged confines, he didn't pause and wait for his mother or brother. He knew the way back.

"Not that way, Akaran," Zurie hollered to his back.

Akaran spun to face her. "It's the way we came—"

"I know a quicker, more secure route to the entrance." Zurie's voice was hushed, and her eyes narrowed. "Most inhabitants don't know of it."

Akaran exchanged a reluctant look with Rowan, who gave a quick nod, indicating they should trust Zurie. If she kept them away from cannibals and the like, he'd follow her up any dark pathway. "Lead on then, *Mother*," he said curtly to her. "We'll follow."

Zurie's way was more secure, but it also was far more treacherous. It involved climbing up rock faces, shimmying across ledges suspended high above bottomless shafts, wading through a frigid stream, and scurrying on their bellies like varmints. With Rowan's and Zurie's more lithe builds, the cramped crawl spaces rendered them little discomfort. Akaran got stuck along the way three times and suffered his brother's laughter each time before he offered the shaft of his spear to help.

"Do try to keep up, Akaran," Zurie said, dipping beneath another jagged stalactite. "One would think you've never ventured deeply underground."

"I'm a pugilist, not a caver, as you so gleefully appear to be."

"I learned to adapt to my environment," Zurie said, strolling forward. "The best survivalists do."

Akaran stooped near his shorter brother who had the luxury of not having to creep around like a hunchback. "Was she this irritating when you met her?"

Rowan shrugged. "We clashed with words a bit, then she tried to kill me. So, I'd say things are going much better this time around."

She tried to kill him? Curses.

Akaran moaned, shaking his head. Yet another piece of information his brother had conveniently left out.

When the saw-toothed roof at last returned to a high, sprawling dome, Akaran stood and stretched to his full height. "I'm glad that's over." He strode up to Zurie, keeping pace with her determined stride. "I find it strange someone of your slim stature would've freely roamed such perilous terrain on your own, not to mention the denizens that could've eaten you for breakfast."

Zurie's lips broke into an amused grin. "You forget I shared the same abilities as Rowan. It's how I became known as the Goddess of Death." Zurie sounded far too dazzled by her deific title. "Did Rowan not tell you?"

Akaran redirected his stern gaze at his brother. "No. He failed to mention that bit as well."

Rowan turned out his palms in a guilty gesture. "I didn't think it relevant."

"One of these days, brother, we'll have a discussion about withheld information, where you'll drink the wine I set in front of you and spill your guts."

Rowan grinned wryly at him. "Now that you've divulged your intentions, I'll make certain to never drink anything you offer me."

"Still sore about the first time I drugged you, huh?" Akaran jested.

"I'm not sure my jaw will ever fully recover."

"Nor mine," Akaran admitted.

Zurie strolled past them, a humorous twinkle in her eyes. It irked Akaran seeing it. What was so amusing to her? He hurled his curiosity aside and marched after her.

"We're almost there," she relayed, hardly breaking a sweat. "There's just one more rock face to ascend."

"It better be the last," Akaran said. He was over this whole adventure.

Luckily, the way up the cliff had a natural stairway and made climbing far less arduous. The occasional hand was required for securing his footing, but once at the crest, a relatively flat path lay ahead. They slipped through a fissure and came back upon a familiar tunnel. The entrance lay close. Akaran dashed the rest of the way with rising elation. When he reached the barred gate, he rattled it, startling the guard on duty.

"Back already?" Gowin showed his teeth. "I expected you would be gone at least another day or forever."

"We had a good guide," Rowan responded with a humble smile.

Gowin pulled the lever, and the gate slid open.

Zurie was hesitant to step into the sunlight. "It's too bright for me." She put her hands over her eyes. Her white lashes fluttered as quickly as a moth's wings.

Rowan removed his sash and tied it loosely around her head, shielding her eyes from the harsh daylight—something she'd not witnessed in eighteen years. He brought her hands around his arm, then bid Gowin a thankful farewell and strolled down the path.

Akaran followed at a close distance, watching the pair. Only days ago, they couldn't stand so close to another person without spreading their curse's toxic infection. The sight softened his heart if only by a small margin.

"How's the state of things back home?" Zurie asked, her voice perking up.

"Much has changed," Rowan said, careening his head to look back at Akaran. "What has changed may come as a shock. There's much to tell." The insistent pull in his brother's gaze bid Akaran to come closer and share their story.

Begrudgingly, Akaran approached the pair and cleared his throat. "We'll start with telling you what happened to your parents."

EPILOGUE

Akaran and Rowan laid their grandparents to rest inside the burial grounds upon the Kamand property with their mother in attendance. Zurie kept quiet, a solemn creature, as if the shock of what became of her parents had left her numb. She was told the truth of their demise, of how they paid the ultimate price for wanting to shield her son from the likes of those who reviled her.

Akaran didn't know what was going through her head, but she seemed overwhelmed by . . . well, everything. Her affair had disrupted and altered the lives of her closest relations, most of whom were dead as a consequence. If she held any guilt for her actions, she didn't show it. Akaran realized his mother was a hard piece of ore to smelt. She was a woman without family or friends, yet her situation didn't seem to bother her. Did her heart have so little to give, much like his own?

He and his brother returned her to Kamand House and hired a maid and manservant for her day-to-day needs and hopefully integrate her back into society. Even though she'd survived on her own for eighteen years in isolation, she was in dire need of human interaction, but not the kind her sons would freely extend. The tunnel had collapsed on that level—at least for Akaran's part. With Rowan's more compassionate nature, he might visit her from time to time.

Rowan and Tahira threw a celebratory feast, and Tahira kindly extended an invitation to Akaran. Not one to shy away from a delectable meal, he attended and actually enjoyed himself. It was a merry affair, with all of the tenants who lived on Rowan's land in attendance. Surrounded by everyone wishing them well, the young couple traded carefree smiles, and the occasional blushful kiss.

Akaran stayed only long enough to enjoy the savory fare they offered before riding to Kamand House to speak to his mother. He found her sitting on the floor before the marble hearth, wearing a clean midnight-blue dress and shawl, her wild curls highlighted in golden tones. She stared deeply into the fire, the world around her forgotten.

Akaran's boots clacked on the unpolished stone floor, drawing her notice.

"Once you brought me here," she said in a subdued voice, "I didn't think you'd ever return to see my face again."

He gave a pithy reply. "Well, as long as you don't turn around, I won't have to."

"I'll accommodate you and get straight to the point. What do you want to hear from me?"

Akaran folded his arms, bracing for the truth. "I want to know about you and my father. Did he neglect you as Rowan says?"

"Yes. Kainan had many qualities one could admire, but alas, not the ones that endeared his heart to mine. Call us selfish creatures, he and I, but from the time you were born, we each chased after our own separate desires. I thought only of myself, and what my heart wanted."

"Which led you to Rorak's arms," Akaran said pointedly.

Zurie nodded, her face unmoved from the fire. "Kainan desired a son, and in you, he got what he wanted most. And curses, did he ever shower you with attention. You could do no wrong in his eyes. He flooded you with gifts and fancy treats."

"And what of his death? Do you bear no guilt for your part in it?"

"Of course, I do. I'm not without a heart."

"Your apathy betrays you."

Zurie sighed, but still no empathy came to her tongue. "Kainan's death was a lifetime ago. The woman who knew him died after giving birth to Rowan. I am a different person. Zamara's curse and Mount

Maldere made me into this severe creature—it gave me a new identity. And now, I've lost even that."

"Don't expect me to pity you," Akaran spat. "Rowan took great risks freeing you."

The edge in Zurie's demeanor dissipated, as though recalling her son's selflessness in freeing her from Mount Maldere had some sort of transformative effect. "He is much like his father, just as you are much like yours. Take solace in the knowledge that you had a father who would've given you the world. He was a far better parent than I."

An unknown emotion stirred in Akaran. Was it that elusive thing called love? Love for a father he couldn't even remember? If what Zurie said was true—and he truly had received such doting from his father—could enough memory exist to reinstall the love he'd once known? If so, perhaps there was hope for his reptilian heart after all. And if not, well, it wouldn't be a devastating blow. He always had Rowan's sassy-mouthed mistress to tease and keep himself amused.

Akaran prepared to leave before any softness exposed him. "I'll never love you," he said without malice, "but perhaps—in time—I'll grow to not hate you."

Zurie's face turned in a subtle gesture, a smile tugging at her lips. "That's the best a bad mother like me could hope for."

Akaran left Kamand House and rode carefree to Castle Crag. From now on, life was whatever he wanted it to be, and he knew exactly what he wanted from it. Prestige and influence. Not like what Adelkar had, but the kind that came from improving himself as a man and the lands around him. He would reopen the mines Adelkar closed, increase his wealth, and employ miners by the droves.

And he had just the friend and brother with whom to partner.

NOT LONG BEFORE MIDNIGHT, WHEN THE SOUNDS OF FEASTING and celebration no longer drifted from the manor's yard, Rowan and Tahira retired to the parlor housing Rahn's cherished plants. The sight of their verdant leaves bathed in firelight brought a bittersweet balm to Rowan's heart. He missed his grandfather sorely, but in this special place where he first met Rahn, Rowan was grateful for the precious time he'd been afforded.

A contented smile formed, and he eagerly looked at Tahira. He budded with excitement for her to notice the new addition occupying the parlor. The opal necklace and earrings he'd given her the night before the feast dazzled against her skin, matching the sapphire shade of her knee-high dress. With a rapturous smile, she drifted toward the table draped with his newest weaving.

Tahira's eyes shone when she beheld its bright colors. "Ah, is this another gift?"

Rowan nodded with a mild blush.

"It's beautiful!" She beamed with pure delight and glided her fingers along its soft threads. "Would you tell me about this weaving? I'd like to understand its message."

"I made it to remind us of our journey together." Rowan came to stand alongside her and cradled her hand within his. "The varying green thread at the beginning signifies the moment I met you outside the Grimwood. The tan hues lulling underneath the green represent our voyage across the Omaran Desert, and this patch of blue thread indicates our time spent at the lake outside of Shandria."

Tahira's rouged cheeks warmed. "I was so jittery bathing under the moonlight."

He teased her with a smile. "At least you weren't seen."

"I have you to thank for that." Her winsome gaze wandered back toward the weaving. "And what of all the streams of color in the middle?"

"That's our life here at Iron Crossing."

Tahira's hand moved to grasp at a row of dark thread. "And the stain of black? What does it represent?"

"When I thought I lost you to Zamara's trickery."

"Before she enchanted me, she said disturbing things," Tahira admitted, her other hand finding his. She grasped it tightly.

"What kind of things?"

A sudden fright came to her eyes, but it abated as she eased against him. "Things I'd rather not voice yet. The whole experience still chills my blood. One moment I was standing before Zamara, and the next, my world became a black void. I was trapped there for what felt like ages, alone in the cold dark. And then, you were there to pull me out of it."

He squeezed her hand, delighted by its warmth. "When you woke, I don't think I'd ever been happier in all my life."

"Until today, I imagine."

"Yes." Rowan smiled, bringing his face in close. "Prepare to imagine more."

"Then tell me the rest," she urged with a delicate whisper to his ear. "What are these rows of red thread?"

Rowan stared deeply into Tahira's alluring gaze, his grin turning roguish. "Can you not guess?"

"Oh, I can," she replied coyly, her smile most engaging, "but I want to hear it from your lips."

"Our growing love for each other." He pulled her into his arms. "Our future adventures." Such closeness was once a far-reaching fantasy. And as his curse no longer stood in their way, he could finally *see* a future alongside his abiding companion.

"I love being held like this—close to your scent." Tahira snuggled against him, her lips skimming playfully against his cheek. "But what I shall love most is having you beside me for years to come."

"If only Rahn or Naja could've lived to see us thrive."

"Rahn knew we would. He left his legacy in the best of hands. Whatever chapter comes next in our lives, we'll never forget his deeds, nor the woman who taught you the skills needed to end your curse."

As Rowan bent his head to sweeten the moment with a kiss, he whispered, "The next chapter, and the next . . ."

THE CONJURER'S CURSE READER'S GUIDE

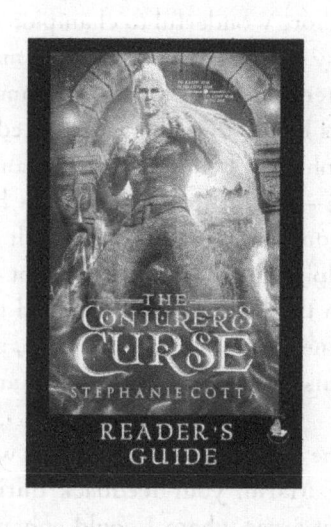

Are you ready for more of The Conjurer's Curse? Check out the Monarch website www.monarcheducationalservices.com for The Conjurer's Curse Reader's Guide. This free educational resource is perfect for educators, librarians, homeschools, small groups, and readers who want more of Rowan and Tahira's story.

ACKNOWLEDGMENTS

This book would not have been possible without the love and support of so many gracious people. First off, I want to thank my publisher, Jennifer Lowry, for believing in me and making this long held dream possible. To have you fall in love with my story was a blessing from above and an answer to my prayer. I could not have asked for someone more wonderful to champion my book!

Thank you to my mother, Brenda, for the many hours you spent reading every chapter and giving them a grammar teacher's editorial eye. You will always be my first and foremost editor! A loving thank you to my father, John, for being the first person who read this book from start to finish—and in less than twelve hours. Dad, you are amazing! Thank you to my sister, Elizabeth, for being my idea soundboard and helping me brainstorm the plot and characters. Your input was crucial in the beginning as I shaped the story. Thank you to my amazing partner, Alan, for all your love, support, and encouragement through this process; and to Alaura and Paul, for all your sweet prayers.

Thank you to the amazing team of editors who helped me polish my story. To Kelly Marin, your feedback during the development edits helped me spot areas where I could enhance the plot, increase the tension, and tighten the stakes. To Pauline Harris, it was a delight to get to work with you again! I knew my manuscript was in excellent hands during your round of edits. To Haley Hwang, your copyline edits helped deliver my prose with sharper eloquence. Thank you for all the advice you gave me as we worked our way through the manuscript. I have learned so much from you!

To all my wonderful beta readers: Kayla Herron, Ashley Davenport, Eli Goergen, Rachel Baker, Betty Walker, and Thomas Perkins. I cannot thank you enough for reading the first draft of my story and giving me invaluable feedback. Each and every one of you helped me improve the content and strengthen my characters' arcs.

Thank you to my two amazing critique partners, Ashley White and Angela R. Hughes. Angela, our coffee meetups and your words of inspiration and encouragement helped keep my head up when I experienced trying days and writer woes. Ashley, an immense thank you for encouraging me to stick with the queries after the rejection letters kept coming in. You came alongside me as a friend, writing confidant, and cheerleader to help open the publishing door for me. I am blessed beyond belief to share this publishing adventure with you!

And finally, to God who gifted me with the creative mind to craft stories for others to enjoy—and who blessed me with a beautiful space to live my dream life as a writer.

ABOUT THE AUTHOR

Stephanie Cotta hails from beautiful Southern Oregon where she resides in a quaint, historic mining town. Growing up, she spent much of her time delving into every new Star Wars book she could get her hands on, which all began at age nine when she bought *The Courtship of Princess Leia* by Dave Wolverton at a garage sale for a quarter. Her love of Star Wars and Sci-Fi/fantasy has been undying ever since. A fine arts major in college, she first embarked into the literary world as a children's book illustrator, then leapt over to the realm of storytelling when she could no longer repress the urge to write the fantasy stories running wild in her imagination. When she's not steeped in writing, she's launching arrows at hay bales, drawing with pastels, reading fantasy, playing an immersive RPG, or watching the latest BBC historical drama.

If you know someone is hurting or if that person is you, please reach out. Talk to school staff, family, and/or a friend. Know you are not alone. You are loved.

National Suicide Prevention Hotline: 1-800-273-8255

Crisis Text Line: Text "Hello" to 741741

National Alliance on Mental Illness (NAMI)
www.nami.org

MONARCH MIDDLE GRADE FANTASY

The Impossible Girl by Ashley White

For fans of Harry Potter and Percy Jackson, meet Ava Jones and join her and her friends on an action-packed fantasy adventure that will be sure to keep readers turning pages and wishing book 2 would magically appear in their hands. Follow www.monarcheducationalservices.com for updates and meet our middle grade author, Ashley White.

CPSIA information can be obtained
at www.ICGtesting.com
Printed in the USA
LVHW091106211222
735625LV00001B/119